EARTHLINGS

EARTHLINGS

SOLDIERS OF EARTHRISE, BOOK II

DANIEL ARENSON

Chapter One
Neon Oasis

Jon fired his gun.

And he missed.

The most important shot of his life—and he missed!

His bullet shattered a lamp. Glass showered like an exploding star. Bargirls screamed and fled the room.

They were in the Go Go Cowgirl, the seediest bar on the seediest world in the seediest corner of the galaxy. The Go Go Cowgirl. A haunt for drug dealers, pimps, prostitutes, and the soldiers they serviced. On this distant planet, so far from Earth, soldiers found their pleasures wherever they could. A neon oasis in the abyss of war, the Go Go Cowgirl welcomed the broken, haunted soldiers limping back from the battlefield. It gave them what they needed. Cold beer. Hot girls. Carnal pleasures in a world of pain. Intoxicating, curvy flesh in a world where flesh so often burned and bled.

The Go Go Cowgirl. The bar where Jon had come to forget. The bar where he found his brother's killer.

There he stood.

The butcher. The torturer. The murderer.

Ernesto "Iron" Santos.

And Jon goddamn missed.

He kept his smoking muzzle aimed at the brute.

"Don't move!" Jon shouted. "Drop your gun!"

They stood facing each other in the bar. Two old cowboys in a saloon. Only this saloon was in a place far wilder than the Old

West. This saloon was on Bahay. A planet of jungles. Of death. Of old scores.

"It's you," Jon hissed. "You're the one they call Iron. The man who killed my brother."

They stared at each other in silence.

Jon—a young Earthling. A private in the Human Defense Force. Sent here to drag this rebellious colony into Earth's empire. Jon Taylor. Slender and pale, his black hair cropped short, his blue eyes haunted. Nineteen years old. Already with blood on his hands. With blood haunting his dreams every night.

Ernesto—a wiry Bahayan. All corded muscles and scars. His skin was bronze, his features sharp, his eyes simmering with fire. A scar cleaved his face, leaving one eye ruined, covered with a milky cataract. His snarl revealed a golden tooth. Ernesto Santos. Rebel against Earth's will. Freedom fighter to some, terrorist to most. The dreaded butcher of the jungle.

"Killed your brother? Maybe." Ernesto spat. "I've killed many of you *pute* weaklings from Earth. Was your brother a scrawny maggot like you?"

The guerrilla held a smoking pistol, the muzzle aimed at Jon. It was an old flintlock, the kind Earthlings had stopped using centuries ago. But it could still put a bullet through Jon.

After all, that gun had just shot a woman through the chest.

Sergeant Lizzy lay on the bar floor, gasping, clutching the bullet hole. Blood dripped between her fingers. Two other soldiers, patrons of the bar, knelt beside her. One was trying to staunch the bleeding. The other ran out onto the street, calling for a medic.

They were Jon's friends. Soldiers he had trained with, fought with. Right now, he barely saw them. Right now, he saw only at the man ahead.

"You killed him," Jon said, voice shaking. "His name was Corporal Paul Taylor. My brother. You murdered him!"

Ernesto smirked. "I've done worse than kill pathetic *pute* soldiers. That woman bleeding on the floor? I raped her. I tortured her. I cut off her hand. Now she's no longer useful. So I put a bullet through her chest." He grinned and licked his golden tooth. "But I've not come here to kill you, little *pute*. You're not even worth the trouble. I've come for that girl who hides behind your skirt. My beloved betrothed. Come to me, Maria!"

Maria Imelda de la Cruz. Once a humble rice farmer from a village by the rainforest. Now an orphan, a bargirl, struggling to survive on these rough neon streets. She cowered behind Jon. A petite woman with long black hair, olive-toned skin, and rare beauty. A beauty that had pierced Jon's heart the first time he saw her.

Maria. The woman he loved. A daughter of the enemy and the brightest light in Jon's life.

She found her courage. She peeked around Jon's back and sneered at Ernesto.

"Your betrothed?" Maria laughed bitterly. "That was never my choice! When I was a child, our parents arranged that. Now our parents are dead. Now our village is destroyed. Now—"

"And now you fuck the Earthlings who destroyed our village!" Ernesto shouted. "You fuck the *pute* demons who murdered our parents! You're nothing but a whore now. You—"

"Don't call her that!" Jon said.

Ernesto laughed—a sound like cracking bones. "Are you one of her clients, *pute*?"

Jon raised his chin. "I'm her husband."

Well, to be honest, Jon had to admit to himself: *We're both right.*

Yes, Jon *had* hired Maria as a prostitute. But only to save her from a cruel man! A brute, a murderer, a man who would take Maria's virginity and leave her bruised and battered.

Still, for all his good intentions, Jon *had* paid for her. And he *had* slept with her. So he supposed that, yes, Maria *was* a prostitute, and he *was* her client.

But there was more to the story. Jon had also married her.

Sure, it had been only a mock service. A bit of fun. A fake wedding dress sewn from a curtain. One bargirl dressed as a priest, a fake mustache on her lip, officiating the ceremony as the guests giggled. A funny little night above the bar. Not a *real* wedding. Not legally binding.

But right now, defending Maria, Jon felt like her true husband. His love for her was stronger than any contract or ceremony. Someday he hoped to marry her for real—on Earth.

He would protect her from this man.

In all of Bahay, of all the girls in all the bars on this godforsaken world, I had to fall in love with her, Jon thought. *With the betrothed of Ernesto Santos, the monster who murdered my brother.*

"Maria!" Ernesto reached out for the girl. "Come to me. Leave this shameful place. You're a proud daughter of Bahay! You don't need to work here. To service the enemy. Come to me, my beloved."

"Your beloved?" Maria shook her head. "No, Ernesto. You don't love me. You beat me. And you scare me. I watched you torture that prisoner. Burn him with an iron. I'll never be your wife! *Never!* Leave now and don't come back. Or Jon will kill you!"

I might kill him anyway, Jon thought.

He pushed Maria behind his back and took a step toward Ernesto. He kept his rifle trained on the guerrilla.

"I won't let you hurt her," Jon said.

Ernesto smirked. "Go ahead, boy. Shoot if you've got the balls." He kept his own gun aimed at Jon. "Let's see who's faster. Old cowboy standoff, like you say on Earth."

Jon tightened his grip on the rifle. At first, when Ernesto had burst into the club, gun blazing, it had been easy to let off a shot. That had felt like an actual battle. And Jon had trained for battles, fought battles in the jungles. But now, like this, locked in a standoff, Jon hesitated. Killing a man like this… it was not a battle. It would be more like, well…

Like murder? he thought.

"Admit it!" Jon shouted. "Admit you killed Paul."

He needed to hear that confession first. To know for certain this was his man. To gain the courage to pull the trigger.

Ernesto wasn't firing either. Maybe he feared his bullet would tear through Jon and hit Maria, who was hiding behind him.

"I told you, *pute*." Ernesto smirked. "I've killed many of your kind. You Earthlings don't belong here. This is Bahay. This world belongs only to Bahayans. Our planet and our women are not yours."

Jon's lip twitched. "I'm not interested in having a political debate, buddy. Tell me you killed Paul!" His voice rose to a shout, and he took a step closer. "*Tell me it was you!*"

On the floor, Sergeant Lizzy raised her head. She was ashen, clutching her wound.

"It's him," she whispered, voice hoarse. "Jon, it's him. I was there. Kill him. Kill—"

"Hey, hey, hey, nobody is killing anyone here!"

The Magic Man burst into the room. The pimp wore a garish purple suit, chains of gold, and glittering rings. Scented oils glistened on his goatee and slicked-back hair. He was a middle-aged Bahayan man, but he wore more jewels than an old French queen.

"Fighting is very illegal!" The pimp tittered nervously. "We don't want to bring the military police in here, do we now? Any violence—please, take it out, take it outside." He stepped closer to Jon and Ernesto, who both still had their guns drawn. Rings glinting, the pimp pushed down both smoking muzzles. Then he winced and put his fingers in his mouth. "Oh, goddammit, I cooked my fingers."

Ernesto's gun was down.

And Jon took his chance.

He raised his rifle and fired.

This time, Jon aimed true.

A chunk of Ernesto's scalp tore off. A piece of skull hit the wall. For a horrible instant, Jon saw the inside of Ernesto's head. A fold of brain. Then just gushing blood.

Ernesto fired his gun. Perhaps just instinct. Perhaps a signal sent from brain to finger before that brain lost its skull.

It was futile. Ernesto was already reeling backward. His aim was off. The bullet shrieked over Jon's head and hit the wall. A few plucky bargirls, who had stayed to watch the fight, wailed and fled behind the bar.

Ernesto screamed. Amazingly, even with his skull shot open, he was still standing.

He even fired a second bullet.

But he could barely aim. This bullet hit the ceiling, shattering a lamp. Glass flew.

Ernesto dropped his gun from trembling hands. He stood, dazed, his skull blasted open, somehow still alive, still standing, still screaming.

Jon was about to shoot again, to put the man out of his misery, when the military police burst through the door.

They wore helmets with dark visors, hiding their faces. They raised assault rifles, sweeping the room with targeting laser beams. The Magic Man stood on the street, peering over the policemen's shoulders. The bastard must have sneaked out the back door to summon them.

"What the hell is going on here?" an MP said.

"Back, back!" somebody shouted. And suddenly medics were rushing in too, barreling through the MPs. They carried a litter, oxygen mask, and medical kits. In the crowded bar, they were trying to reach Sergeant Lizzy, who still lay bleeding on the floor.

"*Kalayaan para sa Bahay!*" rose a cry from outside, and gunfire rattled. *Freedom for Bahay!*

Goddammit! Everything was converging here. Police. Medics. And outside—the goddamn Kalayaan terrorists.

In the chaos, Ernesto stumbled outside.

Jon aimed his gun, but he couldn't fire. Not without jeopardizing the medics. They were blocking his aim.

"Stop him!" Jon cried.

One MP, who stood at the doorway, stared at Ernesto, then recoiled in disgust. "My God, his brain…"

Jon tried to push his way forward. To catch Ernesto. But he slammed into an MP, then into a medic. An oxygen tank clanged onto the floor, and medics cursed. Jon cried out in frustration, worming his way outside.

* * * * *

Sunlight washed the street. At nighttime, the Blue Boulevard shone with neon lights. Not just blue but all the colors of the rainbow. Countless bars filled the neighborhood—not just the Blue Boulevard itself but side streets that branched off like electric twigs. These bars, run and staffed by Bahayans, offered everything an Earthling soldier could want. Booze. Drugs. A girl to dance on the stage. A girl to take into bed.

Or, in Jon's case, a wife.

In the night, the signs all shone, and the barkers all barked, and the pimps prowled, promising delights. Cold beer and hot girls! Lady boxing tonight! Midget wrestling! Shabu shabu, the drug of dreams!

But right now, daylight banished the illusion like dawn banishing a ghost. The neon lights did not shine. And in the searing sunlight of Bahay, Jon could see the decay. The stained, crumbling concrete of decrepit buildings. The roofs of rusty corrugated steel, held down with tires. The filth that filled the gutters. The beggars and orphans and twitching junkies on the sidewalks. The Blue Boulevard, so intoxicating at night, became in day a place of grim awakenings and shattered dreams.

Instead of buskers and barkers, bullets filled the air with their song.

One bullet hit an MP.

More pinged against the ambulance parked outside the Go Go Cowgirl.

One bullet hit the neon sign above Jon's head. The electric cowgirl, the club's namesake, exploded into a million shards.

They were there. In windows and on roofs.

Some called them terrorists. Some called them the Kennys. They had been just peasants once. Today they were the Kalayaan, the great uprising of Bahay, the scourge of Earth. And they were all firing at the club.

Jon ducked behind the ambulance, slung his rifle over the hood, and returned fire.

"Ernesto!" he shouted.

He could not see his nemesis. Blood trailed across the sidewalk—Ernesto's blood! But bullets hit another MP, then a passing *tuk tuk*. The motorized rickshaw crashed into a pole, and more blood spilled, and electricity showered through the air.

Jon squinted, struggling to see through the chaos. His quarry had vanished. Jon wanted to run after the killer, but the bullets kept flying. All Jon could do was crouch behind the ambulance and take potshots at the enemy. He felt helpless as Ernesto got away.

Jon had never wanted to join the army, to fight a war. The desire to avenge his brother had taken him here. Now his hope for vengeance dripped away like blood through a dying man's fingers.

More soldiers streamed onto the street, emerging from bars and brothels. Some were shirtless, and some were hitching up their pants as they ran. One private fell on the street, riddled with bullets. A beer bottle slipped from his lifeless hand.

But most of the soldiers opened fire.

"Kenny raid!" shouted a mustached corporal—as if anyone on the street didn't know. The mustached man was stumbling from a brothel, cheeks pink, pants around his ankles. His polka dot underwear visible to the world, he began firing an assault rifle at the rooftops.

An orphan, one of the myriad who lived on the streets, tried to flee, a bullet in his arm. A shabu addict, only a teenager but already a mother of four, was herding her kids away from the fight, seeking shelter behind a shanty. Over the past twenty years of war, Mindao had swollen to millions of people. Most were homeless. Most were women and children. Widows. Orphans. Refugees of the burning countryside. They had chosen poverty in the concrete jungle over death in the burning wilderness. And now the war had found them here. Now Earth's soldiers and Bahay's rebels littered this neon oasis with bullets.

With a belch of smog, the ambulance took off, carrying Sergeant Lizzy to safety.

Jon, who had been crouching behind the ambulance, was suddenly exposed.

Shadows moved in windows across the street.

Jon ran. Bullets slammed onto the sidewalk around him.

"Jon!" Maria cried.

"Get back into the bar!" he shouted.

A bullet whistled above, leaving his ears ringing. Another hit the concrete wall just above his head. He rolled behind a fallen rickshaw, its driver dead. It wasn't much cover, but better than nothing. Jon looked up.

There! A man in the window, peering between slats of plywood. Not Ernesto. But a Kenny who'd kill Jon just as gladly.

A bullet hit the *tuk tuk* Jon was crouched behind. It glanced off the rickshaw, scraped Jon's arm, and embedded itself in the pavement.

Jon fired.

The man in the window fell, neck spurting blood.

"Jon!"

"Jon, dammit, get to cover!"

Jon turned his head and saw his friends running toward him.

Private George Williams—the largest man in the brigade. The giant stood nearly seven feet tall, and his ample belly swayed over his belt. A brain tumor, pressing on his pituitary gland, had swelled George to gargantuan proportions. He looked like an ogre, and his blazing red hair didn't help. But Jon still saw the boy he had grown up with in Lindenville, New Jersey. A kind, sensitive boy who loved drumming, *Dungeons and Dragons*, and writing science fiction stories.

By the giant's side ran Private Etty Ettinger. The young Israeli joked that her name, with its unfortunate alliteration, made her sound like a superheroine. Peter Parker, Clark Kent, and the amazing Etty Ettinger! Etty joked around a lot. Mostly to hide the pain. A terrorist attack had claimed her entire family, leaving Etty alone in the universe. With her petite frame, smooth black hair, and olive-toned skin, she could almost pass for a Bahayan. But unlike Bahayans, Etty had very round, very green eyes. They were so large and bright people often mocked her, calling her a tarsier—a native animal with bulging green eyes. Etty just laughed along. More laughter to hide the pain.

George and Etty. They were both in Jon's platoon. They were his two best friends in the galaxy.

More bullets shrieked from across the street.

His friends pulled Jon to cover. Under a hailstorm of bullets, they rushed into the infamous Bottoms Up bar, one of the Go Go Cowgirl's competitors. They crouched on the sticky floor, thrust their guns out the window, and fired.

"Why the hell did you run outside, Jon?" George said. "You almost got yourself killed!"

"He was here!" Jon said. "Ernesto! The bastard who killed Paul."

"No shit, we saw!" George said.

"George and I were fucking there in the bar!" Etty said. "I mean—we weren't *fucking* there. We were fucking *there*! As in, we were in the bar, not fucking, and then Ernesto came, I mean he—"

"Shut up, guys, and just kill the damn Kennys!" Jon said.

But the Kalayaan were already retreating. The guerrillas pulled back into alleyways. Into sewers. A few ran across the rooftops, scattering metal sheets and slats of particle board. When a helicopter finally arrived, its machine guns blazing, the last few guerrillas vanished in the urban jungle.

And with them was Ernesto.

"I took off a chunk of skull, but the bastard is still alive." Jon stepped onto the street, blood sluicing around his boots. He balled his fists. "I know he's still alive."

"He'll be dead soon." George wiped sweat off his brow. "Nobody can live long with that kind of injury."

Jon wanted to run through the city, to seek Ernesto, to finish the job.

But then he thought of Maria back in the Go Go Cowgirl. What if Ernesto returned for her? Or one of his men? Jon dared not be apart from her.

He leaped over corpses, making his way back to the bar and the woman he loved.

* * * * *

That night, the Go Go Cowgirl shone with lights, Bahayan pop music pounded, and booze and drugs flowed. As if the place hadn't erupted with violence just hours ago. As if there wasn't still blood staining the wall. Bargirls strutted along the bar, broken angels in high heels and fraying lingerie. Drunken soldiers hooted and hollered from the tables, tossing dollar bills. Soldiers and bargirls copulated on tabletops, on the staircase, even on the filthy floor.

The soldiers were shell-shocked, mere boys plucked from Earth, tossed into war on a distant planet, expelled into the glittering streets for a little sin between battles. The bargirls were refugees, their villages burned and poisoned, their eyes glassy with drugs, their hearts shattered, their children waiting at home for a meal. The Go Go Cowgirl—a hive of sin, pleasure, and broken souls. A place of neon forgetfulness. A place to drown the memories.

But Jon could not forget what had happened, even if the rest of the bar could.

He didn't join the soldiers downstairs. He didn't want to drink or gamble or watch the *unano* dwarfs wrestle. He and Maria sat in her little room upstairs.

I hired her for four days, Jon thought. *I have one more night. And tomorrow I return to the war.*

Jon looked at her. Maria sat cross-legged on the bed before him, so beautiful that his heart hurt. Her black hair flowed like silk, framing a delicate face, the most beautiful face Jon had never seen. She looked back, eyes damp, and smiled tremulously. Jon wondered if this was their last night together.

For dinner, they were sharing a plate of *lumpia* pork rolls and fried rice. But neither one was hungry. They just picked at the food. Suddenly, with a crackling sound, the radio in the room stopped playing the latest Bahayan pop song. A news bulletin began to play, broadcast in English for the benefit of the Earthling soldiers in the city.

"Good evening, free people of South Bahay," said the broadcaster, speaking with a Bahayan accent. "The Red Cardinal, the treacherous tyrant of North Bahay, has launched a major offensive today. His so-called Luminous Army is swarming toward the equator with several divisions of infantry, armor, and artillery. Throughout the jungles, the terrorist organization Kalayaan is aiding them. South Bahayans, this is the most serious aggression we have faced since the war began. Stand strong with our Earthling allies! Together, we will push back the northern traitors, and—"

Maria turned it off. She shook her head. "Propaganda."

Jon didn't know a lot about Bahay's politics. But he knew that Earth had installed a puppet government here in the south. That most Bahayans hated this government, considered its ministers traitors. Jon had come here to fight the north. They told him he was here to liberate the planet. That the Bahayans would welcome him with open arms.

So much for that.

Jon no longer knew who to believe. Which side was right and which was wrong. All he knew was that Ernesto was out there, still alive, and that Maria was here in this room, the most beautiful woman in the galaxy, and he might never see her again.

He caressed her cheek.

Maria, I love you, he wanted to say. *I came here to fight, and I found terror and bloodshed and pain. But I also found you. The past four days have been the best in my life. Because you were with me.*

But he could not utter those words. Feeling too embarrassed. Too awkward. Like a lovelorn boy.

So he just said, "Do you want to play cards?"

She smiled. A true smile. A smile that showed bright white teeth and filled her eyes with joy. "Gin rummy? I bet I can beat you again!"

He poked her with a *lumpia* roll. "Not a chance."

She gasped. "You're on, mister!"

They played a round. He won, and she pouted and pelted him with *lumpia.* But when she won the next round, she celebrated, danced around the room, and blew a raspberry at him. They played a few more rounds. When picking cards, Maria frowned, deep in concentration, tongue sticking out, and whenever she won, she danced and laughed. And Jon laughed too. To savor this last joy. To try to forget the news on the radio, if only for tonight. To try to forget that his leave was ending, that at dawn he would return into the fire.

Finally the music died downstairs. The last few soldiers were probably snoring at the tables or in the beds of bargirls. But Jon and Maria remained awake in her room, sitting side by side, the cards strewn around them.

Jon looked at her, and their laughed faded.

He leaned forward and kissed her lips.

"I love you," he said.

She smiled and a tear flowed down her cheek. "I love you too, my husband."

He brushed her hair, she unbuttoned her dress, and they made love. As he lay atop her, drenched in sweat, Jon felt like he was back in the jungle, that the enemy was all around. He tried to focus on Maria, yet he kept seeing the blood, the dead, and when he climaxed, he felt lost in the dark.

But when he lay on his back, she cuddled against him, and soothed him, and kissed away his tears, and his pain faded.

Tonight, let me just think of her, Jon thought. *Tomorrow I will return to hell. But tonight, here in this hot little room above the bar—this is heaven.*

"I'm scared," she whispered. "Of Ernesto. Of the war. Of everything."

He kissed her cheek. "I'll keep you safe tonight. And I'll return to you. And when the war is over, we'll live together."

"As husband and wife?" she whispered.

He nodded. "As husband and wife. I'll take you back to Earth with me, and I'll give you a good life. You'll never have to work in a bar again. And I'll never have to fight again. We'll be together and happy."

She rolled atop him, kissed his lips, and looked into his eyes. "I love you, Jon Taylor. Promise you'll come back to me. Promise."

Suddenly he remembered.

Kaelyn's words on Earth.

Come back pure or come back dead. Promise me, Jon.

Kaelyn. His muse. His soprano. Singer in his band. He had kissed her under the tree, but Kaelyn was not his to love. Kaelyn had been Paul's girlfriend. And now Paul was dead, and Jon was here, and that old life was gone.

Now there was only Maria in his arms.

"I promise, Maria. I promise."

Finally they slept, holding each other, until the sun rose over hell.

Chapter Two
A Small Light in a Dark Alley

The morning rose, and Jon was gone, and Maria trembled.

The devil is out there, she thought. *Ernesto. He's out there and alive, and he knows where I am, and my soldier is gone.* She looked around her at the seedy club. *There is no more safety here.*

Normally in the morning, you could find Earthling soldiers sleeping throughout the Go Go Cowgirl—slumped over tabletops, on the staircase, and in the beds of bargirls. But not this morning. The entire city was talking about it. A major assault from the north. Fierce battles blazing across Bahay. Every combat soldier had been pulled from Mindao, it seemed. Thousands of drunken, terrified, homesick boys—sent into the meat grinder.

Many, maybe most, would not return.

But Jon would. Maria knew he would. He had promised. Made a sacred vow. He *had* to return.

She just had to survive until then.

The front door banged open, and Maria started, sure it was Ernesto come to grab her. But it was only the Magic Man, his purple suit dusty and wrinkled.

"It's a goddamn mess out there!" the pimp said. "A goddamn mess. The whole city—chaos! Helicopters and planes flying north. Soldiers racing into armored trucks. Goddammit, all my best customers are leaving. My business will be ruined!" He shook his fist. "Curse the Red Cardinal. Curse him!"

Maria had to get out of there. She made a beeline for the door.

"Where are you going, Maria?" the Magic Man said.

"I… I don't know," she confessed.

There wasn't anywhere *to* go. The Earthlings had burned her village to the ground. Her entire family was dead. The city was full of homelessness, drugs, rape, despair.

"You're not going back onto the street, are you?" The pimp took a step toward her. His hands curled into fists spiky with rings. "Remember where you were when I found you. Living in filth! Begging! Eating trash to survive! You have nowhere else to go, girl. You are mine."

"What's the point?" Maria said. "I thought all your customers were leaving the city!"

The Magic Man winced. "You're right. You're right!" He slumped into a chair and covered his eyes. "I'm ruined. Ruined!"

A few of the little people he employed approached to comfort him. They were billed on the poster outside as *The Amazing Unanos—Midget Wrestlers*. But Maria had gotten to know them as kind people, their only curse being born different. They had washed up in the bars for the same reason as her. They had nowhere else to go.

As the little wrestlers comforted their weeping boss, Maria seized her chance. She sneaked outside.

She stood in the back alley. Bottles rolled around her feet. Stray cats hissed, and stray toddlers ran by. Electric cables sagged over the alley, tangled like old fishing nets, buzzing and crackling, and Maria remembered the roar of planes flying over her village.

Trembling seized her.

Jon was off to war.

Her parents were gone.

Ernesto was after her.

She was nothing but a homeless bargirl, alone in the world, and tears streamed down her cheeks.

For a moment, she allowed herself to cry. To be weak. To let it out.

Then she took a deep breath.

No, I'm not alone.

She pulled her best friend from her pocket.

Crisanto hovered above her palm. The little round creature glowed, painting her hand with silvery light. He was a Santelmo. An actual Santelmo she had found in the forest as a girl, had adopted as a pet.

The Santelmos were ancient and wise aliens. They came from a world far across the galaxy. Throughout history, they had shone on Earth, studying humanity. They appeared in folklore around the world. Wills-o-the-wisp in England, mystical beings of the swamps. Saint Elmo's Fire in America. *Chir batti* in India, ghost lights of the marshes. *Aleyas* in Bengal. *Luz malas* in Argentina, believed to be evil spirits. *Naga* fireballs in Thailand, said to be the fiery eyes of monstrous serpents. *Hitodama* in Japan, worshiped as human souls. Almost every culture throughout history knew of these floating balls of light, told their own stories about them.

And the Filipinos, who called them Santelmos, knew them best of all. Centuries ago, back before humans had starships or even planes, the Santelmos had brought a few Filipino settlers here to Bahay, to this distant planet so far from home. Here they still watched over the Bahayans—the descendants of those blessed sailors among the stars.

But of course, Crisanto himself had done none of that. He was only a baby, no larger than an acorn.

"I'm not a soldier like Jon," she told him. "I'm not a warrior like Ernesto. But I'm not helpless. And I have you."

His glow brightened. He bobbed in her hand, perhaps his way of smiling.

Another light flickered in the alleyway—this one orange. A match burning.

A woman stepped out of the shadows. She wore a leopard print miniskirt, a red bra, and high heels, her clothes from last night. Her bob cut, normally black and smooth, was ruffled. Her cross rested between her breasts.

Maria, who was already preparing to flee, relaxed. It was only Charlie, her best friend.

"What you got there, kid?" Charlie said, puffing on a cigarette.

Maria quickly stuffed Crisanto back into her pocket. The Santelmo aliens were allies of the Red Cardinal, arming his northern warriors. If she was caught here in South Bahay with a pet Santelmo… Maria gulped. She had seen traitors hung from cranes in the city square. She did not relish such a fate.

"Just um… a match," Maria lied.

Charlie took a long drag on her cigarette, blew a smoke ring. "Whatever you say, kid."

Maria studied the woman. Charlie Wonder was her stage name. Her given name was Dalisay Cortes, born and raised in the city slums before finding her way into the bars. Charlie was in her thirties, old for a bargirl, and a mother of four. She was also, Maria thought, the strongest, most beautiful, and most intelligent woman in the world.

I've never had a sister, Maria thought. *But if I did, I'd want one like Charlie.*

Sister? Actually, Charlie was the same age Maria's mother would have been today. But it was hard to imagine the woman, with her push-up bra and tiny skirt, as motherly. Four children notwithstanding.

"Charlie, don't tell anyone. About the light you saw in my pocket." Maria grabbed Charlie's arms. "Please."

As she held the older woman, Maria felt them. The little scars on Charlie's forearms. Yes, Charlie injected shabu, the most popular drug in Mindao. It could be injected, snorted, smoked, even eaten, giving different experiences. But the ultimate goal was always the same. The same reason so many bargirls used it.

It dulled the pain. If only for a few hours.

Charlie smiled crookedly and brushed back Maria's hair. "Tell who what?"

Maria sighed in relief. "Thank you, Charlie." She hugged the older woman. "I can't go back to the Go Go Cowgirl, Charlie. Not ever."

Charlie raised an eyebrow. "Because of that Ernesto goon? I'll protect you from him. We've had men barge into the club before, demanding to marry this or that girl. We scare them all off."

"Ernesto Santos is not like other men," Maria said. She remembered how he had murdered a captive Earthling in San Luna. How he had tortured another in the tunnels. How he had calmly shot the pretty Earthling woman in the chest just yesterday. She remembered too how Ernesto used to beat her.

Charlie took another drag on her cigarette. She blew smoke out slowly, gazing at the wall, contemplating. "He's Kalayaan, isn't he?"

"He is." Maria dropped her voice to a whisper. "I was Kalayaan once too. For only a short while. I… I saw things. Things that made me sick. I had to escape them. And now he's after me. He wants to marry me. And he wants to kill Jon. He killed Jon's brother. And…" Maria couldn't stop her tears. "And I don't know why I'm telling you this, Charlie. If anyone knew that I fought for the enemy. If Jon knew…"

"Hush now!" Charlie pulled her into an embrace. "You're safe with me, little one. You're safe with your *Tita* Charlie. And you can stay in my house until things blow over. It's not a mansion. It's only a little shanty by the river. But my home is your home. Until your Mister Jon comes back for you."

If he comes back for me, Maria thought. She remembered the radio reports of the Luminous Army moving south, bombing everything in its path.

And now Jon was in its path.

"Thank you, Charlie." She kissed the older woman's cheek. "Thank you so much. I just wish…" Maria sighed. "I wish there was another way. To fight the Earthlings. To free Bahay. Not with armies like the Luminous Army. Not with torture and kidnappings and assassinations—that's how the Kalayaan fights. But with…"

Maria fell silent. She began to pace the alley, thoughts racing through her mind.

"What, Maria?" Charlie said. "I can hear the gears turning in that big head of yours."

"My mother always did say I have a head that's too big, full of too many questions." Maria smiled shakily and held Charlie's hands. "Charlie, I know what we must do. Not fight as soldiers. Not fight as guerrillas. But we can still resist. We can still free our world."

Charlie's eyebrow arched upward again. "How?"

Maria's smile widened, though fear fluttered in her chest. "Charlie, I hereby invite you to join my little resistance movement. The Bargirl Bureau."

Now Charlie's other eyebrow rose. "Maria, you're a silly little girl, and probably insane. What are you up to?"

She held Charlie's hand, leaned forward, and whispered. Slowly Charlie's eyes grew wider and wider, and then a grin spread across her face.

Chapter Three
Plastic Orchids

Lieutenant Carter ran down the hospital corridor, blinded by terror.

"Lizzy! Where are you?"

The news had reached him not an hour ago.

Lizzy. The woman he loved. His beautiful tigress. Shot.

Since then he had been running. Running through the city. Running down neon boulevards and through shantytowns.

And now he was running through Mindao Military Hospital, seeking the right ward. It was not a large hospital, but Carter felt lost. Trapped in a labyrinth. He felt like he was back in the jungle, seeking her behind enemy lines.

He nearly knocked over a nurse. Her tray clattered. He ran past medics wheeling a wounded soldier, his leg blown off. He finally reached a front desk, awash with sweat.

"I'm looking for Sergeant Lizzy Pascal," he managed, gasping.

The receptionist—a portly corporal with pale blond hair—rifled through his notes. "Lizzy Pascal, Lizzy Pascal…"

"Please." Carter struggled to keep his voice calm. "She was shot. Where is she? What room?"

"Pascal, Pascal…"

Carter's heart pounded. He could remain calm in battle. He had charged at enemy formations without missing a beat. But with Lizzy wounded, needing him, it all flooded back. The terror of last year—his platoon wiped out. Lizzy captured. Tortured. Mutilated. Carter was a decorated officer, a graduate of Julius Military Academy, a leader of men. Some would call him a war hero. And here in this hospital, his insides were falling apart.

"Sorry, sir." The receptionist looked up from his notes. "Wrong department. Try the bottom floor, Patient Care Unit. Ask at the front desk there."

Carter ran. He leaped down the stairs three at a time. He raced into one ward, but he found himself in the ICU. Soldiers lay on operating tables, burnt, blown apart. Wrong ward! Carter ran the other way, finally found the Patient Care Unit, and stood by the front desk, panting.

"Lizzy Pascal, Lizzy Pascal…" mumbled the receptionist, a young woman with a Chinese accent. "Sorry, sir. You were at the right unit before. Upstairs."

Carter nearly tore the hospital down with his bare hands.

He raced back upstairs. He faced the portly blond man again.

"Ah, *Lizzy* Pascal!" said the receptionist. "Sorry, I must have misheard you the first time. Yes, sir, she's with me. Room 404. Just down the hall. No, wait! Room 405. Yes, that way. No, no, the other way!"

And finally Carter was there.

He burst into the room and saw her lying on a bed.

Her eyes were closed. White plastic orchids stood on a bedside table, and white curtains fluttered. For a horrible instant, Carter thought she was dead.

Then she opened her eyes and smiled at him.

"Hey, babe," she said. "What took you so long?"

He wanted to rush toward her. To kneel beside her. To weep. To hug her.

But years at military academy, and horrible years of war, kicked in. He stood stiffly. Remaining strong. Confident. Once more—the leader and protector.

He managed a snort of mock derision. "Hey, I'm busy fighting a war, while you're here resting."

And then the facade crumbled.

And he did rush toward her. And did kneel beside her. And did—gently, because she was bandaged and hooked to tubes—embrace her.

"Lizzy, thank God you're okay. I love you, Lizzy. I'm here now. And I'm just going to chain myself to you, so that we're never apart again, and I can always protect you."

She laughed. "Even when I have to use the bathroom?"

He laughed too. "It can be a long chain." He stroked her hair. "My sweet, fierce tigress. It would take a silver bullet to kill you."

"A silver bullet?" She raised an eyebrow. "What am I—a tigress or werewolf?"

"A werewolf? I'm getting a bit worried now," Carter said. "What with Bahay having two moons."

She smiled, and tears filled her eyes. "Carter, I'm going home to Earth."

He nodded. His voice was barely a hoarse whisper. "I know."

"The doctors said I'll be fine." She touched her bandaged chest and winced. "The bullet sliced between two ribs and pierced a lung. I'll recover. Medicine today is pretty amazing. But I'll never fight again. My war is over. I'm going home."

He held her hand. "I understand. It will hurt to let you go. To fight without you. But I know your war is over."

"Carter." Her eyes were soft. "You can come home with me."

He frowned. He released her hand. "Lizzy, I—"

"Come home, Carter. Come home to Earth. I already spoke to my dad. He said that—"

"You spoke to Colonel Pascal?" Carter lost his breath. "You told him I want to leave Bahay? I'm not a coward, Lizzy!"

"I never said you were! But this is your second tour on Bahay. You've fought enough. You don't have to keep chasing a ghost."

He took a step back. He felt stone doors close the walls around his heart. "Lizzy. I'm not chasing a ghost. Ernesto is alive. I vowed to catch him. To punish him for what he did to you. For how he—"

He bit back his words.

For how he tortured you. Raped you. Mutilated you.

He could not bring those words to his lips. His eyes dampened.

Lizzy stared into his eyes. A tear flowed down her cheek. "Yes, he did those things you're thinking of. And this." She touched her chest. "He's the one who shot me. It was Ernesto. He came to the club where I was drinking with the boys. I confronted him. I thought I could defeat him. And he put a bullet through my lung."

The entire hospital—indeed the entire planet—seemed to crumble around Carter. The news pounded him like a bomb's shock wave.

Ernesto.

He was back.

He had hurt Lizzy again.

Oh God.

"I should have been there," Carter whispered. "Oh God, I should have been there. With you. But I wasn't. And he did this! He hurt you again!" He stood up and gave a wordless roar. "Where is he? I will kill him! Where is Ernesto?"

A nurse walked by the doorway, hushed him, then hurried off, wheeling a wounded soldier.

Carter's heart pounded. He clenched his fists. He wanted to rampage through the city, to find the bastard. He could not believe it. The same man he had come here to catch. The same man who had brutalized his tigress. He had hurt her again!

Carter fell to his knees beside Lizzy.

"I failed to protect you," he whispered. "I'm sorry."

Lizzy shed a tear. "Carter, we came here to fight him. And I got shot. I almost died. We have to admit something. That we lost. That it's enough. That we have to end our war against Ernesto. That maybe Earth has to end its war against Bahay."

Carter sucked in breath. "Never!"

Lizzy closed her eyes. "We should never have come back here."

Carter paced the room. "I'm going to catch him, Lizzy. He's close. In this city. He—"

"Jon shot out half his brains," Lizzy said. "He's probably dying in a ditch somewhere."

"So I'll find him and end the job! We're almost there, Lizzy." He knelt beside her again, held her hand. "I promise you. We're almost done. I—"

"I came here for you, Carter," she whispered. "I wanted to let go. To forgive. I came back because you needed your vengeance. And I lost a lung. Please end this now. Don't lose your life for vengeance."

He held her, and she cried against his chest. And Carter knew that he could not go home. He could not let go.

And she knew it too.

The next day, Carter stood outside on the tarmac. Emery Spaceport bustled with activity around him. Shuttles were rising and descending, some bringing fresh troops to war, others carrying the wounded and dead to space. The motherships were barely visible above, faded gray slivers orbiting this world.

One would be carrying Lizzy home.

Carter wanted to approach. To see Lizzy off. To say goodbye. Maybe she was still on the tarmac, waiting to board a shuttle.

But the pain was too great.

He turned around.

He walked away.

He marched back toward his barracks.

He had a platoon to lead. He had a war to win. He had a man to kill.

Lizzy was gone. But Carter still had Ernesto. Let his hate burn brighter than love.

Chapter Four
Departure

She was going home.

After five years of war and heartbreak, Sergeant Lizzy Pascal was returning to Earth.

She was going home broken.

She was going home defeated.

She was going home with her soul like shattered glass in her chest.

The sun beat down over Mindao City. It was another hot, humid day—like every day on Bahay. Lizzy sat in a wheelchair, wearing a military uniform, an IV attached to her arm. Someday she would be strong enough to walk again. But not yet. Maybe not for a while.

Marco Emery Spaceport bustled around her, a hive of activity. Every few moments, a shuttle descended from the sky, landed on the tarmac, and spilled out green privates—fresh meat for the beasts of war. Just as often, a shuttle rose into space, carrying soldiers toward the motherships that would take them home. Some soldiers were returning as haunted heroes. Others were returning in coffins.

And then there's me, Lizzy thought. *Returning home a broken mess, barely alive.*

The doctors had wanted to keep her longer in Mindao Hospital. Lizzy had refused. The starship *Adiona* was schedule to fly back to Earth tonight. She would be on it. The ship had good doctors, as did Earth. And if she did not survive the journey, well… She had cheated death so many times she could not complain.

I should have died a year ago when Ernesto brutalized me, she thought. *I should have died a few days ago when his bullet tore through me. Maybe I did die. I barely feel alive. I feel hollow.*

Her nurse, a sweet Bahayan woman, pushed her wheelchair forward. "We're a little early, Miss Pascal. I'll find a shady place to wait for your shuttle."

"Thank you, Mary Joy," Lizzy said.

Her nurse was among thousands of *katulongs*—Bahayans who helped Earth. The word *katulong* meant "helper" in Tagalog, the local tongue. Some considered it a derogatory term, a synonym of "slave." But others called themselves *katulong* with pride, loyal helpers in a great struggle.

In the north, the Red Cardinal called the *katulongs* traitors and Uncle Toms. He called upon all South Bahayans to join the Kalayaan, the great uprising against Earth's colonial rule. But not everyone listened. Here in the south, many Bahayans feared the Red Cardinal and his Luminous Army. They chose to assist Earth's military. The *katulongs* served as nurses, custodians, mechanics, maids, and many other professions the Human Defense Force outsourced. Some brave South Bahayans even formed their own militia—the South Bahayan Army—and fought alongside Earth in the field. Some did it for money; an Earth dollar went a long way here. But most truly loathed the Red Cardinal, believing him a *manananggal*—a vampire from Filipino folklore.

"Here, Miss Pascal." Mary Joy pushed the wheelchair under an awning. "We can see the shuttles rise and land from here. It's a nicer place to wait. Would you like me to fetch you a drink?"

"I'm fine, Mary Joy, thank you."

The young nurse smiled. "Of course, Miss Pascal."

If we lose the war, Lizzy thought, *the Red Cardinal will slaughter Mary Joy and thousands like her. The katulongs helped us. For that, North Bahayans see them as traitors. Even sweet Mary Joy with her bright smile.*

"Lizzy?"

The deep voice came from her left.

Lizzy turned her head and saw him.

And suddenly tears were flowing.

"Dad."

He walked toward the awning—that broad, bowlegged walk of his, arms pumping, gut swinging. Joe Pascal had always been beefy and strong. At sixty years of age, he was still powerful, though fat now covered his muscles. His hair was still thick, though it was no longer golden like Lizzy's hair. Age had painted it as white as death's grin. He was a colonel now, a senior officer, and three stars glittered on his shoulders. But he still wore a battlesuit like a grunt, armored and scratched and charred. Even at his age and rank, he still fought amid his troops.

To those troops, he was Colonel Crazy Horse, the hardnosed, plainspoken commander of the Apollo infantry brigade. To Lizzy, he was just her dad. A man she loved with all her heart.

"Sweetheart, I came as soon as I could." He knelt by her wheelchair, and his eyes reddened. "My God, my sweet Lizzy. What have those animals done to you? After last time, to see this again…"

She gave him a shaky smile. "Tis but a scratch."

Joe Pascal shook his head. "This is my fault. I should have insisted. Talked to the dean. Got you back into Julius—"

"Dad!" Lizzy interrupted him. "I told you. I never want you pulling strings for me. Not now. Not then. Not ever. Whatever I do, I must do it on my own."

She saw the pain that caused her father.

I failed him, Lizzy knew. *I hurt him.*

She had been only eighteen, a military brat with a big mouth, a wild streak, and a problem with authority. Her father, the famous colonel, had gotten her into Julius Military Academy. She, Lunatic Lizzy, the wild girl with scraped knees, a pottymouth, and too many tattoos—she was going to the most prestigious military school on Earth!

Normally, they'd never accept her. Most cadets went to humbler schools. You needed to be a genius to attend Julius Military Academy, and Lizzy was no genius. But her father was a colonel. And her father pulled strings. And so Lizzy found herself among the marble columns, hallowed halls, and ambitious cadets of Julius. She wore a fancy white dress uniform. She polished her boots and cufflinks until they shone. She walked around with a goddamn saber on her hip. She was making her father proud.

At Julius, she had fallen in love.

She met another cadet. A handsome boy with serious eyes and quiet determination.

Michael Carter was everything Lizzy was not. His skin and eyes were dark, while Lizzy was pale and blue-eyed. He was raised by a single mother in the inner city, while Lizzy grew up the daughter of a powerful colonel. He was intelligent, ambitious, a true leader, while Lizzy was wild and free and a magnet for trouble. Yet they were both misfits. Perhaps that's why she had fallen in love.

Yes, she was a misfit here. At Julius Military Academy, trouble and Lizzy went hand in hand.

She could never grasp the lessons that came so easily for her classmates. As her grades slipped, she grew wilder. She drank too much, got into fistfights, even punched a superior officer. She skipped classes, dueled with her saber, cursed and spat and questioned every order. She still had a scar from a swordfight.

I don't fit here, Lizzy knew. *I'm too wild and stupid. I'm only here because my dad pulled strings. I'm garbage. I'm not like my dad. I'm not like the other cadets. I'm a loser. And I hate myself.*

She lasted only eleven months at Julius Military Academy before they kicked her out.

So she joined the army with the unwashed masses. She became an enlisted soldier. The daughter of the famous Colonel Crazy Horse—a grunt.

And here she was now, years later—a haunted grunt with one hand, a bullet hole in her chest, and a broken heart. A grunt returning home as a cripple.

Her father knelt before her wheelchair.

"I could have talked to the dean, called in a favor," he said. "You would be dining with officers in Little Earth, not drinking in that sleazy, rundown club in the Blue Boulevard. You'd never—"

"Dad. Please."

"Okay. Look at me, dragging up the past again." The brawny colonel attempted a smile, though pain still filled his eyes. "I love you, my daughter. No matter what. You get back safely to Earth, and you rest and recover. I'll be home in no time, and we'll take a long fishing trip together, okay? Like we used to."

She nodded, eyes wet.

She knew her father was traveling to North Bahay tomorrow, leading the Apollo Brigade to the front line. He commanded five thousand troops, and among them—the Lion's Platoon. Her platoon. Carter, the man she loved. Jon, George, Etty, and the others—soldiers Lizzy had trained, sometimes ruthlessly, but soldiers she was proud of, that she cared for. And Lizzy knew some would never return.

"I can't wait for this all to be over, Dad." She wiped her eyes. "We'll go to Oakthorn Lake, and we'll sit in our old boat, sipping beer, fishing for bass. Like we did when I was a kid."

Now even her gruff, burly father, the heroic colonel, the strongest man she knew—even he had to wipe tears from his eyes. "It won't be long, kiddo. We'll be on that lake again in no time."

He hugged her. He was a bear of a man, but he was so gentle. Lizzy felt warm and protected in his arms.

"Be careful up there, Dad," she whispered. "I love you."

Her shuttle landed. It was time.

She left her nurse and father under the awning. She wheeled toward the shuttle and up the ramp.

Before the hatch closed, she turned and looked back. She wished Carter had come to say goodbye.

Then the hatch slammed shut, sealing her in the shuttle, and the deck thrummed and the engines roared. The shuttle took flight.

Her wheelchair rattled in its harness, nearly knocking her onto the deck. Lizzy clutched a handle and gazed out the porthole. Mindao sprawled into the distance, a mosaic of rusty roofs and twisting alleyways, of jutting cathedrals and shantytowns, of blocky military bases and millions scavenging along rivers and train tracks. A city of beauty and pain. A city of nobility and despair.

As the shuttle rose, the wilderness of Bahay unfurled. The rainforests spread toward glimmering blue seas. As the shuttle got higher and higher, Lizzy could see more islands. Thousands of islands rising from this ocean world. When she had first arrived on Bahay, she had seen cloaks of rainforest draped across every island. Now half the islands were bare. Half the jungles had burned and withered. And then Lizzy could see the entire planet, a sphere of blue water and white clouds floating in space. A beautiful world. A precious jewel. The world where her soul and body had shattered.

I'm leaving Bahay, Lizzy thought. *But I'll forever carry the war with me.*

The shuttle turned away from the planet. Lizzy found herself gazing into deep space. A mothership lumbered into view, shaped like the hull of an old sailing barge. Here flew the HDFS *Adiona*, the starship that had first brought Lizzy to Bahay long ago, that still ferried troops and corpses back and forth between Bahay and Earth. Today it would take her home.

Someday my father, my friends, and the man I love will return home in this ship or one like it, Lizzy thought. *And I don't know if they'll return as passengers or cargo.*

The shuttle entered the mothership. Great engines churned, glowing lavender, filling space with eerie nebulae of light. A warp bubble formed, bending space and time, and the stars streaked into lines. The starship blasted forth, and Sergeant Lizzy Pascal never saw Bahay again.

Chapter Five
The Road North

Jon sat inside the armacar, rumbling toward the northern front.

He was, he decided after examining his feelings, scared shitless.

Sitting beside him, George Williams wiped his forehead. "I feel sick." The giant gulped. "I'm going to throw up."

"Throw up in your helmet if you must," Jon said.

His gargantuan friend was turning green. "Hey, I need my helmet! Especially with us driving toward a million Bahayans eager to fire bullets at my head."

The armacar kept rattling his bones. Armacars were cramped, noisy, clunky vehicles, designed to transport troops over rough terrain. Armored plates covered their walls. There were no windows, only a small dusty monitor showing a view from outside. The Lions Platoon squeezed inside here, backs to the hull, rifles propped between their knees. George needed two seats.

"It reminds me of our childhood in Lindenville," Jon said. "Taking the school bus together. You'd get carsick there too."

"Sure, exactly the same thing," George said. "That is, if school buses were covered in armor and the kids all carried assault rifles."

Etty sat beside the giant, as small as a mouse beside an elephant. She slapped George on the shoulder. "Welcome to the Mechanized Infantry, dear boy! See a new world through a tiny dusty monitor! Visit exotic destinations and blow them up! Travel there in a box of metal, come home in a box of wood! Yes, ladies and gentlemen, in the Mechanized Infantry of the Human Defense Force, every day is an adventure."

Jon rolled his eyes. "We get it, Ettinger."

"Why the hell do we need to drive anyway?" George said. "I mean, this is the HDF! We have starships, for Chrissake! And we're moving through the jungle in glorified school buses."

"Good luck flying a giant starship in atmosphere," Etty said. "That would be like gluing feathers onto your arms and expecting your fat ass to fly."

George growled. "Shut up, pipsqueak. You weigh as much as a feather. We could use shuttles or something. Like how we got down to the planet."

Etty nodded. "Sure. Transport hundreds of thousands of soldiers to the front line with a fleet of a few dozen shuttles barely larger than you. Sounds practical. Especially when the Kennys start firing rockets from the ground."

George fumed. "What I'm saying is that in the twenty-third century, there's gotta be a better solution than rumbling, rattling, bumping, and—" He turned green and covered his mouth. "I'm gonna hurl."

Jon patted his friend on the shoulder. "Hang in there, big guy. Think of something else. Like all the cold beer we'll drink to celebrate after we win the war."

He knew his friend wasn't just carsick. It was also the fear. The all-consuming terror. The kind that dug deep into your belly and spread icy tendrils through your body. They had all fought in the jungles before, but that had been in South Bahay, facing the Kalayaan. In the north, they would face worse than an uprising of skinny peasants. They would face the Luminous Army, a modern fighting force, trained and armed by the Santelmo aliens.

From everything Jon heard, the Lumis made the Kennys look like girl scouts.

Suddenly he felt sick too.

He looked around him. Lizzy's Lions filled the armored car, everyone in battlesuits, their guns oiled, their belts heavy with grenades and magazines. Some of them had scribbled words onto their helmets. Jon read the slogans.

WAR IS HELL

Kill the slits!

Gunslinger

Slit Exterminators Inc

Fighter AND Lover

The Earth Patrol

Just boys and girls, scribbling silly, patriotic, or murderous slogans with trembling hands, laughing and feigning bravado. Few of them were older than twenty. Just scared kids, most of whom had killed already. All of whom had watched friends die.

Lizzy's Lions. Jon's old platoon. But so many were gone. Only last month, half the platoon had fallen in the battle of Surigao Hill. New faces had replaced them, privates and corporals from other decimated units. Lizzy herself, sergeant and eponym of the platoon, wasn't here. She was flying back to Earth

George. Etty. More friends from other fireteams. And Lieutenant Carter was here too, sitting by the armacar's driver, dour and determined.

This isn't going to be like Surigao Hill, Jon thought. *It won't be just the Lions in the wild. An entire brigade is moving north. Thousands of troops. And we'll join with more on the way. There's strength in numbers. We'll win this war, and then Maria and I can—*

Gunfire shattered his thoughts.

Jon stiffened. Everyone looked up. A rotary gun was mounted atop the armacar. It was now roaring.

"Woo! Die, slits, die!"

The voice came from the gun turret, barely audible over the roaring bullets. Finally the gunfire died.

A soldier climbed down from the gun turret.

Heavy boots hit the deck.

"Woo! Killed me some slits! Up to seventy-three confirmed kills in the war." The soldier thrust his hips forward. "Fuck yeah!"

Jon groaned. It was bad enough being at war. It was worse sharing a platoon with Private Clay Hagen.

I've seen evil in my life, he thought. *But nothing like Clay.*

On his first day on Bahay, Jon had seen Clay strafing villagers from a helicopter, celebrating every kill. Who had Clay just shot? Guerrillas? Or more women and children?

The brute strutted down the aisle, thrusting his hips this way and that. He too had drawn letters onto his helmet. His spelled out *slitfucker.* He had drawn a swastika beside the word.

"Yeah, that's right!" Clay said, parading through the armacar, reeking of gunpowder. He tapped his helmet. "Slitfucker. Ain't none of you bitches kill as much as me. They're gonna give me a goddamn trophy from the Guinness Book of Records. Most slits killed."

"Psychopath," Etty muttered.

Clay spun toward her. His strange, wide-set eyes narrowed.

"What you say, Jew?"

Etty snorted. "I said you're a goddamn psychopath. Are you deaf as well as dumb?"

Clay aimed his rifle at her. At once, Jon and George grabbed him, pulled him back.

"Let go of me!" Clay howled.

But they held him back, shoved his muzzle down.

"Enough, Clay!" Jon said. "Cool it."

Clay was a powerful man. But George was even bigger. Through sheer size, George managed to subdue Clay. Jon helped, but he felt a little redundant.

"She threatened me!" Clay said. "You heard it. That tarsier-looking bitch threatened me!"

"Actually, I insulted you," Etty said. "Want to hear another insult? You look like a naked mole rat."

Clay roared and lunged toward her again, but now more soldiers had stood up, were pulling the combatants apart.

"Etty, stop provoking him!" Jon said.

The petite Israeli shrugged. "Eh, he's boring to rile up anyway. No challenge."

Clay spun toward Jon, snarling. "You. Jon Taylor. You feel the need to protect the little Jew, don't you? You like protecting vermin. Just like you protect that slit-slut at the club."

Jon sucked in breath. "Her name is Maria. Don't you call her that."

Clay laughed. "I touched a sore spot, didn't I? The men are saying you hired her for a whole week. That you *married* her." His laughter grew louder, shrill, demonic. "You married a slit whore!"

"Don't call her that!" Jon shouted, grabbing Clay by the collar.

But Clay just kept laughing. "The brave Jon Taylor, saving the innocent little Oriental flower from the cruel, brutish Clay Hagen. Yes, I was going to fuck her then, Taylor. I was going to fuck her for a night, and then never look back. But now that I know you love the whore…" A tight smile spread across his face. "I'm going to go back to her, Taylor. After you die in the jungle. I'm going to find Maria and make her mine. I'll show her what Slitfucker really means."

Jon howled and charged at Clay, fists flying.

For a few seconds, the two soldiers were kicking and punching. Clay's fist slammed into Jon's helmet, ringing his head like a bell. Another fist drove into his chest. If not for his armored battlesuit, it would have cracked Jon's ribs.

And then other soldiers were pulling them apart.

"Cool it, boys, cool it!" a corporal was saying.

A few soldiers started to chant, "Let them fight, let them fight, let them fight!"

Soon everyone was on their feet, some chanting for blood, some laughing, others trying to break up the fight. Jon managed to land a blow on Clay's chin. He took some pleasure seeing blood on his opponent's lip.

"What is going on here?"

A deep voice boomed.

Boots thumped.

A shadow loomed.

Lieutenant Carter stomped toward them. At once, everyone fell silent. A few soldiers even stood at attention and saluted.

Carter was not tall like George. Not muscular like Clay. He looked completely ordinary. A young man with dark skin, closely cropped black hair, and a clean shave. But his eyes were anything but ordinary. They were fiercely intelligent. Determined. Hard eyes, yet haunted. Eyes like iron doors imprisoning ghosts.

"Sorry, sir!" Jon said, saluting.

Clay licked blood off his lips. "The young maestro lost his temper."

The lieutenant stared at them, first one, then the other. Those eyes could make most men wither, but Jon remained standing tall, and Clay only smirked.

"Sit your asses down," Carter said. "You two don't have to like each other. But you do have to fight together—and not each other." He looked at the rest of the platoon. "Save your aggression for the enemy, soldiers. God knows you'll need it."

He returned to the front of the armacar.

George pulled Jon back toward their seats. "Ah, fuck it, man. Clay will probably step on a grenade soon anyway. Let's forget about him and—"

A *pop*.

A blast only an instant long—louder than a shattering planet.

Fire.

Screams.

Jon fell, hit the deck, and white light washed over him. Metal twisted and tore. Shrapnel slammed down around him. His ears rang, his head spun, and smoke filled his lungs. Firelight bathed him, searing-hot.

"We're hit!" somebody shouted, stating the obvious.

"The engine's on fire!"

"Get the men, get them—"

The ringing flowed over their voices. Jon lay on the deck. A corpse lay before him, burning, melting. Another man slumped in his seat, riddled with shrapnel.

Fire was moving closer.

Jon pushed himself onto his elbows.

The fire was spreading through the armacar. Smoke filled the cabin. Jon looked around him, saw Etty lying nearby, eyes closed.

"Etty!" he cried, and he could barely hear his voice.

Through the smoke, he could just make out George. The giant slumped on the deck, blinking, dazed. Blood flowed down his forehead. Other soldiers were scrambling up the ladder, heading toward the top hatch.

"George, up!"

Jon groaned, lifted Etty, and slung her over his shoulder. The girl was tiny. She probably only weighed a hundred pounds. But that was still a lot to carry, especially here. Jon struggled under the weight.

"George!"

The ginger giant was three times Etty's size. No way Jon was carrying him. But he grabbed George by the collar and pulled hard, yanking the giant to his feet.

"George, up the ladder! Go!"

George nodded, stumbled toward the ladder, and climbed toward the hatch in the armacar's roof.

Jon remained below, holding Etty, not even knowing if she was alive or dead. The smoke was everywhere. Jon couldn't stop coughing. The inferno flowed closer like a swarm of fire ants.

Finally George, gut sucked in, managed to squeeze through the hatch. Then Jon climbed the ladder, still carrying Etty across his shoulders. He reached the top, where the hatch was open to the sky.

"George, pull Etty out!" Jon said, hefting the unconscious girl.

George grabbed Etty and pulled her onto the armacar's roof.

Jon looked down. The fire was roaring through the armacar, consuming chairs, corpses—and a few living soldiers.

They were screaming below.

Jon only had a second to make his choice.

He made it and leaped back down into the fire.

He stumbled through the smoke and found Lieutenant Carter on the floor. The officer was still alive, but mumbling incoherently, legs bleeding, lungs full of smoke. He coughed.

"Jon… Jon, we have to get the wounded ou—"

"Right now, that's you, sir," Jon said, dragging his lieutenant out of the smoke.

He helped Carter up the ladder, and George pulled the officer onto the roof.

Jon went back down.

He pulled out another soldier.

And another.

Fire was licking Jon's legs now. The soles of his boots were melting. He coughed, and he was bleeding. He didn't even know what had cut him.

Only one living man remained below now. The armacar driver. The explosion had taken all four of his limbs. He still sat in the driver's seat, burning, screaming. Against all odds, he was still alive.

Jon took a step toward him, but then recoiled from the fire.

The driver's screams finally died.

I'm sorry, friend, Jon thought. *I'm sorry.*

He climbed and emerged onto the roof, coughing, bleeding, barely able to see or hear.

That's when the bullets began to whistle.

* * * * *

They were out there in the jungle. The enemy. Invisible. Ghosts in the brush. And their bullets flew.

One bullet pinged off the armacar only centimeters away from Jon.

Another grazed his helmet. Jon yelped, head ringing. Standing atop the armacar, he swayed.

A third bullet slammed into his armored chest, and he fell.

He slid over the armacar's edge.

He reached out, blinded by dust, and grabbed a handle.

He pulled himself back onto the roof. The bullet had dented his armor, cracked an armored plate, and left him alive.

"Jon, get down!" George cried. He was crouching by the armacar's treads.

Jon looked toward the jungle.

Several other armacars, farther along the road, were firing at the trees.

Jon did not take cover. He stepped toward the machine gun that topped his own burning armacar. A gunner lay there, dead. Ignoring the flames from below, ignoring the blood on the roof, Jon pulled the dead gunner aside.

He gripped the machine gun.

More bullets streaked from the jungle. They pinged off the armacar. One hit the gun turret's shield. Another whistled by Jon's ear.

He remained at his post.

He opened fire.

The machine gun rattled. Bullets roared out, spraying the trees, carving branches off. Along the road, the other armacars were doing the same. Trees collapsed. Trunks burst into flame. They kept firing.

Everything hurt. A bullet was embedded in Jon's battlesuit. The tip pressed against his skin like a lead thumb. The dented armor was crushing his ribs, making it hard to breathe. His head rang. Smoke still filled his lungs. But Jon stayed on the armacar roof, even as the enemy snipers fired from the trees.

And he kept fighting.

And as he fought, mowing down more trees, he thought of his brother.

He thought of Ernesto out there in the jungle.

He thought of Maria waiting for him.

He thought of the lies he had been told.

But mostly, he thought merely of firing more bullets. Of killing more enemies. Of doing his duty.

The battle didn't last long. The enemy pulled back. Like they had in Mindao just days ago.

It was the Kalayaan who had done this. Guerrilla warfare. They came. They struck. They pulled back.

They left death.

Standing atop the armacar, Jon touched his helmet, took it off, looked at it. A bullet had scraped the metal. He touched his scalp. He was fine. Miraculously, he was alive.

He climbed off the vehicle. Fire was still blazing inside the cabin, consuming anyone who hadn't gotten out in time.

George rose from cover. He stared at Jon with wide eyes.

"You are insane!" the giant said. "Standing atop a burning armacar, exposed like that?"

Jon shrugged. "Beats being inside the armacar."

"You go *behind* the armacar!" George shouted, pointing toward where he had been crouching, and where several other soldiers still knelt. "*Behind* the giant box of armor!"

"I had to fight them, George. I had to…" Jon swayed, nearly fell. George had to catch him.

"Etty," Jon whispered, stumbling forward, leaning against George. "Where is she?"

He found her lying by the armacar. Medics were already tending to her. One placed an oxygen mask on her face, and another was bandaging her wounds. The girl looked at Jon, smiled weakly, and gave him a thumbs up.

"Thanks, buddy," she said, voice muffled inside her mask. "You saved my ass."

Jon fell to his knees, then onto his back, and soon medics were treating him too, and he was breathing through a mask. Other wounded lay around him. Lieutenant Carter stood nearby, staring at the forest, ignoring the blood dripping down his leg. A medic approached him, but the officer shooed him away.

"He was there," Carter mumbled. "Ernesto. He was in the forest. I know it. I feel it."

Carter tried to run toward the trees, only for medics to pull him back.

"Sir. Sir! You need to lie down. You probably have a concussion. Sir!"

A horn blared.

"Hey! Hey there, you're holding up traffic!"

Jon looked down the road. Other armacars were lining up. Dozens of them—a line of armor snaking through the jungle. A soldier stood in an open hatch, a smirk on his face.

"You guys gonna clear the road?" the soldier cried down to Jon.

Jon flipped him off. "Shut up, rubberneck."

Then it all became too much, and Jon fell to the ground. He could only lie there, watch the smoke float above, and try to forget the screams of the burning driver.

Chapter Six
The Bargirl Bureau

They gathered in Charlie's house. A dozen bargirls. Proud members of the Bargirl Bureau.

Calling it a *house* was perhaps stretching the truth. Like most people in Mindao, Dalisay "Charlie" Santos lived in a shanty. Her husband had built the place, erecting crude walls of plywood and driftwood. A sheet of corrugated iron formed the roof, rusty and held down by sandbags. The place was built atop another shanty, which in turn balanced atop wooden stilts. A river of polluted water, human waste, and garbage flowed below.

Countless such shanties rose over the putrid puddles, precariously balanced on sticks, always threatening to topple over into the filth.

Fearing the Go Go Cowgirl, Maria had been hiding here for the past few days. Charlie had taken her in. The shanty was humble, yes. But Maria had found a warm home here. A loving family. Charlie's children were intelligent, inquisitive, and happy despite their poverty, and they filled the shanty with laughter. A house? Maybe. Maybe not. But it was certainly a home.

And maybe it's unfair to call us bargirls, Maria thought.

After all, Maria had only slept with one client, one she had then married. At heart, maybe she was still a rice farmer. The other girls too had not begun life as prostitutes. They had been fishwives, farmers, a few trash-sifters from the landfills. They had all washed up in the bars. Driven by poverty or war or loss or drugs. They were like the shanties of Mindao—risen above the trash, but only barely, and only balancing atop the thinnest of supports, likely to fall back in at any moment.

Maria looked around her at the women. A dozen had gathered here, coming from several clubs along the Blue Boulevard. Charlie was the oldest, the matron of the group. The youngest girl was only thirteen, but she already worked the bars, selling drinks—and herself. Her baby boy, a *mestizo*, cried in her arms, always hungry. Many of the girls weren't much older. They were the victims of poverty. Or of war. Or of cruel men.

But today they stopped being victims.

Today they became the Bargirl Bureau. Today they would fight for their world.

"Welcome, sisters, to our first meeting," Maria said.

Charlie raised a cup of wine. "Cheers!"

"Cheers!" the other women cried, raising their cups.

Maria smiled thinly. "Sisters, we didn't gather here to drink! We have our bars for that. We gathered here to discuss how we, the bargirls of Bahay, can defeat Earth."

"We'll drink them under the table!" one girl said. She stood up, raised her cup high, then chugged it down.

"We'll fuck 'em till they die of exhaustion!" said another, thrusting her hips.

Everyone laughed. Maria stifled her smile.

"Sisters, please!" Maria said. "This is serious business. We're not fighters. We're not soldiers. We're not guerrillas. We're not—"

"We're not sober!" a bargirl said, guzzling down another cup.

Everyone laughed again. Maria rolled her eyes.

"We're not victims!" Maria said.

"Hear hear!" said Charlie, raising her cup. Wine sloshed.

"We're not helpless!" Maria said.

"Fuck no!" said the bargirls.

"We can fight Earth," Maria said. "We can secure freedom for Bahay. Not with guns. Not with starships. Not with bombs or bullets. But with—"

"Our *dibdibs*?" said another bargirl, pushing up her breasts. Everyone laughed again.

Maria groaned. "I prefer to say, our womanly wiles."

Charlie laughed and reached toward Maria's chest. "You barely have any wiles."

Maria shoved her hand away, then covered her small chest. "That's not what I mean. We can do a lot with a soft smile. A kind word. A listening ear."

Charlie rolled her eyes. "How are those going to defeat an army of a million Earthlings?"

"And their starships!" added a bargirl.

"And their giant *pute ti-tis*!" said another, holding her hands out wide, then collapsing into a fit of giggles.

The other girls, Maria suspected, weren't taking this quite as seriously as she was.

"They bomb our villages," Maria said softly.

The girls looked at her. They lowered their cups.

"They spray poison on our forests, wilt our fields, and deform our babies," Maria continued.

The girls lowered their heads.

"They rape us," Maria said. "They rape children."

The thirteen-year-old bargirl held her baby closer. A baby who was half-Earthling. A child of rape. Charlie patted the young mother on the shoulder.

"They killed millions of us," Maria said. "These Earthling boys who come into our bars. They do this. They burn, poison, rape, destroy… and Earth doesn't know."

Charlie tossed her wine glass aside. She glared at Maria.

"What do you mean Earth doesn't know? Earth is doing this!"

"Earth's *soldiers* are doing this!" Maria said. "And even they don't always know. Jon didn't know when he came here. He was shocked to learn what's going on, and—"

"Your husband," said one of the girls. She snorted. "He's a filthy murderous *pute*."

"He's not!" Maria said. "He's a good man. Many Earthlings are good. But they're ignorant. Naive. Brainwashed. Especially the Earthlings on Earth. They think they're liberating us from evil aliens. They think we're welcoming them with open arms. They don't *know*."

Charlie snorted. "They know their boys and girls are coming back in body bags."

A few cheers rose. Girls clanked their cups.

"Yes," Maria said. "A hundred thousand—that's how many Earthlings we've killed. Not even one percent of one percent of their population. There are billions and billions of them. Meanwhile they've slaughtered millions of Bahayans. They've probably killed half our population by now. And they're not slowing down. They will keep going until every last one of us is dead."

"And what do you propose we do?" Charlie jabbed Maria in the chest. "How are we to stop this?"

"By exposing the truth!" Maria said. "We need to collect stories. Our stories! And tell them to Earth."

Everyone was looking at her now. They were silent.

"Our stories?" asked the youngest girl, holding her baby.

Maria nodded. "Yes. Kim, you were raped by an Earthling soldier. The same man who murdered your family."

Young Kim wiped her eyes. "I see him sometimes in the bar. He still asks for me."

Maria turned toward another bargirl. She was a young, beautiful woman with tiny arms. Arms as small as a baby's. Her fists like acorns.

"And you, Grace," Maria said. "You watched the Earthling planes spray Mister Weird's poison on your village. You reached into a river of poison to save your son. Only to pull out a little body. And to watch your arms wither and shrink."

The young woman with withered arms couldn't even reach her cheeks to dry her tears. "I would give up my legs too to have my son back."

"And you, Charlie," Maria said. "Do you have a story too? What—"

But Charlie stopped her with a glare. "Don't talk about me."

"Okay. Not all of us are ready to share. But I am." Maria raised her chin. "The Earthlings burned my village to the ground. They killed my parents, killed everyone I ever knew. Only I survived. Do you know what happened when Jon heard about this? His heart broke! And he swore to protect me! He didn't know. He came here thinking Bahayans are just monsters. Slits, they call us. Gooks. Slurs. Names for pathetic subhumans to kill. Not orphan girls from burned villages. Not us. We must share our stories with Earth."

Charlie's eyes softened. "They must see we too are humans."

"And not just our stories," Maria said. "Not just the tragic tales of bargirls. But stories from across Bahay. Every refugee in this city, the millions of them—they all have stories like this. We must interview them. Record them. Collect testimonials. Evidence of Earth's atrocities. And then—we must show them to every person on Earth."

"How will that stop the war?" demanded one bargirl, a saucy little thing, her pigtails dyed red, her striped stockings tattered. Her real name was Angelica Lopez, but an Earthling soldier had once nicknamed her Pippi Longstocking, the name of a character from an Earth story. The nickname had stuck, and now even to her friends, she was Pippi.

"Jon told me that there are elections coming up on Earth," Maria said.

Pippi opened and closed her hand, mimicking a chattering mouth. "Jon this, Jon that."

A few of the girls laughed.

Maria plowed on. "A man named Hale is the current president of Earth. He hates us. He bombs us ruthlessly. But another man is running against him. A man Jon says is dovish, who vows to end the war. He's lagging in the polls, but if Earth knew about us… if they heard our stories… Hale would lose the election. The war will end."

And Jon can come back to me, Maria thought. She dared not say that part aloud, fearing Pippi's scorn.

Charlie tapped her chin. "So basically, we're going to expose President Hale—and bring him down." She nodded. "I like it."

Maria held out her hand. "Are you with me, Bargirl Bureau?"

The others placed their hands atop hers.

"For the Bargirl Bureau!" Pippi said.

"For the Bargirl Bureau!" they all repeated.

Charlie grabbed a new bottle of wine. "Now let's get fucking pissed!"

She popped open the bottle. They all cheered.

Chapter Seven
Hellhole

For weeks, the army slogged through the jungles and wastelands. And for weeks, the enemy harried them without rest.

On the road north, the Apollo brigade joined other units. More brigades mobilized from forts along the way. Soon an entire division was rumbling up the road to Basilica, capital of North Bahay. The land shook. Here it was. The greatest push north since the early days of the war.

The generals called it Operation Jungle Fever. The final invasion of North Bahay. An invasion that could end the war--or lose it.

I just had to be drafted this year, Jon thought with a sigh. *Just my luck.*

The Hades Division, in which Apollo rode, was a force to be feared. They called themselves Earth's Fiercest. Hundreds of tanks. Dozens of helicopters. Ten thousand infantry troops, battle-hardened and eager to kill.

They were, Jon thought, a lumbering elephant. And like hungry wolves, the Kennys constantly nipped at their slow, swollen heels.

Every hour, another armacar rolled over a mine. Sometimes the explosions were so powerful they overturned even these enormous vehicles of armored steel. Jon's ears still rang from the bomb his own armacar had rolled over. And the mines kept detonating. Again. Again. Tearing armored plates open. Burning men alive. The screams never stopped.

And the army rolled on.

Whenever soldiers fled burning vehicles, they were there. Enemies in the trees. Hidden like ghosts. Firing with fury. Burning soldiers ran down the road, only to be riddled by bullets. Boys and girls crouched behind armored trucks, weeping, desperate to scoop up their spilling entrails. Dying in the mud. Calling for their mothers as their blood watered the soil of an alien world.

And the army rolled on.

Planes flew above, bombing the forests along the roadsides. Fire blazed. They moved onward through hell. But the mines kept exploding. And the soldiers kept dying. And still they rolled on.

After a week, the jungles were no more. They traveled over barren landscapes. The planes had flown. The fire and herbicide had fallen. Sometimes the land was burned, and smoldering ash spread to the horizons. Sometimes the land was poisoned, and the ancient rainforest lay in sticky black clumps like tar, and villages rose like fragments of bone from dark wounds.

Jon saw Bahayans traveling this nightmarish landscape. Deformed. Twisted. People whose skin had turned bright red, glowing and pulsing like living magma. People with withered limbs. Mothers carrying babies with no faces. Children with pointy bald heads, with eyeballs that dangled, with hearts that beat outside their chests. Conjoined twins, melted and fused together, crawling across the land, eating insects and worms.

Sometimes the soldiers shot these miserable creatures. Clay took particular pleasure in slaughtering them. And Jon wondered if this was murder or mercy.

We poisoned them, deformed them, Jon thought. *This is what we did to Bahay.*

And the army rolled on.

Jon sat in a jeep, watching the landscape. Few soldiers wanted to ride in jeeps. That meant being exposed to the open air, to poisonous fumes, to enemy snipers.

The other soldiers fought for a seat in an armacar. They felt safer in those massive boxes of steel. Jon did not. He had been inside such a massive box of steel when it rolled over a mine. He had seen that death and fire. Armacars to him now felt more like deathtraps. He had chosen the jeep, and he sat in the back seat, the ashy wind blowing over him.

But watching the land, seeing the deformed and dying, he now missed the dark innards of an armacar.

"It's horrible," George said, gazing at the desolation.

Jon lowered his head. "I remember seeing photos of deformed Bahayans. They told us they were monsters. Demons."

"What happened to them?" George said.

"Mister Weird," Jon said. "Poison. Our planes rain it from the sky. Look."

He pointed. In the distance, they could see it. A plane flying over a last swatch of rainforest, spraying yellow liquid. Where the liquid landed, the forest wilted. So did the people.

"Why?" George balled his enormous fists. "Why do we poison them?"

Jon sighed. "The planes are trying to clear out the forest. To give us safe passage north. To get rid of any hiding places for the Kennys. And…" He swept his hand across the scenery. "This is what happens."

A few Bahayans crawled in the rice paddies nearby. At least, they had been rice paddies once. Now the water was yellow and foamy, and the rice looked like human fingers, millions of human fingers rising from the muck. The peasants raised bloated, eyeless faces. Mouths opened to scream, toothless. Eight arms extended from their swollen bodies. They had become things like spiders, naked, begging.

A child crawled toward Jon's jeep. He had no head, no neck, but his body still moved, and an eye blinked on his torso. A mouth opened. Begging.

"Food. Food."

Jon reached into his pocket for an energy bar. He leaned down, handing it to the poor creature.

But another jeep rolled by. A soldier fired. The deformed child fell down dead. The soldier laughed and his jeep accelerated, spraying mud onto the corpse.

And the army rolled on.

"We're called the Hades Division," Jon said. "Named after the ancient god of death. And that's what we've become. Gods of death risen from the underworld, withering the land."

Etty sat between Jon and George. The young Israeli had been silent for long hours. Her eyes, normally so large and green and glimmering, seemed sunken and dim. Her skin was ashen, and she hugged herself.

Finally, for the first time today, she spoke. "Bullshit poetry."

Jon looked at her. "Etty?"

"Bullshit poetry!" she repeated. "Gods of death risen from the underworld? Fuck that. This ain't some mythological epic. Call this what it is. Genocide."

"Etty!" George recoiled. "You can't say that. Genocide is like something Nazis or aliens do. We're the Human Defense Force! The army that fought the alien centipedes, and the giant spiders, and the cyborgs. We're the good guys."

Etty lowered her head. "We used to be. Back when President Einav Ben-Ari led us. Back when we followed the Golden Lioness to battle. Ben-Ari always rode with her army. Always fought for justice. Now she's gone, and now President Hale sits in his palace on Earth. And we're here. Killing. Murdering. How many millions of Bahayans did we kill?"

George stood up in the jeep. His fists clenched. "Dammit, Etty! The Bahayans joined the aliens. We offered them a place in the Human Commonwealth. They refused! They chose aliens over humans! So, well, we—"

"Decided to kill them all?" Etty said.

"To liberate them!" George insisted.

Etty looked around her. "Do you see adoring crowds welcoming us with flowers?"

They looked around them. At the withered forests. At the miserable crawling things that had once been human. At the soldiers shooting, killing, laughing.

George sat down.

"No," he said. "I see… hell."

"A hell we created," Etty said.

Jon looked at the young woman. He remembered a time at boot camp. They had watched a propaganda film. Ensign Earth, a superhero soldier with a shield painted like Earth, had taught them that Bahay was evil, that heroes had to liberate it. Etty had stood up, dismissed the film, called it lies.

Jon had confronted her then. Had questioned her patriotism.

The slits murdered my brother! he had said.

Now Jon reached over and held her hand. "You were right, Etty. You knew before we did. You tried to tell us. You were—"

The land rumbled.

The ground cracked.

Across the poisoned landscape, a canyon opened like a ravenous mouth, gobbling tanks and jeeps.

Jon watched them fall. And then his own jeep was plunging into the darkness.

*****

Everyone in the jeep screamed.

The canyon opened around them. They fell into darkness. Into hell.

They flew from their seats. Jon slammed his head into somebody above him. The jeep rolled. Etty tumbled out of the jeep and vanished into darkness. More jeeps were falling, and a tank plunged down at their side.

But it was not the sundering world, nor the falling soldiers, that terrified Jon.

It was what lurked below.

The fall was only a few seconds long. But he saw. And he knew he would never forget.

Monsters filled the pit.

Mutations. Beings of nightmares.

Most were animals. Great snakes writhed, as long as pythons, their scales flaking like dry skin, their eyes blazing red fires. Smaller snakes grew from their gums like teeth, hissing and snapping tiny jaws. The beasts coiled like intestines in the belly of the earth. Gargantuan rodents scurried between the serpents, hairless and warty and obese. They were as large as sheep and as miserable as diseased rats. Their jaws opened to shriek, revealing rows of tusks, and their vestigial eyes moved beneath membranes of skin. Strange aliens clung to the walls like starfish, but their arms were human arms, ending with human hands and grasping fingers. They had no faces, but lamprey mouths opened in their centers, hungry for flesh.

Animals? No. They had been animals once perhaps. They had changed. Worms. Pigs. Peasants. Twisted into these strange creatures of the pits. The yellow poison filled their eyes.

The jeep landed among them. And the horrors swarmed.

Snakes wrapped around the jeep, hissing, eyes dripping. Their jaws opened wide, and the smaller snakes inside thrust out like tongues, snapping at soldiers. Fangs tore into one corporal, injecting venom. The man screamed, swelling up like a balloon of flesh. The smaller snakes caught him like hooks and reeled him in. The larger snake opened enormous jaws, tore into the bloating man, and feasted.

Jon opened fire, shouting wordlessly. George was firing at his side. Etty had fallen from the jeep, and Jon glimpsed her among the snakes, screaming, flailing. The terrors surrounded her. Snakes wrapped around her limbs. The mutants drooled and tugged at her hair.

"Etty!"

Without hesitation, Jon jumped off the jeep—and into the horrors of hell.

He landed in the pit of snakes. Jaws rose before him, screeching, full of smaller snakes that grew from blood red gums. Jon opened fire, filling the jaws with bullets. The snake fell, only for a wrinkly boar to take its place and stomp toward him, hooves tearing into the floor of writhing snakes. The beast had two pale, hairless heads, each covered with a hundred red eyes like pomegranate seeds. Its twin mouths roared, full of rotting tusks. Jon's rifle clicked. Out of bullets. He fumbled for a fresh magazine, and the boar charged closer, closer, leaped toward him, and—

Jon emptied his new magazine into the creature.

The mutated boar drove into him, eyes bursting like overripe fruit, grunting and flailing in its death throes. Jon shoved it off, stumbled forward, and waded into the snakes. Etty was gasping ahead, drowning in the swirling sea of creatures. The snakes were pulling her down like quicksand.

Throughout the pit, Jon saw more jeeps, tanks, and soldiers sinking into the monstrous abyss. The creatures were everywhere—filling the pit, covering the walls, emerging from tunnels.

"Etty!" he cried.

She had sunk down to her chest, and she was still sinking fast. She reached for him, gasping for air. Jon placed once foot on a dead boar's head, another on a sinking armacar, and grabbed Etty's hand. He pulled with all his strength, but the snakes had a good grip on her.

"Jon, get me out of here!" Etty cried.

"I'm trying, you weigh a ton!"

He dug his heels into the carpet of mutants, but soon he was sinking too. The creatures were coiling around his feet. Once perhaps, they had been mere earthworms. Mister Weird's poison had seeped into the soil, mutated them, turned them into these scaly monstrosities. Jaws rose from below, widening, reaching toward him. Jon fired with one hand, tearing them down. He kept pulling Etty.

Around them, soldiers were battling more monsters. Jaws sank through flesh. Bullets tore through mutants. Strange bats flew through the pits—creatures with leathery wings and bloated human faces, biting soldiers, whipping them with spiny tails. Every moment or two, a serpent rose from the pit like a cobra from a basket, grabbed a bat, and devoured it.

"Sir. Sir. Please. A coin. A meal."

Hands scrabbled at Jon. Somebody pulled him back, spun him around. He found himself facing a Bahayan peasant. Mister Weird had deformed the woman, melting her face, pulling her eyes down to her jowls. Her children had melted into her body, fusing with her like parasitic twins, reaching out twisted hands, mouths opening and closing, begging.

"Please, sir, please, sir, help, help."

Bullets slammed into the poor bundle of flesh. Into the mother. Into the babies on her torso.

Etty had managed to pull her gun free.

Jon looked at her.

"It was a mercy," she said. "I would do the same to you. And expect no less from you."

"Guys, come on!" George cried, shouting from his sinking jeep. "Get back here!"

Jon finally freed Etty from the squirming mass of serpents. He pulled her back to the jeep, for all the good that did. The vehicle was sinking into the pit of mutants. The soldiers stood on the roof, firing their rifles, trying to hold back the monstrosities.

Jon stared upward. He could see the sky, but it was a far climb.

This is a dream, he thought. *This cannot be real. This is just a nightmare.*

The snakes parted.

A soldier thrust up from below, dripping poison. He was a private Jon knew, had drank with, played cards with. Now he was naked, milky white, and eyeballs blinked across his torso. Another head grew from him, balanced atop his original head, upside down, blinking, trying to speak.

"Help…" the new head whispered.

Jon cringed, turned away.

The snakes pushed up another soldier. A young woman, a corporal Jon knew, had once shared a battle ration with. She smiled at him hesitantly, dripping poison.

"Jon…"

Then her hair slipped off. Then her skin slipped off.

Mister Weird is everywhere here, Jon thought. *He fills the underground. He's pulling us down. Into a nightmare we created.*

"Where are the goddamn helicopters?" George was shouting.

The jeep sank deeper. Now only the roof was visible over the wriggling carpet of snakes. Then the roof was gone, and they were down to their ankles.

"Soon we'll be in the poison," George whispered. "We'll rise again. Just more monsters in this pit."

"And maybe we're already monsters," Etty said, eyes haunted. "As above, so below."

"No." Jon said. "No! I won't let this happen to you. To us."

I must come back to you, Maria. I promised. I won't die here.

They sank to their knees. The sea of creatures swirled around him. Something grabbed Jon's leg. Was pulling him down. More troops disappeared into the pit, rising again, mutated, screaming.

"We're in hell," Etty whispered. "In hell, in hell…" She closed her eyes and whispered a prayer in Hebrew. "*Shma Israel! Adonai elohenu, adonai echad…*"

"There's no way out!" George said. "The goddamn helicopters aren't coming."

But Jon was not ready to give up.

As above, so below, Etty had said.

Jon looked up.

And he saw more of the horrors above. The strange human starfish clung to the cliff walls. The deformed human bats were flying.

"Climb them," Jon said.

"What?" George frowned.

The jeep was sinking faster. They were now up to their waists in the sea of mutants, and the poison sizzled around their boots.

"George, lift me up!" Jon said.

George hoisted him up, and Jon scrambled onto the giant's shoulders.

The bats were swooping, hissing, their bloated faces twisted in sneers. Their eyes bugged out. They had been human once. They still had human spines, human hands at the tips of their wings. The legs had withered, and sheets of skin quivered between their wrists and tailbones.

"To Mister Weird, to Mister Weird!" a bat chanted.

"Be like us, be like us!" hissed another.

One of the bats swooped toward Jon, mouth opening to reveal sharp teeth.

Jon leaped off George's shoulders.

He reached up and caught the bat.

The creature screeched, beat its wings madly, and bit Jon. Teeth sank into his shoulder, and he howled.

But the bat kept flying. And Jon clung on. The serpents were snapping their jaws below, and Jon remembered seeing them feeding on the bats.

"Higher, you bastard!" Jon said. "Or I'll drag you down into the pit."

The bat thrashed, screamed, bit him again. "Let me go, *pute*!"

It had a Bahayan face. That face was bloated, deathly pale, the eyes red. But Jon could see humanity there. Deformed. But not completely erased. Maybe once this poor soul had been a rice farmer. Before Mister Weird.

"Fly back up," Jon said. "Fly above. You don't belong here underground."

The mutated bat looked at him. And suddenly her eyes were human. They shed tears.

"Rise back into the sunlight," Jon said. "Don't die here in the darkness."

Weeping, the bat rose, carrying Jon.

"Rise, sisters!" the mutant cried. "Rise from hell. We were human once! We were farmers! We're not demons. Rise with me! Rise to the sun."

The bats cried out through the pit. Their human souls shone through tortured eyes. Their bodies were deformed, twisted, monstrous, but they still had human hearts.

They lifted soldiers from below. These soldiers from Earth had bombed their villages. Had poisoned their land. Had butchered millions of them. But the bats lifted them nonetheless.

Because they are human, and we are the monsters, Jon thought.

The bat carried him to the surface of the world, then dropped him by the open pit. Another bat carried Etty. It took four bats to lift George, and they struggled and strained, but finally dropped the giant beside his friends.

Other bats were carrying other troops. But not many. Jon didn't know how many jeeps and tanks had fallen, but the canyon spread into the distance. He didn't know if the Bahayans had constructed a huge booby trap, or whether the canyon had naturally opened, a wound in the decaying flesh of the world. Perhaps it did not matter.

This was all our doing, Jon thought. *We mutated this land, and the poor souls who live here still help us.*

"Jon…" Etty pointed. "Your boots."

Jon looked. Down in the pit, his boots had sunk into the poison. Eyeballs now grew from the leather, blinking.

Jon cringed and kicked them off, pulled off his socks, checked his feet. Thankfully he saw no eyeballs or extra toes.

George pulled off his own boots. One had a smacking mouth.

"I'm finally going to be sick for real." George turned green, then spun away and threw up.

For long hours, the army tried to fish out survivors. But in the pits, the soldiers were mutating, screeching, scrambling up, death in their eyes. They had to shoot a few of the poor souls, knocking them back down into hell.

Finally the helicopters came. By now they had nothing to do but drop napalm into the pits. The creatures below squirmed and screamed and died. Jon stood on the edge, gazing down, watching the flames consume hell.

The survivors climbed into beaten jeeps and armacars. Some soldiers grew extra ears and eyes. Some had melting skin. All had haunting memories.

And the army rolled on.

Chapter Eight
The Drumbeat

The road north was long, and every moment chipped off another piece of George Williams's soul.

The Human Defense Force rolled through lands of despair. George drove his jeep. He drove through burnt jungles. Over poisoned fields. He drove past villages where mutated souls crawled and begged, raising heads with no eyes. He drove as enemies fired from charred trees, and bullets picked out soldiers around him. He drove as bombs exploded on the roadsides, destroying jeeps, even the heavy armacars and tanks. He drove as every moment another soldier died. He drove through hell.

George Williams hated it here. Cold sweat kept trickling down his back. His heart kept pounding against his chest. His belly kept roiling with ice. His guilt kept haunting him like ghosts in a castle. But he drove onward, and he never looked back. Because he had made a vow. He had to protect Jon Taylor, and George would drive into hell and back for his friend.

He looked over at his friend. Jon sat beside him in the jeep, manning the machine gun mounted onto the hood. He was staring ahead, eyes dark, face hard.

He's changed so much in this war, George thought.

Only months ago, Jon had been the maestro. The leader of Symphonica. A sensitive boy with long black hair, soft pale skin, and reflective eyes. A boy who spent hours at his piano, composing by candlelight. A poet's soul. But now George saw a stranger. A man with tanned and scarred skin, callused hands, a cold stare. A soldier.

"Hey, Jon. Do you remember the time we met?"

The words just came spilling out. George blushed a bit. Sometimes that happened. He would be thinking to himself, and words just tumbled from his mouth.

Jon glanced at him. "Huh? What's that, buddy?"

George looked back at the road, cheeks hot. "Never mind."

They drove in silence for a while longer. The train of armored vehicles snaked ahead and behind them. Ten thousand soldiers—all moving north, heading through the wastelands toward Basilica, capital of North Bahay. To battle. To death or victory.

George took a deep, shaky breath.

I never wanted to fight a war. But whatever I face there, I will face it bravely. I will do what I've always done. Protect my friend.

Finally Jon broke the silence.

"A blue crayon," Jon said.

George looked at him. "What's that?"

"It was a blue crayon you had," Jon said. "In kindergarten. I wanted to use the blue one. But you had grabbed it first. You ended up breaking it in two, then giving me a half. I believe I drew a dinosaur."

George couldn't help but laugh. "I don't remember that. I thought the first time we met was when you stole my toy truck."

Jon gasped. "I'm not a thief!"

"Oh you were a horrible thief in kindergarten!" George said. "Always stealing everyone's toys. Never sharing. Very possessive."

Now Jon laughed too. "Do you remember that time in first grade? When that big kid—I think his name was Ron—stole my chocolate milk? Now there was a thief! God, I hated that kid."

"I remember that day," George said. "I clobbered the little brat. Pity the milk spilled."

Jon sighed. "Even back then you were protecting me."

"Back then I was a little smaller." George touched the scar on his head, a memento of the brain tumor. "Before my old friend Timmie the Tumor did his work on me."

Those memories kept bubbling up. The painful years following those idyllic days of crayons and toy trucks. Growing larger and larger, passing six feet, growing still. Being ten years old and taller than his father. Doctors and clipboards and medicines. Reaching six foot six, and more doctors, and his mother crying. And growing taller still. Thirteen years old and told he might not reach fourteen. The bullying at school. The name calling. The beatings.

Kill the hippo!

Stomp the elephant!

Beat the freak!

George couldn't help it. A tear fell. Whenever he remembered those years, it happened.

Sitting beside him in the jeep, Jon patted his shoulder. "It was a hard time."

George wiped his eyes. "And you were there for me, Jon. When I kept growing. When the doctors cut the damn thing out of my brain. The long days in the hospital. You were there. So now I'm here for you. And whatever happens in the north, whatever horror we see in the war—I'll be there for you."

A voice rose from the back seat.

"Oh my God, you two dicks! You're going to make me cry, you are. And I fucking hate crying." Etty hopped into the front seat and squeezed between them. "You assholes. I'm teary-eyed now."

The jeep was designed for three to sit in the front. But George was so large that Etty could barely fit. Her slender body pressed against him. Her thigh was warm against his thigh. And George couldn't help it. He blushed again.

Thankfully, if anyone noticed, they were quiet about it.

George glanced at her. His cheeks heated some more.

For a moment—really just a second—he admired her. Her smooth skin. Her silky black hair. Her eyes so large and green. Some people mocked her, said she looked like a tarsier. But to George, she was the prettiest girl in the galaxy.

He looked away hurriedly, cheeks so hot he worried he'd burst into flame.

"So, Etty…" George gulped, trying to think of something to say. "Do you, um, like music?"

She looked at him. "Sure."

"Ah!" George said. "That's interesting. I like music too, you know. Um, music is nice."

He cursed himself. He sounded like a goddamn idiot. Why was the touch of her body breaking his brain?

"Georgie, you okay?" she said. "You need to drink something?"

"I could use a beer," George confessed. "I miss beer. Once we get back to Earth, I'll take you to the Fox and Firkin pub in Lindenville. They have the best damn beer on Earth."

Etty raised an eyebrow. "Are you asking me out on a date?"

George nearly crashed the jeep. He cheeks were definitely on fire now. "No! I'm not! I mean…" He gulped. "If you want to, we can… But no! Of course not. Unless you want to. I mean—Jon can come too! Unless you don't want him to." He winced. "Do you?"

Etty grinned. "Like a threesome? Kinky!"

George nearly fainted.

Jon rolled his eyes. "For fuck's sake, Etty, stop torturing the boy."

Her grin only widened. "But it's fun! I love torturing people. It's my hobby. Sometimes I even—"

A boom shook the air.

Fire blazed ahead.

An armacar tumbled off the road, burning.

A second later, trenches opened along the roadsides. Enemy troops emerged, shouting and firing rifles.

George grabbed Etty, pushed her down, and shielded her with his body. Bullets whistled overhead. George kept driving the jeep, hunched over, protecting Etty.

Jon swiveled the jeep's machine gun around. He unleashed hell, pounding the roadside with bullets. Hot casings flew, clattering to the jeep floor.

Along the road, soldiers died. Blood sprayed. Machine guns rattled. Bullets streaked back and forth.

"George, let me go!" Etty said.

She squirmed free, loaded her assault rifle, and opened fire.

Bullets flew toward her.

"Etty, get down!"

But she kept firing. And George gripped the wheel. The jeeps ahead had stopped. He hit the brakes. They rumbled to a halt, and Etty fell, and the bullets were everywhere, and she screamed, and blood pounded in George's head. Pounding. Pounding. Beating inside him. Beating like he beat the drums in Symphonica's basement so far from here. Etty looked at him, blood on her forehead, fear in her eyes. And George howled.

He leaped out the jeep.

He stood on the roadside.

He raised his rifle and saw the enemy ahead. They were only a few feet away. Three of them, standing in the ditch. Bahayans. Gaunt, fierce, death in their eyes.

They aimed their guns at him. And George was back there. Back at school as the bullies tormented him. Back at home as his father beat him, called him a freak. Back at boot camp as Clay Hagen brutalized him.

And George howled.

He pulled the trigger, firing on automatic.

One Bahayan fell.

Another.

Bullets slammed into the jeep and the dirt road around George. One bullet hit his chest, cracking an armored plate, plowing a wedge of agony across his ribs. Another bullet shattered the armor on his shin, nearly cracking the bone. But George stayed on his feet. And he kept firing. Kept screaming. And the third Bahayan fell.

George stood there, panting, shaking. Staring at three men he had killed. But they were barely more than boys. Younger than him. The youngest barely looked older than twelve.

It was the first time George had ever killed.

The battle only lasted a few moments longer. Earth's superior firepower finished the job quickly.

George looked around him. At the blood. The bullet casings. A dead corporal beside him, a friend George had just played poker with last night.

He shook. He could not breathe. When Jon tapped his shoulder, George jumped.

He spun toward his friends. Jon and Etty faced him, eyes soft.

"George?" Etty whispered. "Are you okay? You got shot in the chest." She touched his dented battlesuit. "That shot could knock down a water buffalo."

George managed a shaky smile. "I'm bigger than one."

Then he had to run around the jeep. He fell to his knees and vomited and wept.

That night, the army camped deep in northern territory. A place where the jungles still grew. A place of danger and savage dark beauty.

Planes had flown here throughout the war, bombing, carving a road through the forest. The soldiers called it the Fire Road, and you could see it from space—a long scar through the rainforest, splitting the world.

The armored vehicles parked along this stretch of ash and death. They would not move again until dawn, and everybody found something to do. Sappers raised metal barricades along the road, while other soldiers lit campfires. Boxes of battle rations were ripped open. Soldiers began to eat and drink. Somebody played a harmonica, and soldiers sang old songs of Earth. Many soldiers sat silently, staring into the flames, while others gazed at photos of loved ones. A few soldiers were quietly weeping. One sergeant, his leg freshly amputated, leaned against a log, puffing on a pipe and reading a book. A petite private with a long, blond braid hugged a stuffed animal, whispering to the fuzzy bear. A turbaned NCO with a glorious white mustache was brewing coffee in a decorative silver pot. Younger soldiers gathered around him, partaking in the ritual, sipping the aromatic brew from silver cups barely larger than thimbles.

There were so many stories here. Thousands of souls, each with their own fears and loves, their homes waiting back on Earth. Soldiers from hundreds of countries and cultures. Soldiers from the glittering towers of New York City, from the rolling farmlands of Manitoba, from Mexican villages and Brazilian favelas. Soldiers from the icy plains of the subarctic and the golden deserts of Africa. Soldiers from the underground cities of Siberia and soldiers from ancient temples on misty mountains. At boot camp, the sergeants had tried to break them, to crush their individuality, to turn them into machines. But here spread a panoply of humanity.

George stood in the camp. Silent. Still. Everything spun around him.

"Hey, Georgie!" a corporal cried. "Join us for a drink? We got grape juice and can pretend it's wine!"

A private slapped him on the back. "Hey, it's George the Giant, slit slayer extraordinaire! Heard you killed three slits today. Popped your cherry, huh?"

Even Lieutenant Carter walked by and gave George a nod. "Good job, Private Williams. Killed three Kennys, did you? I always knew you had it in you. I'm proud of you. I see a promotion in your future."

They were all there. Patting him on the back. Celebrating his kills. They all spun around him, their faces blending together, becoming demonic, deformed, all laughing, eyes everywhere.

And he saw *their* faces.

The faces of the three Bahayans he had killed. Skinny young faces. Just boys.

And George couldn't take it.

He barreled between his fellow soldiers and stumbled toward the forest.

He shoved his way through the brush, ripping vines, ferns, and curtains of moss, banging into trees, moving deeper and deeper into the darkness. He left the campfires behind. He left the sounds of laughter. The taunting faces. The laughter and slaps on the back.

All light faded. He moved by touch alone. The rainforest wrapped around him, and his eyes stung, and animals scurried and hooted and hissed around him. Finally he tripped over something, perhaps a root, and fell down hard in the darkness.

George lay on the forest floor, panting, tears in his eyes.

The rainforest closed on him like a coffin. The humid air was like a living being, swallowing him, digesting him. The darkness wrapped around him like a shroud. When George placed his hands on the soft soil, he was touching the faces of the dead men. His fingers sank into cheeks, eye sockets, brains. He pulled his hands back, alarmed, and fell onto his side. But now they were gazing from above. Ghostly wisps of mist. Staring with accusing eyes.

You shot us.

You murdered us.

We are just boys.

You are condemned.

"Go away," George whispered.

Creatures hooted in the darkness. Ghosts moaned.

You're a murderer.

"Go away!" George howled.

He stood up, trembling. He still could see nothing. He pawed blindly in the forest, hit a tree, and banged his nose. He stumbled back, slammed into another tree. He grabbed at branches, tugged, tore them free. The wood snapped. He stood in the forest, clutching the broken branches like spears, and howled.

He began to beat the sticks against the trees. Again and again. Pounding at everything in the darkness.

"Go away!" he roared, thrashing the ghosts. "Leave me! I didn't mean to." He wept. "I'm sorry. I'm sorry…"

He found something hard in the dark, maybe a boulder. He began to beat it with his sticks. Banging again and again like banging on a drum. Back home in Lindenville, whenever the pain grew too great, he would beat his drums. He had broken several drum kits. Jon would play his keyboards, and Paul the guitar, but George had always been a drummer. Always been one to beat his fury into sound.

At school—always so meek, the gentle giant, taunted and beaten by the bullies. At home—so afraid, shrinking as his father railed. But in the basement, with his drums, the beast came out. And now the beast roared in the jungle, and George pounded the boulder until both branches shattered, and he kept pounding with his fists until they bled.

Finally he fell to his knees. He knelt, head lowered, fists bleeding. And he realized he could see. A light shone from behind.

George spun around and squinted. A ball of light glowed in the air.

A Santelmo!

He raised his gun. "Hold back!"

Two huge green eyes gleamed in the dark. George frowned. A tarsier?

"Whoa, whoa! Georgie, cool it! It's me."

George squinted and lowered his rifle. "Etty?"

She came closer. The light was coming from her flashlight. Her helmet was askew, and her black hair spilled from the sides. Her eyes shone like two lanterns.

"Yes, it's Etty!" she said. "What did ya think, that I'm a tarsier? Yeah, I get that sometimes. I just came to make sure you're okay. And that you don't destroy the entire rainforest."

George managed a weak smile. "I had to blow off some steam."

Etty stepped closer, dropped her flashlight, and pulled him into an embrace. He held her close. Her head only came halfway up his chest, and he wrapped her in his arms, protecting her, giving her his strength, and taking strength from her.

I'm four times her size, he thought, *but we're both full souls. And hers shines brighter than her eyes.*

"I know it's hard," Etty whispered. "I'm so sorry this happened to you."

"I killed them, Etty," he said. "They were just boys. But I had to. They were firing on you and Jon. I had to protect you."

She caressed his cheek. "They were firing on you too, you know."

George snorted. "They *hit* me too! I'm big and tough. I can take it. But you and Jon, well… you're so little. I was always so ashamed of being so big, Etty. So I tried to make myself very small. I hunched over a lot. I sat in a lot of corners. I thought there was something wrong with being so big. But here in Bahay? Let me use my size. To keep the little ones safe."

Etty hopped up, grabbed his shoulders, and tugged him downward. "Ugh! Get down here, ya' big idiot!"

He knelt before her, coming to eye level, and Etty kissed his cheek and mussed his hair. "You're a giant sweetie."

George looked into her eyes. "Etty, I would love to take you to the pub. Just you and me. A date. Will you go with me?"

She grinned. "Of course, you big galoot. I'd love to." She lifted her flashlight and pointed the beam at the shattered branches. "By the way, you're an excellent drummer."

"I even broke my drumsticks!" George said. "That's how badass I am. Just like Keith Moon."

She tilted her head. "Keith who?"

George grinned. "I have some things to teach you. Come on, Etty. I'll walk you back to camp."

She looked around her. "I dunno. I kinda like it here in the rainforest. What say we sleep here? Hell, beats sleeping on the dirt road with thousands of soldiers drooling and farting all around us."

George raised an eyebrow. "And if we oversleep and the army rides without us?"

She shrugged. "So we'll stay here forever. We'll live like Adam and Eve in the forest."

"Deal!"

They found a soft patch of moss and fallen leaves, and they lay down. George lay on his back beneath the rustling canopy, and Etty curled up against him. She slept in his arms, her breath soft against his chest. George stayed awake a while longer.

He gazed up at the night, and he saw a thousand little lights, spinning, floating like fireflies. He didn't know if they were Santelmos or some luminous bug of the forest, but they were beautiful, and he felt that he floated among the stars. He stared at the lights, trying to forget the faces of the three boys.

Chapter Nine
Shantytown Blues

Maria sat in the alleyway, listening to the orphans tell their tales.

Her camera rolled.

One child sat before her on an overturned plastic bin. He wore rags, and mud coated his bare feet. All around him spread the despair of the slums. Walls of rotting plywood topped with tarpaulin lined the alleyway, forming crude shanties. Trash covered the road, and rats scurried. Tangled webs of electric cables sagged above, nearly hiding the sky, buzzing.

The boy, one among a million who lived on the streets of Mindao, gazed into the camera with huge dark eyes.

"I lived in a village. A green village. There were farms. Rice and trees. And there was always food, and I ate it all, and my mom made the food, but then the bad guys came. The bad guys from Earth. Planes roared in the sky. *Roar. Roar!* Like that. And the bad guys flew them. And they dropped bombs on our village, and there was fire everywhere, and my mom died, and I saw her, and I said to her: Wake up, wake up! But she didn't wake up. Because the bad guys from Earth burned her until she was dead." His tears flowed. "That's what my cousins say. I want her to come back to me. Maybe someday she'll come back to me."

Maria shed tears too. She recorded every word.

The bargirls had pooled their money. The girls who took shabu, a drug to dull the pain, scaled back their habit for a few days, collecting more money than they ever had. Other girls took coins from secret stashes under floorboards. Some hustled, dancing in one club, pleasing men in the other, working harder than ever. A few, Maria had a feeling, picked pockets.

Twelve bargirls. The Bargirl Bureau. With their combined savings, they bought a single small camera. A precious weapon for their war.

With this little camera, Maria thought, *we will bring down President Hale. With these stories, we will free Bahay.*

She walked by the river. Many women were there, sifting through the trash, trying to find scraps to bring home. The sun beat down, and the garbage rotted, and children scurried over the hills of decay.

"The Earthlings came to my village," said a woman, her braid hanging across her shoulder, her eyes sunken into nests of wrinkles. "They killed the men. Then the elders. They raped the women before they killed the children. I had five children. Now I'm here in Mindao alone, trying to find food, to feed the orphans who live here. The farms are gone. The forests are gone. There are some scraps. The Earthling army dumps their garbage here. We sift through it, eat what we can, fix what is broken. We survive."

Maria sat on a concrete staircase behind a bar. The concrete was stained, crumbling, and stray cats hissed. An overpass stretched overhead, rumbling with jeepneys, mopeds, and the odd truck. A girl sat on the steps, wearing flip-flops and rags. She held a baby. Toddlers lay behind her, too weak to even brush off the flies.

"My name is Nina," the girl said. "I'm twelve. The Earthlings flew over my village. They rained fire. Many people died, but I escaped, and I took my brothers and sisters with me. My parents were too slow and they burned. I burned too." She turned around, pulled up her shirt, and showed scars on her back. "I walked for weeks before I reached Mindao. One of my brothers died on the road. He was so hungry. He starved. Now

Earthlings visit me here in the alley. They sleep with me. And they pay me."

"Why do you do this?" Maria whispered from behind the camera.

The girl looked into the camera. "So that I can buy food for my little brothers and sisters, and maybe someday, I can send one of them to school. And he or she can get an education. Find a good job. Feed the rest of the family. I'll be dead by then. The Earthlings gave me some disease. They put it between my legs, and the old healer lady by the river said I'll die in a few years. But maybe I can make enough money to save my family."

Maria walked along the Blue Boulevard strip, a thousand neon signs shining around her. Purples, blues, yellows, a psychedelic galaxy, glittering and promising endless delights. They were all in English, sometimes misspelled, calling out to Earthlings.

Angles of Holywood Dance Club

Bottoms Up: Come All Earthlings

Paradise Lost: Beer from Erth, Girls from Bahay

Pinoy Pleasure: Find You're Princess

Arabian Nights: The Most Exotic Dancers

Go Go Cowgirl: Midget Boxing Tonight!

Shabu Secrets: We Won't Tell

Manila Nights: Brekfast & Girl In Bed

Maria sat inside one of these glittering dens, hiding in the shadows, recording. A young soldier from Earth sat before her, holding a beer, not drinking. Strippers danced around him, but he didn't even watch. He was too timid to even look into Maria's camera. But he spoke. He told his story.

"The Kennys dug pits, filled them with spikes, and hid them with grass. The booby traps killed three of our men. We could never catch the Kennys, but our lieutenant, he said they came from a village nearby. We went there. There were no men.

The men were all in the jungles, fighting, or dead. There was a school, maybe fifty kids inside, just a little building of bamboo, and I could see the kids in there. Little bamboo desks and a blackboard. Somebody had drawn two suns and two moons on the board. Just kids, you know? But our lieutenant said they'll become Kennys someday, and that Kennys were probably hiding in the walls, and he told us to shoot. He told us to shoot and kill them all. So we shot." The soldier finally looked into the camera, but he seemed to be staring ten thousand miles away. "We shot them all. We shot the ghosts in the walls. We shot the kids. Every last one. I shot them. I shot them. Oh God, I shot them."

He lowered his head, weeping. Maria filmed his tears.

* * * * *

Finally, at dawn, Maria returned to Charlie's apartment. The rest of the Bargirl Bureau gathered there. They had been twelve members yesterday. Tonight they were eighteen.

"I recruited more girls at the Bottoms Up club," said Pippi. The tiny girl wore an even tinier schoolgirl uniform. Her pigtails were dyed bright orange, and she had drawn freckles on her face. She had come straight from dancing at the club. "They all want to help."

"I was made to understand there would be free wine here," said one of the new bargirls.

Her friend elbowed her hard. "Shut up, Joyce. We're here to help Holy Maria defeat the *putes*, not indulge your endless thirst."

Joyce crossed her arms, looked at Maria, and scrunched her lips. "Is that really the Holy Maria, the one they said shot a

Kalayaan in the *titi*, and he got so angry that his skull exploded, and his brain fell out?"

"Yes, it's her!" said another girl. "You know she slept with ten men in the club, but somehow, she's still a virgin. She's blessed by Jesus."

Another girl snorted. "No she's not! Don't be silly. It's her baby who's holy. They say that a *pute* fucked her in the bottom, but she still got pregnant." The girl waved her arms in the air. "It's a miracle!"

The girls all laughed. Maria sighed.

"We're here to win the war," Maria said. "Not to get drunk and tell jokes."

But Charlie was already popping open a few bottles of wine, pilfered from the clubs. The girls began to drink.

"Can't we do all those things together?" Charlie raised her cup, splashing a few drops. "To Holy Maria and her magical bottom!"

The girls all raised their cups, cheering.

Maria blushed. But she forced herself to stand up, to face the others.

"Today I walked throughout Mindao, and I collected stories." She pulled the camera from her pocket. "They're here. Stories from refugees. From child prostitutes on the streets. Even from Earthling soldiers. This is evidence of war crimes. This can bring President Hale down."

Charlie raised her cup again, sloshing more wine. "Down with that old *pute* bastard!"

"Down with Hale!" called the other girls, raising their cups. They had to open a few more bottles of wine.

"Last time we met," Maria said, "I asked you to search for more evidence of Earth atrocities. What did you find?"

Charlie spoke first. "I found a *pute* captain, a pretty high rank for the boulevard. He came into the Go Go. We normally just get the grunts, not the officers. I think he likes me. He squeezed my *dibdibs* a few times. I told him to come back, and I'll take him into my bed. Maybe I can get some intelligence from him. Something useful we can pass to the Kalayaan." She dropped her voice. "My brother is in the Kalayaan. Whatever I learn from Captain Pute, maybe it can help."

"I don't want us to help the Kalayaan!" Maria said.

"Why not?" demanded Charlie. "My brother is a noble warrior. The Kalayaan are killing many *putes*. They're heroes."

"The Kalayaan are the best fighters we have!" said another girl.

"Let's help them!" A curvy bargirl stood up and wiggled her bottom. "I will intoxicate this Captain Pute and learn all his secrets. No offense, Charlie, but your bum is far too small. The soldiers like women like me who eat too much and grow big like *pute* women."

"You *drink* too much!" Charlie said. "That's where you get your fat."

The curvy girl nodded. "That's true." She drained another cup of wine.

Everyone was laughing again, talking about their curves or lack thereof, and arguing about who could do a better job seducing the Earthling officer.

"Ernesto Santos is in the Kalayaan!" Maria said, speaking over them.

They all turned toward her and fell silent.

"Ernesto Iron Santos," Maria continued, voice softer now. "He tortures people with a clothing iron. I saw it. He beat me. He came to the Go Go Cowgirl to kidnap me, to force me to marry him." She shuddered. "It was Jon who saved me. Who blew open his skull with his gun. But Ernesto is still alive, a hole in his head. And Jon is out there, fighting him in the jungle. If we help the Kalayaan, we will help Ernesto kill my husband."

For a moment, everyone was silent, just looking at her.

Finally it was Pippi who spoke. "Too bad. You should never have married a filthy *pute*."

Maria slapped her.

Pippi screamed and lunged at her.

Soon the two were scratching, clawing, wrestling. Pippi bit Maria's leg, and Maria tugged the girl's pigtails until she squealed. The other bargirls had to pull them apart.

"Enough, enough!" Charlie said. "Save your violence for the *putes*, girls! All the *putes* other than Mister Jon. Otherwise Maria is likely to slap you." She winked.

Maria finally settled down, rubbing tooth marks on her leg. She forced a deep breath, trying to calm her heartbeat. Pippi sat down with a huff, straightened her skirt, and fixed her bright orange pigtails.

"I'm sorry, Pippi," Maria said. "I lost my cool."

The pigtailed bargirl laughed. "You slap like a little girl. It's okay. The *pute* soldiers smack me every night, much harder than you."

Maria held Pippi's hand. "Then I'll record your story too. So that the people of Earth know."

Pippi reached into her purse and pulled out a camera. "I already recorded myself. And a bunch of other losers like me with sob stories to sway the hearts of sentimental Earthlings."

Maria gasped. Her eyes widened. "Pippi! Where did you get another camera?"

The bargirls all crowded around, reaching out to touch the new camera.

"Oh, this is a Magica DSLR camera!" Charlie said.

"Much nicer than Maria's camera," said a girl.

"Hey, take some photos of me!" Joyce made a sexy pose. "Show the Earthlings something beautiful from Bahay, not just war." She made kissy lips at the camera.

Maria sighed. "Nobody wants to you see you looking like a duck, girl. Sit down." She turned toward Pippi. "Where did you get this camera, Pips?"

"I stole it." The pigtailed bargirl shrugged. "What do you think?"

Maria groaned. "I think I'm going to slap you for stealing! Don't you know it's a sin?"

"We're already doomed to hell." Pippi laughed. "You're talking about sins to a group of prostitutes."

Maria shook her head. "No. We're more than that. We're farmers and fishwives. We're mothers and daughters and sisters. To Earthlings, we're just slits—good for killing or fucking, that is all. We'll show them that we're human."

Pippi embraced her. "You are wise, Holy Maria."

"Even when I slap you?"

"You just slap sense into me, that's all." Pippi tapped a button, and a video began to play on her camera's monitor. "See some of what I recorded. Is this any good?"

The bargirls crowded together, watching.

Pippi had recorded heartbreaking testimonials. She had interviewed orphans on the streets, some only toddlers, who spoke of Earth planes burning their villages. She recorded a girl burnt beyond recognition, her face a map of scars, who lived in an alleyway behind a Jolly Joy Chicken, who spoke of Earthlings burning her. Pippi had recorded Earthlings too, soldiers weeping in her bed, confessing their sins as Pippi soothed and caressed them.

Maria wiped tears from her eyes. "There is so much tragedy in this war. So many dead. So many who still live but are dead inside. And we're all humans. Not just Earthlings and Bahayans, putes and slits. We are one, and we are suffering. And this must end."

The girls embraced her.

"It will end," Pippi said.

"We'll send these stories to Earth and show them the truth," Charlie said.

Maria smiled tremulously. "Yes, there's so much suffering here. But there's also us. There is friendship and love and hope, even in the bloodiest of wars. There is beauty in ugliness. There is nobility in tragedy. There is purity in struggle. That's what these stories show. That's why we must tell them." She finally poured herself a cup of wine, then raised it overhead. "To the Bargirl Bureau!"

"And to wine!" Charlie announced, and they all laughed and drank. Even Holy Maria.

"There is, of course, one problem," Pippi said. "How do we get these videos to Earth?"

The bargirls looked at one another. For a moment, silence filled the hovel. They all looked at Maria, who only bit her lip, lost for words.

"Fuck," Charlie said.

Chapter Ten
Basilica

After a journey of blood and fire and shattering steel, they saw it at last.

There in the north.

A black mountain, and atop it a city of stone.

Basilica. The Black City. Capital of North Bahay.

The first Filipino colonists, three centuries ago, had built a cathedral upon this mountain, constructing it from the black basalt found on the mountainsides. They had named their city Basilica after their cathedral, envisioning a shining beacon in a new world.

But Basilica had changed.

Over the years, the people of Basilica began to construct more and more from those basalt stones. Walls within walls. Guard towers. Churches that sprouted steeples like blades. Snaking alleyways with glimmering cobblestones. Looming black archways like the mouths of beasts. A labyrinth of rock and shadows.

Jon lowered his binoculars. To the naked eye, the city was a black smudge on the mountaintop. A shudder ran through him, clanking his battlesuit.

The Human Defense Force rolled across the burnt land. Along the road north, they had swelled to three divisions. A mobile city dedicated to destruction. They swallowed the land like a swarm of locusts.

The jungle had once grown here, draping the lowlands with a dizzying alien ecosystem. The jungle had burned. The tanks, armacars, and jeeps rolled over charred brush, burnt logs, and the skeletons of dead animals. Ash rose in clouds behind them.

They had lost many lives along the road. But thousands of soldiers still rode here, bandoliers slung across their chests, guns clutched in nervous hands. They wore battered battlesuits and dusty helmets. A few were smoking cigars. One soldier rode in a tank's open hatch, his helmet off, revealing a spiky mohawk. A few soldiers in jeeps raised Earth's flags, and another jeep was blasting a rock song. There was a lot of bravado. But everyone was scared. They had all seen friends die. Now they were riding toward the great battle of their lives.

Thousands of armored vehicles roared forth. Hundreds of planes and helicopters shrieked overhead. Drones flew everywhere like swarms of bees. There were more soldiers here than could fit inside the largest arena on Earth. It was the largest assault Bahay had seen in years. Here was Earth's full fury on display.

"This battle will win or lose the war," Jon said. "If we take Basilica, North Bahay will fall."

"Thank you, General Taylor, for that insight." Etty rolled her eyes.

"What, you don't believe me?" Jon said.

Etty chewed her lip, gazing at the city ahead. "Win, lose… I just see a place to die."

The fireteam sat in an open-roofed jeep. George was driving, while Jon manned the jeep's machine gun. They both shuddered at Etty's words. They all stared at the city ahead.

There it was.

Basilica.

A black city atop a black mountain.

This was nothing like Mindao. The southern capital was a sprawling hodgepodge of river and coast, a city of plywood, corrugated steel, concrete, and tarpaulin. A city of neon lights and palm trees, or human misery and sin, home to millions of lost souls.

But Basilica was different. Basilica was harsh. Unforgiving. A city in black basalt, its cathedral crowning the mountaintop like a fortress. There was no color here. No rivers or ocean. No trees. A city like a labyrinth. Smaller than Mindao. Only a tenth the size. But unyielding like an aging knight defending his territory to the last breath.

Jon peered through binoculars, seeking the enemy. But the city seemed dead.

Another jeep roared up beside them, crammed full of troops. Lieutenant Carter leaned out. He spoke over the roaring engines, the shrieking wind, and the clatter of skeletons snapping under their wheels.

"Soldiers! Are you ready to win this war? I bet you we find that bastard Ernesto hiding here."

There was a hint of a smile on the lieutenant's face. A touch of madness in his eyes.

He's obsessed, Jon thought, looking at his officer. *Not even obsessed with winning this war. But with his own vengeance. Ernesto murdered my brother. But I just want to go home and forget. Carter will never have a home until he destroys his nemesis.*

"From hell's heart, I stab at thee," Jon said softly. Too softly for Carter to hear from his jeep.

The lieutenant slapped the side of his jeep, nodded, and grinned—a grin more like a grimace, all its joy twisted. His jeep rumbled onward, raising clouds of dust over the barren landscape.

As they drew closer to the mountain, the last charred trees and animals disappeared. They rode over basalt plains. The volcanic stone flowed in hardened rivulets like wrinkled skin. The mountain must have once been an active volcano, spewing lava across the land. Now that lava was as hard and black as death, and if any fire rose from this volcano today, it would be the fire of war.

"Our lieutenant is mental," George muttered, gripping the steering wheel. "I swear, for him this whole war is a personal vendetta."

"Ernesto did kill Paul," Jon said. "And he threatened Maria. Is it so crazy to want him dead?"

George shrugged. "Well, you did put a bullet through his brain."

Jon sighed. "I know. But Ernesto is still alive. Maybe Carter is right."

He was playing devil's advocate now. Perhaps it was best to turn around. To end this whole war. To go home to Earth and forget this world ever existed. What was in Bahay for them? Vengeance? Victory? Maybe Etty was right, and there was only death in this place. Nothing more.

We've become mad here, Jon thought. *With bloodlust, or the will for vengeance, or pain, or shell shock. There is only madness here.*

"You're right, George," Jon said. "But this is our last battle. It's our chance to end this war. To defeat the Red Cardinal once and for all. And go home." His eyes dampened. "We can go home, George. Back to Lindenville. To Kaelyn. To our families."

And suddenly it was too much.

In this black, lifeless place, Jon remembered Lindenville's peaceful streets, the maples and oaks rustling.

In this world of death and despair, he remembered kissing Kaelyn outside the church, and evenings playing Monopoly with his family, and nights in his soft bed with posters of Nightwish and Epica on the walls. He remembered waking up on Christmas morning, running downstairs, and finding presents. He remembered pumpkins on the patio. He remembered the people he loved.

In this place of so much hatred, he remembered Maria back in Mindao. A little room above the club. Holding her in his arms. Kissing her lips. Talking to her all night, playing cards, tickling, giggling, making love.

I'm going home soon, Jon thought, tears in his eyes. *And I'm taking you with me, Maria. We'll live together in Lindenville. In a green, good place. In a house of joy and laughter and music. Far from this horrible place.*

He looked at his friends, and he saw that George and Etty were also crying. Perhaps they too were thinking of home.

Look at us, Jon thought. *The mighty soldiers of Earth—just homesick kids with tears on their cheeks.*

But Jon imagined that throughout history, the bravest soldiers had been like them. The soldiers who had stormed the beaches of Normandy—they had been just scared, homesick teenagers too. The soldiers who had stormed Abaddon, the alien planet of the scum—they had been just terrified kids, tears in their eyes. The soldiers who had risen up against the Marauder Invasion, freeing Earth from alien occupation—they had been like Jon and his friends. Just terrified kids.

And they had all been courageous.

They had all been heroes.

The greatest heroes in history have been scared, homesick kids, Jon thought. *We put our lives on the line, and we storm the beaches of war, because we know there is beauty back home. That it's worth fighting for. Even dying for. It's worth charging into the fires of hell to protect the meadows of heaven.*

In one way, Jon was not like those old heroes. Those soldiers before him had fought honorable wars. Against Nazis. Or aliens. Or vicious cyborgs. Perhaps Jon was fighting on the side of evil. He was the alien invader now.

But he still fought to return home.

He still fought for the woman he loved.

Perhaps many years from now, looking back at his role in this war, at his unjust fight, that would bring him some comfort. That would soothe the guilt. That perhaps would let him live with himself despite all the blood on his hands. That perhaps would offer a hint of redemption for his soul.

I fought an unjust war, but I fought for love, he thought. *If anyone remembers me, let them remember that. That I fought for her.*

"Hey, guys?" Etty said. The little Israeli stood up, frowned, and raised her binoculars to her eyes. "Look, on the city walls. Is that—"

A streak.

A whistle.

The jeep beside them exploded.

Fire blazed. Severed human limbs flew. Shards of metal pattered down.

The shock wave slammed into Jon's jeep. George screamed and tried to wrestle the steering wheel, but they were spinning, screeching across the basalt. Jon grabbed the jeep's machine gun, teeth clenched. A boot tumbled through the air, then thumped down beside him. Jon just hoped it was empty.

"What the hell is going on?" George shouted. They were still careening.

"Artillery on the walls!" Etty shouted. "Artill—"

Nearby, a tank exploded. Fire roared skyward.

Then an armacar went up.

Then another jeep.

George finally steadied the wheel, and their jeep pointed toward the city again. And Jon could see it now. Cannons on the city walls.

More shells streaked toward them. They were moving so fast. Faster than bullets. Mere luminous streaks like lightning strikes, then another jeep exploded, and another, and troops screamed and blood sprayed the basalt.

Jon opened fire. His machine gun rattled in his hands. His bullets streamed toward the city. But they were still too far. Several kilometers away.

"You're wasting ammo!" Etty shouted. "They're out of range!"

Another tank exploded.

A few soldiers emerged from burning vehicles. They began to flee on foot, wreathed in flame. A shell landed by a running squad. Men screamed and a mist of blood sprayed. Chunks of flesh, cracked helmets, and burning boots pattered down across the plains. A severed hand landed inside Jon's jeep. It was still clutching a cross.

"Those are fucking railgun cannons!" an officer was shouting somewhere. His arm was gone, ending with dangling red tissue and a jutting bone. "How the hell do the slits have railguns? They shouldn't have this tech! They--" He swayed, then collapsed.

"The Santelmos must be here!" a major cried. "The aliens are arming the little yellow bastards!"

"All armored units halt!" shouted another officer, speaking through a megaphone. "Artillery units—roll out!"

"Tanks ahead, jeeps behind!" somebody was shouting into a radio.

Chaos reigned across the army.

Another jeep exploded.

Another.

"They're butchering us!" George shouted.

A streak ahead.

"George!"

Jon leaned down and shoved the steering wheel. Their jeep jerked. The vehicle behind them exploded. Blood pattered. A loose tooth clattered down at Jon's feet.

It took only moments for Earth to return fire.

But those were agonizing moments of hell. Of people dying. Of fire and screams and blood and body parts everywhere.

Finally Earth's tanks responded with shells of their own. Finally the cannons of Earth dug down, aimed their bores, and began bombarding the city.

Jon stared at Basilica upon the mountain. Boom after boom rocked the enemy city. Fire bloomed over the basalt walls and towers. A black tower crumbled, then collapsed with a cloud of dust. Shell after shell pounded Basilica.

And the Basilicans kept firing back.

Even under massive assault, their shells kept flying.

George hit the brakes, joining the other jeeps of their brigade. The vehicles crowded together upon the plain. Carter stood in a jeep ahead, shouting something. The tanks formed a wall before them, pummeling the enemy, but more shells flew from Basilica, and—

"George!" Jon shouted, pointing.

A missile streaked from the city.

Heading right at them.

"Our jeep is stuck!" George shouted, gripping the steering wheel so tightly it cracked. Tanks and other jeeps surrounded them.

They had no time to think.

They leaped from their jeep, and—

Fire washed over Jon.

The explosion deafened him.

A shock wave pounded him.

Jon slammed down hard, and his face hit stone, and he tasted blood.

Stars floated around him. Dwarves filled his head, pounding his skull with little hammers. Blood dripped down his arm.

And then everything went dark.

Chapter Eleven
Scattered Pages

Kaelyn Williams was only seventeen, too young to be drafted. She never imagined she would end up fighting the Colony War here on Earth.

But there were many realities she had never imagined.

She had never imagined she would become a soprano, a singer in a symphonic metal band.

She had never imagined she would fall in love with the guitarist, a boy named Paul Taylor, a boy with black hair and laughing eyes.

She had never imagined Paul would be sent to fight on Bahay. That he would come back to her in a coffin.

She had never imagined that Jon and George, keyboardist and drummer for Symphonica, would leave for war just days after Paul's funeral.

She had never imagined that she, Kaelyn Williams, would remain alone here in Lindenville, New Jersey. A girl with wild red hair. With mismatched eyes, one blue and one brown. With so much grief and fear in her heart. The last member of Symphonica, like some princess from a tale, the last survivor of her kingdom.

She was Kaelyn Williams, and she was alone.

Lindenville Military Cemetery was a place of sad beauty. Maple and oak trees rustled around her, their leaves turning red and gold. Sunbeams fell between the boughs, mottling the tombstones with beads of golden light. Flowers bloomed, filling the air with sweet scent. The crisp breeze ruffled the grass, billowed Kaelyn's long red hair, and scattered dry leaves around her feet. She shivered and tightened her coat around her.

Yes. A beautiful place. A place of marble statues, gurgling fountains, and singing birds. A place of death and so much life. A place for so many of Lindenville's boys and girls.

They had come home from the horrors of the jungle. They rested around Kaelyn Williams, with only the autumn breeze to carry their whispers.

She walked between the graves. Row by row.

This was an old cemetery. Many of the graves were from the Alien Wars a century ago. Hundreds of Lindenville's youths had died in those wars, repelling wave after wave of alien invasion, fighting under the banners of the legendary President Ben-Ari, the Golden Lioness from the history books. Many of the graves were even older, dating back to the twentieth century, that century of man-made slaughter. Hundreds of these graves contained heroes of the world wars, youths who had died on the battlefields of Earth, some even younger than Kaelyn.

And there were new graves too.

Row after row.

White tombstones like soldiers.

Most featured crosses. Some were engraved with Stars of David, moons and stars, or a circle to symbolize Earth. Different faiths. Different backgrounds. But all were the same in death. All had given their lives for Earth.

The dead of the Bahay War rested here.

"You are all heroes," Kaelyn whispered. "But only the heroes of the Bahay War died in vain. Some of you gave your lives to defeat Nazism. Some of you gave your lives to cast back the aliens. But you, heroes of the Bahay War… you died for no reason."

Those words hurt to speak. Those words shattered her heart into a thousand pieces like shards of glittering glass. But those were words she had to speak here. Not just to the dead. But to herself.

She finally came to it. The grave she visited every day.

She read the epitaph engraved in the stone.

Paul Taylor
HDF Corporal
The Bahay War
2204 – 2223
Purple Heart

That was it. A rank. A war. A medal. A name and some numbers. Paul had given his life to the military. And this was all they could give him. A few stats.

"You were more than this, Paul," Kaelyn said. "They didn't write that you played the guitar. That you jogged in the mornings, painted on the beach, and loved the sea. They didn't write that you loved me. And that I still love you."

Sudden guilt filled her.

The memory resurfaced. The bench under the tree by the church. Sitting there with Jon. Kissing him. A kiss goodbye before the war.

And with her guilt—terror. Terror that Jon should return to her dead like so many in this cemetery. That she would come here every morning to visit two souls she loved.

"Symphonica is broken, and so is my life," Kaelyn whispered.

But Symphonica's music was still in her soul. The band was broken, but she had never forgotten Jon's music.

You are my muse, he would tell her, composing songs for her to sing. Even back then, Kaelyn had known. That the younger Taylor brother loved her.

Paul was taller, stronger, faster. An athlete, a guitar player, a hero in this town.

Jon had always been different. Thinner. Introverted. Reflective. When Paul was leading the swim team, Jon was at home, composing on the piano. When Paul was shredding his guitar on stage, a god of music preening for his adoring fans, Jon was playing keyboards in the background, barely visible in the shadows, the phantom in the cloisters. They were Jon's own songs, yet the maestro would shy away from the limelight.

And Kaelyn had known that he loved her. That the songs he wrote, cryptic as their lyrics might be, were love songs about her. She knew it broke his heart that she had chosen Paul. Perhaps Jon himself had never known. Perhaps he had lied to himself, told himself that Kaelyn was perhaps his muse but not his love.

But Kaelyn knew. She had always known.

And now she sang "Scattered Pages," one of those songs Jon had written for Symphonica. The overture for *Falling Like the Rain*, his uncompleted rock opera. A song he had written for her voice.

A dead boy cries
His tears fall cold
On the scattered pages of a poem untold
Do not weep
For notes already played
For symphonies composed
For prayers prayed
In the silence they echo
Marble halls they haunt
Death is only dry ink
Of notes written for naught
A dead boy cries
For those fallen young

On the scattered pages of a song unsung
Do not weep
For notes already played
For symphonies composed
For prayers prayed
A dead boy cries
His tears fall cold
On scattered pages for a dead boy's soul

Kaelyn sang those words. That song Jon had composed for Symphonica, for her to sing.

A soft song. A bittersweet ballad. Her voice rose high in the cemetery, a voice that brought Jon to tears so many times. A voice he had once called clear as a beam of moonlight trapped in crystal.

She sang. The song was part of *Falling Like the Rain*, Jon's uncompleted masterpiece, ostensibly the tale of a dead soldier looking back upon his life. But Kaelyn had always known. That dead boy was Jon, for he felt dead inside, lost without her love. She had chosen Paul, and she had killed a part of him. That part emerged with the music that he wrote.

Now, as she sang here, this song took on a third meaning.

It became a song for Paul.

It became a song, perhaps, for all the dead in this war.

And thus it came full circle. A song of the dead, looking back upon life. And Kaelyn prayed that she would never have to sing this song about Jon.

She heard a song behind her. A new song. An old song. This one sung by deep baritone.

She turned to see a funeral procession moving through the cemetery. A priest was singing, leading the mourners. Pallbearers carried three caskets, each draped with the blue flag of Earth.

Kaelyn approached, and she stood with the mourners. Three youths of this town. She had known them well. All three killed on Bahay. All three buried here in this beautiful place.

Scattered pages for a song unsung, Kaelyn thought. *And their song is done.*

Chapter Twelve
Blood and Basalt

"Help. Help!"

A voice called through the fog.

Jon blinked and opened his eyes.

I was unconscious, he realized.

He found himself lying in blood. A battle raged around him. Basilica mountain loomed above, a demonic shadow overseeing rivers of carnage.

The voice returned. "Help. Please. Help…"

A soldier was crawling toward Jon. A young man from his platoon.

His name is Patrick, Jon remembered in a haze. He recognized the private's freckled hands, which were clutching his rosary beads; he always held them, even in battle. *Patrick from Ohio.*

Patrick didn't have a face anymore. Just a hole above his mouth. But still he begged.

"Help. Help…"

Jon knelt beside him. Patrick was bleeding from the chasm in his head.

How do I stop this? What do I do?

More explosions bloomed all around. The earth shook. Another jeep exploded nearby, the tanks kept bombarding the enemy, and fire hid the sky.

In a daze, Jon pulled off his boot, took off his sock, tried to stanch the bleeding on Patrick's face. His sock sank into the skull. And then Patrick fell, gurgling, dying. He died in Jon's arms.

A shell exploded overhead. Shrapnel rained, pattering around Jon, sinking into corpses. He crawled. He crawled through gore. Though mangled bodies. Through screaming, wounded soldiers. He crawled over severed limbs. His hand sank into mush, and he realized it had once been a soldier. He couldn't tell who.

Oh God, is it Etty? Is it George?

With a shaky hand, Jon tore off the soldier's dog tags. Corporal Alissa Campbell. Jon had just talked to her that morning.

"Jon!"

Etty limped toward him, covered in blood. Her helmet's visor had shattered. Shrapnel had seared a sizzling line on her thigh. Her eyes were huge, green, and dazed, peering from a face covered in ash.

"Etty, where is George?" Jon shouted. He could barely even hear himself.

She pointed, and a tear streamed down her cheek, carving a line through the soot.

George lay nearby, buried under an overturned jeep.

Jon's heart shattered.

He ran.

He ran as shells rained all around. As people screamed, shouted, died. He ran toward his friend.

The blast must have lifted the jeep, then slammed it down onto George. He lay pinned under the heavy machine, the door pressing against his chest.

"Etty, help me!" Jon shouted.

He grabbed the jeep, strained. Etty helped, but it wasn't enough.

"We need more help!" Jon shouted.

A few more soldiers approached. They heaved together. Two soldiers grabbed a fallen cannon's bore and used it as a lever. They lifted the jeep.

George moaned. He was still alive.

"Etty, help me pull him to cover!" Jon said.

"I'm helping, I'm helping!"

They grabbed the giant, dragged him across the battlefield. All around the fire rained, the shells exploded, and bullets rattled. They pulled George behind a tank, seeking cover from the shelling. The tank's cannon faced the city, shelling the basalt walls again and again. The entire tank kept jerking. They huddled behind the thundering mass of metal.

"I don't see any injuries!" Etty shouted to be heard over the noise. "The damage could be internal."

"George, buddy!" Jon touched his friend's cheek. "You with us?"

The giant moaned. "Ow."

George's battlesuit was cracked and dented. But amazingly, it had withstood the jeep's weight. George even managed to stand up. Then take a step.

Jon gazed in wonder. "Fucking hell. A goddamn jeep fell on you, and you're walking."

"That's because he's bigger than a fucking jeep," Etty said. "Fat bastard."

But then she was crying and hugging George.

The giant winced. "Ouch, ouch, I'm tender! I think I cracked a rib."

Jon shook his head. "Goddamn, George, that thing should have crushed every bone in your body. I forgot our friend is an elephant. I—"

A shell exploded nearby.

Then a shell hit the tank they hid behind.

It burst into flame. Mangled metal clattered to the ground. The friends ran together through the barrage, hunched over. Shrapnel pattered their battlesuits, embedding in the armored plates. They found shelter behind an overturned armacar. More shells streaked, etching red lines across the sky like claws through sallow flesh. The dead lay strewn over the land.

Roars sounded overhead. Jon looked up to see HDF planes blaze toward the city. Blasts bloomed in the basalt streets. A tower collapsed. Anti-aircraft fire rose from beyond the walls, and a plane caught fire, then crashed into the city. Smoke blazed skyward, more defensive fire rose, and the surviving planes scattered.

"Hey!" shouted a sergeant wearing heavy earmuffs. "Hey, you privates! Get over here, we need more gunners!"

Jon looked. The sergeant was standing by an enormous cannon on wheels. It was the size of an oak tree. A few dead soldiers lay around it, mangled.

"We're not gunners!" Jon shouted. His ears kept ringing.

"You are now!" the sergeant shouted. "Get over here, we need more! I'll talk you through it."

Jon, George, and Etty approached the cannon. They dragged the dead gunners away, then took position and accepted earmuffs.

A bit too late to save my ears, Jon thought ruefully. They still rang.

The sergeant barked orders. George and Etty loaded a shell—it was the size of a fire hydrant. Jon pulled the massive chain.

The cannon jerked, shaking the world.

A blast roared.

Smoke and dust and fire blazed.

Jon watched the shell fly. It streaked overhead, crossing several kilometers within a split second, and slammed into the walls of Basilica.

Atop the mountain, the walls shook. A hole ripped open in the basalt.

Etty cheered, and even George managed a smile. Jon felt sick.

"Again!" the sergeant barked.

They loaded another shell. They fired again.

Around them, hundreds of tanks and cannons were firing too. Hundreds of shells slammed into Basilica. They bombarded the walls. The mountainside. Some shells made it into the city, and fire raged, and smoke billowed over the mountain.

The volcano is active again, Jon thought. *But this is our fire.*

They kept firing.

They fired all day, and they fired through the night. There was no darkness that night. There was no rest. There was the red fire, and the red blood, and the endless bombing.

The soldiers dug trenches. They huddled behind sandbags as the shells flew. The tanks kept firing. The cannons kept booming. The soldiers kept dying. A red night. The longest night of Jon's life.

Dawn rose with more fire.

The shells from the city kept flying.

"The goddamn enemy is desperate," Carter said.

The lieutenant had joined his platoon in the trench. They shared a bleak breakfast of battle rations under enemy fire. Every few moments, a shell hit nearby, and dirt and stones and chunks of metal pattered into the trench. Jon brushed dust off his tin of coffee.

"They don't seem desperate to me," Etty said. "With all due respect, sir, they seem to be kicking our asses."

Carter snorted. "They know the end is near. That's why they're using every last bomb they have. They're emptying their reserves. They want to go out with a bang." Carter climbed to the edge of the trench and stared at the city. "You're in there, Ernesto, aren't you? Yes. You're there. You're waiting. We'll meet again soon."

"Sir." Jon shivered in the dawn even as fire blazed all around. "Ernesto Santos is probably still somewhere in the south. He's Kalayaan, remember. We're fighting the Luminous Army here, not the—"

"I know who we're fighting, goddammit!" Carter spun toward Jon, his eyes burning. But then his face softened, and he placed a hand on Jon's shoulder. "I know, Jon. But Ernesto isn't a normal Kenny. Not some scrawny little rice farmer lost in the jungle. No. He's clever. He's strong. He's more than human. He survived a bullet to the skull. What kind of man can survive that? Tell me, Jon. What kind of man can survive a bullet to the skull?"

"I don't know, sir," Jon said. "George survived being crushed by a jeep, though."

The lieutenant turned toward George. He slapped the giant on the back. "Yes, you're a strong soldier. The biggest goddamn soldier in this army." He turned toward Etty. "And you're fierce. You're Israeli, aren't you? Like the old president. You're a race of elite warriors. The modern Spartans!" He turned back to Jon. "But you, Jon… you're special. For you, it's personal. What Ernesto did to your brother…"

"Sir—" Jon began.

"Yes, we're going to do it together!" Carter said. "We're going to find Ernesto. He's here in this city. Our platoon! We're going to find him! We're going to stab the bastard right in the chest."

"Sir!" Jon said. "This isn't about vengeance. Not for me. Not anymore. Don't become Captain Ahab, sir. Don't die fighting a whale."

"Ernesto is not a whale, Jon." Carter looked at the dark city, and he spoke softly. "He's a demon. He's woven of pure evil. He's a creature from the biblical darkness, risen from chaos like Leviathan. And we're going to end him."

"Leviathan was a whale," Etty muttered under her breath. The lieutenant didn't hear.

For three days and nights, they bombarded the city of Basilica.

For three days and nights, the enemy refused to die.

When dawn rose on the fourth day, it revealed a wasteland. Husks of armored vehicles spread across the basalt plains. Craters sunk into the stone, filled with blood, shrapnel, and scraps of shattered battlesuits. The corpses were everywhere. A few medics moved over the killing field, trying to collect the dead. It was impossible to distinguish soldier from soldier. Some bodies were fused together in death, melted and reformed in the fire.

And on this fourth blessed day, the bombardment ended.

Both sides were too beaten to continue.

Jon rose from his trench, coughing, shaking. His platoon rose around him. They stepped across the smoldering landscape, around bodies, shards of metal, and craters, and they stared at the city on the mountain.

Basilica had once been beautiful, in its own way, at least.

Now it was a ruin.

Half the defensive walls had fallen. Towers had crumbled. Scattered fires crackled.

But the cathedral on its crest still rose tall, surrounded by cannons. Even the mighty fury of Earth had not toppled it.

"The city still stands," Jon said.

"Not for long," said Carter. "The orders just arrived. We're moving into the city. Lions Platoon, gather around me!" The lieutenant grinned savagely. "It's time to enter the city. Let's find the rat in the maze."

"Sir!" Jon said. "Hang on. Why?"

Carter wheeled toward him. "What do you mean—why?"

"Why must we enter the city?" Jon said. "Can't we just . . . keep bombing it? Until we win?"

Carter shook his head. "Not gonna work. The bastards are hiding in tunnels. We softened up the city. But we need to move in. To fight dirty. Street by street. House by house. We need to rat them out."

Jon grimaced. "I hate to say this, but we could just nuke the whole mountain. Leave a crater here."

Carter snorted. "We're here as liberators, Private. Nuking a city would look bad." The lieutenant winked. "Come on, Taylor. We got this."

Under the red dawn, Earth's army collected its ragged remnants—and rolled toward the mountain.

They left ruin behind. Hundreds of charred vehicles, some barely more than twisted heaps of metal. Fallen planes and helicopters. Countless dead.

But thousands of armacars, tanks, and jeeps full of soldiers remained to fight.

They rumbled over the basalt, dipping in and out of artillery craters, and began the journey up the mountainside. A journey into the capital of North Bahay. A journey into the heart of hell.

Chapter Thirteen
Slum Predator

Maria was deep in thought when the wall crashed open and the devil burst in.

As if tonight hadn't been stressful enough already.

Charlie, Pippi, and the other girls had left hours ago. Some were dancing at the Go Go Cowgirl tonight. Others were stripping at Manila Nights or Bottoms Up. Some simply prowled the streets, too low on the totem to even work a club.

That left Maria here in the shanty. Well, Maria and a handful of insane children.

The Go Go Cowgirl was no longer safe. Maria could never work there again. Not now that Ernesto knew to look for her there. Skull blown open or not—he would stop at nothing to find her. To conquer her. To break her. Maria knew this.

And so Charlie had opened her heart and home. Maria now lived under the older bargirl's roof. It was a rusty, leaky roof, just some scrap metal secured with zip ties. But it was a roof over a warm home. And it was an act of remarkable kindness, one Maria would never forget.

It came at a price, of course. Maria had gone from bargirl to babysitter.

She sat among Charlie's children, trying to get them to sleep. Two were *mestizos*—half Bahayan, half Earthling, the gifts of soldiers at the Go Go Cowgirl. The other two were the children of Charlie's late husband, who had joined the Kalayaan and died fighting Earth.

All four were very much awake.

"*Tita* Maria, we don't want to sleep!" said one.

"We want to jump!" said another.

"Yay, jumping, jumping!"

Soon all four children were jumping on their bed. They shared a bed, all four of them. Charlie and Maria shared the second bed. There wasn't room for much else in the shanty. It was a hot, cluttered room, the plywood walls crudely cobbled together. There was no plumbing, but there was a toilet over a hole, and a gutter flowed below. The rain pattered the corrugated steel roof, raising a din like gunfire. It was probably too loud for sleep anyway.

Through the window, they could see the rain falling in sheets, washing over the shantytown, perhaps cleaning some of the illness and stench from this place. Rivers of trash flowed, churning around the wooden stilts which held the shanties aloft. Lighting flashed, and a shanty burst into flame, then fell into the river. It soon vanished in the darkness.

"It's often like this in the City of Angels," said Jasmine, Charlie's eldest child, a girl with wise, dark eyes. "The rains come at night. Wind and lightning knock shanties down. In the dawn, we collect the plywood and steel, raise new stilts, and have homes again."

Maria looked at the girl. "City of Angels?"

Jasmine nodded. "That's what we call the shantytown. There are angels here. They keep us safe. They bless us. My mom says it's hard here, but we're happy, and that's something amazing about us. She says we're the most amazing people in the galaxy."

Maria smiled and mussed the girl's hair. "She's right. We're Bahayans. Nothing dampens our spirits. Not even the monsoon."

She looked out at the dark, rainy night. The shantytown spread before her. Some shanties cluttered together on solid ground. Others rose from rivers and the sea, balanced atop stilts, for the shantytown always spread, grew, multiplied, a living thing, and a little water certainly could not stop its bloating. They were poor. But they were not helpless. Bundles of twisting, tangled electric cables draped across the shantytown like a huge blanket of cobwebs, and lamps shone everywhere, a field of stars in the night.

When the air was clear, countless people moved about the shantytowns, millions of them crammed in together, most of them children, despairing and bustling. Cats would hiss and fight, roosters would crow, and dogs would bark. When the rain fell, the people huddled inside their makeshift shelters of plywood and tarpaulin, and even the stray cats hid. Only the rats still scurried in the darkness, seeking higher ground, many falling and drowning. The rivers overflowed, and the sea rose, and the shanties were like flotsam and jetsam from crashing fleets, bobbing on the water.

"It's tragic but beautiful," Maria said, holding Jasmine's hand. "It's a scene from hell but also a miracle. There are three dark places where the human spirit shines brightest. In a hospital room. On a battlefield. And in poverty. In these three pits, you find the most horrible despair—and the most beautiful courage."

In this dark, swaying scene—a singular figure.

A man in black, tall and thin, slinking through the shantytown.

Maria frowned. Then a blast of lightning hit a bundle of cables, and the shantytown plunged into darkness, and the figure disappeared.

The light bulb in Charlie's shanty burst. Darkness cloaked the room. The rain suddenly seemed even louder, pounding the metal roof. The wind gusted, rattling the slats of plywood. Through the window there was only darkness.

The kids screamed.

"There's an *aswang* coming!" one child said.

The younger ones wept in the darkness. "*Aswang, aswang*!"

"There's no such thing as *aswangs*!" said Jasmine, the eldest. "Those demons are only stories from folklore."

Maria rummaged around in the darkness. "Where is the oil lantern? And the matches?"

She had seen them earlier. She stumbled blindly, pawing at toys, bottles, cans, clothes. Finally—an iron cylinder. The lantern. But where were the matches?

The wind blew louder. The moldy walls shuddered. The rain banged on the roof like the hoofs of the devil. The kids kept weeping.

"A monster is coming!" one said.

"Maybe it's a *pugot*, a monster with a giant mouth!"

"No, it's an *aswang*, a demon!"

"No, it's a *penanggalan*!" said Jasmine. "It's a flying severed head, with the spine dangling, and all the inner organs like the heart and lungs and entrails are still attached to the spine, so that when the severed head flies, all the organs drag behind like a disgusting banner, and—"

"Jasmine!" Maria said, finally finding the matches.

"Sorry, sorry! But the little ones were annoying me, and look, I scared them silent."

Indeed, the children were silent now.

In fact, the rain died to a drizzle, and the wind faded to a breeze. For a moment, the shanty was eerily quiet.

"The storm is over," Maria whispered.

She lit a match.

The flame flickered.

And the wall shattered open.

A lanky dark figure appeared through the cracked plywood. Eyes shone, one black, the other searing white. A toothy jaw opened in a cruel, red grin.

The children screamed.

"Demon!"

Wind gusted into the shanty, and the match guttered out.

The stench of blood and rot wafted. A voice boomed, filling the room.

"Hello, Maria!" The floor creaked. "I've returned for you!"

In the darkness, she could just make out a few smudges. Long arms, reaching out, fingers clawing at the walls. Dark legs like a spider's legs. A thin torso, and a golden tooth, and a white eye like a ball of shattered glass, like a dead Santelmo in the shadows. He was creeping closer. Closing in on her. Engulfing the room, a blooming arachnid. And she was the fly.

"Ernesto," she hissed.

She lit a new match, and he was right before her, looming above her, his face only inches from hers. The match lit him, painting him a hellish red, casting long shadows. His mouth opened in a lurid grin. His blind eye blazed furious white. His skull, she saw. His skull! Somebody had screwed in a metal plate, replacing the chunk of skull Jon had blown out. But the job looked crude, the bolts rusty and scratched. The metal plate still had a serial number on it; it was a piece of an artillery casing.

"Demon!" the children cried in fear.

And Maria could not contradict them. Here before her rose a demon. A creature of metal and flesh. A strange spider god of the shantytown. Ernesto the man was gone. Only this beast remained.

Maria screamed and hurled her match at the creature. It landed on his shirt. The fabric caught fire, but Ernesto barely seemed to notice. He only laughed, head tossed back, and grabbed her.

"You are mine, Maria! You hurt me. You broke me. You are mine forever!" He laughed, chest shaking, spraying saliva. "I'm whole again. I'm a man again! They say your lover took a piece of my brain. I'm insane now, Maria. I'm mad with lust for you. Be mine!"

She kicked, struggling to free herself. He leaned in to kiss her, and Maria swung the unlit lantern. The iron slammed into his face with a *crunch*. Ernesto fell to the floor, limbs curling inward like a wounded spider. And still his clothes were burning.

"Children, run!" Maria cried.

As Ernesto curled up on the floor, Maria herded the four children toward the window. They began to jump outside, one by one. The eldest, Jasmine, held the youngest, who was only a toddler.

Ernesto rose again, flaming, laughing.

"Come to me, Maria. Let us be married tonight in my camp."

He grabbed her arm.

Maria swung the lantern again. It shattered against him, spilling oil. The fire roared with new fury. It enveloped Ernesto and spread throughout the shanty, consuming clothes, magazines, and—

The cameras!

The Bargirl Bureau only had two cameras. Both were in the back of the room. The fire was spreading toward them.

All the stories, the interviews, the evidence—it was all loaded into those two precious devices.

Heartbreaking stories. Tears and souls. She needed to show them to Earth, so she could bring President Hale down. Just as importantly—she needed to preserve these memories. These testimonials. For proof of Earth's crimes. For history's tears and condemnation. As the fire spread, Maria realized that her goal was not only to stop the war, not only to shame Earth. But to preserve forever the cry of her people. To never forget.

She lunged forward, trying to reach the cameras.

But Ernesto blocked her way. He grabbed her wrist.

"Let go, Ernesto!" She pointed. "I need those cameras!"

The fire spread across his clothes. It seared Maria's wrist. She screamed, struggling, kicking. Ernesto didn't even seem to mind the heat. He must have become a true demon, immune to the inferno. Any last semblance of man had burned away.

"You will suffer for me, Maria."

He twisted her wrist, nearly crushing the bones.

Maria snarled.

She was much smaller than him. All her life, she had been small. Weak. A victim. Letting him beat her. Letting him scare her.

No more.

She roared and barreled forward. With all her strength, she drove her head into his stomach. Her hair burned. She kept pushing, springing off the floor, driving into him like a battering ram.

He wobbled backward, arms windmilling, and Maria slammed him against the wall.

The scraps of burning plywood shattered.

And they were falling.

Wreathed in fire, they tumbled, tore through a tarpaulin sheet, smashed through a hodgepodge of wooden slats, and finally crashed into the water.

Maria thrashed in the river, coughing, blinded. Her head went under. She reached up, pawing for anything to hold. She felt only floating scraps of paper, cans, diapers.

She kicked wildly, her head broke the surface, and she found herself in a world of flames. The fire was spreading over the shantytown. Charlie's children stood on a rickety bridge nearby, holding one another.

"Run!" she said. "Run to—"

Something underwater grabbed her.

It yanked her down, and she vanished under the surface.

She tried to kick, but the creature was gripping her legs. Maria opened her eyes in the water. It stung, and she could see nothing, only blackness. The grip tightened around her ankles, and he was pulling her down. Down into the depths. Down to cold death.

His voice reverberated through the darkness.

"Be mine…"

Maria pulled Crisanto from her pocket.

He burst into light. Brighter than she had ever seen him. So bright that he lit the water all around. Maria could see the trash floating above. A drowned rickshaw crumbling to rust. A skeleton covered with crabs, still sitting in a sunken boat. And below—the beast.

And Ernesto. He was there—skin burnt, the piece of metal embedded in his skull. Somehow still alive, pulling her under, a creature of the depths ready to feast. His jaws opened.

But Crisanto's light blinded him. He closed his eyes, and his grip loosened.

Maria kicked furiously, freed herself, and shot upward.

She burst through the surface and gulped down air.

She swam, and Jasmine reached down from the rickety bridge. It was really just a few wooden boards slung between two hills. Maria climbed up, coughing and shivering. The other children gathered around her, the firelight reflecting in their eyes.

"Where are you, Ernesto?" Maria whispered, scanning the water.

He was gone. Perhaps he had drowned. Perhaps he had escaped her again. And perhaps his darkness would still claim her.

The flames were spreading from shanty to shanty. Rats scurried over the bridge, squeaking. People soon followed. They emerged from the flames and swam through the water, fleeing the devastation. The sky cracked with thunder, and the rain returned. The flames battled the water, and steam and smoke filled the air. Maria stood in a realm of chaos, no sky or earth, no land or water, but a swirling inferno of all the elements of earth and heaven.

Maria pulled the children close to her and lowered her head.

Her videos were gone.

Chapter Fourteen
The Basalt Gates

Battered, bruised, and bloodied, the remains of Earth's army rumbled up the mountainside.

Basilica loomed like a gargoyle. Capital of North Bahay. Stronghold of the enemy. There it rose, a city like a fortress. Its walls and towers had taken a beating. The artillery had carved deep cuts. But the city was still mighty. The enemy had built these walls from basalt, hardened black lava spewed from the heart of this very world. Here was a city constructed from Bahay's molten core. It would not easily fall.

We're fighting the planet itself, Jon thought. *This isn't just a war against the Bahayans. It's a war against an alien world.*

He sat in a jeep with his squad. He rode shotgun—or, more accurately, machine gun. The heavy firearm was mounted onto the hood in front of him, slung over the cracked windshield. George was driving. Etty sat between them, as small as a child between her parents.

It was a dented jeep, the hood cracked open, both doors gone. But it was in better shape than hundreds of jeeps that smoldered on the black plains. The crew too was beaten and battered. Bandages covered George and Jon, and both still complained of ringing ears. Etty had sawed off one leg of her battlesuit, and layers of gauze covered her injured thigh. She didn't seem to mind. She was leaning back, chewing bubble gum. Every once in a while, her pink bubble popped.

"Goddamn it, Etty," George muttered, gripping the steering wheel. "Can you stop that? Every time you pop a bubble I think the enemy is shooting at us."

She twirled the gum around her finger, then flung it at him. "Pow."

George grimaced. "Etty, you got it in my hair, dammit."

She shrugged. "You should be wearing your helmet."

"Don't make me pull this jeep over!" George said.

Etty popped more gum into her mouth. "Are we there yet, Dad? Are we there yet? Are we there yet?" She flung the gum at his head, getting even more stuck in the giant's red hair.

Jon turned away from the bickering pair. He stared at the city again.

If I survive this war, he thought, *this is how I'll remember the Battle for Basilica. Riding in a jeep with no doors and two lunatics.*

"Fine, fine, I'll put on my helmet!" George said. "But the damn thing is so tight." He squeezed it onto his head and winced. "Ow! See? It fits like a—"

A *ping.*

A moment of confusion.

"George!" Jon said. "A bullet just ricocheted off your helm—"

And suddenly more bullets were flying from above.

Screams rose across the convoy of jeeps.

"Down!" Jon shouted.

Etty hit the floor. George ducked as well as he could, still trying to steer. Jon seized the machine gun and opened fire.

He didn't know what he was firing at. He aimed blindly at the city above.

More bullets pinged off the jeep. On the mountainsides around them, bullets tore through soldiers. Only those in tanks and armacars were protected.

"Onward, soldiers!" Carter called from his jeep as it roared by, eyes flashing and grin wide. "Onward to the city, with me!"

"Goddamn lunatic," George muttered, pressing down the gas pedal.

The jeep roared up the slope. Thousands of other vehicles rumbled around them.

"There!" Etty said, pointing. "Jon, look!"

He turned his head. He saw it.

A hole carved into the mountainside. It looked like a simple cave, barely large enough for a man.

But bullets were streaming from it.

Jon fired his machine gun. His bullets peppered the basalt around the cave.

"Aim properly!" Etty shouted.

"I'm trying, I'm trying! It's like a goddamn carnival game."

"Well, you better win me a stuffed animal!" Etty said.

Finally Jon managed to send bullets into the cave. The barrage from inside died. A corpse rolled out.

They kept driving.

Ahead, a hidden doorway swung open on the mountainside, and a rocket flew.

George tugged the wheel.

The rocket slammed into the jeep behind them. In the rearview mirror, Jon saw it explode. Saw the soldiers inside burn.

"Onward!" Carter was shouting. He was standing in his jeep, pointing at the city. "Is that all you've got, Ernesto? I'm coming for you!" The lieutenant laughed. "I'm coming to kill you, you bastard!"

The enemy filled the mountainside like termites in a hive.

Every few meters—they were there.

Hatches opened on the lava slopes, meticulously carved to blend in when closed. Bahayans emerged, shouting, firing guns.

Earth's forces kept storming upward. Cannons booming. Machine guns rattling. And every step along the way, the enemy resisted them.

For the first time, Jon saw soldiers of the Luminous Army, the military of North Bahay. He had fought the Kalayaan before, but the Kalayaan was just a peasant uprising. Those guerrillas warriors slunk through jungles, wearing rags and straw hats, covered with mud, most of them half-starved. But now Jon saw actual Bahayan soldiers. They wore armored black uniforms and helmets. They carried assault rifles. Insignia was stitched onto their sleeves.

Most looked very young.

Most were probably younger than Jon, and he had just turned nineteen. Some of the enemy soldiers looked as young as twelve.

But they were old enough to become Luminous soldiers. To fire guns on Earth's forces. And so they were old enough to die.

In the chaos of battle, of shrieking bullets and exploding shells, of rumbling engines and the screams of dying men, it seemed to Jon that Earthlings and Bahayans became indistinguishable. The Bahayans were smaller, yes. Most stood a good foot shorter than the Earthlings. And they wore black uniforms, while the Earthlings wore navy-blue battlesuits. But those were just superficial differences.

We're all humans. We're all stuck here on an alien planet. We're all killing one another for no goddamn reason.

Jon understood this. Yet he still fired his machine gun.

And he still killed.

He was part of an invasion force. He was fighting on the wrong side of this war, if there was a right and wrong side. But he fought to survive. He fought to someday go home, to see Lindenville, Kaelyn, and his parents again. He fought for Maria.

And perhaps that gave him courage. And perhaps, even among all this evil, it gave him nobility.

I wish I could be like the heroes before me, Jon thought. *Like the heroes from the stories of the Alien Wars. Like Marco Emery, the War Poet, who fought the alien centipedes. Like Addy Linden, after whom my town is named, who raised Earth in rebellion against the marauders. Like Einav Ben-Ari, the Golden Lioness, who had repelled alien invasions and turned Earth into a galactic empire. But I'm not like them. I don't have a just war to fight. I am fighting fellow humans. Fellow youths. And I just want to go home.*

A hatch opened on the mountainside.

A squad of Bahayan soldiers emerged, screaming.

They ran toward the Earth forces. A few scrawny young soldiers—running toward jeeps, armacars, and tanks.

"*Kalayaan para sa Bahay!*" they cried.

Jon had been on Bahay long enough to understand some Tagalog, the ancestral language of the natives. They were shouting: Freedom for Bahay!

A soldier in a nearby jeep fell, head torn open. Bullets sparked against jeeps and armacars. Another man fell.

And then Earth's soldiers opened fire.

The enemy ran into the hailstorm of bullets, screaming, firing, dying.

They were all dead before they reached the first jeep.

The army kept climbing, heading toward the smoldering city on the mountaintop.

Another hatch opened. Bahayans emerged, screaming, and charged at their foes. Their cries echoed.

"*Kalayaan para sa Bahay! Kalayaan para sa Bahay!*"

And they died upon the mountainside.

Another hatch.

Another enemy squad emerged from a tunnel.

They stormed toward Jon's jeep, and he couldn't do it. He couldn't fire. They came closer, howling for glorious death. Their guns boomed, and bullets pinged against Jon's jeep, and he wanted to shout at them: *Turn back! Stop!*

But they kept coming. It was a Kamikaze attack. They knew it. They had chosen this death.

Perhaps that only made things harder.

Finally Jon opened fire.

He mowed them down. They fell before him, twitching, and he knew he would never forget their dying faces.

"Why are they doing this?" George said, hand shaking. "They can't take on our armored divisions."

"They must be out of rockets," Jon said. "All they have left is bullets. Death in battle is better than surrender. To them at least. And—"

A Bahayan popped out of a tunnel ahead.

He was holding a rocket launcher.

Jon opened fire, and George swerved, and the rocket landed between two jeeps.

The explosion lifted Jon's jeep. They slammed down on their side. Everyone screamed. They fell onto the mountainside, and more hatches swung open, and more Bahayans came bubbling up from underground.

Jon glimpsed a tunnel swallowing an entire tank, and then a host of screaming Bahayans charged toward him.

He was on the ground, could not reach the jeep's machine gun. He ducked for cover behind the overturned vehicle, unslung his assault rifle from his back, and fired.

More rockets streaked.

Jeeps flew into the air, slammed down hard, crushing soldiers.

Earth's infantry spread across the mountainside like scattered toy soldiers spilled from a bucket. Their lines broke apart. Their wounded cried out for mercy, for their mothers. And the enemy kept coming. Wave after wave came like fire ants from a disturbed hive. Bullets and rockets streaked back and forth.

But Earth did not turn back.

Through death and terror, the soldiers of Earth moved forward.

As their jeeps burned, as their brothers and sisters fell, they charged into the fire.

"Clear out those tunnels!" a captain was shouting.

"Bring out the flamethrowers!" somebody cried. "Bring the fire!"

Under a hailstorm of bullets, soldiers ran forth, tanks of fuel on their backs. They approached the tunnels, only for bullets to fly from within, to mow them down. One man crashed, rolled, and came to a stop by Jon's feet.

Etty and George crouched behind a fallen jeep. A bullet hit George's shoulder, knocking off an armored plate, and he roared.

Jon moved without thinking. He knelt by the dead soldier. He gripped the man's fuel tank and grabbed the tube and nozzle.

Armed with the flamethrower, Jon marched up the mountainside.

"Jon, what are you doing?" Etty cried from behind.

"Saving your asses!" Jon shouted back.

Bullets whistled around him. More soldiers ran, only to fall on the mountainside.

"Not without me you're not!" George cried. Wounded shoulder, cracked ribs, and all, the giant ran up beside Jon. He roared, spraying the enemy with his assault rifle.

"Oh, fuck you guys!" Etty said, running to join them, even with her bandaged leg. She fired her rifle. "I ain't letting you die without me!"

Soldiers fell all around them, both Earthlings and Bahayans. Jon stepped over corpses, around smoldering jeeps, and reached a tunnel opening.

A Bahayan charged out. George and Etty mowed him down.

Jon thrust his nozzle into the tunnel and unleashed hell.

His flames boiled into the tunnel, a furious torrent, and it seemed to him almost like liquid fire, as if lava were flowing here again, this time entering the mountain rather than spewing out. Screams filled the tunnels. Enemy soldiers howled, wept, begged. A few came charging toward Jon, only to fall at his feet, burnt black and red.

And he knew there was no salvation for his soul.

They kept climbing the mountain. Foot by bloody foot. And every step along the way, they fought.

Jon kept firing his flamethrower. Filling tunnel after tunnel. He became an agent of death. Heartless but grieving. Murderous but mournful. Tears filled his eyes, but the fire dried them.

Because I have to survive today, he thought. *I have to come back to you, Maria. I made you a promise. That I'll bring you with me to Earth. That we'll be husband and wife. We'll have a beautiful little house in Lindenville on a street with many trees. We'll be so happy. So I must burn them, Maria. I must become an angel of death and make this world into hell. To come home to you, I must burn them all.*

He saw the fear in the eyes of his enemies.

And he saw the fear in the eyes of his friends. As he blew his fire, pumping the mountain full of death, he saw the terror in George and Etty. Not just terror of the enemy. But of him. Of what he had become. Like Moses, he had climbed a mountain and had been transfigured. But Moses had become a prophet of God, and Jon had become an angel of death. And instead of witnessing a burning bush, Jon cast living fire.

We've become new gods, Jon thought. *Gods of this alien world, Nephilim who descended from the sky, woven of furious vengeance, smiting the land.*

All day, they climbed the mountain. Filling tunnels with fire. Slaying the Bahayans who emerged, burning and screaming, to die in battle. The enemy made their choice. A death in fire over shame in shadows.

As the sun fell, Earth's soldiers finally reached the gates of the city.

The walls of Basilica rose tall, built of black bricks. They were mighty walls. Even under the horrible bombardment, they had stood. The artillery fire had dented them. Cracked them. Punched gaping holes. Guard towers had crumbled.

But those wounds were skin deep. The walls had cracked but not fallen. The city still stood.

The Lions platoon regrouped. Ragged. All of them covered in dust and blood. Many had not made it this far; their corpses lay mangled across the mountainsides or burnt in the charred jungles. Some had vanished, perhaps dead in a ditch, perhaps captives of the enemy, never to return.

Lieutenant Carter was here, covered in ash, a madness in his eyes.

George and Etty were here, dearest of friends, most loyal companions.

Jon was here, feeling so numb, his rifle held in cold hands.

His heart sank to see that Clay Hagen had survived this far. The brute was a corporal now. He had earned his promotion after killing more Bahayans than anyone in their company. He wore a chain of severed ears like a bandoleer, and scalps hung from his belt like wineskins. He smirked at Jon.

So many good people died, Jon thought. *And that monster is still here. We took this monster. We trained him. We gave him a gun. And we unleashed him on this world. Now the dead lie strewn upon the mountainside.*

How many more people will Clay Hagen kill? And how much more blood will stain my own hands? Maybe I'm no better than him.

"Hey, Taylor." Clay pointed at him. "When we get back south, I'm going to fuck that whore of yours. Don't worry, I'll leave her alive. But maybe I'll cut off her ears too. Add them to my collection."

Only a few weeks ago, Jon might have ignored the taunt. Might have feared the fight.

But he had killed men. Killed boys. He had faced death, dealt death. And he had no fear left.

He lunged at Clay, roaring.

The other soldiers leaped forward. They pulled the two apart.

"Let him be an asshole," George said, pulling Jon back. "Don't let him get to you."

Jon struggled to free himself, to pummel Clay. All the rage, all the guilt, all the horror and terrible violence—it all gushed inside him. This war had kindled violence in him, a terrible dark fire. The poet had burned. The killer awoke. Jon had been killing Bahayans, mere children defending their home, when he should be killing monsters like Clay. And the bastard stood there. Smirking.

"Enough!" Lieutenant Carter said, stomping between them. "Soldiers! Don't spoil our glorious moment of victory. The top brass says we can take this city, win the war. But more importantly—we can find Ernesto Santos. Come on, Lions! For all those we lost. For Lizzy. For Earth. Let's win this war!"

The first tanks rolled into the city. Earth's flags billowed from their antennas, flashes of blue in a world of black and red.

Jon stood for a moment, ash blowing around his feet.

Come back pure, Kaelyn had told him. But she had said that to somebody else. To a boy who had died.

Here I have become death, Jon thought. *Layer by layer, they stripped away who I was. They skinned me alive. This is all that remains. A man and a gun. The heart of a killer.*

The Lions platoon had no jeeps left. They walked, guns held before them, dented helmets on their heads. They stepped over rubble and charred bodies, and they entered the gates of Basilica.

Chapter Fifteen
Gravedwellers

"They're lost," Maria said. "The videos. The testimonials of refugees, widows, orphans, and soldiers. Their hearts and souls and tears and secrets. They all burned in the fire."

The other bargirls huddled around her. They sat in church, occupying the last few pews. The service had ended. The priests had gone home. But perhaps there was still some safety here, some sanctuary for lost souls.

"The important thing is that you're safe, Maria," Pippi said. The fire had spread across the shantytown, leaving nobody unscathed. Pippi's pigtails were singed at the tips, and burns had eaten holes in her stockings.

"And my children." Charlie hugged the little ones close. The family shared a pew. Even in her miniskirt, fishnet stockings, and halter top, Charlie was a devoted Catholic and doting mother.

"Too bad that fucking Ernesto didn't get his *titi* burned off!" Pippi said, rising to her feet. "If he comes in here, I will rip it off myself, then stick it up his own ass!"

Her voice echoed through the nave. One last priest was shuffling by, legs old and bent, sweeping the floor. He looked up, startled.

Pippi cleared her throat, sat down, and pressed her hands together. "I mean—I love you, Jesus!" She gulped.

Maria waited for the elderly priest to pass.

"Girls, we can record more videos," she said. "But you must do it without me. I must quit the Bargirl Bureau."

"What?" Pippi gasped and stood up again. "But you are Holy Maria! You founded the Bargirl Bureau! Besides, what else will you do? Your *dibdibs* are too small to be a good stripper, and you have an ass like a—"

The priest shuffled by again, holding the collection plate.

Pippi cleared her throat. "I mean—Holy Mary, mother of our lord!" She gave several curt bows. "Bless you, holy mother, bless you…" She watched the priest disappear around the corner, then turned back toward Maria. "Seriously, why are you leaving us?"

Maria heaved a sigh. "I don't have much of a choice. I must leave Mindao altogether. Ernesto knows I'm here. He found me in the Go Go Cowgirl. Then he found me in Charlie's house. No matter where I go in Mindao, he'll find me. I must flee into the wilderness."

"Oh, please!" Pippi pulled her into a protective hug. "Stay in my place. You too, Charlie! I have a nice little apartment. If you don't mind all my pet cats, that is."

"Kitties!" Charlie's children said. "Mommy, Mommy, can we live with the kitties?"

But Maria only lowered her head. "Thank you so much, Pippi. But I can't. I would put you in danger. If Ernesto found out that I'm staying with you…"

"Well, stay with Pippi for one night!" said Blessica, a slender bargirl in a leather miniskirt. "Then with me the next night. I have a little room over the Manila Nights club. I can take a night or two off, share my bed with you instead of the *putes*."

"And stay with me the night after that!" said Darna, a petite bargirl with unusually pale skin. She claimed that her ancestors in the Philippines had been part Chinese. "My place is small, just a little hovel under a bridge, but it's comfortable and warm and dry."

"And you can stay with me!" said another bargirl.

"And me, don't forget my place!"

"I just live above the Bottoms Up bar," said a girl. "My room is very loud most of the night. You can hear the music from downstairs, and the Earthlings grunting in the other rooms. But you can stay anytime. Just bring cotton for your ears!"

Everyone offered their place for a night or two.

Warmth filled Maria. She sniffed and wiped her eyes. "Thank you so much, sisters."

Charlie pulled her into an embrace. "The Bargirl Bureau is a sisterhood. We don't abandon one of our own. So it's settled! You'll move from one place to another. You'll never spend more than one night in one place. Ernesto won't find you this way."

"And if he does—" Pippi stood up, voice booming, then glanced around nervously. The priest was gone, and she continued. "—we'll cut off his *titi*!"

Everyone laughed.

"So long as we're armed," Maria said. "We don't have guns. But we can pilfer knives from the clubs."

"We can pilfer guns too," Charlie said. "God knows enough Earthling soldiers pass out drunk between my legs. They have guns that can conveniently disappear."

"The *putes* have guns like their *titis*," Pippi said. "They're big and hard and shoot their loads into Bahayans, and we bargirls can always get our hands on them. I'll steal some guns too."

Maria nodded. "The Bargirl Bureau will be armed."

When Ernesto came to me in the club, I hid behind Jon, she thought. *When he came to me in the shantytown, I was helpless. But now I will defend myself. I know how to kill.*

And suddenly—the memories were back. Flashing before her.

Her time in the Kalayaan, fighting in the jungles.

Her knife sliced a man's throat, and blood washed her.

Her gun boomed, and a man fell.

Yes. I've killed before. I sit in a church, a cross hanging from my neck, but my hands are bloodstained. I'm a murderer.

"Maria!" Charlie stroked her hair. "Are you alright? You're trembling."

Tears flowed down Maria's cheeks. She looked up at the crucifix above the altar, at the tortured figure hanging there. And for a moment, she did not see her savior on the cross. She saw David, a young soldier from Earth, chained in a tunnel, calling Maria's name as Ernesto burned him with his iron.

"Forgive me," she whispered, and knelt before the altar. "Forgive us all."

The bargirls knelt in prayer, and suddenly many were crying, perhaps remembering their own unspeakable sins. All but Charlie. She stood apart, arms crossed, staring aside.

* * * * *

The next day, the bargirls gathered in the graveyard.

It was a cluttered place with no tree, no flower, nor blade of grass. Dead from many generations were buried here, resting deep in cold soil. But the earth had run out of room. In recent years, the people of Mindao had begun to intern their dead aboveground. Crude sarcophagi filled the cemetery, stacked one atop the other, forming a city of stone. The cemetery was only a few blocks wide, but it was a city of its own, a hidden realm in the heart of Mindao, home to countless lost souls.

This is where we all end up, Maria thought.

She stood between the stacks of stone coffins. The dead were below her. The dead surrounded her. And someday she would find her eternal home among them.

It was a cluttered place, perhaps haunted with ghosts, but Maria found it peaceful. The sarcophagi were crude, but stone was better than rotting particle board or rusty corrugated iron. Ironically, these were better constructions than the shanties. The dead were frightening, but the orphans who filled the rest of Mindao broke her heart. There was no trash in the cemetery, no despair, and the only rot hid within stone. The cemetery soothed Maria. It was a quiet place. A good place. A place to remember. But also a place to forget.

The other bargirls gathered around her. Most still wore their miniskirts, halter tops, and high heels. Pippi was an exception, draped in black, even a veil.

"Pippi, why are you dressed like a giant garbage bag?" Charlie nudged her. "We're here for a Bargirl Bureau meeting, not a funeral."

Pippi glared from behind her veil. At least it seemed so. It was hard to see her face. "I have respect, Charlie! I'm not like you, parading around the dead with my *dibdibs* sticking out."

The veiled bargirl reached for Charlie's breasts, only for the older woman to shove her hand away.

"Look, don't touch!" Charlie said. "These puppies cost two hundred pesos to squeeze."

"Do you have them?" Maria said. "Do you have the guns?"

Charlie adjusted her breasts. "I sure do."

The girls tittered.

"Girls!" Maria rolled her eyes.

"Yeah, yeah, I got 'em," Pippi said. "Why do you think I'm really wearing this stupid big black robe?"

She pulled her robe open.

Maria's eyes widened. Everyone oohed and aahed.

Pippi had a dozen pistols hanging inside her coat, like some sleazy salesman selling counterfeit watches.

"How did you get all those in one night?" Charlie said. "I only got one, and I had to drug the damn *pute* to get him to sleep. Did you fuck the whole tenth division last night?"

Pippi raised her chin, pigtails swinging. "Hey, don't hate me because the *putes* like me more." She snorted. "And don't ask too many questions. You know me, *Tita* Charlie. I have ways. I can get you anything."

"You're going to get the syphilis at this rate," Charlie said, smacking Pippi on the head.

"Hey, don't you mess my hair!" Pippi adjusted her brightly-dyed pigtails.

The girls each took a gun. Maria chose an Albion, a lightweight pistol made by Oakeshott Industries on Earth. It was a small gun, but when Maria held it, she felt powerful. She felt safe.

If you come to me again, Ernesto, I'll put another bullet in your head. This time in the center.

Pippi cleared her throat. "And, ladies, for the *pièce de résistance*… I got two new cameras!" Pippi pulled them from her purse. "Check out these babies! Not too shabby, huh? Not the best cameras on the market. But it's all I could get on such short notice."

Charlie rolled her eyes. "What, if we gave you another day, you would get us a whole film crew? A Hollywood director for our movies?"

Pippi puffed out her chest. "I'd get you goddamn Ensign Earth to act in them too! Hell, I'll pull Charlie Chaplin from the grave and revive his career. I can get anything. You know me. Whatever you need, you come to Pippi. I always get the job done."

"That's what the Earthling soldiers all say about you," Charlie muttered.

A bell clanged. The sound reverberated through the cemetery.

Birds fled. The girls turned toward the sound.

The bell clanged again.

A Latin chant rose, deep and beautiful, rolling like thunder over the cemetery. Monks were walking among the stacked coffins, chanting. They wore dusty robes and hoods, and the monk at their lead clanged his bell again. It made a deep, reverberating sound like the birth of some primordial giant crying out in a subterranean lake.

The monks were wheeling forth several wooden carts, and inside lay the dead.

They were youths. Sons and daughters of Bahay. They were so young. Many seemed barely older than ten. But crimson scarves were tied around their arms, denoting their status. Here were warriors. Martyrs of the Kalayaan.

Some of the bodies were burnt and mangled. They had no limbs, no faces, sometimes no skin. But other bodies seemed unhurt, almost beautiful, the dark skin of Bahay become milky white in death, pale and pure as the moonlight. They had been child soldiers. They were as fallen angels, eyes finally closed to the horrors of the world.

The monks had scattered flower petals upon the bodies, and they swung thuribles of incense. The sweet scents mingled with the stench of death. As the monks chanted, pushing the carts forward, mourners walked behind them. Grieving mothers, still reaching for their fallen children. Weeping widows, tearing at their clothes, calling for their husbands.

The procession moved on through the graveyard and passed the Bargirl Bureau.

"Let us pay our respects," Maria said to her friends, "and let us mourn the fallen sons and daughters of Bahay."

She was no friend to the Kalayaan. Ernesto still wore the crimson scarf, hunting Maria's husband. But still, these dead were her brothers and sisters. They had been proud patriots, fighting for freedom. Perhaps lied to. Perhaps led by cruel men. Perhaps plunging Bahay into deeper pits of despair. But they were her brothers and sisters, nonetheless. And Maria mourned them.

The bargirls followed the mourners. They walked on high heels. They wore miniskirts and halter tops. They wore too much makeup to hide the bruises and weariness. Some had teeth stained with shabu, eyes that darted nervously. And they too were fighters, and they too were martyrs, and they too mourned.

In the heart of the cemetery, by a statue of a weeping angel, the monks halted the procession. The bell stopped clanging. A solitary monk sang a plaintive requiem. Maria could not understand the Latin, but the melody spoke to her. She understood the sound of grief and loss. It was the sound of rending hearts. It was the sound of planes flying overhead, and fire raining onto villages. It was the sound of children plucked too soon from the ephemeral luminosity of life. It was the sound of girls beaten in alleyways and bars, forced to spread their legs for the strangers who butchered their sons and brothers. It was the sound Maria's own heart had made as San Luna had burned. It was the song of Bahay.

Sarcophagi rose everywhere, scattered like so many dominoes, some piled four or five high. The monks began pulling off stone lids, revealing the skeletons inside.

Maria gasped. Some coffins held two, even three or four skeletons.

One monk arranged and lit bowls of incense, and aromatic smoke wafted, doing little to disguise the smell of the dead. The other monks carried the fallen youths from the carts, then placed them into coffins. The skeletons creaked beneath the weight of fresh bodies. The dead were small. Maybe even smaller than Maria. They could easily share their eternal beds of stone.

"Why are they sharing?" Pippi whispered, watching with wide eyes. Among the bargirls, she was the only one dressed appropriately.

"The cemetery is like the rest of the city," Maria said. "Overpopulated."

Pippi clutched Maria's hand. "When we die, let's share. I don't want to end up in a grave with some stranger." She turned her head. "Hey, Charlie, you want to share with us?"

Charlie snorted. "With how often you bang the *putes*, the syphilis will kill you in a year. I intend to live a long life." She looked at the sky. "And when I die someday, at the age of ninety-nine, I will be on Earth. With my new Earthling husband, who is twenty-three years old, and who bought me a big house with a spiraling staircase. Like in the movies from Earth that the soldiers watch."

Pippi leaned against her. "I hope it comes true for you, Charlie. And that you let me live under your staircase."

Charlie laughed and wiped tears away. "It's only a dream. If any one of us ever reaches Earth, it will be Maria. She has a real Earthling husband. Mister Jon will buy her that house. Then the rest of us will live under her stairs."

Maria looked up at the sky, trying to imagine it. Earth. The world from the stories. She had heard so many tales of Earth, even seen Earth in the old movies the theaters played, the ones the Earthlings had brought with them. Earth. The cradle of humanity. A place of peace and prosperity. A world where everyone lived in a house like a palace, not a shanty. Where you could buy any food you wanted for almost no cost at all, and people were never hungry.

"It's funny," Maria said. "We're fighting Earth, yet we all want to live there."

A voice cried out in terror, filling the cemetery, startling the bargirls.

Maria spun around, already reaching for her gun.

A monk had just pulled the lid off a sarcophagus. He stumbled back, dropping the stone lid, which cracked and shattered.

"A *multo*!" the monk whispered, face pale. *Ghost.*

Maria approached the sarcophagus. A man inside the coffin rose, blinking and brushing dust off his hair.

"A ghost!" Pippi cried and drew her gun.

Maria waved her down. "It's all right!" She turned back to the man in the coffin. "Are you okay?"

The dusty man looked around, dazed. "I was just sleeping. Why did you interrupt me?" He rubbed his head. "A piece of stone hit me on the noggin."

Maria tilted her head. "Why were you sleeping inside a coffin?"

"There's nowhere else to go," the man said. "I don't want to live on the landfills. Squatters line the train tracks. The countryside is full of fire and poison. The cemetery is quiet, and a stone box is better than a rotten shanty. Now leave me alone. This is my home."

Maria looked inside the coffin. She could see old bones below. "Who's that?"

The man shrugged. "How should I know? I only live here."

The monk was still clutching his chest in fright. But he managed to swing his thurible like a mace. "Leave this place and beg God for forgiveness, sinner!"

"Sinner?" The dusty man bristled. "Who do you think maintains the cemetery? Who do you think prays for the dead every morning and night? Who keeps the place clean and scares off the animals? We do. The people of the graves."

Another coffin lid slid off, and a woman crept out, slender and dusty, her hair wild. "I scare away the rats every day. Sometimes they make off with a finger bone." She cackled. "Thankfully, never mine."

Another coffin lid creaked open nearby. A bearded man emerged. "I clean the dead. I make sure they have nice places to rest. In return, they let me stay here."

More and more gravedwellers rose.

"I was a farmer once," said a man.

"I was a fishwife."

"I was a soldier."

"I was a hunter."

"Now we're all gravedwellers. The living hurt us. So we dwell with the dead."

Maria listened to their stories. And as they spoke, she kept her new camera rolling. They shared stories of war, of woe, and Maria captured every word.

As they spoke, two things became clear to Maria.

First—the Bargirl Bureau was back in business.

Second—she would not endanger the girls by living in their homes. Not after what Ernesto had done to Charlie's house.

Maria had just found her new home.

Chapter Sixteen
Dead Boy's Soul

Clutching his rifle, Jon walked with his platoon through the black city.

Basilica. Capital of North Bahay. A city of death.

"Where are they?" Jon whispered, eyes darting.

"Are they all dead?" George whispered, his rifle shaking. It looked barely larger than a pistol in his mighty hands.

"Hush, you two!" Etty whispered. "The enemy will hear you."

George rolled his eyes. "Ettinger, we have tanks rolling with us. They can already hear us. Trust me."

"Your footsteps are louder than tanks," Etty said. "Because you weigh more."

"Yeah, well, you weight as much as my sweaty underwear," George said. "Especially your brain!"

Jon tried to ignore his friends. They were bickering because they were scared. Banter was how they clung to normalcy in hell.

He looked around and shuddered.

Basilica was a city of walls. They lined every street. Surrounded every tower and well. Some walls were thick and towering, topped with battlements. Others were squat and crude. Some had fallen. Others withstood the bombardment. All were built of basalt. All were birthed from this very volcano. A black city. A city spewed from the belly of Bahay, taking twisting forms.

It's a labyrinth, Jon thought. *Or maybe it's a jungle. A new kind of jungle. Not one of trees and roots, but a jungle of hardened magma, just as wild and dangerous as the jungles we burned.*

A tank rumbled ahead of them. An armacar rumbled behind. But most of the troops were walking. A hundred thousand soldiers had come to assault this city. Many had fallen upon the mountain. But most were still alive. Wounded, haunted, covered in blood and dust—but still ready to fight. They spread out through the labyrinth.

Their orders were simple.

Sweep through every street in this city. Find the enemy. And kill them.

Yet as Jon and his friends walked along the cobbled street, they saw no sign of that enemy. Of any Bahayans at all, civilians or soldiers.

Did they all flee north? he thought. *Did they all die on the mountainsides? Do we just need to pluck this city like a ripe fruit?*

He was a soldier in a vast army. But here in this stone alleyway, he could only see his own platoon. The labyrinth of Basilica had segmented the grand Human Defense Force into small units. A squad here. A platoon there. Jon could barely even hear the rest of his army. He knew that hundreds of tanks and armacars were traversing the streets, but the basalt walls muffled the sounds. When the tank ahead rounded a corner and trundled off, the city became almost silent.

Jon shivered.

He looked up at the cathedral on the mountaintop. It was all he could see from down here.

It was larger than he had thought. It loomed. Larger than Earth's famous Notre Dame. Pitch black. Its gargoyles hunched over, leering, tongues sticking out. Its towers rose toward the red sky. Smoke still wafted over the city. The tower perched like a demon lord, spreading ashy wings.

Nobody knew who ruled North Bahay. They said that a cardinal lived in that cathedral. The Red Cardinal, his robes woven from Christ's shroud, still stained red with ancient blood. They said that the Red Cardinal ruled this world. That he was only half human. That he had changed. Become something greater than mere man.

But no Earthling had seen him. There were no photographs of the Red Cardinal. Only stories.

"Is he in there?" Jon said. "Watching us?"

It seemed to him, from this distance, that he saw a shadow moving in the cathedral's windows. But it was still so far. Perhaps just a trick of his imagination.

They entered a courtyard, a black well in its center. Dour basalt buildings glared from all sides with windows like eyes. A tower had fallen here, and bricks littered the cobblestones. A Bahayan corpse sprawled atop the bricks, her long black hair strewn around her head like a puddle. She gazed with blank eyes toward the smoky sky.

Jon couldn't help but stare. The corpse wore a Luminous Army uniform. But she looked so much like Maria.

A few soldiers from the platoon approached the corpse.

One of them, a private with a pockmarked face, pointed at the dead Bahayan. "Look at this bitch. Artillery must have killed her from the mountainside."

Another soldier, a mustached sergeant, whistled. "She's pretty hot. Think she'll show me her tits?"

Soldiers laughed. More approached the body. Some whistled and even thrust their hips at the corpse. The mustached sergeant knelt, began to unbutton the dead woman's uniform.

She's lying on top of the bricks, Jon realized. *Not below them.*

His eyes widened.

He saw it. Cables dangling from the woman's sleeve.

The mustached sergeant pulled open her shirt, revealing a ticking pipe.

"What the—"

"Run!" Jon shouted.

He slammed into George and Etty, knocking them to the ground.

An explosion rocked the courtyard.

Windows shattered all around, scattering shards like a million jewels.

The city shook. Ringing filled Jon's ears. And then the dead began to rain down. Chunks of flesh pattered everywhere.

Jon looked back toward the pile of bricks. The Bahayan corpse was gone. So were the mustached sergeant, the pockmarked private, and a handful of other soldiers.

"That'll teach 'em," Etty muttered, but then she stumbled aside and vomited, and when she looked back at Jon, tears were rolling down her cheeks.

Lieutenant Carter entered the courtyard. He looked over the scene. At his dead, mutilated soldiers. He walked through the gore, around the piles of bricks, and toward the next alleyway.

"Come, soldiers! He's not here." The lieutenant sneered. "We'll find him."

They kept moving through the city.

The higher they climbed, narrower the streets became. Coiling. Branching off. Jon felt like a rat in a maze. He couldn't see the rest of the city. He could barely see a few yards ahead. Just twisting streets like tunnels. There wasn't even a sky above. Just a pall of red smoke. Jon didn't know if it was night or day, whether sunlight or firelight lit his path. The world was black and red like a burnt man.

The city is alive, he thought. *And we're parasites inside its stone veins.*

And always the cathedral was there. Rising on the mountaintop, casting its long shadow. It guided them onward. And always in those distant windows—a red shadow, moving back and forth.

"Jon!"

Etty grabbed him, pulled him back. She pointed.

Jon stared ahead. He inhaled sharply.

A cable stretched across the street. Barely wider than a cobweb. Jon could see only glints when the light caught it.

The Lions Platoon climbed carefully over the cable. They continued down the street, rounded a corner, and saw another platoon heading down a road. Jon recognized the stars drawn on their helmets—they were the Starfire platoon from the same company.

"Starfire, watch out for cables!" Jon called out. "We found a cable a road back, no wider than a fishing line, and—"

A soldier looked at Jon, tilted his head, but didn't slow down. He walked into a shimmering line.

An explosion roared over the street.

Fire blazed.

Soldiers screamed and the brick walls caved inward.

Jon and his friends leaped back. They huddled down, covered their heads, as bricks rained.

When the dust settled, Starfire platoon was gone.

Scattered fires burned. A few charred limbs rose from the ruins.

"The bastards boobytrapped the whole city," George said. The giant shivered. "Goddamn it. This place is a death trap. Everything here is a bomb. Even the dead! We're going to die here. We're going to die here! I want to go home, Jon. I want to go home."

Nearby, Clay smirked. "Wuss."

Jon placed a hand on his friend's shoulder. "Keep it together, George. We'll get through this. I promise you, buddy."

George took a deep, shaky breath. Surprising Jon, he pulled him into an embrace.

"It's horrible here, isn't it, Jon?" the giant said. "But I promised to look after you. To bring you home. I had to come here with you. I had to."

Jon tilted his head. "What do you mean, George? You were drafted with me. Remember? We didn't have a choice."

George took back a step. He looked at Jon, eyes solemn, haunted.

"Jon… I got an exemption."

Jon felt the blood drain from his face.

"What?" he whispered. "George…"

The giant nodded. "Because of my brain tumor. The one the doctors took out a few years ago. Anyone who had an issue like that. Even if they're better now. They don't draft you. I volunteered."

"George," Jon whispered.

"I had to volunteer, Jon. To come here with you. To look after you. To make sure you come home. Not like…" He sniffed. "Not like Paul. I promised to bring you home. But now I'm so scared. Now everyone is dying all around us. But I have to be strong. For you."

Jon stared in silent astonishment. Nearby, other soldiers were staring too. Etty had tears in her eyes.

"Oh, George." Jon pulled his friend into a crushing embrace. They held each other for a long time as ash rained and blood flowed between their feet. "I'm so glad you're here, George. I can't believe you did that! But in this horrible place… I'm glad you're here."

George sniffed. "Not me, buddy. Not me. I was an idiot for enlisting."

Jon couldn't help it. He laughed. "Yes you were, George. I love you, you big noble idiot."

George grinned. "Right back at ya, buddy."

Etty approached them, smiling through her tears. "And I love both of you, you big dumb—"

"*Kalayaan para sa Bahay!*"

The cry rang across the street.

From buildings everywhere, the enemy stormed out, guns blazing.

Soldiers screamed and fell.

Jon and his friends opened fire.

More blood sprayed. More soldiers died. No, this city was not abandoned. This city was death.

As Jon fought, killing men and women, he remembered the words Kaelyn had spoken long ago.

Come back pure. Or come back dead.

A Bahayan ran toward him. Just a boy. But he was old enough to fire a gun. And he was old enough for Jon to kill. And Jon knew that he could not keep his promise to Kaelyn.

Because I'm already dead, he thought. *I still breathe, and my heart still beats, but I'm dead. I died somewhere on the road from Mindao to this wretched place.*

The enemy died. A few Earthlings died with them. The survivors continued on.

A dog ran toward them, barking madly, wires strapped to its underbelly. They shot it. It exploded too close, killing two soldiers.

They walked onward, and a building blew up, shedding bricks, burying a soldier.

They kept going, and more enemies surged over walls, screaming, firing, killing, dying. Death became a dance, and the world became a fever dream.

Jon and his friends kept moving. Fighting for every block. For every step. For every bloodstained cobblestone. And as he fought, Jon remembered the music he had composed long ago. The songs he had written for Symphonica. And even as his gun roared, as more and more blood stained his hands and soul, he sang softly. He sang the overture to *Falling Like the Rain*, his magnum opus. Desperately trying to cling to the boy he had been. Knowing that boy was dead. Knowing that his song, written about a fictional soldier, was now about himself.

A dead boy cries
His tears fall cold
On the scattered pages of a poem untold
Do not weep
For notes already played
For symphonies composed
For prayers prayed
In the silence they echo
Marble halls they haunt
Death is only dry ink
Of notes written for naught
A dead boy cries
For those fallen young
On the scattered pages of a song unsung
Do not weep
For notes already played
For symphonies composed
For prayers prayed
A dead boy cries
His tears fall cold
On scattered pages for a dead boy's soul

Chapter Seventeen
Dance of the Dead

All day Maria moved through the city, clad in white robes, speaking to the downtrodden.

"Holy Maria!" the children said when they saw her.

"Bless you, Holy Maria." Old women kissed their crucifixes, then touched Maria with the wooden amulets, bestowing her with blessings.

Even the Earthling soldiers learned her name. Holy Maria, she who had been a prostitute, who now walked among the poor. The soldiers no longer catcalled or reached out to smack her bottom. They bowed their heads. They too whispered blessings.

"God bless you, Holy Maria," said a burly sergeant.

Another soldier pressed his hands together. "Bless you, Angel of Bahay."

Maria knew it was dangerous. If people recognized her, spoke of her, Ernesto would soon find her.

She did not try to stand out. She had fashioned the white robe from a shroud, linen she had found in the cemetery, replacing her tattered old dress. Big mistake. It only made her look like some biblical prophet. Once people started bowing before her, she ditched the robe, and she borrowed clothes from Pippi. Maria began to explore the shantytowns wearing jean shorts, flip flops, and a purple tank top. The outfit was a bit more revealing than Maria liked, but these were the most conservative clothes Pippi owned. Maria now looked like any other Bahayan girl. Slender and short, her skin light brown, her eyes curious and dark, a little cross hanging from her neck. Like a million other girls here.

But still they recognized her.

As Maria moved through the shantytowns, listening to the poor share their tales, they touched her reverently. They kissed their prayer beads. They called her Holy Maria.

When she walked through the landfills, the garbage people rose from the trash they sifted through, recycled, sold, ate. They lived in the shadow of a glittering blue cathedral, a place of heaven whose gates were closed to them, and they bowed before Maria, she who walked among them through hell.

"Angel of Bahay," they called to her, filthy and shivering and diseased. They blessed her, and Maria thought them the most noble fighters in Bahay, facing battles as cruel as those in the north.

She walked in the alleyways that framed the Blue Boulevard, dark veins branching out from the glittering neon strip. Children sat on concrete steps, wearing rags. A girl held her starving brother, trying to feed him some milk from a damp rag. Toddlers raced down the alleyway, swinging wooden sticks. A child peered from the corner, gnawing on a bone. He was badly burned, but the scars were old.

Maria spoke to them. Recorded them. Even the sleaziest bars would not employ child prostitutes, but here in the alleyways, men found their pleasure with the urchins and refugees. The children shared their stories with Maria. Many of them dying, diseased. Many would remain children forever, and their slender bones would rest in the cemetery among the gravedwellers.

Not all of this was Earth's fault. Maria knew this. She knew that Bahay too shared much of the blame. She knew that South Bahay's president lived in a palace, a puppet of Earth, and that Bahay's bishops lived in the glittering blue cathedral amid the shantytowns, sucking the wealth of this land like a dying child sucking at a damp cloth. She knew that the priests outlawed birth control, that population kept growing and growing, even as Earth culled them. She knew that the people spent too much time praying, too little time learning the science that the Earthlings understood.

We too bear the blame, Maria thought.

It was hard to separate these stories from the tragedy of war. Every child here, abandoned by Bahay's priesthood and president, bore the scars of Earth's bombs, some on the skin, others much deeper. Some people had come here as refugees, fleeing the burning countryside, swelling the ranks of the wretched. Yet many of these homeless, hungry souls had been born into poverty before the war. Charlie had grown up in a landfill before Earth's first starships had ever sailed into Bahay's blue sky. And there were many like her.

Perhaps this was a tragedy Bahay had planted the seeds for. But Earth had poured so much water onto these seeds, and Earth had watch them bloom into trees of misery.

We are both to blame, Maria thought. *And I don't know the way out.*

And so Maria would record these stories. To show Earth her sins. To show Earth the humanity of those she oppressed. To show that here on Bahay lived more than the evil Kennys, than the wily slits. That humans lived here. Humans descended of Earth. Humans with souls no different from those that filled any Earthling.

Yes, we're smaller than Earthlings, Maria thought. *We're dark and skinny and poor, and we don't have mighty starships or pretty dresses or stores that sell all the foods you might desire. But we still yearn for Earth, for she is our ancestral homeworld. We are all Earthlings.*

That night Maria returned to the cemetery. She felt safe walking between the stacks of stone coffins. There was no electric grid here, but Crisanto hovered before her, lighting her way. Bahay was a city of violence and bloodshed, a city where thieves, rapists, and murderers lurked in every shadow. But she was not afraid here. Nobody dared enter the cemetery at night, fearing vengeful spirits.

Nobody but the gravedwellers.

At night, with no mourners in the cemetery, the gravedwellers emerged from their stone coffins. They sat between the tombstones, rolling dice, playing cards, and smoking cigarettes. Candles burned around them, casting warm light upon hard, craggy faces. A few gravedwellers were passing around a skull full of booze. Another was playing a bone flute, and a few men danced, their necklaces of fingerbones clattering.

"Hello, Maria!" they called to her.

"Will you dance with us?" said one, a man with a skull mask.

Many of them had woven bones into their clothes, had become like skeletons themselves. They danced and clattered and drank in the candlelight like a skeleton feast.

"Why do you do this?" she asked.

One man grabbed her hand. "To unite with the dead. I wear the bones of my slain wife."

"To unite our world and the world beyond," said a woman. She held Maria's other hand. "Here the living and dead are one."

"We are the undead," said an old woman, hunched over, a spine rattling across her back.

"You're not undead!" Maria said. "You're alive."

But they shook their heads.

"We died long ago. We died in the fires of our villages. We died in battlefields. We died in the poison rain. Now we rise again among the bones."

The flautist began playing his bone flute, and another gravedweller played a ribcage like a xylophone. One man swung femurs like drumsticks, beating a drum kit of skulls. The gravedwellers danced, holding hands, ring within ring of dancers, clockwise and counterclockwise, a dizzying mandala. They pulled Maria with them, clinging hard to her hands, and she danced too. She danced the dance macabre. Round and round the tombstones danced the gravedwellers, and in the night, Holy Maria became a spirit in white.

As they danced, these dwellers of the cemetery, so did the dead. The true skeletons rose from their tombs, and they too joined hands, forming a great circle. The ring of skeletons danced around the living, until death and life became as one.

In the daytime, this was a place of reality. Of the hardship and grittiness of this world. But at night, it had become a place of dreams. Of dark beauty. Of song. And this was not like the music of the day, that symphony of tears and blood, that song of her people. This was a song of the night. And this song was of truths that predated man. Of the spirits and wonder that had flowed over Bahay long before humans had ever set foot there. It was a song of magic. Of dreams and whispering souls.

She danced all night with the dead, and at dawn, Maria found herself waking up in a sarcophagus. She did not remember entering the stone coffin, but here she lay, curled up against an old skeleton. The lid was ajar. She pushed it off and rose into the sunlight.

The cemetery sprawled around her, but the revelers were gone. No more skeletons danced here. No more band played instruments of bones. Once more this was a place of this world, of dust and the distant rumble of the city.

She pulled her Santelmo from her pocket. "What happened to us, Crisanto?"

But the little ball of light could only bob, a tiny moon in her palm. She pocketed him again, for perhaps he too was a creature of the night. She lifted her camera and her gun, and Holy Maria left the land of the dead to walk among the dying.

Chapter Eighteen
The Hunt

Night fell and Earth had only claimed the first few streets of Basilica City. After hard weeks of fighting through wastelands, mountainsides, and the urban labyrinth, the Human Defense Force dug down.

"We're spending the night, soldiers!" Lieutenant Carter told his platoon. "Time to get some beauty sleep before the big push tomorrow."

Jon panted, his battlesuit splashed with his enemies' blood. He had barely slept in days. He bled from countless cuts, ached with countless bruises. The other survivors of the Lion's Platoon huddled in the shadows, nursing their wounds. One private was crying. Another private was leading his fireteam in prayer. Black walls surrounded the platoon. Black cobblestones spread below their feet. They stood in the heart of Basilica City, a labyrinth of stone. The entire city was like a huge network of trenches, and they were fighting to claim each narrow canyon at a time.

Jon looked toward the mountaintop. It was the only place in the city visible from the alleyway. The cathedral loomed there, never closer, always somehow larger. Darker. Watching them. Above its gates, a circular rose window beamed like a malevolent eye, watching the city.

Like Ernesto's white eye, Jon thought and shuddered.

The cathedral was still miles away. But it was calling him. Binding him. He felt like there was no distance between them.

Like the weight of that monolith could crush him. Like the searing white eye could burn through him.

They had found no civilians in this city. Only a few last Luminous Army soldiers, hunkering in tunnels and abandoned buildings. But even a handful of the enemy here was wreaking devastation upon the Human Defense Force. The Bahayans had inferior firepower and smaller numbers. But they knew their city. They knew every brick and cobblestone. Every shadow to hide in. Every manhole cover and tunnel. They knew this labyrinth of blackened magma like they knew the jungle. And they fought hard for every stone.

Part of Jon wanted to keep going. To reach the mountain tonight. To win this city. Maybe even kill the Red Cardinal and win this war.

But he was also exhausted.

Everyone was. Jon looked at his platoon, which filled a brick alleyway. They looked like beaten cats. They looked like roadkill. They looked like soldiers throughout the ages. George was hunched over, wheezing. Etty sat in a corner, knees pulled to her chest, rocking gently. A few soldiers were praying, and others were weeping. One soldier kept whispering that he wanted to go home, that he wanted his mother, and his tears flowed. Only Clay Hagen seemed content. The brute sat on the cobblestones, smirking. He was busy stringing a fresh severed ear onto his grisly chain of trophies.

"Come, soldiers!" Carter said. "It's every platoon for itself tonight. Let's find a hideaway to sleep. Jon, scout us a place."

Jon nodded. "Yes, sir."

He walked up the block, encountered a wire, and paused. He pointed it out. Unfortunately, the battalion had lost its bomb disposal robots on the road north. The platoon sapper rushed forward instead. She wore thick padding over her battlesuit, but she kept her visor raised, so she could keep puffing on her cigarette. She said it calmed her down. Her hands steady, the sapper dismantled the explosive.

"No boom for you, bitch." She cut the hairline cable and stomped out her cigarette.

If detonated, it would have killed us all, Jon knew.

He walked to the end of the block, turned a corner, and found a tall dark building. A doorway loomed. The place looked imposing, like a mausoleum. But when Jon peered through a window, he saw rows of tables and chairs. Blackboards. Propaganda posters on the walls.

"A school." Jon turned around, beckoning the others. "This is a safe place."

They set three soldiers to guard the first shift. The rest settled down in a classroom to spend the night. There were no children here. Jon had seen countless children in Mindao, but none here in Basilica. They must have evacuated before the HDF could arrive, for which Jon was grateful. Basilica had become a city for killers and the dead. For demons and ghosts.

Jon sat in a corner. He leaned against the wall, legs sprawled out, and took slow deep breaths. He would have given the world for a hot shower, a hot meal, an actual bathroom, a clean uniform, a night in a real bed. They were little things. But even in a war zone, a place where death lurked around every corner, Jon missed his creature comforts. Even with thousands dying around him, the smallest things—a nourishing meal, a hot shower, clean socks—became as important as a soldier's gun. Acquiring them sometimes felt as difficult as conquering a world.

It's not only my body that's hurting, he thought. *This war is cutting my soul again and again. Carving off one piece at a time until nothing is left.*

George and Etty flopped down beside him.

"I'm so exhausted I could hibernate all winter." George yawned.

Etty poked his belly. "Well you already look like a big hairy ginger bear."

He growled. "Watch out or this bear will savage you, tarsier."

"Nah, you're just a big teddy." She leaned against him.

Delicately, more like a mother bear than a deadly grizzly, George wrapped his arms around the petite girl. Both closed their eyes. Both whispered soft nothings. And within moments, they were asleep.

Across the dark classroom, other soldiers were lying down. A few prayed. Others wept. One soldier was mumbling incessantly about demons in the dark. One soldier had lost his hand. He cradled the bandaged stump, crying for his mother. Finally they all slept.

All but Jon.

Weary as he was, Jon could not sleep. He lay there, leaning against the wall, eyes open in the darkness.

And suddenly he missed battle. Because in night, the fear filled him, sour like poison. It flowed through him. Curdled his belly. Stung his eyes. Fear of death. But also guilt. He could see them in the shadows. The faces of the people he had killed. They had been soldiers, yes. But were they truly different from him?

Yes, they were different, he decided. *They were defending their home. And I killed them. And I'm dead inside.*

He noticed a figure sitting apart from the others. A man by the window, staring outside.

Giving up on sleep, Jon approached. It was Carter. The lieutenant was sitting very still, gazing at the dark street. A corpse still lay outside, trapped in a beam of moonlight like a mummified fly in a web.

Carter did not turn his head, did not look at Jon. But he spoke softly.

"It's a strange thing, isn't it?" Carter kept staring at the corpse on the street. "Back home, you kill a man, you end up in prison. Here you kill a man and you get promoted."

Jon stared at the dead man outside. "Sir, I think he was one of ours."

"They all look the same in death," Carter said. "Earthlings and Bahayans. Who can tell? Peel back the skin, and we're the same inside. The same bones. The same hearts. The same red, red blood. Here on the battlefield, that's all we are. Bones and blood." He finally turned toward Jon. "Have you ever seen a dead man? Before the war."

"Yes. My grandfather's service was open casket. I… I never saw Paul's body. His casket was closed."

"Soldiers' caskets usually are. Now you know why."

Jon cringed. He didn't want to imagine Paul like one of the mutilated corpses throughout this city.

"Sir, maybe we should sleep," Jon said.

"Have you ever killed a man, Jon? Back home on Earth, I mean. Did you ever kill a man in anger?"

Jon frowned. "Not on Earth, sir."

But I've killed so many here, he added silently.

"I grew up not far from you." Carter gazed outside again, but now he seemed to be seeing a distant world. "On the rough streets of New York City. Just across the river from your town. But it might as well have been across the galaxy. It wasn't quite as rough as Basilica or Mindao. But it was rough enough. My mother tried to raise me. Mostly it was gangs who raised me."

Jon wasn't sure what to say. So he only said, "I'm sorry, sir. That must have been hard. I grew up spoiled, I guess. Two parents who loved me. An older brother who was my best friend. A house at the end of a cul-de-sac, surrounded by trees. A comfortable home in a middle class town." He sighed. "I had to come to Bahay to see poverty. What I saw in Mindao shocked me."

"We're not so different, Jon," Carter said. "I lost a sibling too. A younger half-sister."

"Sir, I'm sorry. I had no idea."

Jon didn't know why the man was opening up like this. Carter was a lieutenant, a commissioned officer. Jon was one of his soldiers. There should be distance between them, even in a war. But perhaps it was lonely, being the platoon's sole commander. Perhaps Carter was missing Lizzy who was recovering back on Earth. Perhaps he just needed a listening ear in a dark, quiet place.

And perhaps he's gone mad, Jon thought. *Perhaps we've all gone mad. Bahay is an insane asylum the size of a planet, and we're the inmates.*

"She was a sweet girl," Carter said. "I loved her with all my heart. One day she was walking home from school. A man grabbed her. Pulled her into an alley. Raped and murdered her."

"God," Jon whispered.

"You know why he did that, Jon? Mistaken identity. That was all. That bastard, rapist, murdering son of a bitch—he thought she was another girl. The daughter of an enemy from another gang. I found out who did it. His name was Richard Saxon. A scumbag from a white supremacist gang that ruled a nearby neighborhood. The scum saw a little black girl and to him, they all looked the same."

"That's horrible." Jon didn't know what else to say.

"For months, I tried to find him. It consumed me. I hung a photo of him in my bathroom mirror. Every time I stepped inside. To piss. To shave. To shower. I saw him there. Staring back at me. Richard Saxon. And I vowed to find him. Finally I tracked him down, Jon. And I put a bullet in his head."

"Jesus," Jon whispered.

"He survived." Carter sighed. "He currently lives in an infirmary, a vegetable. I suppose that's a fate worse than death. I was only sixteen at the time. The judge took pity on me. I only spent a few months in prison. And when I got out, Jon, I could find no rest in my neighborhood. My life was shattered. My sister was gone. So I studied hard. I studied with the same insane passion that drove me to find Saxon. And I got admitted to Julius Military Academy. The first person from my family to become an officer. Aside from my estranged father—and he's no family to me."

"That's an inspiring story," Jon said. "But sir, I can't help but notice the parallels. You were obsessed with hunting down Saxon. Now you're hunting again. Now you're hunting Ernesto, a man who hurt Lizzy, a woman you love. And sir, if I may be so bold—you seem obsessed again. Maybe, for your own peace of mind, you need to let go."

Carter leaned against the wall. He gazed up at the dark ceiling. His voice was soft, almost a whisper.

"I can't let go, Jon. Not after what Ernesto did. I must hunt him. I must hunt him until he's dead. I hunted him through the jungle, and I hunted through the neon canyons of Mindao, and I hunt him now in Basilica, and I'll hunt him through the depths of hell before I give him up. This is why I'm here, Jon. This is why you're here. Why I brought you here, brought all of you. To hunt Ernesto across this cursed planet, and we'll hunt him until his body lies at our feet."

"You sound like a certain captain obsessed with a whale," Jon said. "That did not end well."

"It ended with the whale's death."

"And the captain's!"

Carter turned to look at him. A haunting look of endless shadow. "I would gladly give my life to take his."

"Would Lizzy want you to?" Jon said. "Sir, he killed my brother. He threatened my wife. I have every reason to hate Ernesto. But what I see in your eyes, sir, how you're talking, I—"

A gunshot sounded outside.

A man screamed, then fell silent.

Not a second later, men burst into the classroom, screaming and firing guns.

Bahayans!

Everything happened so fast.

A bullet slammed into a sleeping soldier. Then another.

A few soldiers woke up, dazed, only for bullets to pound into them.

Jon scrambled for his rifle. It was hanging at his side. Not even loaded. He had removed the magazine before bed. He managed to lift the rifle, to aim it, but had to paw for a magazine, and a Bahayan came running at him, pistol drawn, and Jon knew he wouldn't make it.

Carter leaped.

He slammed into Jon, shoving him back.

The Bahayan's pistol rang out.

Carter screamed, and blood sprayed from his side.

The lieutenant crashed to the ground, and Jon finally pulled his trigger. He fired on automatic, mowing down the incoming enemy. Within seconds, George and Etty were at his side, firing too.

The Bahayans fell.

Four men. All dead and leaking over the classroom floor.

Jon looked down at his lieutenant. Carter moaned, clutching his side. The platoon's medic ran toward him.

"I'm fine, Doc!" Carter said, waving him away. "Tend to the others. Save them."

But it was too late for some. Three soldiers were killed in the attack.

And I almost died with them, Jon thought.

He knelt by Carter, rummaged through his pack, and pulled out a medical kit. He pulled up Carter's shirt, revealing the wound.

"A bullet grazed your side," Jon said. "Right between two ribs. Only took out some muscle and skin. I'm no medic, sir, but I think you were lucky."

He held a thick bandage to the wound. Blood soaked it.

Carter coughed weakly. "Good. A flesh wound. A drink of medicine, and I'll be all right." His voice was raspy, his eyes sunken. "They couldn't even hit any organs. The bastards couldn't take me down."

"Sir, you saved my life," Jon said. "You took a bullet for me."

With a bloody hand, Carter gripped Jon's arm. "I failed to protect my sister, Jon. I failed to protect Lizzy. But I will always protect my soldiers. You are my soldier, Jon, and so you are my brother. Always."

Jon nodded, eyes stinging. "Always."

No one slept any more that night. They all kept their guns loaded and clutched in their hands. Finally dawn broke, red and ashy. They emerged from the school like dazed prisoners, seeking sunlight after an eternity in hell. But there was no sunlight here. Only whatever the pall of smoke let through. The city had become a crimson wasteland.

A heavyset man with thick white hair stomped toward the platoon. He had three stars on each shoulder. A colonel. It was rare to see such high ranking officers up close. Everyone stood at attention and saluted. Even Carter, bullet wound and all.

Jon recognized the white-haired man. He had spoken to him back at the Old Mig, their southern base. Here came Colonel Joe "Crazy Horse" Pascal. Lizzy's father.

"You part of Horus Battalion?" the beefy colonel barked.

"Yes, Colonel Pascal, sir!" Carter said. "Lions Platoon, Cronus Company, Horus Battalion. That's us."

The colonel turned toward him, and his face split in a smile. "Lieutenant Michael Carter! I didn't recognize you with all the blood and shit covering you."

Carter managed a smile. "It's me, Joe. I'm not that easy to kill."

The colonel embraced the lieutenant. They seemed overly familiar to Jon. But he suspected there was a long history there.

Carter is dating his daughter, Jon reminded himself. *And maybe Carter, rejected by his own father, sees the colonel as a father figure.*

The colonel looked around him, then back at Carter. "You're in the wrong goddamn neighborhood, son. You should be on the eastern slope."

"I know it, sir," Carter said. "I'll reconnect with the battalion and—" He flinched and clutched his wounded side.

Colonel Pascal frowned at the lieutenant's bloodstained bandage. "What the hell happened to you, son?"

"Bit of a war going on, sir," Carter said.

Jon stepped forward. "Colonel Pascal, sir! He took a bullet for me, sir. Saved my life."

"It's all right," Carter began. "The bullet just grazed me. Didn't even need a medic."

"Sir, he deserves credit!" Jon said. "An enemy was aiming his pistol at me. I was distracted. Too slow. Lieutenant Carter jumped in front of me. He's a hero, sir."

"Is that so?" The colonel raised his bushy eyebrows.

"Yes, sir!" Etty ran up. "I saw it! Lieutenant Carter saved Jon's life, sir. Ask anyone here."

Colonel Pascal clasped Carter's shoulder. "Good work, son, and congratulations. You're promoted to captain."

Carter tightened his lips. He saluted. "Sir! Thank you, sir."

"You deserve it. And not just because you're dating my daughter." The colonel winked. "We need more captains. Too many are dying. Including the captain of your own company. In fact, I'm not just promoting you, son. I'm assigning you command of Cronus Company. Are you well enough to carry out your duties? Or do you want to withdraw behind the front line?"

"I'll continue to fight, sir." Carter raised his chin. "It's an honor."

The beefy colonel nodded. "Good. Good! Excellent." He looked at the privates who were gathering around. "And you lot. You're all corporals now. You've seen enough blood and guts to earn a little promotion yourselves. Now get back to your battalion! We still have the rest of this city to win."

"Yes, sir!" they all said.

They headed along the street. Bloodied. Haunted. Exhausted and shell shocked. They traveled through the labyrinthine streets toward the cathedral on the mountaintop. Toward death or victory. The hunt continued.

Chapter Nineteen
Goodbye Kisses

"So what do we now?" Charlie said, puffing on her cigarette. "You never told us, Maria, how we're to get these videos to Earth."

They sat in the Jolly Joy Chicken, Mindao's most popular fast food chain. It was a strange place. The walls were bright red, the stools were yellow, and the plastic trays were blue. Even the menu, which hung on the wall, was all garish bright colors.

It looks like a jeepney threw up in here, Maria thought.

During her homeless days, Maria had eaten from trash bins outside Jolly Joy Chickens. She was still broke. But today the other bargirls pitched in, and they bought her a meal. Two pieces of fried chicken, the batter crunchy. A scoop of mashed potatoes. A scoop of peas. The menu bragged that it was Earth fare, and indeed, most of the clientele were Earthling soldiers.

Beefy soldiers walked back and forth, carrying trays laden with chicken. They were huge men who ate huge meals. It seemed that an Earthling could eat an entire bucket of fried chicken, all in one sitting, while Maria was struggling with just her two pieces. The soldiers devoured their food, licked their fingers, and guzzled down sickly sweet black liquid. They belched, blasted Earth music on their radios, and bragged of their victories in battle.

"Why did you want to come into this place?" Pippi nibbled on her chicken, winced and put it down. "This is *pute* food. Where are the noodles? Where is the rice? Where is my lechon or adobo?" She sniffed her mashed potatoes, then pushed her tray away. "It's bad enough I have to fuck the *putes* for money, I don't have to spend that money on their food."

"I wanted to come here," Maria said. "This is an Earth restaurant. I wanted to try it."

Pippi snorted. "Well, after Mister Jon takes you to Earth, this is all you'll eat." She took another bite of chicken, her freckled face scrunched up, and she forced the bite down. "Oh, Maria, we need to move with you to Earth, so we can open a real restaurant and show the *putes* how to cook."

Charlie slammed down her cup of fizzy pop. "Will somebody answer me? I am, you know, the oldest of the bargirls, and the prettiest, and the smartest, making me your leader. And you all ignore me. All the time."

Pippi leaned against the older woman and kissed her cheek. "Oh, Charlie, we can't help it. You are just *so old*."

Charlie slapped her. "I'm only thirty, you dumb little thing!" She sighed. "Okay, thirty-one. Maybe thirty-two but that's it! Stop laughing! Regardless of my age, I'm still prettier than all of you together. So answer me! How are we going to get our videos to Earth?"

Maria opened her mouth to speak. Before she could say a word, a group of Earthlings sauntered toward the table. They held trays of chicken and plastic cups so large you could hide artillery shells in them.

"Hey, babies." One soldier waggled his eyebrows. "Want to nibble on a real bone?"

His friends laughed and high-fived him.

"Want to get lost?" Charlie said.

The soldiers squeezed into the booths beside the bargirls. Charlie groaned as they jostled her aside, squeaking across the cheap plastic upholstery. Another soldier squeezed up against Maria, who grimaced and wriggled away.

"I know you," a soldier said, placing his hand on Maria's knee. "You dance at the Bottoms Up."

One of his friends snorted. "How can you tell? All these slit-sluts look the same."

"They're all beautiful," said a third soldier. "How much?" He pulled open his wallet. "You do me right now, you get ten bucks, what do you—"

"Go away!" Maria said, rising to her feet. "All of you Earthlings. Go! Leave us."

The soldiers growled. They stood up, knocking over the girls' trays. They towered over Maria. She didn't even reach their shoulders.

"What did you say, you little bitch?" a soldier demanded.

Maria balled her fists. "Go away! We're not working now."

The soldier reached out, grabbed her wrist, and twisted it painfully.

With her free hand, Maria lifted a fork from the table and stabbed the soldier.

It didn't cut the skin. But it must have hurt like hell. The soldier howled, released her, and stumbled back.

Maria thrust her fork. "Go away or I'll stab you again!"

"Yeah!" said Pippi, raising her own utensil. "Me too! Get lost, you big stinky *putes*."

"Get out of here!" Charlie added, shaking her fist, then dropped her voice. "You can visit me later at the Go Go Cowgirl. I take twenty dollars for the night, and if you want to marry me and take me to Earth, I—"

"Charlie!" Maria rolled her eyes.

The soldiers departed. The stabbed man grumbled while his friends laughed uproariously, already reenacting the scene. Maria expected that for the rest of his service, this soldier would be mercilessly ribbed.

"Anyway." Maria looked back at her friends. "You wanted to know how we get our videos to Earth?" She pointed her thumb at the retreated Earthlings. "With them."

Charlie's eyes widened. "With the *putes*? They'll never help us."

"They'll be our mules," Maria said.

Charlie tilted her head. "A mule? Like a little cow?"

"No, no, you stupid city girl!" Pippi slapped the back of Charlie's head. "A mule is a kind of big pig. You know, like *lechon.* I know because I grew up on a farm."

"You grew up two blocks from me, you dumb idiot!" Charlie slapped her back. "A mule is a cow! Like a cow that still has its balls, so it has horns."

Pippi groaned. "A cow with balls is a bull, you dumb bitch. Like they fight in France. You know, the country shaped like a boot? That's on Earth, in case you don't know, you uneducated gutter rat."

Maria cleared her throat. "Actually, a mule is…" She thought for a moment. "To be honest, I'm not sure what a mule is. But I know you use them to deliver things. And that's what the Earthlings will do for us. Deliver our videos. Like mules."

"I've never seen a pig delivering anything," Pippi muttered.

"Besides, like I said, the putes will never help us!" Charlie said. "You know, these videos would never survive military censorship. The soldiers can't just report anything they want, you know. It's all classified. Everything that happens here. Any soldier who agreed to be a delivery pig would just end up in prison."

"A *mule*," Maria said. "Not a pig. And they don't need to know they're mules."

"Because even they don't know what a mule is!" Pippi said, gnawing on a chicken leg.

"I told you when we founded the Bargirl Bureau," Maria said. "That we would not fight as soldiers or guerrillas. But as bargirls. And what are bargirls best at?"

"Drinking?" said Charlie.

"Fucking?" said Pippi.

"Charming," said Maria. "Specifically, charming men. More specifically, charming Earthling men. Follow my lead, girls. Let's go kissing."

*****

"Roll up, roll up!" Charlie announced, swaying her hips. "Roll up for your kisses, boys!"

The bargirl queen was a picture of seduction, wearing denim cutoffs, fishnet stockings, and a cowgirl hat. Her tiny flannel shirt barely hid her breasts, and her lipstick was a bright red beacon.

"Step right up, boys!" Pippi leaned forward and blew a kiss. "Get your goodbye kisses, oh brave cowboys!"

Pippi wore a revealing schoolgirl uniform, including striped stockings. Her pigtails were freshly dyed, the orange hue so bright it could give people seizures, and she held an oversized novelty lollipop. To complete the picture, freckles were painted on her face. She began to sing "On the Good Ship Lollipop," swaying seductively across the stage, drenching an innocent song with liquid sex. A few Earthling soldiers approached, practically drooling as they watched Pippi dance.

Twenty other bargirls were strutting on stage, wearing their most revealing outfits, ranging from sexy nurse uniforms to bikinis. The sunlight reflected in their sunglasses, and their skin glistened with sweat, but the heat did nothing to dampen their spirits. They kept calling out.

"Step right up!"

"Free kisses for all brave soldiers!"

"Come and get 'em!"

A banner hung above the stage: GOODBYE KISSES. Hearts were drawn around the letters.

The stage rose outside Marco Emery Spaceport. The MES was Earth's gateway to and from Bahay. Every day, shuttles landed here, carrying fresh troops from motherships in orbit. Teenage boys and girls emerged into the sunlight and heat, blinking and afraid, fresh meat for the jungles. And every day, some shuttles rose, heading toward the motherships. And these shuttles carried soldiers away from Bahay forever.

There were different reasons soldiers left Bahay.

Some simply completed their five years of military service. They could return to Earth now, haunted and broken after half a decade of war.

Others returned home disabled. Some burnt. Some missing limbs. Some missing faces. Some were fine physically, but something had broken inside their souls, and they walked in silence, staring ahead with blank eyes.

And many soldiers returned home dead.

As Maria strutted on stage with the girls, watching the Earthlings carrying coffins toward shuttles, she prayed that Jon was not inside one of them.

Unlike the other girls, she wasn't dressed revealingly. She wore a white dress, like the one she had worn on her debut at the Go Go Cowgirl. It was virginal and she was no longer a virgin. But it still seemed appropriate. To the soldiers, indeed to all of Mindao, she had become a figure of legend. Holy Maria, she who walked among the poor. She who had gone into the shantytown fire a whore, who had emerged transfigured and pure.

She did not fear standing here. Not before this crowd. If Ernesto was still in the city, he would never dare come here. Not to a place with hundreds of Earthling soldiers. This was probably the safest place for Maria on Bahay—here with those who had destroyed her world.

"It's her." A soldier pointed. "It's Holy Maria. The saint of Bahay."

"Holy Maria!" whispered another, his eyes wide, as if he had seen an angel.

Hundreds of soldiers were walking below the stage, heading toward the spaceport. They wore tattered, bloodstained uniforms. Some were walking, carrying rucksacks and weapons. Some rolled in wheelchairs or hobbled on crutches. Some lay on litters. But they all had haunted eyes.

They are a grand empire, Maria thought. *They spread across the stars. And we humble Bahayans hurt them. We hurt them so badly.*

The soldiers stared at the Bargirl Bureau. A few men whistled, catcalled, even thrust their hips. But they all had haunted eyes. Eyes that gazed upon two worlds: the world around them, and the world they had left in the jungle. Maria knew that even back on Earth, even on that distant world of comfort and plenty, they would forever see the ghosts of war.

She knew because she herself still saw them. Her dead parents, their faces gone. The burning corpses. The men she had killed. Forever they danced around her like the dance of skeletons in a midnight graveyard.

"Get your goodbye kisses!" Charlie said, strutting on her high heels. She blew kisses at the soldiers. "Brave soldiers, you fought to liberate Bahay from the evil Red Cardinal! Let us southern girls send you off with a goodbye kiss. Free goodbye kisses, hottest in town, come and get 'em!"

Charlie Wonder. She was famous, billed at the Go Go Cowgirl as the most beautiful woman on Bahay. Few soldiers would dispute that, and fewer would turn down her lips. And the other girls were no eyesores either. The soldiers approached, nudging one another. A few officers came with them. Even a few female soldiers fluttered toward the stage, licking their lips.

The bargirls teetered toward the edge of the stage, where ramps had been set up. Each ramp led to a different girl. Soldiers lined up, climbed the ramps, and leaned in for kisses.

Charlie was first to kiss a man—a stubbly sergeant with one arm. She kissed him deeply, passionately, and Maria noticed what nobody else did. Charlie slipped a little device into the sergeant's pocket, then whispered something in his ear.

"Holy Maria, I want a kiss goodbye."

Maria turned to see a soldier climbing the ramp toward her. He was a young man, probably no older than her. He was walking on crutches, barely able to get up the ramp. One of his legs was gone.

"What's your name?" Maria said.

"I'm Sergeant Dennis Harrison, from Nebraska, Earth." He blushed. "Maybe that sounds too official? I'm Dennis. Um, hi." His blush deepened. "You're very pretty."

He was so nervous. He almost reminded Maria of herself on her first night at the Go Go Cowgirl. She was loyal to Jon, and she loved Jon with all her heart. But she leaned forward and kissed this young soldier, and as their lips touched, she wondered how many Bahayans this boy had killed.

As they kissed, she pulled the little device from her pocket.

A codechip.

It was no larger than a fingernail. A little computerized square. Maria didn't know much about computers. That was Earth technology. Pippi had stolen a whole bag of these codechips from an electronics store outside an HDF base. Soldiers used them to store movies, books, video games, and photos, which they could then plug into their miniature computers.

To Maria it all seemed like magic. But Pippi was clever with Earth's strange machines, and she had filled hundreds of codechips with the Bargirl Bureau's videos.

Interviews with refugees.

Testimonials from soldiers who had killed civilians, who had spilled their hearts before the camera.

Photos of scars. Of deformities.

Stories of atrocities.

Stories to make Earth ashamed. To make Earth vote down President Hale. Stories to end this war. Each codechip only contained a single video interview—these were codechips made in Bahayan shops, crude compared to Earth technology, and it was all they could hold. But together, they could bring down an empire.

And so, as she kissed Dennis, she slipped the codechip into his pocket.

She pulled her lips back, stroked his cheek, and whispered into his ear. "I put something in your pocket, Dennis. A gift from me. A special little video. Keep it secret. Keep it safe. Don't watch it until you're back on Earth. And then share it. With everyone."

He looked at her. "What's on it?"

She stared steadily into his eyes. "Truth. Goodbye, Sergeant Dennis Harrison."

You killed Bahayans here, Sergeant, she thought. *You're just a boy, but you're a boy who raped and brutalized my world. Now share your secrets with your world.*

He left, heading toward the shuttle that would carry him to his mothership—and from there across the galaxy, all the way home to Earth.

Another soldier stepped up. She was a tall sergeant with black hair, icy blue eyes, and a scar on her cheek. Her sleeves were rolled up, revealing many tattoos on her arms. Red star tattoos. Maria had seen such tattoos on Earthling soldiers in the clubs. Each one represented one Bahayan killed.

This sergeant killed dozens of us, Maria thought.

The sergeant brushed back Maria's hair and smiled crookedly. "I fought hard to liberate you southern girls from the scourge of the north. Do I get a kiss goodbye too? Or do you only kiss the boys?"

Maria had only kissed two people in her life, Jon and Dennis, both of them boys. But she let this tall, tattooed sergeant kiss her. Despite the sergeant's gruff demeanor, her kiss was soft. Surprisingly soft. And when she pulled back, the sergeant had tears in her eyes.

"I'm sorry," the sergeant whispered. "For what we did to you."

Maria slipped a codechip into the tall woman's pocket. "Take this with you. Show this to Earth. They must know."

More soldiers lined up. Hundreds of them. After years of war, of bloodshed and heartbreak, of killing and watching friends die, they wanted this last kiss goodbye.

And most of them lined up to kiss Maria.

She was not the prettiest. That was Charlie. And Maria was certainly not the sexist, what with her flowing white dress and skinny body. That honor went to Pippi. But Maria realized that the soldiers were not lining up here to fulfill a sexual urge.

They came, and they kissed the bargirls, because they wanted to feel that they had done right here.

That they were appreciated.

That they had fought as liberators. Not as a conquerors or killers.

Deep down, perhaps they all knew that they had sinned. That they had come as an alien imperial force. That their leaders had lied to them. They had flown here like Jon, young and idealistic, believing in the justice of their cause. Believing that they must kill the evil slits to protect the justice of the Human Commonwealth.

They had found themselves in hell. And they had discovered that they were the demons.

And so now they sought to kiss angels. Now, during their last few moments in this war, they sought forgiveness. Redemption. A moment of fantasy. See! they told themselves. We are heroes! We are liberators! See how the daughters of Bahay kiss us, grateful for how hard we fought to protect them!

But all these daughters of Bahay had lost brothers and fathers to the cruelty of Earth. And while they kissed these departing soldiers, comforting them for a moment, they also gave them codechips full of horrifying truths. Truths which would haunt them for a lifetime.

This is how we fight, Maria thought. *Not as soldiers. As bargirls. This is how we will win.*

She kept kissing them. Kept giving out codechips. And she saw that while she was not the prettiest, nor the most alluring, she had the longest line of soldiers. Because while the other girls were curvier, prettier, and intoxicating, she was Holy Maria, an angel in white, and only she could offer absolution.

As the day went by, and she kept kissing soldiers, Maria just hoped Jon would forgive this infidelity.

I'm doing this to end the war, she thought as the men kept stepping up. *Fight like a soldier, Jon. I'm fighting like a bargirl.*

Chapter Twenty
The Cardinal

Carter moved through the black city, hunting, relentlessly stalking, seeking his prey along twisting cobbled roads.

I will find you, Ernesto. I'm coming for you. Your end is near.

He had lost half his platoon already. Twenty-five of his soldiers lay dead in the jungles, upon the mountainside, and in the alleyways of Basilica. But Carter kept going. He would never turn back. There was a bullet hole in his side. There was fire in his belly. There was hatred in his heart. He kept fighting, firing his gun, killing for every step, seeking his enemy.

You're here, Ernesto. I know it.

And suddenly Carter was back there.

Two years ago. His first tour of Bahay.

Lost in the jungle, the only survivor of his platoon.

Back then, he had not stopped either. He had kept trudging through the forest, day after day. Week after week. Hunting. Dwindling away. Alien bugs had lain eggs under his skin. He puked blood. But he kept going through that jungle, tracking the man who had wiped out his soldiers. Who had taken Lizzy.

And I found you.

Carter roared, fired his gun, and sprayed bullets down the basalt street. Bahayans fell, riddled with lead. But none of them were a man with a scar on his cheek, a metal plate on his head, and one white eye. None of them were the only enemy that counted.

I found you a year ago. I will find you now.

Carter narrowed his eyes. They stung. The pain clutched his heart.

He still remembered it. Finding the lair a year ago. Finding Lizzy in a bamboo cage. Covered with burn marks. Raped. Her hand severed. Dying. The woman he loved more than life—mutilated.

He had saved Lizzy's life. He had fled with her.

He had given Lizzy his full attention—and let Ernesto get away.

"Not this time," Carter swore, moving down another dark road. "We end this now."

His eyes burned with tears.

He thought of General Ward, his father—rejecting him.

He thought of Lizzy, the woman he loved—flying home. Leaving him.

He had nothing left. Nothing but his need for vengeance. A deep hunger inside him, all-consuming. And that hunger would be sated.

"Sir!" Jon Taylor was racing after him. "Sir, we're moving too far from the rest of our company."

Carter stared ahead.

He saw it there.

A flutter of movement. A red shadow.

"Here's there, Jon!" Carter cried. "I see him. Ernesto is there! With me, Lions Platoon! For Lizzy! For Earth! He's there!"

"Sir!" Jon cried, falling behind. "I saw nobody there. We should stay with the heavy armor. We…"

But Jon's voice faded. Everything faded. The world, the war itself—all blurred.

There ahead! A man in crimson robes. Hooded. Staring from an alleyway.

"Ernesto," Carter whispered.

All noise died. The rumbling tanks. The shrieking planes overhead. The rattling of bullets. All faded.

The red figure vanished around the corner.

Carter ran. Every sound seemed magnified in this silence. His breath, rasping. His heart, beating. He could hear the ghosts of his past, haunting. Lizzy moaning, close to death, smiling weakly in his arms. His own howl of rage. His vow of vengeance.

As Carter ran through the basalt city, those ghosts surrounded him. Peering from the windows. Replaying the old terrors over and over as shadows on the walls, passion plays of his torment.

But the red figure was gone. Vanished into the labyrinth.

"Ernesto!" he howled.

His voice echoed, bounced back to him a thousand times, each echo speaking with a different voice. Mocking him. Laughing. Ernesto! Ernesto! Ernesto! The name of his tormentor—tossed at him like a thousand arrows.

And there! The hints of red footprints in the dust. The wind scattered them in a crimson whirl. Carter ran in pursuit.

He spun around a serpentine minaret, raced down an alleyway, and ran up a coiling staircase carved into the mountain. Walls rose around him, filled with arrowslits like eyes. The stairs zigged and zagged, passed under archways, dove through tunnels, climbed slopes under a red sky.

Carter's bullet wound throbbed. His breath sawed at his lungs. His injuries were slowing him down. But he kept running.

There he was! A flutter of crimson cloth. Just ahead!

In his memory, blood sprayed.

A long shadow vanished around a corner.

In his dreams, countless shadows filled the jungle.

Carter kept moving through the labyrinth, panting. His wound reopened. Blood leaked through the bandage, leaving a trail behind him.

He was climbing higher up the mountain. The streets became narrower. The walls closed in around him. Stone doors led to hidden chambers. Windows were bricked up. Carter felt like he had two years ago, lost in the jungle, hunting Ernesto.

This time Lizzy is safe on Earth, he thought. *This time it's just you and me, Ernesto.*

The red footprints led onward, scattering in the wind, vanishing one by one as Carter pursued.

The rest of his platoon was far below now. The war seemed eras and light-years away. He could no longer hear nor see the Battle for Basilica. He had come here with a hundred thousand soldiers.

But it was now down to two. To Ahab and his whale.

Carter turned a corner, and there it was, rising ahead.

The cathedral.

He stopped dead in his tracks, panting.

The cathedral was larger than he had thought. From a distance, it had appeared like a church, the kind Carter would visit as a child on Earth. But this place was larger. Towering. Imposing. Covered in gargoyles and battlements. Its arrowslits peered like reptilian eyes, filled with firelight.

Carter took a step closer.

He hesitated. For a moment the weight of the cathedral seemed to crush him. He felt so small in its shadow.

"How did the Bahayans ever build this?" he whispered.

He knew the history. Centuries ago, the glowing Santelmos had visited Earth. They had chosen a handful of Filipino colonists, saving them from the ravages of the Philippine-American war. They had flown them here to Bahay, an alien world. A place to build a new homeland, safe from colonial powers. Basilica cathedral, the stories said, was the first structure built on this new world.

How did a handful of scared nineteenth-century rice farmers build such a marvel of architecture?

Carter forced himself to stand upright, to resist that invisible weight. He took another step toward the cathedral. His boots scattered black ash.

He frowned.

Flying buttresses rose around the cathedral, supporting the walls. Carter approached one of the arched buttresses and touched the polished basalt.

He pulled back his hand as if bitten.

This was not basalt. It was metal.

Carter took a few steps back.

My God.

Those weren't buttresses.

"They're a chassis," he whispered.

He took another step back. He stared up at the cathedral. Yes, there were gargoyles. There were bell towers. There were basalt bricks. But those were all additions, cobbled on years later.

The central structure was a starship. An alien starship.

"It's the ship that brought the colonists here," Carter whispered.

He had never seen a Santelmo starship. The glowing balls of light were mysterious beings, shying away from humans, helping or harming them from afar. They aided the Bahayans—gave them knowledge to build and arm a modern military. But until now, Carter had never seen Santelmo tech. Before him rose a starship to rival anything Earth could build.

Wind moaned.

Whispers sounded within the cathedral, echoing, flowing out like mist.

Carter looked up. A circular rose window glimmered, watching the city like an eye. Perhaps once it had been an airlock. The intricate round window reminded Carter of the beautiful rose window of the Notre Dame cathedral, which he had seen in picture books. Except Notre Dame's rose window was full of colorful stained glass, forming a mandala of greens, blues, and yellows. Here at Basilica Cathedral, the rose window was frosty white glass, etched with circles. Circles within circles. White within white. Perhaps this stained glass was meant to represent the Santelmos, glowing bulbs of alien light. But to Carter this rose window seemed like an eye coated with a cataract. Like Ernesto's eye.

A voice fluttered through the gateway, barely more than whisper.

Come to me. I am here.

A red shadow flitted behind the white stained glass. A figure moving, robes fluttering.

Come to me, Carter. I'm here.

"Ernesto," Carter whispered.

He slammed a fresh magazine into his assault rifle, yanked back the cocking handle, and approached the cathedral gates.

The gateway loomed like a mouth. This gateway alone was taller than most buildings in Mindao. Statues stood along its arch like pilgrims on a bridge, solemn figures in stone robes, their faces hooded. They had no eyes. But Carter could feel them staring.

The wooden doors were decaying. With his bayonet, Carter tore off chunks of wood, carving an entrance. He stepped into the nave.

He found himself in a vast chamber of shadows. Larger than he imagined it would be. A nave the size of a world.

Carter pulled out his flashlight and swept the beam from side to side. Columns lined the nave, carved from black stone into the likeness of hooded monks. Shadows filled the vaulted ceiling. As Carter walked, his boots scattered ash, revealing names engraved into stone tiles. The names of the dead.

I'm walking over the bones of the original colonists, he realized. *This is a mausoleum.*

As he walked, he read some of the names and dates engraved below his feet. Filipino names. Born on Earth in the nineteenth century. Interred here on this alien world three hundred years ago. Colonists. Saints.

And one tile—

Carter froze.

He stared down, belly churning.

He pointed his flashlight at the tile beneath his feet. He read again what was engraved there.

Michael Carter
Captain
May 14, 2199 - October 14, 2224

His name.

His date of birth.

His date of death—today.

He looked up, sneering.

"What is this?" he shouted. "Ernesto!"

Around him, a thousand statues echoed his voice.

Ernesto! Ernesto! Ernesto!

A thousand stone monks, glowering from their hoods. All chanting the tormentor's name. Firelight blazed in the distance, filling the nave, painting the statues blood-red. All around him, the statues spun, pointed, accused, laughed. Carter knelt, covered his head, and shouted wordlessly as the statues chanted around him.

I am Ernesto!

No, I am Ernesto!

I am him!

"Stop it!" Carter howled.

His voice shattered into a thousand echoes. Each fragment of sound fluttered off like a bat. And the nave fell silent.

It's his temple, Carter thought. *A temple to Ernesto. He's the Antichrist. He's the devil himself.*

"Cart. Cart, are you there?"

A voice from the depths of the cathedral. A female voice. A beautiful voice.

Carter inhaled sharply.

"Cart, help me! Cart, I'm here. He has me again. Cart!"

"Lizzy," he whispered.

His head spun. No. No! It was impossible! Lizzy was back on Earth, recovering. Ernesto had shot her back at the club. She had gone home the next week. She wasn't here!

"Carter, please! He's hurting me. He's burning me. Please."

He could not help it. The cry spilled from his mouth. "Lizzy!"

Carter ran, scattering dust from the engraved tiles. Some tiles were loose. His boots pushed some up like trapdoors, cracked through others. Skeletal hands reached from beneath. Bony fingers grabbed his boots, lacerated his legs. He ignored the pain and kept running, kicking through the sea of skeleton hands.

He ran past two mighty statues—towering sentinels, shaped like dragons with blazing fire in their jaws. And before him he beheld a dizzying array. A grand ceiling soared above, adorned with magnificent frescoes, painted larger than life upon the canopy.

It was his story.

In one painting, Carter was a child in the slums of New York.

In another, he walked the manicured lawns of the palatial Julius Military Academy, a young cadet with squared shoulders and fire in his eyes.

But the artwork became darker. As did his life.

In one enormous painting, Carter was battling ghosts in the jungles. In another, he was killing innocents. In the largest fresco, directly above, Carter was holding Lizzy in his arms.

Lizzy. Painted above him, her beauty displayed across the ceiling. Limp. Her eyes closed. Her left hand was gone in the painting, the stump dripping.

A drop splattered onto Ernesto's boot. Another drop wet his hand, then his hair. Carter wiped the liquid with his fingers, examined it. Blood. It smelled like real blood. The ceiling was bleeding. *Lizzy* was bleeding.

And there in the fresco…

Carter gasped and aimed his rifle at the ceiling.

It was hard to see in the shadows. But unmistakable. The painting depicted a jungle behind the wounded Lizzy. A figure lurked in the trees like Satan in the Garden of Eden. A figure of shadows. Grinning maliciously. A man with one dark eye, the other blazing white like the rose window. A beam of light shone through that white eye, and Carter realized it was an oculus. A small round hole in the ceiling, peering down at him.

The beam of light fell upon an altar.

Carter froze.

The stone altar dominated the room. Carter climbed the stone stairs toward it. Atop the altar he found a shattered stone sword. The altar was cracked. Perhaps the sword had cleaved it, and both had broken, now lying here together in death.

More blood dripped from the ceiling. Pattering around the sword. The blood seeped between the altar's cracks and trickled down the stone stairs. An organ loomed above the altar, several stories tall, its black pipes rising toward the ceiling like gargantuan serpents of myth.

Carter turned around, sweeping his gaze across the room.

"Lizzy!" he shouted, and his voice echoed. "Lizzy, where are you?"

"I'm here, Carter."

A voice behind him.

Carter spun around.

A figure came walking up the staircase, clad in crimson cardinal robes. The head was lowered, hidden inside a hood. The cardinal held a swinging thurible, spreading aromatic smoke.

"Lizzy?" Carter whispered.

"It's me, Carter. It's me."

But her voice came from everywhere now. It bubbled up from the floor, dripped from the ceiling, flowed around the columns.

The robed figure stepped onto the altar and pulled back its hood.

Carter found himself staring a sharp face, its angles like shattered stones. Mocking thin lips. A scar along the cheek. One blazing black eye, the other searing white.

Ernesto.

Carter raised his rifle.

Ernesto grabbed the barrel and yanked it aside.

A shot rang out. A bullet slammed into a column.

Ernesto gripped the rifle tightly. His fingers were long, tipped with red claws. Carter refused to release his own hold. He fought, trying to wrestle the gun free, while Ernesto grinned, teeth bared. Sharped teeth. The fangs elongated. Vampire teeth.

"You are the devil," Carter hissed.

Ernesto laughed, yanked the rifle back, then swung it.

The butt slammed into Carter's chin.

He fell.

He crashed down the altar's stairs and landed on his back.

Ernesto swooped. Carter rolled and came up swinging. His fist slammed into Ernesto, but—

He was gone.

Ernesto was gone.

Where—

Claws clutched Carter from behind, digging into him, drawing blood.

Carter screamed, spun around, and saw his enemy. He grabbed Ernesto by the throat.

"You captured her!" Carter shouted, eyes burning.

He squeezed. Squeezed tighter. Crushing the windpipe, and—

The red robes fluttered to the floor, empty.

A shriek sounded above.

Carter looked up to see a figure swooping, wings spread wide, one white eye blazing. An enormous bat, hiding the fresco on the ceiling. A bat with Ernesto's face.

The creature landed on Carter. Claws sank into flesh. Fangs pierced Carter's shoulder.

He howled, ripped the creature off, and shoved it away. Then he lunged right back at it. He barreled into his enemy, slamming the demon against the altar.

"You raped her!" he shouted.

The altar cracked. Blood leaked from the stone. One of the sword's shards clattered to the floor.

Carter lifted the shard.

A piece of a stone sword. But that stone was glimmering obsidian, filled with fire.

"You mutilated her!" he cried, almost blind now.

With all his fury, Carter drove the obsidian into his enemy's chest.

Ernesto screamed.

A hideous scream. Growing louder and louder, higher and higher pitched. A scream like steam fleeing a kettle. Like demons fleeing hell. Smoke rose from his wound. With his claws, Ernesto pulled the shard from his chest, then fell to his knees.

Carter aimed his gun at the beast.

"It's over, Ernesto. You captured her. You raped her. You mutilated her. Now you will die."

Kneeling by the altar, Ernesto threw back his head back and laughed.

His robe unwove, each thread becoming a red serpent. The snakes hissed and fled. His skin melted, revealing a new face.

And suddenly it was not Ernesto kneeling there.

It was an old man. A stranger. An old man with white hair. With black sacks beneath blacker eyes. An old man with discolored fangs. A Saint Peter's cross hung around his neck, blazing with black fire. The snakes returned, weaving a new robe. A finer robe than before. A blood-red robe trimmed with gold, woven with inverted crosses.

"The Red Cardinal," Carter whispered. "Lord of Bahay."

The cardinal moved so fast Carter could barely see it. With fingers like claws, he gripped Carter's gun, yanked it free, and hurled it aside.

Before Carter could react, the old man clutched him. Those bony fingers tightened around Carter's arms. The nails pierced the skin. The old man was so strong. The cardinal licked his lips, then sank his fangs into Carter's neck.

Carter struggled. He tried to shove off the vampire. But the fight had fled him.

It's not Lizzy. Not Ernesto. Just an illusion. A shapeshifter. A trap. My war—for nothing. This quest—in vain.

He fell to his knees before the altar. His strength was seeping away with his lifeblood. He fell onto his back, and the vampire knelt above him, clutching, sucking, drinking and drinking like a glutton.

Everything was fading now, but when Carter looked up at the ceiling, he could see her. Painted larger than life. Lizzy.

And she was no longer mutilated. No longer a bleeding, brutalized woman with one hand.

She was the beautiful woman he would walk with in the garden. Kiss under the elm tree. The woman he wanted to marry someday.

I love you, Lizzy. I tried to avenge you. I failed. I'm sorry.

Across the ceiling, he saw them painted. Dozens of men and women. No—just boys and girls. The fallen soldiers of the Lions Platoon. All those he had led to death. All those who had died for nothing. For his own quest of meaningless vengeance.

And he saw the multitudes. The hundred thousand Earthlings dead in this war. The millions of dead Bahayans. And in the distance, so faded—a greater, more brutal war, looming like storm clouds, inching ever closer.

"I'm sorry," Carter whispered. "For what we did. For why we fought. I'm sorry, my soldiers. I'm sorry, Earth."

The Red Cardinal kept drinking. Carter's head rolled back, and the world faded to black.

Chapter Twenty-One
A Rising Light

Jon ran through Basilica City, lost in the labyrinth, seeking his captain.

"Jon, slow down!" George called somewhere far behind, wheezing.

But Jon would not slow down. He had to find Carter. To save him. A madness had seized the captain, driving him blindly onward. Jon had heard of such things. Battle madness. Blood madness. Brought on by combat trauma. It often ended with soldiers running into enemy fire, dying in glory and insanity.

You saved my life, Captain Carter, Jon thought. *Now I must save yours.*

The labyrinth coiled, branching this way and that, but Carter was still bleeding from his bullet wound. Red drops splattered the basalt cobblestones. Jon followed the gruesome trail.

The red trail led him to the cathedral.

The enormous building loomed before him, scratching the red clouds. For a moment, Jon had to stop and stare. The cathedral towered. Punishing. Crushing. A dark god, making Jon feel so small. The gargoyles leaned over the stone spouts, staring like vultures waiting for their victim to die.

But Jon had no time for terror. The trail of blood led inside.

He ran through the cathedral gates.

He raced down a dark nave. Columns stood all around, shaped as robed monks. Shrieks rose from ahead. Jon ran past the statues, kicking up dust, until he burst into a rotunda. Frescoes of demons and angels covered the round ceiling, circling an oculus.

A stone altar dominated the room. An enormous organ rose behind it, pipes soaring several stories tall.

Carter lay atop the altar like a sacrificial lamb, eyes closed. A figure hunched over him, clad in crimson robes.

The Red Cardinal?

Jon froze. He aimed his gun at the stooped figure.

"Step away from him!" he shouted. "And raise your hands!"

The figure straightened, and his red hood fell back.

Jon froze.

Fire and ice flowed through him.

His hands slipped from his rifle. The weapon dangled from its strap.

Jon's heart lurched. Cold sweat washed him.

"No," he whispered. "No, it can't be. You're dead. You're dead…"

But there he stood before him.

Paul.

"I'm alive, little brother!" Paul smiled. "I never died. I've been here all along. Waiting for you."

He took a step toward Jon, beaming, arms wide.

Tears dampened Jon's eyes.

Memories flooded him. Playing with Paul in their backyard, running around the three apple trees, pretending they were deep in a forest. Fishing with Paul at the river, catching little sunfish and bringing them home for their father to cook. Camping outside, roasting marshmallows, laughing as the little treats caught fire, then blowing them out and feasting. Playing music with Paul, keyboards and guitar weaving together as Kaelyn sang.

Paul. His older brother. His best friend. Here before him on this alien world.

"I saw your coffin," Jon whispered. "We buried you."

Paul shook his head. "No, Jon. That wasn't me. That body was burned so badly. Face melted off. Skull cracked. They thought it was me. But I survived. They abandoned me here on Bahay. You came for me! Put down your rifle, Jon. The war is over. Let's go home. Come closer. Come to me and give me a hug."

Jon took a step closer, then froze.

"Paul, you're bleeding from your mouth."

His brother wiped his lips. And Jon caught a glimpse. Just a split second. But the image seared itself into his mind. Sharp teeth behind the lips. Fangs. Vampiric and bloodstained.

Jon looked past his brother. Looked at Captain Carter, who still lay on the altar.

There were holes in his neck.

Jon looked back at his brother.

"Sing the overture to *Falling Like the Rain*," Jon said.

Paul frowned, took another step closer. "What?"

"The song I wrote!" Jon said. "Sing it! You remember it. We played that song a million times in the basement. With Kaelyn and George. Sing it for me, Paul!"

"I'm no singer." Paul laughed. "You know that. I—"

"You don't know the song, do you?" Jon said.

Paul's eyes narrowed. His lips peeled back, revealing the fangs.

"You should never have come here," he hissed, this creature in Paul's skin. "This is *my* world! Die now!"

The shapeshifter leaped toward Jon, robes fluttering, claws extended. It shrieked for blood.

Jon raised his rifle and fired.

A bullet slammed into the creature's chest.

It fell at Jon's feet. Bleeding. Shrieking. The illusion vanished. It was just an old man with thinning white hair, with beady black eyes, with sharp teeth and no lips.

"The Red Cardinal," Jon whispered. "Ruler of North Bahay."

The old man glared, blood flowing from his chest. He tried to rise, then fell again. He coughed blood.

A hoarse, choked voice moaned like wind from a deep cave.

"Jon…"

But it wasn't the cardinal speaking. The voice came from atop the altar.

Carter!

Jon ran toward his captain, leaving the wounded cardinal. He leaned over the altar.

He nearly fell backward.

Jon felt the blood draining from his face.

My God.

Carter seemed fifty years older, a hundred pounds lighter. He lay there, shriveled and wrinkled, almost desiccated. The holes in his neck were still bleeding.

The captain coughed. "He took everything from me, Jon." His voice was hoarse, barely audible. "My blood. My life. Even my soul. He took it all. Ernesto isn't in this city. But the devil is. I fought him, Jon. I fought the devil so hard. But he was too strong."

Jon tried to lift the captain. But as soon as he touched him, a bone snapped. Carter groaned.

His bones are like hollow reeds, Jon thought.

"Sir, I'll get a medic," he said. "I'll be right back, I—"

"It's too late, Jon," Carter whispered. "I can feel myself fading… Whatever remains of me… it's trickling away. Jon… lean closer. It's hard… to speak."

Jon leaned down. "I'm here, sir."

Carter looked up at him. His eyes were sunken. Eyes like water in deep wells.

"Take care of Lizzy, Jon," he rasped. "Tell her I love her. Tell her I'm sorry. And Jon…" He clasped Jon's hand. His fingers were like talons. "Let Ernesto go. Let the war go. Don't die like me. The best revenge is living well. Living well means knowing when to let go."

And then Carter's eyes closed, and he let go.

"Sir?" Jon said. "Sir! Carter!"

He shook his officer. He pounded his chest. But Captain Michael Carter was gone.

Jon lowered his head, mourning the loss of his leader.

"The truest of all men was the Man of Sorrows," he said to his captain. "Herman Melville wrote that in *Moby Dick*. You were true, and you were sorrowful. I don't know if you lived well. But you died well. Godspeed, Captain."

For a moment, Jon just stood in silence, holding the body.

Then a low chuckle filled the church.

The Red Cardinal crawled toward the altar, leaving a trail of blood.

"You fool!" the old man hissed, blood dripping down his chin. "You don't know what you did. Only I keep them contained. Only I control their wrath. Now I will unleash the light of God!"

The cardinal managed to stand, though a hole gaped in his chest. He stumbled toward the altar, shaking, coughing, and grabbed the hilt of the stone sword.

Jon laid his fallen captain down. He raised his rifle, ready to fight.

But the cardinal was not aiming the sword at him. He held the hilt over his head. Only half the stone blade thrust out, ending in a jagged break. The obsidian shards still lay on the altar around the dead captain.

The cardinal cried out, voice echoing through the cathedral, "Behold his light and cower, mortals!"

The cardinal slammed the broken blade into the altar.

The altar, already cracked, split open like a walnut.

Every pipe in the cathedral organ blared. Every note rang out, pealing, filling the nave.

The broken halves of the altar crashed down, revealing a gaping hole. A shaft plunged deep into the cathedral. Into the ground. Into the very heart of Bahay.

"Here they come," the Red Cardinal whispered and licked his bloody lips.

The organ pipes lit up, blazing white, soaring toward the ceiling like naked oaks in a lightning storm. The light was so bright Jon winced, fell back a step. The music pounded him with pulsing waves of bass.

The church began to shake. A column cracked. A statue fell. Cracks raced along the floor. Stained-glass windows shattered, raining a million glittering shards, revealing the fiery sky.

And from the broken altar, they emerged.

Sphere after sphere of glowing orbs. Furious. Blinding white. Some no larger than marbles. Others as big as a blazing furnace.

The Santelmos.

Jon turned and fled the crumbling cathedral.

Chapter Twenty-Two
Shattering Glass

Jon fled the black cathedral, and the furious alien lights followed.

He ran across the courtyard, heart thudding. When he glanced behind him, he saw them emerge from the cathedral. Hundreds of them. Maybe thousands.

Santelmos.

Glowing balls of white light.

Aliens.

Everyone on Earth had heard of them. Some called them the wills-o-the-wisp. Others called them Saint Elmo's Fire. The Filipinos, ancestors of the Bahayan nation, called them Santelmos. For thousands of years, these effulgent aliens had monitored Earth.

And now here on distant Bahay their fury woke.

As they stormed from the cathedral, they slammed into walls, towers, buttresses. A gargoyle fell to the courtyard, breaking into chunks of gleaming obsidian. A flying buttress crumbled. The rose window, an enormous work of stone and stained glass, blew out in a rain of glimmering shards.

The entire cathedral was crumbling. The aliens, buried for centuries, were emerging.

And they were angry.

The aliens couldn't speak. They had no facial expressions—no faces at all. But anger was the universal language. And they were blazing their anger with blinding white vengeance.

Jon raced down a cobbled road, arms pumping.

From here on the mountaintop, he could see the rest of the city. Basilica draped over the mountainsides—a black labyrinth. The mountain was shaking. Towers and walls were falling. Across the city, the Human Defense Force was still busy fighting rebels. Tanks, armacars, and thousands of soldiers were moving along the cobbled streets. Soldiers pointed at the mountaintop. Cannons swiveled toward the light on the mountain.

As he ran, Jon looked over his shoulder. Basilica Cathedral still crumbled. The Santelmos were gushing out, each alien a drop in a fountain of white fury.

The volcano is erupting again, Jon thought. *This time with alien fire.*

He ran down a street, and he saw George and Etty, racing toward him. A few other soldiers from the Lions platoon stood farther back.

"What the hell did you do in there?" Etty shouted.

"Run!" Jon said.

"What?" George said. "Jon, what are those things?"

"Run!" Jon shouted. "Shut up and run!"

The friends turned to flee.

But a few soldiers, perhaps too brave for their own good, stood their ground, raised their rifles, and opened fire.

Bullets slammed into the horde of pursuing aliens.

The balls of light flashed brighter. A few Santelmos exploded like suns, bathing the city with searing beams. Walls collapsed. The ground cracked.

One Santelmo, barely larger than an apple, blazed forward and crashed through a soldier's chest. The glowing orb emerged from the man's back, leaving a trail of blood and light. The soldier collapsed.

Another Santelmo, this one the size of a basketball, plowed through another soldier. The poor corporal fell, a mangled mess, barely anything left of him.

All over the city, the aliens were swarming, flowing, leaving trails of light, driving into soldiers. With the labyrinth walls falling, Jon could see it all. The slaughter. A massacre. Some soldiers were fighting, firing on the aliens, desperate to hold them back. A few Santelmos exploded like supernovas. But most still lived, plowing through soldiers left and right, devastating platoons, even carving through tanks and armacars.

The heroes died this day. The brave fell. The cowards—or perhaps the wise—fled.

Jon and his friends were among those fleeing.

We cannot beat this enemy, he knew. *We can kill humans. We can tear through Bahayans with our superior weaponry. But we can't stand up to these creatures.*

"Where are we going?" Etty cried, running beside Jon.

"Out of the city!" he said. "Anywhere but here is good!"

"How about back to Earth?" George suggested, wheezing and panting. "Ideally, Hawaii."

"Enough banter and just run!" Jon said.

An officer was shouting somewhere through a megaphone. *Fall back! Fall back!* He hardly needed to. The Human Defense Force, which had so courageously fought into this city, was crumbling like the cathedral. It became a rout. Earth's mighty host—fleeing, dying in the light, their blood spilling over the black streets of Basilica.

Jon looked back to the mountaintop one more time.

The cathedral was gone. But he thought he saw a solitary figure. A man in red robes standing before the geyser of light.

And then Santelmos raced toward Jon, blinding him, and he ran again. All around them, soldiers fell.

They were moving fast, approaching the city gates, and Jon was beginning to feel hopeful when that hope shattered against a wall.

Literally.

A building had fallen over, blocking the road. A wall of crumbled basalt lay across his path.

Jon skidded to a halt.

The barricade was too tall, too steep. He'd never be able to climb it.

"A dead end!" Etty cried.

Jon spun around, his back to the barricade.

They streamed forth. The Santelmos.

A storm of glowing balls, tearing through soldiers. Corpses lay beneath them, gouged with holes, burned with white fire.

"Jon, come on!" George shouted. The giant was trying to climb the barricade, only to fall. "Etty, push me!"

"Dammit, George!" she shouted. "I'll climb, you push, you big dumb hippo!" She looked at Jon. "Jon, hurry! They're coming!"

A few last soldiers stood farther down the street. They were firing, standing their ground. A last stand. The Santelmos mowed through them. One alien was the size of a pumpkin. He burst through a soldier's torso. The head and four limbs thumped down. The torso was gone.

The aliens were only a second or two away now.

George and Etty, still scrambling to climb the blockade, raised their guns.

"Wait!" Jon said. "Don't shoot."

He stood, rifle lowered, and raised his hands.

He faced the Santelmos.

The aliens slowed. They hovered before him. So close he could reach out and touch them. Dozens of them. Balls of glowing light. But they were not beings of pure energy. When Jon squinted, he could see vague shapes within the glowing spheres. They had physical bodies in there. He could detect little more than hints—round abdomens and long, skinny limbs, like a hundred spider legs stretching out from a central lobe.

"I know one of you," Jon said. "A young one name Crisanto."

The orbs glowed brighter. Jon squinted. George and Etty knelt behind him, covering their eyes.

"I know that you're kind," Jon said. "That you're looking after the Bahayans, your adopted people. Like Crisanto looks after Maria. Maria is my wife. If you care for her like Crisanto does, let me see her again. And let me share your story with my people."

The Santelmos floated closer.

One of them, a small being, no larger than a heart, swirled around Jon. It bobbed forward and bumped into him. It was the slightest of touches. Jon flinched, expecting searing pain. But he felt only warmth.

A few other Santelmos swirled around George and Etty, curious, tapping them.

"We're with him!" Etty said, pointing her thumb at Jon.

George nodded vehemently. "We're his best friends! He'd be *devastated* if aliens killed us."

The aliens circled the fireteam once more. Then one came to hover directly before Jon's face. It seemed to be staring. And through the glare, Jon could see its slender, thread-like limbs swaying inside the ball of light. It reminded him of a neuron emitting electricity. He wondered if the Santelmos formed a hive brain, whether Crisanto himself formed a part of this great consciousness, watching him now.

Jon heard words in his mind.

Let her go. You will bring her only sorrow.

"Do you mean Maria?" Jon said.

Never see her again. You bring tragedy, son of Earth. We are the children of light, and we are merciful. We will spare your life today. Spare her life tomorrow.

With that, the Santelmos swerved around the companions, leaving trails of light, and slammed into the barricade of stone. The wall shattered. Bricks flew every which way. The luminous aliens roared forth like a river through a crashed dam, drowning fleeing soldiers.

But they all flowed around Jon and his friends. Fireteam Symphonica stood like an island in the torrent.

And then the light died.

The last soldiers were fleeing to the foothills.

The Santelmos rose to hover above the city, forming a protective dome like glowing clouds.

Jon and his friends walked through the smashed barricade, down the streets, and toward the city gates. They passed through ruins. Toppled buildings. Fallen walls. And everywhere the dead—corpses of Bahayans and Earthlings alike. Mostly Earthlings. Corpses burnt and mangled.

At first, Jon knelt to take their dog tags. He collected a bundle, mementos of the dead. Finally Etty placed a hand on his shoulder, looked at him sadly. And Jon nodded. He understood.

There were too many dead.

They walked on by. They left them behind. Perhaps, if the Santelmos left the sky, the army would send in teams to collect the corpses. Perhaps the dead would remain here forever, ghosts in the labyrinth.

And you will remain, Carter, Jon thought, looking back at the mountaintop.

The cathedral was gone, burying Captain Carter's body. But even from here, Jon thought he saw movement among those distant ruins. A flutter of red cloth. He could feel a dark presence.

You're still alive, Red Cardinal. Jon balled his fists. *You lost your cathedral. But you won this battle. This is not over yet. Someday we'll meet again.*

Jon turned away and left the city.

Chapter Twenty-Three
The Blood of Lindenville

Kaelyn walked through Lindenville, New Jersey, grieving for her beloved town.

Stars hung in the windows of houses. Golden stars for soldiers serving on Bahay. Purple stars for soldiers fallen. Every home—with stars. With children killing or dying. This town was affluent. The colonial houses were lovingly maintained, many predating the Alien Wars. Pumpkins rested on patios, their carved faces mocking. Red and gold leaves rustled on elms and birches, and apple pies were cooling on windowsills, filling the streets with the scent of cinnamon and nutmeg. American flags fluttered on whitewashed porches. A beautiful town. But there was no more happiness in Lindenville. It was a broken place.

A hearse drove down the road. A military funeral. Kaelyn stood, watching it go by, and saluted the fallen soldier.

Do they have funerals on Bahay? Kaelyn wondered. *Or are there too many dead?*

A hundred thousand Earthlings had fallen in the jungles of Bahay. But Kaelyn had heard that millions of Bahayans had died. She wondered if they had cemeteries like the one here. Whether mourners sang for the dead. Or whether the millions rotted in pits or burned in great fires. She wondered if the Bahayans had stars on the windows of their homes. Whether they had homes at all, or whether they lived in shanties like in the propaganda reels.

Bahayans were short, twisted, ugly things, barely human at all. Kaelyn had seen the reels. She had heard President Hale's speeches. Yes, the Bahayans were primitive, closer to monkeys than men. But Kaelyn still felt sorry for them. Even if they were primitive, even if they were *monsters*, it seemed wrong to fight them, to kill so many of them, to lose so many soldiers on such a distant world.

Kaelyn passed her house. It was smaller than many houses in Lindenville. It was a humble bungalow, painted white, nestled among elms. Once this had been a house of such joy. When Kaelyn looked at it, she could still see herself running through the yard, playing with her brother George, or looking out her bedroom window, waiting for Paul to visit.

But now her beloved Paul was dead. And George was fighting on Bahay. And this house seemed so empty. So cold. It had become a place of sadness, a golden star in the window. A star for George, a son at war.

Kaelyn could not bear it. She turned away. She could not enter that home now, deal with her mother's fear, with her father's hopeless eyes. With that ever-present, silent horror. The house was still beautiful, but it was no longer a home.

She walked away.

She walked along Main Street, passing cafes, antique shops, barbershops, the little businesses of this once-thriving town. The war was everywhere. A man rolled down the street in his wheelchair, both his legs gone. He wore his medals pinned to his ratty coat. A young man sat on a bench, talking to a woman. A burn mask covered his face, translucent, revealing smudged hints of horrible scars. A group of soldiers in dusty uniforms lined up at a bus station, the insignia of corporals and sergeants on their sleeves. They had fought a tour in Bahay already. Their short leave on Earth, earned after so long at war, was over. Their eyes were dark as they began their journey back into the fire.

Posters hung in the windows of shops and cafes. She read some of them.

SMACK 'EM DOWN! Join the mechanized infantry today!

STICK IT TO THE SLITS! Become an artilleryman!

LOOSE LIPS BLAST STARSHIPS! Spies are among you!

Ensign Earth wants YOU for the Human Defense Force!

WE'LL GIVE 'EM HELL! Earth tanks will win the war!

THE HOME FRONT FIGHTS! Buy WAR BONDS to arm our boys on Bahay!

You can SLAP A SLIT with WAR BONDS!

The posters all featured drawings of Bahayans. The enemy was hunched over, wily. They had buck teeth, eyes so narrowed they were merely slits, sickly yellow skin, and Fu Manchu mustaches. In one poster, Bahayans were depicted clutching the Statue of Liberty with their claws, making her bleed. In another poster, a Bahayan was gripping all of Earth, sinking his fangs into the planet and drinking the blood. A third poster showed Bahayans cowering and sniveling around the heels of Ensign Earth, who was smiting them with his mighty shield.

Kaelyn had never seen a Bahayan in real life. But she knew they were descended from Filipino colonists who had moved to Bahay centuries ago. There were no more Filipinos in Lindenville, of course. Once there had been many Lindenvillians of Filipino heritage. President Hale had ordered them all imprisoned years ago, accusing them of loyalty to Bahay.

Kaelyn still remembered her schoolfriend Carlo, a gentle boy of Filipino ancestry. She had visited his family for dinner many times. That family had not looked anything like the goblins in the posters.

One time, Kaelyn had asked her teacher about that. "Aren't the Bahayans just like my friend Carlo?"

"No," her teacher had told her. "Not at all. See, young Kaelyn Williams, on the planet Bahay, the original Filipino colonists interbred with aliens. They became monsters. Nothing like little Carlo at all, you see. They're goblins now. And we must fight them."

"Then why were Carlo and his family sent to prison?" the young girl had asked.

Her teacher had laughed. "They're not in prison, silly girl! They're merely in a monitoring camp. A pleasant place full of trees and butterflies. A place to wait out the war in safety. Just to be safe. Just to make sure no spies betray our planet."

Twenty-three schoolchildren had disappeared that year across Lindenville. Along with their families. All of Filipino heritage. As did her grandfather's nurse. And the kindly old man who had once driven an ice cream truck. And the local pharmacist who sometimes gave Kaelyn a free lollipop. All of them—off to the peaceful camps with trees and butterflies. Their houses given to widows of war.

As Kaelyn stood here, years later, looking at the posters, she was filled with new questions. And she had nobody to ask.

"War no more! War no more!"

The chant rolled across the street.

Kaelyn turned to see protesters marching down Main Street. This was not unusual. They marched often these days. She had sat several times in Bagshot Coffeehouse, her favorite haunt on the sunny side of Main, watching them march. Usually she just let them march on by.

But something was different today. Today the protesters were holding v-signs. Videos were playing on the electronic placards.

Kaelyn stood on the sidewalk, watching with wide eyes. The protesters were all chanting. "War no more! War no more!" But Kaelyn barely heard them. She focused on the videos playing on the placards.

They were just short clips. A few seconds long, looping over and over. There were dozens of clips here, a different one on every placard.

One clip showed a beautiful young Asian woman. She was speaking. The placard's speakers were grainy, the words weren't in English, and it was hard to hear anyway over the chanting. But subtitles appeared on the screen.

"The Earthling planes flew over my village. They dropped fire. My brothers, my sisters, my parents—they all died." The woman lifted her arm, which was badly scarred. The fingers had been burnt off. "They left me this memory."

Kaelyn frowned. Why were planes bombing Asia?

As the protesters walked by, Kaelyn looked at another placard. This one featured a young HDF corporal. He sat in a dusty bar, head lowered, then looked up at the camera with haunted blue eyes.

"We entered their village. We killed the men. We found a girl we liked. Everyone in the platoon agreed she was the prettiest. We tied her down, and… we all took turns." He sobbed. "I did too. I'm so sorry. I have sisters. I'm so sorry."

Another protester marched by, holding another placard. An Asian boy appeared in this video, disturbingly skinny, maybe starving. He held a baby in his arms. The baby looked even thinner, close to death.

"The Earthlings bombed my family farm," the boy said. "All our fields—gone. I watched my parents burn. Do you have food, Holy Maria? Please some food for my sister."

Kaelyn tilted her head. Since when were fields burning in Asia? What was going on? The Alien Wars had ended years ago! Why was there such despair on Earth?

And then she understood.

It suddenly snapped into place.

No, it couldn't be. Impossible! And yet…

"They're Bahayans," she whispered. Trembling seized her. "Bahayans aren't monsters. They're human."

She looked at the posters on the walls, depicting bucktoothed, slanty-eyed goblins. Then at the true Bahayans in the videos. Speaking of their loss. Of a tragedy beyond anything Maria had ever envisioned. She had heard generals brag about killing millions of slits, and she had imagined monsters exterminated.

"But we are the monsters," Kaelyn whispered.

"I know what I saw on Bahay!" rose a voice. "I saw slaughter! I saw soldiers murder babies! War no more, war no more!"

Kaelyn looked toward the source of the voice. A woman in a wheelchair was holding a megaphone. She wore a military uniform. It was shabby and battle-worn, but medals jangled across it. One of her hands was a metal prosthetic, and her shirt was unbuttoned, revealing bandages on her chest. She wore her golden hair in a braid.

"I am Sergeant Lizzy Pascal!" the woman said into her megaphone. "I fought in Bahay. I was captured. Tortured. Burned. Shot. I sacrificed everything for my planet. And I tell you: this war is pointless! Meaningless! Senseless!" Tears flowed down her cheeks. "We cannot win in Bahay. We can only burn, bomb, destroy. Kill and die. Year after year. Enough have died! War no more!"

"War no more!" the others chanted. "War no more!"

Kaelyn inhaled sharply.

Sergeant Lizzy Pascal?

The name tickled something in her memory… Of course!

George had called her after graduating basic training. Just before blasting off to Bahay. He had mentioned Lizzy.

Kaelyn ran toward the demonstration.

"Sergeant Pascal! Sergeant Pascal!"

The sergeant halted her wheelchair, and her medals clinked. Her body tensed. Her hand reached toward her waist, instinctively reaching for a gun, but she found no weapon. Her lips peeled back in a snarl. But then she noticed Kaelyn, her body relaxed, and she took a deep breath.

A soldier's instincts, Kaelyn knew. She told herself not to run shouting toward any veterans again.

"Sergeant Pascal," she said again, voice softer now. "My name is Kaelyn Williams."

The protest was continuing. People were still marching down Main Street, chanting and raising their placards. Caught in the flow, the sergeant had no choice. She propelled her wheelchair along with the crowd.

"Well, for fuck's sake, make yourself useful, Kaelyn Williams," the sergeant said. "Push me so I can hold my megaphone properly. And call me Lizzy. You're not one of my soldiers."

"Yes, Lizzy!"

Kaelyn almost saluted. She caught herself and began to push the wheelchair. It was amazing how commanding this sergeant could be, even wounded and wheelchair-bound. No wonder George had spoken of her with such awe.

The protest kept moving down the boulevard. People were emerging from their shops to stare. A few spat.

"Traitors!" a barber called.

"Slit-lovers!" shouted the baker, a veteran with one leg.

But many were watching the video-placards. The townsfolk were, perhaps, seeing Bahayans for the first time.

"Lizzy." Kaelyn licked her dry lips, afraid to ask, but she forced the words out. "Do you know my brother? Private George Williams?"

Lizzy twisted around in her wheelchair. She stared at Kaelyn, eyes narrowed.

"A big fucker? Seven feet tall? Ginger?"

Kaelyn couldn't help but grin. "That's him!" Her smile faded, and her heart galloped with fear. "Is he okay? Is he…?"

Dead? she wanted to ask. *Wounded? In a wheelchair too?*

But she could speak no more, overwhelmed.

"He's fine." Lizzy patted Kaelyn's hand. "At least when I left Bahay a few weeks ago, he was fine. He has a good friend watching over him."

"Jon Taylor," Kaelyn said.

Lizzy smiled. "You know them both. Yes, I had several soldiers from Lindenville in my platoon. Clay Hagen is from here. And Etty Ettinger lived in the next town over. It's why I chose this place to protest." She shook her head in wonder. "Kaelyn Williams. I never imagined that giant ginger could have a sister who's so small."

Kaelyn laughed. "I'm five-foot-five. Average height. I only seem small next to George. He had a brain tumor, do you know? It's why he grew so big. It was pressing on his pituitary gland. If the doctors hadn't removed it, he'd be even bigger. Oh gosh, Lizzy, *thank you* for the update. And thank you for…" She looked at the video placards that rose all around. "For this."

"Earth has to know," Lizzy said.

"How did you get this past military censorship?" Kaelyn asked. "My grandfather was an officer in military intelligence. The stories in these videos… they must be more classified than a presidential sex tape. My God, the army must be *pissed* at you, Lizzy."

The sergeant smiled thinly. "Actually, I didn't smuggle these videos from Bahay. A young Bahayan girl did. They call her Holy Maria, and—"

Hundreds of thudding boots interrupted her.

Kaelyn stared between the placards, and her heart sank.

An army of policemen were marching down the road toward the protesters, clad in riot gear.

Sirens blared. Several police cars raced onto the street, surrounded the protesters, and blocked all exits.

One policeman rode a heavy black horse, and protesters recoiled from the thundering hoofs.

"All protesters, you are under arrest!" announced the mounted policeman, speaking into a megaphone.

Kaelyn gasped. "What? No! On what charges?"

Nobody heard her. The protesters all began to boo, to shout. A chant began to rise.

"Pigs get lost! Pigs get lost!"

They waved their placards. But nobody was looking anymore. Everyone in town was retreating into the shops.

The police marched closer. There must have been a hundred policemen here, all in riot gear, faces hidden inside their helmets, their shields tall. They carried mean batons. The mounted policeman led the officers like some medieval knight leading his infantry.

"This is bullshit!" Lizzy shouted into her megaphone. "We have a right to assemble!"

The mounted policeman spoke into his megaphone. "You are broadcasting classified material. You are all under arrest. Raise your hands and offer no resistance."

"Fuck you, pigs!" somebody shouted.

"Pigs get lost!" A protester hurled a can at the police. It splattered beer against a shield.

And the police swarmed.

The horse charged through the protesters. They fell back, shouting. Electronic placards fell and shattered. The faces of the Bahayans, telling their stories, vanished in showers of sparks and smoke and twisted metal.

"We refuse to be silenced!" Lizzy said into her megaphone. "War no more, war no mo—"

The mounted policeman leaned down, reached toward the wheelchair, and grabbed Lizzy's megaphone.

Kaelyn rushed toward the rider. "Hey, let her speak!"

The policeman swung his fist.

Pain exploded across Kaelyn's face.

She fell. The policeman had struck her! She could barely register it. Surely it was a mistake. She tasted blood.

Rough hands grabbed her, lifted her.

"Let me go!" Kaelyn screamed, spat, and kicked. She managed to free herself and scampered back, pulling Lizzy with her.

All around, protesters clashed with police. Shields plowed forward, bloodying faces. Batons swung, crushing bones. A protester fell beside Kaelyn. A loose tooth clattered over the pavement.

Kaelyn froze.

She stared around in horror.

No. Oh God, no.

Everywhere around her—violence. Blood. A baton cracked a man's head, and he fell, blood matting his hair. One protester was throwing rocks. They bounced off shields and visors. Another protester managed to grab a baton from a policeman, to swing it, to shatter the officer's leg.

Here in Lindenville—a war zone.

"I… I'm not a part of this," Kaelyn whispered. "I…"

"Burn the pigs down!" a protester cried, lit a Molotov cocktail, and hurled it at the police.

The bottle landed among the policemen.

Fire blazed. One policeman screamed and fell, fire sweeping over his uniform.

Another Molotov cocktail flew. Another policeman burned.

A tree caught fire. Then a shop awning. Smoke filled the air.

A policeman managed to reach Kaelyn, to grab her arm. Another policeman grabbed Lizzy and pulled her from the wheelchair.

"Leave us alone!" Kaelyn shouted, kicking and screaming.

"Don't touch her!" Lizzy cried. "The girl's not part of this. She just came off the street! Don't fucking touch her!"

Wounded as she was, Lizzy struggled hard. It took three policemen to twist her arms back, to handcuff her.

Kaelyn retreated into the smoke, coughing. The town was burning around her. She could barely see anything but fire and smoke.

But on the ground, she found one vid-screen. It had not shattered. A video was still playing across it.

The young Bahayan girl with the burnt arm. Speaking of Earth bombing her village.

Kaelyn lifted the sign.

She raised it overhead.

She began to chant. "War no more! War no more!"

Across the street, people joined her. Protesters, some still fighting, others handcuffed. And city people too! Shop owners. Students. Regular townsfolk. They chanted with her.

"War no more! War no more!"

As the fire spread, so did the chant.

Kaelyn looked through the smoke, and she saw the policeman on the horse. Their leader.

He had raised his visor. And she saw fear in his eyes.

She looked into those eyes, and she raised her chin, and she spoke directly to him.

"War no more!"

The rider snarled, raised his rifle, and opened fire.

*****

The bullets flew.

Kaelyn screamed and ducked for cover.

A bullet slammed into the pavement beside her, ricocheted, and scraped across her leg with searing agony.

A bullet slammed into a protester beside her.

Another man fell.

"They're shooting us!" somebody shouted. "They're killing us!"

Another policeman opened fire. Then a third. Bullets flew and protesters fell.

Kaelyn lay on the ground, playing dead, trembling. Her leg was bleeding. The bullets whistled above.

Here in Lindenville. Here in this beautiful town. Fire. Bullets. Bodies.

A corpse lay beside her. A young man with shaggy hair. With glassy blue eyes.

She crawled away, and she bumped into another corpse. A woman. Her face locked in a silent scream.

And Kaelyn knew she would remember these faces forever.

"Up you go, you little bitch." Strong hands grabbed her, wrenched her up. "Ah, there you go. See? You can cooperate when you're taught to behave."

Kaelyn found herself facing the policeman again. The one who had ridden the horse. Who had struck her. Who had fired on her. He stood on the ground now, clutching her so tightly he almost broke her arms.

She read his name badge.

"Officer Miller." She fixed him with a steady gaze. "You murdered people today."

He laughed and spat on her face. "Fucking hippie."

He handcuffed her. Kaelyn had lost the will to fight.

A few moments later, she found herself in the back of a police car. As it drove through the burning town, Kaelyn lowered her head.

How has it come to this? she thought. *This is Earth! This is America! We fought the Nazis, the communists, the terrorists. We fought back waves of alien invasions: the scum, the marauders, the grays. We fought under the banners of the Golden Lioness. We're the good guys!*

But President Ben-Ari, the Golden Lioness, had disappeared years ago. The Colony War burned in space. And now Lindenville burned too.

Now Kaelyn didn't know who she was. Who they were. How they had strayed so far from the righteous path.

Later in her life, she could never remember arriving at the police station. Or being manhandled inside. Or the reporters surrounding her, snapping photos that would appear next morning in news around the world. Everything was a daze to Kaelyn, and her ears wouldn't stop ringing.

Finally she found herself in a jail cell. The door slammed shut, sealing her in darkness. Kaelyn thought of the dead and wept.

Chapter Twenty-Four
A Rising Fire

On the basalt plains, the Human Defense Force licked its wounds.

Outside the smoldering ruins of Basilica, they buried whatever bodies they had managed to pull from that hellish city.

"We lost this battle," Jon said, gazing at the city on the mountain. The ashy wind fluttered his hair and stung his face, hot and scented of death. "We killed nearly every Bahayan who hunkered down inside the labyrinth. We demolished the cathedral on the mountaintop, symbol of Bahayan freedom. But we lost. Historians might write that the Battle of Basilica was our greatest defeat in this war."

George slung an arm around him. "But we survived. That's gotta count for something, right?"

Did we survive? Jon wondered.

He felt dead inside. Hollow. He could barely feel a thing. His body had survived, yes. Perhaps his soul had died upon that mountain. Died when he pumped the tunnels full of fire and heard the men inside scream. Died as he moved from street to street, gun booming.

I wish I could be like the old heroes, he thought. *The ones from the stories. They fought monsters. They fought aliens and robots and cyborgs. They never had to shoot people. Never had to shoot boys too young to shave.*

He lowered his head.

He didn't know how many of his fellow soldiers had died in this battle. But it was thousands.

Most still lived. But none had survived unscathed.

Even those of us who lived—we will carry this inside us forever, Jon thought. *We will forever remember the Battle for Basilica.*

He embraced George, silent, just needing his friend. Etty joined the embrace. They stood together as jeeps rolled around them, as medics worked to save the wounded, and as helicopters rumbled above.

Even louder roars drowned out the helicopters. Thunder boomed.

Jon and his friends looked up.

A squadron of Firebirds, the dreaded starfighters of the HDF, were shrieking toward the city. Their fury shook the world. The legendary Firebirds had fought in every human war over the past century, dominating space and sky. Today they stormed over Basilica, engines roaring like dragons of old.

Their bombs fell.

Balls of fire bloomed across the city. Mushrooms clouds billowed. White light flooded the landscape.

On the basalt field, everyone knelt and covered their eyes.

The *booms* hit them a few seconds later—the sound of falling titans.

"They nuked the city," Etty whispered. "My God, they nuked it."

When the light dimmed, Jon looked back at Basilica.

Little of the city remained.

Every wall and tower had fallen. Even chunks of the mountainside had collapsed. Some of the basalt melted back into magma. Once more, lava trickled down the volcano.

He shook his head. "No, they didn't nuke it. Not with us so close. Those were conventional explosives. Just… big ones."

Etty rubbed her eyes. "But the white light…"

"The Santelmos," Jon said. "The white light was them. Their death throes."

Etty hung her head low. "How horrible."

A jeep rumbled by. A potbellied, mustached NCO stood inside, bellowing into a megaphone.

"All soldiers! Into your units! All soldiers—into your companies, into your battalions, stand for inspection! All soldiers—form ranks!"

It took a while to organize. The army had shattered. Units had collapsed. Many platoons had been demolished, some down to only a handful of survivors. Some soldiers could not even move, just lie on litters, screaming, weeping, or begging.

For a long time, NCOs rumbled back and forth in their jeeps, desperately trying to reorganize the survivors into something resembling an army. Finally Jon stood with the rest of the Lions Platoon.

It was so small.

They had been fifty soldiers once. They were twenty now.

Sergeant Lizzy—on Earth, recovering from the bullet Ernesto put through her chest.

Captain Carter—his body cremated in the explosion.

The rest—fallen on the mountainside.

You served in this platoon too, Paul, Jon thought. *Before me. You too are gone.*

The vision of Paul in the cathedral haunted him. A shapeshifter. A cruel trick. The memory stabbed him.

He looked at his friends. At George and Etty. And Jon realized that, along with Maria, they were the most important people in his life now. He loved them more than he had ever loved anyone. Here in this horrible place, with death all around, his love overwhelmed him. He had never felt such love—as bright and abounding as dawn after rain. He pulled both friends into another embrace.

Unfortunately, Clay Hagen was among the survivors. He stood nearby, still wearing his grisly necklace of severed ears. The brute ruined the moment by snorting and muttering something about them being gay for one another. Jon tried to ignore him.

Boots thumped.

A familiar figure stomped toward the Lions Platoon—a burly man with white hair. Jon recognized Colonel Pascal, Lizzy's father.

The survivors of the Lions Platoon stood at attention and saluted. Even Clay saluted, and he almost never saluted officers. Maybe it took a colonel to put some discipline into him.

"You boys, I recognize you," Colonel Pascal said. "Lions Platoon. The platoon my daughter once served in. Where's your captain? Where's Michael Carter?"

Jon lowered his head. "He fell in battle, sir. He died a hero."

Pascal blanched. "Carter is dead?" he whispered. "Goddamn. He was a good man."

"The best of men," Jon said.

For a long moment, Pascal was silent.

"Michael Carter wasn't just another soldier," the colonel finally said, voice grainy with emotion. "He loved my daughter. He would have married her after the war. He was like a son to me."

"I'm sorry, sir," Jon said.

Clay stepped up. "With all due respect, sir, war culls those who don't have that true killer instinct. Carter was a good man. A brave man. But he didn't have what it takes. He wasn't ruthless. Not like me." He puffed out his chest. "I'm a natural born killer, sir."

Eyes rimmed with red, the colonel turned to Clay.

"What the hell are you wearing around your neck, soldier?"

Clay raised his chin. "Trophies, sir. The ears of slits I killed. Even got the skull of a slit general in my rucksack. I killed more slits than anyone else in my platoon. They all goddamn know it."

"Is that so?" the colonel said.

"Yes, sir! I hate the bastards. After all, they killed the captain." Clay smirked. "If you ask me, sir, we should nuke every last one of them gooks from orbit. But hell, I kinda enjoy going into their hidey holes in person. Killing them close up and personal is fun."

The colonel looked at the rest of the platoon. "Is this son of a bitch telling the truth? Is he a natural born killer? Killed more slits than anyone?"

Nobody could deny it. They had all killed people. But nobody relished it like Clay. Certainly nobody wanted to brag about killing. So they just remained silent and nodded.

The colonel looked back at Clay. "Son, what's your name?"

"Corporal Clay Hagen, sir!"

"I'm giving you a battlefield commission, son," Colonel Pascal said. "You're a mustang now. An officer who never went to an academy. We do that sometimes. Especially when too many officers are wiped out in battle. You're now Lieutenant Clay Hagen."

Jon stared in silent shock.

His world seemed to shatter.

What? Clay Hagen—the brute, the murderer? The psychopath who mutilated his victims? An officer in the Human Defense Force?

"Colonel, sir—" Jon began.

But Pascal waved him silent. His face was a storm of emotion, and his eyes were still damp. Perhaps it was Carter's death. Perhaps the colonel was going mad with grief.

Pascal clasped Clay's shoulder. "From now on, Lieutenant Hagen, you command this platoon. Make me proud, son." He stared down at Clay's chest and shook his head in disgust. "But for God's sake, man, get rid of that disgusting chain of ears."

With that, the colonel stomped off to bark orders at another platoon.

Jon remained standing there in silent horror. He looked at George and Etty. He saw the same terror in their eyes.

Clay approached them. *Lieutenant* Clay. New commander of the Lions Platoon.

A thin smile stretched across his face. His wide-set eyes narrowed with malice. The fires of insanity burned in those pale blue eyes.

"You're mine now." His grin widened, demonic, revealing sharp teeth. "We're going to have so much fun."

Chapter Twenty-Five
Awakening

Kaelyn spent a cold, miserable night in jail.

And she knew she was lucky.

The police had opened fire on the demonstration. As she sat behind bars, many protesters lay in morgues.

And that was nothing compared to the bloodbath in Bahay.

"Is it true, Lizzy?" she said. "The videos on the placards. Did you see these things?"

The sergeant sat on a concrete slab, sharing the little jail cell. Her medals hung from her dusty army coat. She took a long, deep drag on a cigarette, then blew a ring of smoke.

"It's true, kid." She tapped the cigarette, scattering ashes. "It's all true."

It was only them in the cell. The male protesters were kept separately. Kaelyn had no idea what was happening outside the jail. Whether the town was still burning. Whether bullets were still flying. In here, it was just her, Lizzy, the shadows, and memories.

Kaelyn lowered her head. "They told us we were heroes. That Earthlings flew to Bahay as liberators."

Lizzy snorted and puffed on her cigarette. "If you believed that, kid, you're dumber than I thought." She sighed and leaned back. "I suppose that makes me an idiot too. I believed that shit once. I went to Bahay to fight evil. But that's bullshit. This ain't another war between humans and aliens. The Santelmos are barely involved. It's humans versus humans in the jungle. And that ain't right."

Kaelyn sat beside her. "Tell me about Jon and George."

Lizzy took another long drag. She smiled wistfully. "They're good men. I hope they come home soon."

"Men?" Kaelyn tilted her head. "And you call me a kid."

The sergeant seemed to gaze ten thousand miles away. "Whatever Jon and George are now, they're no longer kids."

Kaelyn pursed her lips. She saw again those images. The bullets flying. The people dying. The corpses beside her.

"I'm not a kid either," she said. "I was this morning. Not anymore. Lizzy, if what I saw in the videos is true…" She shook her head slowly. "It's a horrible crime. A stain on the legacy Einav Ben-Ari built for Earth. It's…" Her voice dropped to a whisper. "Genocide."

Lizzy nodded. "Yep, it's fucked."

"We must stop it!" Kaelyn paced the cell. "We'll raise hell. We'll protest again! I'm not afraid. Those videos from the placards? We'll upload them to the internet. Make them go viral. It's an election year. We'll make President Hale lose. We'll end this war!"

Lizzy snickered. She lit another cigarette. "It's pointless, kid. Lost cause. Didn't you see what happened out there on Main Street?"

"Yes!" Kaelyn said. "I saw it. A proud demonstration for peace. I saw you, a soldier, a decorated war heroine, speak out against the war. That inspired me. That made a difference." She crossed her arms. "And don't call me *kid*."

"All right, Ginger." Lizzy lay on the concrete slab and shut her eyes. "Keep telling yourself that. I'm going to sleep."

"Lizzy!" Kaelyn knelt beside the older woman and grabbed her arm. "How can you sleep now? We must plan the revolution!"

Lizzy rolled over, turning away from Kaelyn. "Listen, Ginger, leave me alone. I was just shot a few weeks ago. I'm still in pain, and I'm fucking tired."

"You can't give up, Sergeant Lizzy Pascal." Tears gathered in Kaelyn's eyes, and her voice trembled. "Please. You inspired me. And you can inspire millions. If you give up, what hope is there for us?"

"None!" Lizzy sprung to her feet, wounds and all. "You saw what happened, dammit! I protested. I led that protest. And people died! Ten, twenty—maybe more! The cops shot 'em. Because of me."

"And millions are dying on Bahay!" Kaelyn shouted. "And our soldiers—"

"Pipe down in there!"

A voice boomed from outside. A baton rattled against the bars. A guard glared at them, then walked on, muttering something about goddamn hippies.

The rest of the night passed quietly. Lizzy lay very still, facing the wall. Kaelyn sat on the cold concrete floor, staring at the bars, thinking of Jon and George, of the videos she had seen, and of her own oncoming conscription.

In just a year, when I'm eighteen, I'll be drafted too, she thought.

She had to end the war by then. Somehow. But what could she possibly do? How could she possibly take down the leader of the Human Commonwealth?

Finally, in the morning, keys rattled in the lock. The barred door swung open. The guard was back, his uniform wrinkly. He muttered something about "damn hippies" under his breath between sips of coffee.

"Here, sign this release form." He shoved a tablet into Kaelyn's hands. "Just a thumbprint! For God's sake, I don't need your John Hancock. Goddamn hippie."

Lizzy signed it next. And just like that, they were free to go.

"Later, kid," Lizzy said. "Try not to cause any more riots."

The veteran winked, gave Kaelyn a sad smile, and wheeled out of the jail. A bus rumbled to a stop, belching smog. Lizzy lit a cigarette as she rolled up the ramp, and then she was gone.

Kaelyn stood in the jail's doorway, daring not take another step, like some broken animal fearing freedom after too long in a cage. She almost wanted to turn around, to return to her cell.

But with a deep breath, she stepped onto the sidewalk.

She had hoped to feel optimism, to savor her freedom. Instead her heart sank.

Her dad was waiting to pick her up.

The commander, as people called him, sat in his car, facing forward, face stern. He was not in the military anymore. He had retired years ago. But Henry Williams, retired HDF captain, was still every inch the military officer.

Kaelyn debated walking home. She even toyed with the idea of running away.

If she had shown some courage yesterday at the protest, it all faded now. Perhaps a night in jail had broken her.

So she entered the car. She sat beside her father.

He began to drive. He still did not look at her. He did not say a word. His mouth was a thin line.

They pulled off the highway and into Lindenville. Kaelyn could see the damage now. Charred shops. Blackened trees. Even a few overturned cars. The protest must have grown into a riot overnight, but it was over now. Only ashes remained. And tomorrow there would be more graves in the cemetery.

Finally Kaelyn could not bear the silence.

"Dad."

The commander stared ahead. He did not speak.

"Dad," she tried again. "Are you going to say anything?"

His hands tightened around the steering wheel.

"Dad, I wasn't involved. I mean—not at first! I was just walking by, but when I saw the videos, when I heard them, I had to know more. And then the police came, and—"

He slapped her.

He actually slapped her.

She gasped. He had not hit her since she'd been a child.

"You dared march with traitors!" he said, teeth bared. "Our boys are fighting in space. And you dared march against them! For the enemy!"

"Dad, no!" She clutched her burning cheek. "That's not what's happening. The war is wrong! I met a sergeant. Her name is Lizzy Pascal. She fought in the war, and won medals, and she told me we're killing innocent people. Babies. And—"

"I will not hear this!" Father said. "I—"

"Dad, you have to listen! I—"

He pulled over.

"Get out."

"Dad!"

He spun toward her, sneering. His face was red. Demonic. "I served in the military for years. I would still be there if not for my wound. I taught you and your brother to respect the HDF. George respects it! He enlisted. I didn't think that fat piece of shit had it in him. I know he's soft. But he manned up and he enlisted, and now he's there, fighting the enemy! While you're here betraying him! Putting him in danger. *Get out*!"

Kaelyn got out of the car. She stood on the roadside, watching her father drive off.

She stood for a long time as cars drove by.

Finally she turned and walked. But she did not walk home. She walked to the church on the hill, and she sat on the bench under the maple tree. The place where she had often played with her friends. The place where she had kissed Jon.

She sang softly the song he had written for her.

A dead boy cries
His tears fall cold
On the scattered pages of a poem untold
Do not weep
For notes already played
For symphonies composed
For prayers prayed

The wind scattered dry leaves and billowed her long red hair. The robins sang. It was a beautiful place. A place of bittersweet memory. And Kaelyn knew that she would not be a soldier. She would not fight in the battlefields like Jon and George.

But she would be a warrior.

She stood up, tightened her lips, and began to walk.

She had to find Lizzy Pascal. She had to end the war.

Chapter Twenty-Six
Every Last One

"Clay Hagen is our commanding officer." George's face was pale as a ghost. "That psychopathic, murderous, evil *monster* commands our platoon. How the hell did this happen?"

Jon and Etty sat with him, silent and shocked. It was bad enough to have survived Basilica, a battle that left them all broken and haunted, maybe forever.

Being at Clay's mercy made things much, much worse.

The army bivouacked fifty miles west of Basilica, recuperating from the battle. Officers and NCOs rumbled back and forth in jeeps, reorganizing their units. Some platoons had been butchered down to just a handful of survivors. They joined together, forming new units. Many officers, especially the younger ones, had perished. Battlefield commissions and promotions were being handed out like candy, minting new commanders.

The Lions Platoon wasn't just under new management. It had also absorbed thirty stranded soldiers from other units. All strangers. This platoon had been like a home to Jon. Now it felt like a house full of strangers, its closets full of monsters.

"What do we do?" Etty whispered. "We can't tolerate this. We *can't*. He'll kill us. That psychopath will kill us and eat our hearts."

Both the giant ginger and the petite girl turned toward Jon, waiting for his advice.

"Why are you looking at me?" he said.

"You're our leader," George said.

Jon sighed. "Seems like Clay is our leader now."

George shook his head. "No. Never! That's bullshit. We're Fireteam Symphonica. We're friends. We're the only thing that matters. And you're the leader of that."

"I'm not your leader," Jon insisted.

"Yes you are, Jon!" George said. "You led Symphonica back home. And you lead Symphonica here. Maybe we're not a band anymore. But Symphonica has always been more than just a band. We've been friends. A family."

Etty nodded. "Hell, I wasn't even part of Symphonica the band, but I'm proud to be part of Fireteam Symphonica. So what do we do, fearless leader?"

Jon looked around him at the camp. Thousands of soldiers, jeeps, armacars, and tanks sprawled across the coast. The ocean spread to one side, the jungles to the other. Helicopters roared above. Clay stood by a nearby palm tree, chewing out a few new troops. Enemy skulls dangled from his belt like canteens, and his new officer insignia shone on his shoulders.

Jon looked back at his friends. "We keep our heads down. We survive the next few days. When the dust settles, when we're back at Fort Miguel, we can ask for a transfer."

"Or we can frag Clay!" Etty said, eyes lighting up.

"No fragging people, Etty," Jon said. "Not even him. We're not murderers."

Though privately, he wondered. He had already killed so many people in this war. He had shot so many Bahayans. True, that had been in battle. They had been charging at him, guns blazing. But they had not been evil, merely defending their homes. If he assassinated Clay, would that truly be worse? After all, he'd be ridding the world of a monster.

His mind reeled. For killing enemy soldiers, Jon had been promoted to corporal. If he killed more enemies, he might even earn a medal. Yet if he killed a monster like Clay, he would be a murderer.

Some world, he thought.

"Fine!" Etty rolled her eyes. "So we won't frag the bastard. *Yet.*"

Boots thumped. A shadow fell. Clay Hagen strutted toward them. Scalps dangled from his vest like lurid tassels.

The beefy lieutenant—it made Jon sick to think of him as lieutenant—smirked.

"Hello, *corporals.*" Clay spat out that last word as an insult, like some medieval lord spitting out the word *peasants.*

Etty placed her hands on her hips. "Oh, you're really savoring this, aren't you?"

Clay stepped closer, looming over Etty. He snarled and leaned so close their noses almost touched. Their helmets clanked together.

"When you see your commanding officer, *corporal*, you stand at attention and salute."

Etty sprung to attention. Her chin rose so high she was almost staring straight up. She gave the stiffest, most ridiculous salute in the history of warfare, more like a karate chop to her forehead than anything.

"Oh yes, mighty sir!"

Clay twisted her collar. "Are you mocking me?"

"Hey, lay off, man." Jon approached and grabbed Clay's shoulder.

The newly minted officer spun toward Jon. "Well, if it isn't little Jon Taylor the slit-lover."

Jon refused to cower. Clay might be an officer now, but he was still the same lowlife.

"We've decided to accept your command, Clay," Jon said. "We don't want trouble. So don't cause any."

Clay's lips peeled back, revealing blood on his teeth.

My God, Jon thought. *Who did he bite?* He glanced at the skulls hooked to Clay's belt. *Did he… eat the corpses?*

"You don't *accept* my command, Taylor," Clay said. "You *suffer* it. Now get down and give me thirty."

Jon scoffed, but inside a chill washed him. "This isn't boot camp, Clay."

Clay stepped closer, growling. "You call me *sir*. Now get down and give me thirty, corporal, and shout out *sir* every time."

Jon stood still. He crossed his arms.

Clay shoved him. Hard. With both hands. Jon stumbled back a few steps, and Clay guffawed.

"Come on!" Clay shoved him again. "Come at me, slit-lover." He punched Jon in the shoulder. "Come on! Fight back. Swing at me." Another shove. "You wuss. You know what I'm going to do to that slit whore you married? I'm going to fuck her first. Then make every man in my platoon fuck her, one by one, as you watch."

Fury exploded through Jon. George and Etty could only stand there, watching with wide eyes.

"Don't hit him, Jon," George whispered.

Clay shoved Jon another time, knocking him into the mud, and kicked his side. "Come on! Stand up and fight like a man."

Jon balled his fists. Rage bloomed inside him like a nuclear bomb. If he struck an officer, he knew what would happen. They all did. He would stand trial. Spend time in the brig. Maybe be dishonorably discharged.

To hell with it. Jon had faced the Luminous Army in battle. He could face a court martial.

He stood up, pulled back his fist, and prepared to smash Clay's pasty face.

"Lions Platoon!"

A jeep rolled up with a cloud of dust. A stocky, white-haired man hopped out, his battlesuit dented and scratched, his assault rifle slung across his back. It was Colonel Pascal, the very man who had promoted Clay and plunged the platoon into hell.

Pascal was an idiot, if you asked Jon. But he *was* a colonel. Both Jon and Clay sprung to attention. Clay stood especially rigid, his salute particularly brisk. Clay perhaps hated everyone else. But he seemed to adore the beefy colonel who had crowned him king of the lions.

"Sir!" They both saluted.

"Get your asses to Apollo field. Join your company. We're about to deploy."

Dark sacks sagged under the colonel's eyes. His left boot was unlaced, and stubble covered his jowls. The man had lost half his NCOs in Basilica, according to the scuttlebutt. He was now handling twenty jobs at once—including rallying his troops. And yet, beneath the weariness, a fire still burned in the burly man's eyes.

He loves this, Jon thought. *He was born for this. For me, every moment of this war is hell. But Pascal fucking loves it.*

"Yes, sir!" he and Clay said.

And then the colonel was off, his jeep rumbling toward another platoon. There was something almost comical about the sight. Colonel Pascal, a sixty-year-old man, a decorated colonel, commander of an entire brigade… bustling back and forth in a beaten-up jeep, moving from platoon to platoon like a mother hen rustling up her chicks. Any other time, Jon might have laughed. But the news stabbed him with an icy spear.

We're deploying again. So soon after Basilica—another battle.

He barely had the will to move.

The platoon trudged toward the field where their company mustered. Their boots scattered ash, burnt branches, and skeletons of both animals and humans. Once this land had been verdant. Once Jon too had been full of life. Both land and soldier were now charred husks.

I can't do this anymore, Jon thought, barely able to even hold his head up. *I can't keep killing. I can't keep watching friends die. I can't fight this war anymore.*

He knew that he was Jon Taylor of Lindenville. That last year, he had been a composer. A keyboardist. A quiet, reflective boy who wrote poetry and music for his friends. A boy who loved walking alone in the woods—a place to think and imagine and create. That he had been happy in his own melancholy way.

He knew all these things logically. But it seemed bizarre now—to connect this current beaten soul, this bruised body, with that boy from another world.

They had taken that boy. They had locked him in a space station, a tube of metal, and they had broken him. They had taught him to kill. They had made him a machine of killing. A machine that could only obey, run, kill, die.

They had killed Jon Taylor in that space station. In that factory in space. Whoever had emerged from the other side—it was not human. It was a robot. Mechanical. Programmed to inflict maximum destruction.

In the dark jungles. In the decaying streets of Mindao. In the basalt labyrinth of Basilica. In these levels of hell, the machine had hunted. Killed. And more and more of Jon's soul had died. There was nothing left now. Just a bruised, bloody husk with a wisp of despair trapped inside.

And then he thought of Maria.

Like an angel, her image emerged through the bleak miasma of his mind.

He saw again her bright smile. Her laughing eyes. He felt again her smooth black hair, flowing between his fingers, and her lips pressing against his.

And something Jon had thought dead and burnt flickered inside him. Faint. Nearly drowning in the murk. But it was there, a beacon in the black wilderness.

Joy.

There was still joy in him. Maria was keeping that flame alive. And if he could return to her, Jon thought that she could nurture that flicker, grow it into a roaring fire. Perhaps he would always be damaged. Perhaps his hands would forever be bloodstained, his soul forever shattered. But perhaps there was a chance, the slightest of hopes, that she could wrap around those shards inside him, could piece them back together. She could not heal him. He was beyond healing. But perhaps she could collect the scattered pieces of his soul. The Japanese practiced the art of *kintsugi*, collecting pieces of broken pottery, and gently gluing them together with molten gold, making what was broken more beautiful than before. Perhaps Maria could do the same to him. Perhaps she could be like a melody holding together the fluttering notes of a dying song.

So I must keep going. I must keep fighting. I must survive. For you, Maria. I love you. I'm dead and broken and full of ghosts, but I love you. You keep my life inside me.

He wiped a tear off his cheek. George noticed and slung an arm around him.

"I'm with you, buddy," the giant said. "Always. No matter what."

Etty leaned against Jon. "Me too. Always. We're a family. We'll always be a family." She smiled at Jon, eyes glistening with tears. "And someday Maria will be with us again."

"And Kaelyn," George said. "My sister is part of our gang."

Jon managed a weak smile. "We'll get through this. We'll get back home. We'll all hang out at my house. We'll play music in the basement. Maria and Kaelyn will be there. And we'll forget all of this."

He knew that last part was a lie. They would never forget.

But maybe, with Maria's smile, I can live with the memories. Maybe, with her love, I can live with the guilt and shame and the blood on my hands.

*****

They approached a dusty field surrounded by tanks and armacars. Thousands of soldiers were mustering here—the entire Apollo infantry brigade, affectionately known as Pascal's Punks. Pascal himself was still riding around in his jeep, herding the last few scattered units to the field. The brigade's banners fluttered in the wind, featuring golden suns on blue fields.

Apollo was the most infamous of infantry brigades. Even back on Earth, during his civilian life, Jon had heard of them. They were not the elite soldiers. In fact, Apollo was known for taking almost anyone. They were the grunts. The lowly soldiers nobody else wanted. Yet Apollo fought on the front line of almost every major battle. They were the expendables. They were the heroes. They were the dumb kids who couldn't get into elite units, trudged through mud and fire, and won wars.

They were, in short, cannon fodder.

The brigade was divided into several battalions, each commanded by a lieutenant-colonel. Jon and his friends approached Horus Battalion. It was easy to find; Horus raised distinctive banners featuring falcons clutching quivers of arrows. The battalion was divided into several companies, each containing two hundred soldiers, each commanded by a captain or major. Jon soon spotted lightning bolt banners. Here was Cronus Company, home to four platoons—including the Lions.

They formed rank—Lizzy's Lions, still bearing the name of their wounded sergeant. This little unit of haunted soldiers. This family.

And Clay Hagen stood before them, a smirk on his face.

"Every family has one asshole," Jon muttered under his breath.

Clay was only a junior officer. He commanded a mere platoon, the smallest unit an HDF officer could command. But it still sickened Jon to see the psychopath wearing an officer's insignia. It sickened him even more to serve that officer.

When the entire brigade was assembled, Colonel Pascal stepped onto a makeshift wooden stage. A young, blond private hurried onto the stage too, her ponytail bouncing. With a dimpled smile, she handed Pascal a microphone. Jon couldn't help but notice that she wore a very tight uniform. Those buttons were clinging on for dear life. The colonel smiled, winked, and patted the private on her sizable backside, much to the delight of the soldiers, who hooted and catcalled. The curvy private gave the troops an adorable salute, blew them a kiss, and swayed offstage.

"I'm in a goddamn loony bin," Etty muttered.

The colonel watched his private shimmy away, a smile on his face. He lost his smile as he turned toward the troops.

"All right, you sons of bitches!" he said. "You're here because the top brass has still got use for your asses. We dealt the slits a major blow. We wiped their goddamn capital off the map."

Cheers rose from the brigade. Jon thought the celebrations inappropriate.

We lost too many soldiers. This was a Pyrrhic victory. If it was a victory at all.

The colonel waited for the cheers to die down, then continued. "But the enemy still fights! According to our boys in Military Intelligence, the Red Cardinal escaped the city. The bastard is in hiding. But he's still commanding his army. Even worse, the goddamn Santelmos have woken up. The aliens are bombarding our forces across this whole godforsaken planet."

A few troops booed. But an uneasy silence fell over the rest. They had all seen the Santelmos fight in Basilica. Seen the aliens rip through their friends. Fighting humans was one thing. Fighting glowing balls of searing energy was quite another.

Isn't this what I wanted? Jon thought. *To fight aliens instead of humans?*

He thought of armies of Santelmos plowing through HDF brigades, and he changed his mind very quickly.

"We're the Apollo Brigade!" Pascal said. "They call us Pascal's Punks. You know why? Because they think we're useless. They think we're cannon fodder. They think we're the most miserable sacks of shit in the army. And they gave us a new mission. A mission they think is a punk mission. But one I happen to be proud of! Our new mission, my dear punks, is to wipe out the Kalayaan once and for all."

Massive cheers erupted from the brigade. Perhaps it was because, after years of war, these soldiers hated the Kalayaan with a passion. Perhaps they were just glad they wouldn't be fighting Santelmos anymore. Facing those glowing balls of death once had been quite enough, thank you very much.

"My dear punks, this is a turning point in the war," Pascal said. "Until now, we were fighting a limited war. A war of attrition. We were in first gear. Call it what you will, we weren't giving it our all. But now things have escalated. The Santelmos are no longer just advising and arming the Red Cardinal; they're fighting at his side. The Luminous Army isn't just defending the north; they're attacking our bases across the equator. The Human Defense Force is, in turn, ramping up its own operation, determined to liberate this whole damn planet this year. In short, my dear punks, shit just got real."

Etty muttered something under her breath about shit always being plenty real to her.

"Dear punks," the colonel continued, "we'll be moving deep into Kenny territory. I don't mean the damn southern jungles where they sneak around like rats. I mean their home bases. Territory where the cockroaches have been free to train, build, breed, and overall fuck shit up. We're gonna hit 'em where it hurts!"

"Hell yeah!" Clay cried. "I'm a slitfucker, says so right on my helmet. I'm going to fuck every last one of those slits."

A few other officers glared at him. Judging by the fury in their eyes, they didn't appreciate a brute like Clay joining the officer class. Especially not as a mustang—an enlisted man given a battlefield commission, never having gone to officer school or a military academy. Officers still held themselves to a higher standard, which Clay was pissing all over. But the colonel ignored the disruption.

"The Kalayaan don't have proper military bases," Pascal said. "The Kennys are far too wily for that. They're hiding in villages among the women and children. Like cowards. Every platoon in this brigade will be assigned a Bahayan village. Your job is to mop up the villages and kill every last damn Kenny you find. Any questions?"

Jon raised his hand. "Yes, sir! I have a question."

All eyes turned toward him. Jon felt a moment of dismay. He wasn't used to thousands of people looking at him. It was funny. He had faced thousands of enemy guns, and he was nervous about thousands of eyeballs.

The colonel nodded. "Speak, son."

"If the Kennys are hiding in villages, they'll be disguised as farmers or fishermen. How are we to tell who's a peaceful villager and who's a Kalayaan guerrilla?"

"Excellent question, Corporal!" the colonel said. "And I salute your morality. Did everyone hear the corporal? How can we tell who's an innocent Bahayan to liberate, and who's a Kenny to exterminate? Well, let me tell you. If they run toward you, they're the enemy. If they run *from* you, they're the enemy. Anyone who moves is your enemy! You will find the enemy and destroy him. Kill every last one. Any more questions?"

There weren't.

"All right, punks!" the colonel said. "Go out there and kill some Kennys!"

With rumbling jeeps, roaring armacars, and trucks full of ammo, Apollo Brigade rolled out. They headed north. To war. To madness. Farther and farther away from Maria and any semblance of civilization or sanity.

Chapter Twenty-Seven
The Shattered Sword

She slept in a stone coffin, the dead all around, and she dreamed.

In her dream, Maria was wandering the rainforest. The trees were tall and dark, and mist floated between the boughs. Many eyes peered from the shadowy branches like the candles of monks marching through catacombs.

The forest was dark, but a silver stream guided her, slender and undulating like a serpent. She followed the silver thread, passing through shadows where monsters peered, over battlefields where dead soldiers lay, and through the skeletons of dead giants, their ribs rising like cathedral columns. Through all the horrors of the world this silver path led her. And Maria followed the light, even as all around her the monsters snorted and sniffed, and demons hissed.

Finally she came to a forest clearing. Palisades of black trees circled a crater. Cobblestones covered the crater floor, mossy and crumbling, engraved with ancient runes. Dry leaves and lizards scuttled between creeping roots, and when the wind moaned, acorns rolled like dice. An altar rose in the center of the crater, draped with ivy, and upon it lay a shattered stone sword.

Maria stepped closer, and she saw that the altar was bleeding. The sword must have struck the stone with great strength, cracking the altar but also shattering the blade. Blood dripped across the altar, staining the shards of the broken sword. The hilt lay on the bleeding stone, shaped like a phoenix.

A cry distracted her. A baby lay upon the altar, bloody like a newborn. It looked at her and wept and wept. A baby with pale skin, trapped in a beam of moonlight.

Maria lifted the newborn, and it nuzzled her and sucked from her breast.

When it was full, the baby looked up at her, milk on its lips.

"I was born from sword striking altar," the baby said. "I was born of stone and blood."

Maria bolted up, gasping for air.

She found herself back in Mindao Cemetery, sitting upright in her stone coffin, the one she shared with a child's skeleton.

It was morning, but she felt dazed, as if she had barely slept at all. The dream kept tugging at her. She could still hear the rustling leaves on the cobblestones. Hear the baby's cry.

Other gravedwellers were only now retiring to bed. They shuffled through the cemetery, weary souls, dressed in rags and coated with ashes. Men with skinny legs and long white beards. Dour girls with pale faces and dark eyes like bottomless pits. All night, perhaps, they had been dancing with the dead. Now they climbed into their coffins, sharing them with the skeletons, and pulled the lids shut.

The night of dark magic and strange dreams was over. Cold reality dawned.

But Maria could not forget her dream. Even as she walked along the city streets that day, recording stories on her camera, she thought of that crater in the forest. Of a sword with a phoenix hilt, shattering against a bleeding altar. Of a baby suckling at her breast.

And Maria realized that she had missed her period.

That she was, in fact, quite late.

She placed her hand on her belly.

No.

A trembling seized her.

It can't be.

She began to pant. How could this happen? She had only slept with Jon a few times!

We did not use a condom, she remembered, feeling faint. Condoms were illegal on Bahay, a devoutly Catholic planet, but sometimes soldiers brought them from Earth. Jon had not.

I was a virgin. So was he. We thought ourselves safe.

She tightened her lips. It was surely just her stress, her hunger. Couldn't those cause a girl to be late? Maria did not know. Her mother had never taught her these things.

Charlie will know, she thought.

She broke into a run.

*****

Maria ran through the shantytowns, past an army base, around a refugee camp, and finally along the Blue Boulevard. It was early. The neon lights were off. The bars, so luminous at night, huddled like frightened beetles in nests of concrete and electric cables. But already Earthling soldiers were prowling the strip, determined to spend their short leave drinking booze, smoking drugs, and banging bargirls. And those bargirls were already out in force, seeking their first catches of the day. They strutted along the boulevard, their short skirts like fishing lures, drawing patrons into the clubs. There they could earn a commission for every drink sold—and extra if they took a soldier to bed.

But Maria avoided the main strip now. She was no longer a bargirl, could not be a bargirl. Not with Ernesto after her. She had become a creature of shadows, and she slunk through the back alleys, avoiding the bright boulevard. She moved with the rats, the stray cats, and the thousands of orphans who lived in these side streets, struggling like the animals to survive.

She reached the back of the Go Go Cowgirl. The alley was strewn with paper cups, condom wrappers, and beer cans. Bundles of cables sagged above, shattering the sunlight into a thousand motes like broken glass. Music and laughter drifted from the club like echoes of a dream. The jukebox was playing "Memories of Manila," a popular Bahayan ballad. Somebody was singing bad karaoke.

Maria sneaked through the back door, entering the kitchen.

At once she leaped back and hid.

He was inside. The Magic Man.

Her old pimp still wore his garish purple suit, and golden chains jangled around his neck and arms. His hair was still oily and slicked back, his goatee neatly trimmed.

"What is this?" the pimp was saying, voice leaking into the alley. "You call this a cheeseburger? This tastes like crap!" Dishes shattered. "My clients are *putes*, and they demand proper *pute* food!"

"But Magic Man, all the Earthling food tastes like crap!" the chef was objecting. "That's how it's *supposed* to taste."

"Well, you're supposed to be dead in a trash heap, but I gave you a job. Now cook them again, damn it!"

Maria heard a hand slap flesh, a yelp, then the Magic Man stomping off.

She crept back into the kitchen. The chef was there, picking up pieces of shattered plates, grumbling under his breath.

"I should kill him!" the portly man was saying. "I should kill him, then get work at the Cockatoo Club. It's cleaner too, and—" He gasped and dropped the shards of plate. "Maria de la Cruz! You're back!"

Maria cringed. "Shh! Oscar, please. Be quiet."

But he was already rushing toward her, his ample belly swaying. Chef Oscar was probably the only fat man in Mindao, no doubt achieved by pilfering quite a few meals. He pulled Maria into a warm embrace.

"Welcome back, *Nini*! Can I cook you anything? Just tell *Tito* Oscar."

"Please, Oscar, keep it quiet! He'll hear."

She glanced toward the door that led to the common room. The music was still pounding, but she could hear the Magic Man schmoozing the guests, recommending this or that lager, this or that girl. It was still early, and there were probably only a handful of Earthlings here now, but the bar would be full to bursting tonight.

"Sweet Maria." Oscar brushed back a strand of her hair. "I'll cook you a meal. Not this silly *pute* food." He gestured at a few clumsily made cheeseburgers and pizzas. "How about a nice chicken adobo and some rice?"

Her belly rumbled. She had not eaten all day.

And my child needs food, she thought. She shivered, reminding herself why she had come.

"I would love that, *Tito* Oscar. Soon. Right now, I need to see Charlie. Can you call her please?"

The door banged open, nearly giving Maria a heart attack.

But it wasn't the Magic Man. Charlie came strutting into the kitchen. Even with ridiculously high heels, she moved with feline grace. She wore lacy lingerie and a cowgirl hat, and a cigarette dangled between her brightly-painted lips.

"I could hear you from across the club, you fat fuck." Charlie smacked Oscar's head. "Thankfully the Magic Man is busy singing karaoke and did not hear. Be careful next time, you stupid idiot!" She turned toward Maria, and her voice softened. She held out her arms. "Come to *Tita* Charlie, *Nini.* Give me a hug."

They shared a quick embrace.

"Charlie," Maria whispered. "I had to talk to you. I need help. I…"

Suddenly tears were flowing, and she was trembling. Maria cried like she had never cried, not even in the jungle.

Charlie cooed over her like a mother bird, drying her tears. She peeked into the common room. The Magic Man was on stage, belting an off-key rendition of Frank Sinatra's "My Way." Earthling soldiers were booing and pelting him with beer cans and chicken bones.

"Come on, *Nini*," Charlie said. "Now's our chance."

She pulled Maria into the common room, where they slunk along the wall, sticking to the shadows.

"I did it *myyy wayyy*!" the Magic Man was crooning.

"Get off the stage!" an Earthling cried and tossed a bottle.

As the Magic Man fled the stage to the sound of laughter, the two women hurried upstairs. Soon they heard cheers from below. The bargirls must have replaced the Magic Man on stage for the day's first striptease.

Maria and Charlie walked down the hallway, stepping around a few drunken Earthlings, a sleeping dog, and a couple of bargirls snorting shabu. They entered Charlie's room.

It was a small concrete cell. Charlie's four children were here, sitting on the floor, doing homework. Outside the window, the strip was slowly coming to life. The neon sign of the Bottoms Up club was flickering, prostitutes were prowling, and music was playing, but the children didn't seem to notice. They were busy with their notebooks, studying English and math.

"This ain't no place to raise kids," Charlie said. "Above a club like this. And the kids have to go into the hallway and wait when men fuck me here. But since that bastard Ernesto burned down my house, well, here we are."

Maria's heart melted. "Oh, Charlie, I'm sorry. It's my fault."

Charlie shrugged. "Eh, it's not too bad. And it's not your fault. Besides it's only temporary. Soon enough a kind Earthling man will marry me. Like Jon married you. And he'll take me and the kids to Earth. I know it. We'll have a big house with a spiraling staircase. Like this."

She pointed at a photo on the wall, perhaps ripped from a magazine, showing a huge Earth-style house. It probably included *at least* three rooms, maybe four. At first, Maria mistook it for a hotel. Surely a single family did not need a mansion this size! Compared to Bahayan huts or shanties, it looked like a palace. But Jon had told her that many Earthlings lived in big houses like that. That he himself had grown up in one.

"If that doesn't happen, Charlie," Maria said softly, "maybe you can come with Jon and me. Earthling houses are big. There will be room for you, I'm sure."

Charlie snorted. "We're not Mormons. He can't marry both of us. And you need a visa to go to Earth. Only a soldier's wife can get a visa." She pushed up her breasts and adjusted her bra. "Not to worry, *Tita* Charlie's still got it. I'm going to woo a husband with these puppies tonight, you just wait and see."

Maria sighed. "I wish I had big *dibdibs* like you. Yours are almost like an Earthling woman's." She looked down at her own humble breasts. "Mine are like tiny baby Santelmos."

Charlie laughed. "You didn't come back to the Go Go Cowgirl to talk about tits. What's on your mind?"

They sat on the bed. Maria was trembling again. And she told Charlie. About sleeping with Jon but not using protection. About her period being late. About her dream.

Charlie frowned. "Why didn't you use a condom, silly girl?"

Maria blushed and clutched the cross that hung around her neck. "They're illegal on Bahay."

Charlie snorted. "Oh, please, so is shabu, but since when do bargirls give a damn? And the Earthlings brought more condoms here than bullets."

"I don't know then!" Maria said. "I… I didn't know much about sex. My mother never taught me, and…" She covered her face. "I feel so stupid."

"You didn't know how babies were made?" Charlie said, eyebrows rising.

"I suppose I did! Somewhere. In the back of my mind. I don't know, Charlie! I fell in love with him, okay? I was scared that night. Scared and in love. And I'm stupid. You know how stupid I am."

Charlie sighed. "You're not stupid, Maria de la Cruz. You're just young. And… No, okay, you *are* stupid. But hopefully *Tita* Charlie can teach you a few things." She rummaged through her purse. "Here, try this, stupid girl. Take this stick. Go pee on it."

Maria looked at the stick. A pregnancy test.

She took it to the toilet. She came back crying.

Charlie looked at her. She looked at the stick.

A positive sign.

"I'm pregnant," Maria whispered.

She sniffed, shaking, as Charlie embraced her.

"Oh, sweetie," Charlie said. "Don't cry. It's okay! Children are a joy. Other than my useless brats, that is." She looked toward her kids and shook her fist. "Get back to your homework, you useless little idiots, or do you want to grow up like me?"

Maria wiped her eyes, but she could not stop shaking. "Charlie, I'm scared. What if Jon doesn't come back? What if I'm left alone with a baby, and we're homeless and hungry? What if the war just goes on and on, and I end up like—" She bit down on her tongue.

Charlie placed a hand on her hip and raised an eyebrow. "Like me?"

"I didn't mean—"

"Yes you did." Charlie sighed. "And you're right. You don't want to end up like me. An aging whore. Who would?" She held Maria's hand. "Mister Jon will come back, Maria. I know it. He's not some stupid *pute* who would run into gunfire, trying to become a hero, and only become a corpse. He's careful. And he knows you're waiting. He'll come back, and he'll take you to Earth, and the baby too." Tears smudged Charlie's makeup. "You'll live in a big house with a green yard, and a spiraling staircase, and you'll be so happy."

That night, Maria walked for hours, along train tracks and highways, through bustling boulevards and decaying shantytowns, until she reached the end of the city.

She stood in the darkness, facing the edge of wilderness. Behind her Mindao perched on the land like a boil—bloated, glowing, rotting. Before her spread the darkness, a living, whispering being, guarding the beasts of flaming war. Maria stood here between neon and fire, looked to the northern distance, and placed a hand on her belly.

"Are you thinking of me too, Jon?" she whispered. "Do you miss me too?" She looked up at the twin moons. "Do you look upon the same moons, and do you wish we were together?"

She closed her eyes, and she imagined he was here. Holding her hand. Laughing with her. Playing cards. Hugging and kissing her. Telling her it would all be okay.

She opened her eyes and gazed into the darkness.

"I love you, Jon. Come back to me. Come back to our child."

Chapter Twenty-Eight
Village of Roses

Lieutenant Clay Hagen, ears dangling around his neck, led his platoon to battle.

Their jeeps rumbled over the charred landscape of this shithole world. This maggot-infested wasteland. This playground of mutilation. Clay watched the landscape roll by, his blood bubbling hotter, hotter, his cock hardening in his pants, his lust for the killing blazing like an inferno in his belly. He loved this feeling. He lived for this feeling. Planet Bahay. The galaxy's premier hunting ground.

Clay had gone hunting many times as a child. He would roam through the town of Lindenville, hunting squirrels. Stray cats. Sometimes dogs he snatched from yards. He loved the thrill of the chase. Loved the fear in the animals' eyes. He loved how they squealed as he dissected them. As he pinned their skin into the ground. As he pulled out organs and watched them pulse and quiver and bleed over his hands. He delighted in keeping his projects alive as long as possible. He was a scientist of pain.

Sometimes Clay would collect trophies from those animals. In his bedroom, he had drawers full of them. Dog teeth. Cat paws. Squirrel tails. Sometimes he left mementos for the families whose pets he hunted. A severed cat head in a yard. A beheaded dog on a driveway. Why should only he enjoy his beautiful creations?

Yes, Clay had adored those hunts. But here in Bahay… Here was a different sort of game. Here was something more wonderful, intoxicating, sexual.

Here you could hunt men.

True, the slits weren't *really* humans. Not like he was. They were more like Jews or mongrels. Subhuman. But that made the hunt even more fun. Because Clay was not doing this just for the thrill. Clay was doing something noble here.

Clay was purifying.

He was purifying this planet from the subhuman slits. He was purifying the very galaxy from the inferior races. He was purifying his very soul, scouring it with the blood of his victims.

Back home, he had been nothing. Just an amateur. Back home, he had only ever killed one man. But here, on Bahay?

Here Clay Hagen was a god.

Sitting in the rumbling jeep, he looked over his shoulder. The rest of his platoon rode behind him, crammed into several other jeeps. The platoon he now commanded. Most of them were good men. Good killers. Clay had insisted on commanding the best killers.

I am a god, and these are my angels.

His eyes strayed toward one jeep. A dented old vehicle trailing behind the others.

His platoon was not fully pure.

They were in there. The giant. The Jew. And the stuck-up musician, the worst of the three. They were sinners. They were heretics. Clay would keep them alive for now. He would show them the glory of the hunt. He would wash them with blood. He would break their souls, their spirits, their very humanity. Only then would he break their bodies.

He grinned and licked his teeth.

I will mutilate your corpses, sinners. But first I will shatter your souls into a thousand pieces.

He saw it ahead now. A slit village. The one Colonel Pascal assigned to him. Santa Rosa village.

"My playground," Clay hissed and licked his lips.

The jeeps rumbled closer. They were in northeast Bahay, exploring a remote island. Most slits lived on Bagong Palawan, the largest island on Bahay. But there were thousands of smaller islands like this one, full of more rats. The war hadn't burned this place yet. This was virgin territory. And Clay intended to take that virginity with full force.

The jeeps passed by palm trees and hills lush with rainforest. This land was still sickeningly green, infested with vermin. Clay would cleanse it. As his driver focused on the dirt path, Clay scanned the trees around him.

There!

Movement in the trees!

Clay grinned. The hunt was on!

He aimed his rifle, fired, and—

An *ungoy* thumped down dead—an alien monkey with six tails.

Clay groaned, spirits crashing. Just a goddamn monkey. Not a slit at all.

"Got a Kenny there?" his driver asked.

Clay snorted. "A monkey."

The driver, a private named William, lit a cigarette. "Same thing. The slits are just monkeys, you know."

"Shut the fuck up, soldier," Clay said. "I didn't come to this world to kill monkeys. I can kill monkeys at home. I came here to kill slits, and that's what I'll do."

"Hell yeah!" said William. "I'm with ya, man. I mean—sir. Sorry, sir, still not used to you being an officer."

Yes, Clay was an officer now. A commander of this platoon. His chest swelled. Back home, they had locked him in jail for killing a man. Here he had killed many men and earned a commission.

By the time I'm done with this village, he thought, *I'll be a goddamn general.*

The jeeps left the rainforest. They rumbled down a dirt path between rice paddies.

Euphoria leaped in Clay. He hardened at once with desire.

There they were. There in the rice paddies.

His prey.

A handful of Bahayan women stood in the paddies, the water up past their ankles. They wore white dresses, but Clay could already imagine their naked bodies. Straw hats topped their heads, but Clay could already imagine their long, silky hair in his hands, imagine tugging it, ripping it out.

The peasants just stared. Frozen. Deer in headlights.

Clay aimed his gun and fired.

One woman fell down dead.

"Um, sir?" William said. "Didn't the colonel say to kill them only if they run away or toward us?"

Clay shrugged. "The others are running now."

Indeed, the other farmers had gotten the message. They were fleeing toward their village. Dumb bitches! They should be fleeing toward the jungle. This would be easier than Clay had thought.

He fired. Again and again.

The farmers fell. Their blood flowed through the rice paddies.

"Woo!" Clay rose to his feet in the jeep, rifle raised high. "Five slits down so far! Hunting season is open, boys!"

He grinned. Blood pumped through his veins.

In the distance, he could see it. A cluster of bamboo huts with thatch roofs. Hundreds of slits would be in there. Hundreds! It would be a glorious day. The best day of his life.

The jeeps stormed forth like chariots, and the gods of Earth descended in all their wrath and glory.

Chapter Twenty-Nine
The Tears of Santa Rosa

Jon stared from his jeep.

Cold sweat washed him. His heart burst into a gallop.

"He's killing civilians," Jon said. "He just shot farmers."

George and Etty were in the jeep with him, faces pale.

"That bastard." George clutched the steering wheel so tightly he nearly broke it. "That fucking bastard."

The giant's face turned red. He pressed down on the gas. Their jeep roared down the dirt road, racing between the rice paddies. And Jon saw them now. Corpses in the paddies, half sunken in the water.

Farmers. Women. Unarmed.

And Clay was ahead, leading ten jeeps toward the village. All full of soldiers.

George swerved off the road. He took a shortcut through the rice paddies, spraying water everywhere. Soldiers in the other jeeps cursed and shouted, soaked. But George kept racing until they were driving alongside Clay's jeep.

"Clay, dammit!" Jon leaned out his jeep. "Don't shoot the civilians."

Clay looked at him from the other vehicle. Madness filled his eyes. Those strange eyes were nearly bugging out, the pupils like pinpoints. The eyes of some strange bird. His mouth stretched into a deformed grin. A demon grin.

"They were running away!" Clay laughed. "They're the enemy. They're all the enemy! And we're going to exterminate them."

"Clay!" Jon shouted. His jeep bucked beneath him, rumbling alongside the road, splashing water and scattering seeds. "We're here to shoot Kennys. That's it! Kalayaan fighters and nobody else."

They didn't have time to argue any more. The jeeps had reached the village.

One villager, a young woman in a flowing white dress, began to flee toward the hills.

She looked so much like Maria.

And Clay shot her.

She fell down dead.

"Clay, dammit!" Jon shouted. He clutched his rifle. His hands trembled. He didn't know what to do.

Should I shoot Clay? Should we turn and drive away? What do we do? How do we stop this?

"Everybody in the village—freeze!" Jon shouted, not sure if they understood English. "If you run, he'll shoot you. Freeze!"

His eyes burned. His heart thudded against his ribs. He had to calm Clay down. Right now, the lieutenant was like a mad wolf, ready to rip into prey. If the villagers ran, he would see them as prey. He would hunt them down. If the villagers stood their ground, very still and confident—they might survive.

Clay has animal instincts, Jon thought. *He's a rabid predator. But rabid predators can be understood. Can be controlled. I must control him.*

The jeeps rolled into the village common, a sward between the huts. Their wheels tore up vegetable patches, crushed a handful of chickens, and knocked over carts of fruit. Mangoes and coconuts rolled across the grass. A pineapple crunched under a tire.

Many villagers were already here for market day. Wooden stalls rose on the grass, displaying a cornucopia of fresh fish, tropical fruit, fabrics, spices, and sundry other items. Two or three hundred people were here to haggle and gossip. They wore the traditional clothes of the provinces—tunics woven from pineapple leaves and straw hats. Several girls were carrying baskets of bananas on their heads. Exotic birds squawked in bamboo cages, and a small, leashed monkey hopped about.

Jon saw mostly women and children. A few villagers were old men, bent and crooked. But no young men. Every young Bahayan man was probably off fighting—or dead already.

The villagers froze and stared at the jeeps.

Don't run, Jon prayed silently. *Don't run or he'll shoot you. Just stand still and we'll get through this.*

Clay hopped out of his jeep. He strutted across the village common, chest thrust out, his rifle hot in his hands.

"All right, you goddamn gooks!" he shouted. "Everyone—out of your huts! Out of your stinking paddies! All slits—gather here for inspection!"

Jon stepped forward. "They don't speak English."

Clay spun toward him, smirking. "So *you* tell them, slit lover. You speak gook, don't you?"

Jon had learned a few words of Tagalog, but not nearly enough to communicate clearly.

He took a deep breath. He would have to do his best with English. Hopefully the villagers would understand his tone and gestures if not his words.

"Everyone!" Jon said, arms held open, gun hanging at his side. "We won't hurt you. Gather here!" He pointed at the village square. "We're just looking for the Kalayaan, that's all."

That word—Kalayaan—they understood.

An elderly man stepped forward, hobbling and bent over. His hair was white, his eyes sunken into nests of wrinkles. His knobby fingers clutched a walking stick.

"No Kalayaan!" the old man said. "Just village. No Kalayaan! Just rice." He mimicked eating. "Just rice. Fish. Fruit. No Kalayaan."

Clay approached the peasant. He grabbed him by the collar. "Where are you hiding the Kennys, old man?"

The peasant shook his head. "No Kalayaan! Only village."

Clay snarled and shook him. "You're lying! Where are they? You're hiding them. Answer me!"

"Hey man, lay off him." Jon stepped closer. "He barely speaks English."

Clay spun around, face twisted with fury. "I told you to call me sir! I'm an officer now. And you're my soldier, Taylor." He gestured at the Bahayans. "And these are all liars!"

The old man shook his head again. "No! No lie. No Kalayaan. Village, village! You go. You go away!"

Jon's heart sank.

Don't argue, old man. Please don't argue.

But the old man kept going. He gestured at Clay, then at the village. "No Kalayaan here. Only village. Kalayaan there!" He pointed at the jungle. "Only there. No here. You go there now. You go there! You leave village."

Clay spun toward the old man. "Did you just tell me to get lost, old man?"

"No Kalayaan here! This peace village. You no belong here. You go now. You—"

Clay roared and drove his bayonet into the old man's belly.

The man screamed. Clay twisted the blade, then pulled it free. Blood sprayed.

The other villagers screamed.

The old man gurgled, clutched his lacerated belly, then fell to the grass. Clay kicked him hard in the face, snapping his neck. He spat on the corpse.

"You got off easy, old man."

Jon stood frozen. Blood roared in his ears. His heart pounded. Beside him, George and Etty let out small strangled sounds. A few other soldiers smirked. One imitated the screaming women and laughed.

Everyone in this village is going to die, Jon thought. *Unless I can somehow save them.*

He stepped toward Clay.

"Clay, enough. I'm calling an end to this." Jon turned toward the other soldiers of the platoon. "Hear me! There are no Kennys here. There aren't even any men of fighting age. We can search the huts. But we must leave the villagers alone! We—"

Powerful arms wrapped around him.

Goddammit! Stupidly, he had turned his back to Clay. And now the brute was holding him, wrestling him down.

"Let him go!" George howled.

But several soldiers leaped onto George too. They looked like wolves piling onto a bison. The giant fell. One soldier pulled out a taser. He electrocuted George again and again, laughing as the giant bellowed.

Etty ran to help him, but soldiers grabbed her too. The petite girl fought fiercely, kicking and screaming. But at sixteen, barely weighing a hundred pounds, she was no match for the men holding her.

Jon struggled against Clay's grip. It was futile. Jon was not a small man, but Clay was much larger and stronger. Pain stabbed the back of Jon's knee. Clay was digging his boot there, forcing Jon to kneel.

"Good," Clay hissed, still gripping him. "This is how I like to see you. On your knees."

Jon roared and spun around, only for Clay to kick him.

Pain exploded across Jon's face.

Blood filled his mouth. Stars floated everywhere.

He hit the ground, and then blows were raining on him. In the distance, he heard villagers scream and soldiers laugh.

Chapter Thirty
Mad God

"Lock them up!" Clay shouted. "Lock the three traitors in a hut!"

Across the village, slits were screaming, weeping, pointing at the dead old man. Clay would deal with them later.

He stared at the traitors who lay at his feet. Jon. George. Etty. All three were bloody and gasping for air. Jon especially was in bad shape, his face already swelling, coughing on blood. Good. It was beautiful to see. Soldiers stepped on their backs, pinning them down. It took three beefy soldiers to secure the giant.

Clay admired his handiwork.

"There you are. Finally on your bellies before me." Clay spat on them. "Three traitors. I'm going to court martial you for this."

William, the jeep driver, approached. "Sir, we should kill them. Put bullets in their heads. Nice and easy."

Clay shook his head. "No. I want them alive. They are mine to torment. Lock them up! I'm not nearly done hurting them."

His soldiers grabbed the traitors. Jon wasn't even able to stand. Clay watched, smirking, as his men manhandled the traitors into a bamboo hut.

You will suffer, he vowed. *So very much. But first I have a village to purify. I will show you what remains, Jon. I will show you all the death and destruction before I break you.*

Clay turned toward the villagers. With the traitors out of the way, it was time to have fun.

The old man lay dead on the grass. The other slits surrounded him, too fearful to flee or attack. They just stood there like the useless herd animals they were.

All but one woman. A young woman. Pretty, if a bit skinny. She knelt by the old man, weeping.

"*Lolo. Lolo!*" She clung to the body. "*Lolo.*"

Clay guessed that meant *grandfather.*

He grabbed the girl, pulled her off the corpse. "Get away from him, you whore. He stinks."

She faced him, tears on her cheeks. Clay couldn't help but notice how her chest heaved as she wept.

He clutched her shirt. He ripped it open, exposing her breasts.

Soldiers catcalled and hooted. The woman covered her nakedness and shrank away.

"No," she whispered. "Please. No."

"Come here." Clay pulled her close. "You ever fucked a real man? An Earthling?"

She spat on his face, then clawed his cheek.

Clay hissed, raised his hand to his cheek, felt blood.

His soldiers all laughed. Their laughter rolled around Clay. They were mocking him! His blood pounded. His fury flowed over him. The world was red.

"Woo, she's feisty!" said a corporal.

"Watch out for cat-scratch fever, sir!" said another.

Clay saw red. His fists trembled.

"Shut up!" he shouted. "Stop laughing! Nobody laughs at me!"

The laughter died at once.

Clay grabbed the woman. There was blood on her fingernails.

She spat on him again. But this time there was no laughter.

Clay clutched a handful of her hair. He dragged her over the grass. Hair ripped from her scalp, but enough remained for him to pull. She screamed all the while. A few villagers rushed forward to help, but his soldiers held them back with thrusting bayonets.

Clay dragged the woman toward the village well. Still gripping her hair, he faced the other villagers.

"This is what happens to anyone who defies me!"

He lifted the woman and shoved her into the well.

She screamed as she plunged down.

Clay dropped a grenade in after her. An explosion shook the well. The screams inside cut off.

When Clay looked down into the well, he couldn't help but laugh.

"You'll be drinking red water for a while, slits!" he said.

The villagers all stared in horror. Farther back, screams rose from a hut. His soldiers were inside, beating Jon and his traitor friends to a pulp.

I'm going to have so much fun here. Clay licked his lips. *This village is mine. Here I'm more than an officer. I am a god.*

He breathed deeply, nostrils flaring, smelling the fear. The blood. The sex.

And he was a child again, hunting along the streets of Lindenville. He grabbed cats and dogs. Skinned them alive. Dissected and studied their organs and savored their screams. He now knew why he had hunted so many animals.

He had been practicing for today.

"All right, slits!" he shouted. "You're going to do what I say. I am Lieutenant Clay Hagen, an officer of Earth. You are going to kneel before me now. You are going to worship me. Or—"

He frowned, biting down on his words.

What the—?

He heard a sound from deeper in the village. A chant. A prayer.

He inhaled sharply.

"Guard these villagers," he said to William. "If anyone runs, shoot them."

Leaving the village common, Clay walked between the huts. A few other villagers were hiding inside, peering through cracks in the bamboo walls. He would get to them later.

He still heard the chanting ahead. He followed the sound toward the largest building in the village. And the only building of stone.

A church.

The walls were crude, just stones gathered from the surrounding fields and mortared together. A wooden cross rose from the roof. The chanting came from inside.

Clay kicked down the door.

About twenty Bahayans were inside, all women and children. They knelt around candles, praying and crying. Incense was burning, and a painting of Christ hung on a wall.

When Clay entered, the villagers turned toward him, tears on their cheeks. A few of the women clutched prayer beads. Children cowered behind them.

"You dare worship another man," Clay hissed. "*I* am your god. I am your only god. And heretics must die."

He raised his rifle.

The women screamed.

Clay opened fire.

He emptied his magazine. He loaded another. He emptied it too. He loaded a third magazine and unleashed his wrath.

Blood flowed across the church floor.

The last infidel crashed down dead.

They lay there before him. Twenty corpses. Women still huddling over their children. There was so much blood.

It was beautiful. He had become holy. A savior standing above hell, reaching to heaven.

A child crawled out from under its dead mother.

Clay shot the brat in the chest.

He left the church and returned to the village market. One woman was already stripped naked. Her children lay dead around her. A group of soldiers dragged the woman behind a hut, and Clay heard her scream. Other villagers were running toward the rainforest. Soldiers fired, tore them down, and laughed.

Gunshots filled the air.

Death was everywhere.

Clay smiled, walking through his domain.

"Now I am become Death, the destroyer of worlds," Clay whispered, and a shudder swept through him.

A woman ran past him, carrying two children. She was heading toward the hills.

Clay shot her in the legs. She fell, spilling her children. The brats lay there, weeping. They looked at Clay. They whispered something. Maybe begging.

Clay shot them. A shot to each little chest. They both fell.

The mother screamed and wept and lifted her dead children. Clay grabbed her.

"Hey, soldiers!" he said. "I got a fresh one for you!"

He tossed the woman to a few sergeants and corporals. The men laughed, ripped her clothes, and dragged her behind another hut. It was barbaric, if you asked Clay. But let the men have their fun. They had earned it. Clay was a good lieutenant, and he took good care of his soldiers.

He knelt by the two dead children. Two fresh experiments. Clay drew his knife.

He whistled as he worked. He scalped his victims. He cut out their tongues. He carved off their ears. He stuffed the trophies into his pack. He would clean and preserve them later, souvenirs from his conquest.

He walked through the village. A few people were fleeing their huts. He shot them. They were easy shots. Most of the villagers soon smartened up. They were staying indoors, cowering behind flimsy bamboo walls.

Well, that wouldn't be a problem. As he sauntered through the village, Clay pulled out his lighter. Hut by hut, he kindled thatch roofs. The huts caught fire so quickly. So beautifully.

Villagers emerged, screaming, some burning. And Clay shot them too. He knelt, carving them up. Collecting ears, scalps, tongues, fingers. A few heads he would boil later for the skulls.

Let the other men rape the women. Clay was not interested in such crude pleasures. He was not some animal. There were more beautiful uses for flesh.

His pack was already brimming with trophies. But Clay kept exploring the village. Kept loading new magazines. He wandered by a farm, and he shot the oxen. Pigs squealed in their pen, slamming at the fence, mad with terror. Clay emptied his magazine into them. Killing animals was not as fun as humans. But it was fun enough.

Clay was soon out of bullets. Spirits high, whistling a tune, he walked toward his jeep to grab more ammo. As he passed through the village common, he saw more naked women on the ground. Men were queuing up for their turns. Children lay dead everywhere. Nearby, a squad was lining up more villagers. The poor bastards were on their knees, begging.

"No Kalayaan here!" one woman said, tears on her cheeks, before a soldier shot her through the head. And soon the entire squad was firing, and bodies hit the grass.

Humming an old song, Clay grabbed more magazines and reloaded.

"Save some slits for me, boys!" he said.

His platoon laughed. Some other soldiers were collecting trophies too. They were jealous of Clay's necklace of ears. Most of the corpses were mutilated already, ears and scalps removed. One sick bastard was violating a corpse. Pervert. Even Clay wasn't that depraved.

"You sick fuck," he muttered, kicking the necrophiliac as he walked by.

Clay looked around, seeking new targets. So many villagers were dead already. But there! A few children crawled away from their dead mothers, trying to escape. *Bam. Bam. Bam.* Clay shot them dead. A group of other villagers were running toward the banana grove. Clay tossed a grenade, and they fell.

He lost count of how many he butchered. Dozens? No, surely hundreds by now. This was the best hunt of his life. This was, he decided, the best day of his life. Here in Santa Rosa, this beautiful village on Bahay, Clay Hagen became a true god.

Chapter Thirty-One
A Few Small Lights

Jon struggled against the ropes, desperate to free himself. He could hear it outside the hut. Gunfire. Explosions. Screams.

It was a massacre.

And here he was, tied up inside a nipa hut, helpless.

He tugged harder at the ropes, groaning, then collapsed. He could barely see. His left eye was swollen shut. He tasted blood. Bruises covered his body. Clay's fists and boots had bloodied him.

But Jon didn't care about the pain. He kept seeing the image of the Bahayan woman running. Clay shooting her. A woman who looked so much like Maria.

I have to stop him. I have to, or he'll kill every Bahayan in this village. And he'll find Maria and kill her too, like he promised.

He looked at his friends. George and Etty sat nearby, gagged and tied up. They too were bruised and bloody. Blood was dripping from Etty's forehead. George's nose was bashed up. Both were straining against the ropes, unable to free themselves. The platoon had unarmed them, taking even their pocket knives.

The screams continued outside. The gunfire rattled. Villagers were begging, screaming, dying. A baby wailed, a gunshot rang out, and the baby's scream was cut short.

Jon shouted into his gag.

Clay will murder everyone in Santa Rosa, then torture me and my friends.

He cursed himself. He should have killed Clay when he had the chance. But he had spared the monster. Shown him mercy. The blood of Santa Rosa was on Jon's hands too.

Another scream sounded outside. Footfalls thudded, and a woman begged for mercy. Gunfire roared. A body slammed into the hut, cracking the wall, and blood leaked between the bamboo stalks. Outside, the killer laughed.

Jon stared at the bloodied wall. One of the bamboos stalks was cracked. A splinter thrust out like a bayonet.

Every movement ached. Every breath sawed at his lungs. But Jon forced himself to move. He wriggled across the floor, ankles bound, arms tied behind his back. Thankfully, there were no guards inside the hut. Everyone was outside, enjoying the killings.

Jon pushed himself up, then slid his tied wrists around the sliver of bamboo. He moved his wrists up and down, sawing at the rope. It took an agonizingly long time. As he worked, George and Etty watched with wide, hopeful eyes. All the while, the gunfire and screaming continued outside.

Finally—the rope tore.

Jon's arms were free.

He removed his gag and took a deep breath. The ropes around his ankles were tight. He kicked the wall, broke off a shard of bamboo, and sawed at the rope, finally freeing his legs. With his wooden blade, he cut George and Etty free too.

The friends shared a quick embrace.

"What do we do?" George whispered.

From outside the sounds of gunfire, screams, and laughter continued.

"George, Etty—you two run." Jon took a deep breath. "I'll face Clay."

"We're not going anywhere," George said. "We'll face him together."

Etty balled her fists. "We're Fireteam Fucking Symphonica, and we stick together."

"If we face these soldiers unarmed," Jon said, "we'll probably die."

George clasped Jon on the shoulder. "Then we die together."

"If George and I ran, we'd regret it forever," Etty said. "In this war, we killed for nothing. Let's go die for something."

They left the hut and stepped into hell.

For a moment, they could only stare.

Hundreds of corpses filled the village. They piled up along the roadsides. Women. Elders. Children. Even babies. Many of the women had been stripped naked. Many of the corpses had been mutilated—scalped, ears cut off, hands severed.

The three friends just stood there, staring. For a moment nobody could speak.

"We have to show the world," Etty finally whispered. "We have to show them what happened."

Jon looked around. His heart pounded. His head spun. A few soldiers stood nearby, mutilating corpses. Other soldiers gathered between burning huts, laughing about something.

Jon could not move. Could barely breathe.

A massacre. Genocide. This was genocide. And it seemed to him that every corpse here had Maria's face.

"How can we show them?" Jon said. "Nobody will ever believe this."

George was pale, trembling, but he managed to snarl. "Yes they will."

His hands shook badly, but the giant managed to pull something from his pocket. It was a phone.

Jon's eyes widened. "George! We're not allowed to own personal phones."

"I know." George wiped away a tear. "I smuggled it with me. All the way from Earth. It has photos of my family on it. I look at the photos sometimes at night." He gave a shaky growl. "And now we'll take more photos."

The giant raised the phone, which seemed as small as a matchbox in his massive hand. He aimed the camera at a pile of corpses. But his hands trembled violently. He dropped the phone.

Jon lifted it. "Here, George."

But the giant was pale, shaking. He shook his head. "My hands are shaking too badly. Besides, I got fat fingers. You'll have to do it, buddy." George covered his eyes. "I can barely look."

So Jon began to take photographs.

He moved along the dirt road. Between the burning huts. Along the papaya grove and rice paddies. To the marketplace. The bodies were everywhere. Hundreds of them. He saw no bodies of Kalayaan, no bodies of fighting-aged men at all. All innocents.

Most of the soldiers gathered farther away, pointing at the ground, and laughing. But a few soldiers were walking through the carnage. They were collecting trophies—bead necklaces, folding knives, body parts. They saw Jon taking photos. Some looked away, suddenly ashamed, but others laughed. A few soldiers even smiled and posed for the camera.

Jon kept moving through this vision of hell. He photographed it all. Every victim. Then he hid the phone in his pocket.

He took a deep breath, glanced at his friends, and nodded.

They stepped between the burning huts and toward the laughing soldiers.

Most of the platoon was gathered there. Clay stood among them. The soldiers surrounded something, leaning down, laughing.

Jon stepped closer, and he saw it.

The soldiers surrounded a hole in the ground.

"I knew it, soldiers!" Clay was saying. "I told you we'd find enemy activity here. A bunker! A bunker to store Kennys!"

Jon stepped closer.

"Clay!" he shouted.

The platoon stopped laughing. Everyone turned toward Jon and his friends.

Clay looked over the rim of the bunker. His lips curled into a predatory smile.

"Ah, you've come just in time, Taylor," he said. "Do you enjoy what you see here?"

"I see murder!" Jon said, standing across the bunker. "I see a massacre! I see genocide!"

Clay tossed back his head and laughed. "Wrong, Taylor. You see victory. We found a bunker! Enemy activity. The Kalayaan are here."

Jon shoved his way between soldiers. He stared down into the bunker.

It was just a hole in the ground. Barely larger than a well. A handful of women and children cowered below, weeping. They were probably the only survivors of the village.

Jon looked back up at Clay. "This isn't a bunker. This is just a little cellar. A place they store seeds and supplies. It's just women and children down there. Not Kalayaan. Everyone you murdered here today, Clay—they were innocent."

Clay pulled a grenade from his belt.

"Watch them die, Jon Taylor. Enjoy the show."

Jon took a step back, eyes widening.

Clay laughed and pulled the pin.

Jon ran, vaulted over the cellar, and slammed into Clay.

Both men fell onto the grass. The live grenade thumped down beside them.

Soldiers ran, cursing.

Jon lifted the grenade and hurled it into the distance. It exploded among the burning huts.

"George, Etty, get the villagers into a jeep!" Jon shouted. "Get them to safety! And tell Colonel Pascal what—"

Clay barrelled into him, knocking him down. Jon nearly fell into the cellar.

Clay's beefy hands closed around Jon's throat. The lieutenant smirked, drooling, his eyes bugging out. His hands tightened, and Jon gurgled, unable to breathe.

"I'm going to kill you nice and slow," Clay said. "You're going to die like a slit, and I'm going to piss on your corpse."

Jon drove his knee into Clay's stomach. As hard as he could.

The brute recoiled, groaning. He reached for his rifle, which hung across his back.

Jon kicked. Hard. His boot connected with Clay's shoulder, knocking him backward. The beefy officer fell onto his back, pinning down his rifle. He roared.

Vaguely, Jon was aware of George battling other soldiers, holding them off, howling. Of Etty lowering a rope into the cellar, coaxing the women and children out.

But Jon had no time to take a closer look. Before Clay could aim his rifle, Jon leaped onto him, pinned him to the ground, and began raining down blows.

His knuckles cracked. Maybe they broke. The pain was agonizing, but Jon kept punching. Clay's face bled, but he just laughed.

The brute kicked wildly. His knee drove into Jon's ribs. Pain bloomed. Jon fell. For a moment both men lay on the grass, panting.

Jon glimpsed Etty pulling more villagers out. George was roaring, tossing soldiers back. The huts were still blazing, and smoke rolled through the village.

And then Clay was rising, aiming his rifle. Jon grabbed the gun. A shot rang out. A bullet hit a tree. The muzzle burned Jon's hands.

Both men wrestled for the rifle. It still hung across Clay's body on a strap. Jon yanked it hard, pulling Clay off balance. Another shot fired. A branch shattered and fell. Jon's ears rang.

Jon kicked his opponent in the shin. Clay crumbled, and Jon pinned him down, managed to unhook the rifle from its strap, and—

Clay's boot slammed into his chest. The same spot as before. Right in Jon's solar plexus.

Jon fell, unable to breathe. Stars exploded across his vision. Still he struggled to hold onto the gun.

Another boot hit him. Jon howled in pain, and the rifle tumbled into the cellar.

Before Jon could recover, Clay was on him, and the blows rained. Jon raised his arms, desperate to protect himself. His head dangled over the pit. Clay was laughing above him, blood covering his face—dripping from his nose, his mouth, splashing onto Jon. He had become a demon. If there had ever been any humanity in Clay, it was gone.

"You're going to die now, Jon Taylor," the beast said. "I wanted you to live long enough to see the dead. You saw. You suffered. Now I will grant you mercy and let you die."

Jon tried to fight, but Clay pinned his arms down. His beefy fist rose.

Another blow came down.

White light flashed.

Jon's head tilted back. Blood flowed from his nose, his mouth, his forehead.

He saw the world upside down. And he saw Etty load villagers into a jeep. Saw her driving them away to safety.

So many died, Jon thought. *We failed to save this village. But we saved a few lives. We saved a few at least.*

"Still alive, Taylor? You're showing some spirit." Clay leaned closer and whispered into his ear. "You will die soon, don't worry. Before you die, know this. I'm going to Mindao next. To the Go Go Cowgirl. Me and my platoon. We're all going to take turns with your whore before I scalp her. I'll keep her scalp as a trophy. Goodnight, Jon."

Clay's fist rose high, prepared to deliver the killing blow.

Jon roared, freed his arm, and drove his fist into Clay's chin.

Clay fell back.

Jon grabbed him.

For a moment they struggled, rolling around by the cellar. The huts burned all around. The other soldiers watched.

A blow hit Jon's cheek.

In the white light, he saw Maria's bright smile.

He saw her kind eyes.

He heard her laughter. Felt her kiss.

He rose to his feet, panting, dripping blood. Clay stood before him, bruised and laughing.

"Ready for more, Taylor?" the brute said, a tooth loose.

With a wordless cry, Jon ran, barreled into Clay, and slammed him into a burning hut.

Jon stumbled back, coughing, and watched the fire spread over his enemy.

For a moment, Clay just stood there. Burning. A living torch. He stared at Jon from the inferno. He did not fall.

He really is a demon, Jon thought.

And then Clay began to run. Burning, screaming, he ran toward the huts and vanished into the smoke.

Jon did not follow. He could not run, could barely even walk. But he had done enough.

Let the fire end him, he thought.

Bleeding, coughing, barely able to stand upright, Jon stumbled in the opposite direction. He limped down the dirt road, leaving a trail of blood. Soldiers stepped aside, letting Jon pass. He had defeated their leader.

"Jon!"

A jeep roared up beside him. George leaned out, gesturing for him. A few Bahayan women and children were sitting in the back, trembling. Etty was farther ahead, driving a jeep of her own.

Stay conscious, Jon, he told himself. *A moment longer.*

He climbed into the jeep, George hit the pedal, and they rumbled away from the burning village.

Jon sat in the back. The women began tending to his wounds. He closed his eyes, and he could see it again. A vision of Clay burning, a demon risen from hell, racing into the smoke. Jon didn't know if Clay was alive or dead. He didn't know if you could kill a demon with fire.

He pushed that hellish image away, and he thought instead of Maria. He imagined himself back in her room above the club. She was smiling, eyes bright. He finally passed out with a memory of her smile.

Chapter Thirty-Two
Wildfire

They sat in the heart of the jungle.

Jon. George. Etty.

They sat in silence, heads lowered, and shed tears for the dead.

The rainforest was a living being, wrapping around them, cloaking, hiding. A place of mist and shadows and motes of light. The roots coiled like petrified serpents, and the trunks soared like buttresses, supporting a cathedral of dark green and gray. Iridescent insects moved along branches, tiny emeralds with fluttering wings, and glowing pollen glided between vines, ferns, and mushrooms. Yellow eyes peered from holes and branches, watching but not judging. The forest was alive. The forest was a single great being, breathing, withering. All over this planet it was dying. Here in the last beating chambers of its pulsing raw heart they hid.

It began to rain. The canopy rustled. A gleaming blue bird glided between the branches, resplendent with raindrops, and vanished into a hole in a trunk. The raindrops pattered ferns and moss and fallen logs, forming curtains woven from ten billion reflective beads. The forest was weeping. It was weeping for Bahay.

They sat there. Three friends. They were all hurt. Bruised. Cut. Burnt. But the physical pain was nothing. Their bodies were nothing. The agony came from within. The memories had been seared into their hearts with fire and anointed with blood.

The people they had saved sat with them. Sixteen women and children. The only survivors of Santa Rosa. Five hundred people had once lived in the village, they said. They were the last.

The children curled up and slept, and the women tended to the soldiers' wounds. They knew the ancient medicine of the forest. They picked purple flowers, squeezed out nectar, and applied a healing ointment to deep cuts. Instead of stitching the wounds with needle and thread, they used ants. At first, they peeled bark and leaves off twigs, then used the rods to fish ants from hives. Next the plucked the pincers off the ants. Even severed, the pincers still clasped the wounds tightly, sealing them shut like staples. Finally, the women placed broad leaves over the wounds, gluing them down with sap.

The village women were as skilled as any Earthling medic. As they worked, they wept. For the loss of their families. For their fallen home. For their sundering world.

"You are angels," said a village woman, tending to a wound on Jon's forehead. Her accent was thick but her English was flawless. "You saved our lives. We'll always remember you."

Jon looked into her kind dark eyes.

"I wish we could have saved more." A sob fled him. "We should have stopped Clay earlier. We should have shot him at once. We should have done more. We could have saved five hundred."

He lowered his head, overcome with grief.

Etty held his hand.

"The world must know," she whispered in the shadows. "We must show them. Do you still have the photographs?"

Jon pulled out the phone. He scrolled through the photographs of Santa Rosa. He could barely look at them.

Photographs of soldiers slaughtering, raping, mutilating. Photographs of the piles of corpses.

"Any photographs of Bahay are highly classified," Jon said. "If we show these to Earth, we would become criminals. We would get life in prison."

"Not if we leak the photographs anonymously," Etty said. She took the phone from him. "Let this be my task. I'm good at this. Find me a computer, and I'll make sure everyone on Earth sees these."

George, who had been silent for hours, finally spoke. "Etty, if the army catches you leaking these… Oh God, Etty. You'd die in prison."

"I'm already dead," Etty said.

Jon embraced his friends. "Let's make a promise. That when we return to Earth, we leave the pain here. That whatever we saw, whatever we did—that it remains on Bahay. Someday we'll be on Earth again. I believe that. And when that day comes—let us not be soldiers anymore. Let the soldiers die. On Earth, we will be reborn."

Etty and George looked at him, eyes damp.

"What if we can't?" Etty whispered. "What if soldiers is all we are now? What if there's nothing left of who we were?"

"I don't believe that," Jon said. "When facing the massacre, we did not succumb to barbarism. The other soldiers in our platoon, almost fifty of them—they lost their humanity. They followed Clay. They raped and murdered, because they had become nothing but machines of destruction. We three stood against them. Our humanity is not dead. Maybe it's brighter than ever."

George sighed. "There's only one problem. We're stuck here in the middle of a jungle. Where do we go now?"

Jon rose to his feet and balled his fists. "Back to base. To find Colonel Pascal. And we're telling him everything."

* * * * *

Jon stood in the colonel's trailer, hands clasped behind his back, and told the tale.

He told everything. From his first moment in Santa Rosa to the last. He told of every atrocity. As he spoke, he stood still, voice steady, feeling numb. He spoke almost in monotone. His insides had shattered. And everything was spilling out.

As Jon spoke, Colonel Pascal sat behind his desk. The white-haired man listened silently. At some points, he leaned forward. At others, he frowned. His lips tightened when he heard the worst atrocities. And when Jon finished his tale, the colonel heaved a long, deep sigh.

For a moment, the two men were silent.

Finally Pascal spoke. "Is that all, corporal?"

"That's all, sir. That's what happened in Santa Rosa. That's what Lieutenant Clay Hagen and his men did."

He handed the colonel the photographs. He had printed copies.

The colonel stared at them in silence for a long moment.

Jon left out just one detail. That Etty still had the original files. That she was hiding them on George's illegal phone. That she planned to leak them to Earth. This Jon could not reveal. Not if he wanted to see daylight again.

Moment by moment ticked by. And Pascal just sat there, looking through the photographs.

Finally he lifted his phone and made a call.

"Debbie? Let me talk to the Sergeant Major." He waited a moment. "Bob, that you? Yeah, this is Joe. Can you hear me? *It's Joe Pascal.* Yes, the colonel! Send word to all battalions. To every officer in the goddamn brigade. We're halting Operation Search and Destroy. Bring everyone back to base. Right now. Get moving."

He hung up and looked at Jon.

"Sir, is it over?" Jon said.

Pascal rose from his desk. He stood for a moment, facing the wall. "It's a terrible thing, war. It's a terrible, terrible thing that we do. Necessary, yes. We join the army. We learn to kill. We do this because the galaxy is full of so much evil. We become monsters so that we can defend our families from monsters. We are soldiers, and we make the ultimate sacrifice. We sacrifice our souls to protect the innocent. But sometimes… sometimes this necessary mechanism goes haywire. We are like a campfire that holds back the wolves. Sometimes this fire spreads and consumes and burns everything in its path. In this war, we've become a wildfire."

"Sir, when I joined the army, I thought I could become a hero," Jon said. "Like the heroes from the stories. That I could fight monsters. But I didn't see monsters in this war. And I began to wonder if I was the monster."

The colonel clasped Jon's shoulder. "Son, you showed remarkable courage in Santa Rosa. You didn't just save those sixteen women and children. By coming here, by telling me, you halted the entire operation. You made sure no more villages would be destroyed by men like Clay Hagen. You saved thousands of lives, Corporal Jon Taylor." He heaved a sigh. "I'll probably end up in deep shit with the generals. But fuck it. And fuck them."

Jon couldn't help it. His eyes dampened. Not only from relief that the operation was halted. Not only for the knowledge that he had saved thousands of lives. But mostly for learning that there was still goodness in the Human Defense Force. That not all his commanders were evil. That there was decency and nobility to humanity along with all the cruelty. In Santa Rosa, Jon had seen the depravity of man. He had seen the pits of evil humanity can sink into, had sunken into so many times in history. But here in this trailer, he saw an act of nobility. Of compassion. And Jon shed tears because it meant he was not serving evil, that perhaps the soul of humanity could still be salvaged.

He wiped his eyes, trying to collect his thoughts.

War shows us the evil that men do, but it also shines a light upon all that is noble in man. In the shadows of war we see the most wicked of man's demons, but we also see angels shine their brightest. If I ever make my way home, that is what I'll remember of this war. That I saw darkness and light. That I saw cruelty and compassion. That I saw the worst of man but also his finest.

He saluted. "Thank you, sir."

The colonel gave him a long, hard look. "One more thing, Corporal Taylor. And you're not going to like it." He lifted the photos, then held a lighter to them. They burned in his hand. "I'm going to need the camera that took these photos. I'm going to need every copy of these files. Nobody must see them. Or we're all screwed."

Chapter Thirty-Three
Leave-Taking

Etty walked through the dark camp, lips tight, horror in her heart.

She had never felt more lost.

This place was nothing like Fort Miguel in the south. Down at the Old Mig, there had been concrete buildings, a little temple open to all faiths, a mess hall, a commissary. Down there, there had been some innocence. Some joy.

She missed it.

But Etty was now in North Bahay. And Camp Apollo, where her brigade bivouacked, was a circle of hell. The ground was littered with charred brush and animal skeletons. The only solid structures were wooden palisades topped with barbed wire. Soldiers slept under the sky, many clutching their trophies of war—Bahayan daggers, jewels, even sickening mementos like ears. By a fallen log, a soldier dropped a severed head into a pot of boiling water. It was how some soldiers collected skulls as souvenirs. They boiled off the flesh.

Etty kept walking through the camp. It was a dark night. Smoke rolled over the twin moons. Darkness fell, and the horror around Etty faded into shadows. But in these shadows new horrors rose.

"No," Etty whispered. "Stay away! Not you. Not now. Not again."

But they wove around her. Caressing. Taunting.

"Leave me!" she said.

But she could not banish them. Not tonight. Not after the trauma of Santa Rosa. They rose like demons from a crypt.

Her childhood memories.

She saw again her homeland.

Rolling dunes under a yellow sun. A mountain rising between coast and desert. Walls of ancient bricks and gateways from a time beyond memory. Standing here on a forsaken world in deep space, Etty returned to a lost land of milk and honey.

She ran down the cobbled streets of Jerusalem, a little girl in a white dress. It was Yom Kippur, the holiest day of the year. A garland of wheat adorned little Etty's hair, and she carried a straw basket full of pomegranates. She felt like a princess.

Jerusalem had been destroyed so many times. By cruel empires. By wild tribes. By invading aliens. Yet for thousands of years, people had continued to live here, stubbornly clinging to these ancient roads and halls of limestone. The cobbled streets were narrow, and brick homes and temples rose everywhere, forming labyrinthine walls. But this was not a dark, twisting place. It was a place of light, of gold and copper and life. The bricks had been carved in biblical times, and nobody could determine their color. They were golden at dawn, brilliant white under the searing noon sun, and pink tinged with blue at sunset. Jerusalem was a city of a thousand generations and the countless colors of the desert.

There were no cars driving along these ancient streets. Not on a sacred day like today. The people of Jerusalem all wore white, a color of holiness and rebirth. A rabbi blew a ram's horn, and people prayed. It was the Day of Atonement, but despite the solemnity, it was a day of joy. Children all in white ran along the streets, laughing, playing. Etty and her friends spent hours collecting pine nuts, cracking them open with rocks, and feasting. They played with apricot seeds like marbles, and they built little boats from olive leaves—one leaf for the hull, the other for the sail. They were poor, but they found joy in every leaf, nut, and stone. To them, it was a city of wonder.

"Etty! Etty, come! It's time for synagogue."

It was her mother calling. Etty looked up. Mother stood across the courtyard where Etty was playing with the other children. Like Etty, she wore a white dress, and a garland of wheat adorned her hair. Father stood beside her, also in white, the strongest man Etty knew, yet kind, smiling at her, a twinkle in his eyes.

Etty blew them a raspberry. "I don't want to. I still want to play."

Mother rolled her eyes. "Okay, Etty, five more minutes and—"

The shock wave lifted Etty into the air.

She hit a brick wall, and white light and fire blazed.

Shrapnel pattered into the wall around her, embedding in the ancient stones.

She remembered sitting there in a daze. Bleeding. Seeing body parts all around. A child's severed leg in an olive tree. Pools of blood. But she did not see her parents. The suicide bomber had stood too close, and almost nothing remained.

She remembered the years that followed. The days in the orphanage. The long flight to America. Her aunt's big, creaky house among the maple trees. A strange town in a strange land, so cold and different from everything Etty had ever known. A house of memory and quiet despair and slow death. A house where her aunt lay in bed, ravaged by cancer, leaving Etty alone again, a husk of wheat scuttling in the wind.

"You've always had something to fight for, Jon and George," Etty whispered. "But I never did. I have no home waiting for me."

She wiped her eyes, and she kept walking through the dark camp.

She had joined the army. Volunteered. Lied about her age. She was sixteen, orphaned, broken. She had come here. To be a soldier. To be like Einav Ben-Ari, her heroine, the great warrior of legend.

But she had found evil, and not among the enemy.

She had found terror, and not in the battlefield.

At Santa Rosa, Etty had gazed into the eyes of orphaned girls. Their parents murdered. She had stared at herself.

"And I've had enough," she said to the shadows.

She walked onward, small and silent, sneaking between rows of tents. Finally she reached the edge of Camp Apollo. A wooden palisade rose here, topped with barbed wire. Beyond spread the jungle, cloaked in night.

Guards patrolled the defensive palisade. But Etty had memorized their shifts; they were now patrolling another area of the camp. She pulled wire cutters from her pack. She had given a pair of panties to a sergeant for these. A small price to pay for freedom.

She approached the palisade, prepared to climb the wooden stakes, cut the barbed wire, and flee into the night.

"Etty!" An urgent whisper sounded behind her. "Damn it, Etty, what are you doing?"

She spun around, placed her hands on her hips, and glowered. "Don't you try and stop me, George. Don't you dare!"

He stood before her, a blob in the darkness. He stepped closer.

"Etty? What?" He gasped. "You're not sneaking away, are you?"

"Shh!" She glared, grabbed him, and pulled him behind a charred tree—one of the few that remained standing in the devastation. "Shut up, will you?"

Just then, a guard came by, patrolling. Etty and George stood in the shadows, not even daring to breathe. The guard was a young corporal with a shabby uniform, ill-fitting helmet, and a joint between his lips. He was whistling a Santana tune as he sauntered by, wreathed in smoke. The enemy could probably smell him for miles away. George and Etty waited until the guard passed around a patch of brush, then exhaled shakily.

"Etty," George said, holding her hand, "you can't just leave us. Where will you go?"

"Anywhere but here," she said. "If I must live in the jungle like an animal, that's better than here!"

"Etty!" George knelt, bringing himself to eye level with her. "Don't go AWOL. If you do, and they catch you, they'll toss you into the brig for a very, very long time."

Her eyes burned. "The brig is better than this!"

"No it isn't," George said. "Because I won't be with you."

Etty went limp. She embraced the giant, shed tears onto his shoulder. "Oh, George, I can't stay here. I can't. Not after what happened in Santa Rosa. When I was a child, George… You know what happened. To my parents. I swore then that I'd always fight evil. But now I find myself fighting *with* evil. The HDF, the proud army that fought the aliens… it lost its path. This is no longer the noble army that Ben-Ari once led. This army destroyed families like my family was destroyed. And I can't serve here anymore. I can't wear this uniform anymore. I have to go. To run. Even if I run for the rest of my life. I can't stand another single day here."

George took a deep, shaky breath and squared his shoulders. "Then I'm going with you."

Etty stroked his hair. "My sweet ginger giant. You can't. You have to stay here for Jon. He needs you more than I do."

George deflated. "But how can I let you go?"

She whispered into his ear. "I need to smuggle out these photographs. You heard what Jon said. The colonel tore up the prints. He confiscated the phone with the files. But I have a codechip in my pocket, carrying copies of the photographs. I need to make my way to Mindao in the south. To find a spaceport. To smuggle myself off this world and bring these photographs to Earth. I'm not just going AWOL, George. I'm going on a mission. To show Earth what's happening here. And to end this war."

George gave a little whimper. "But Etty, I've always been there for you. To help you. Protect you. And… No, it's not that. You've always been here for *me*. To protect *me*. Or maybe we protect each other. The point is, Etty, I love you. I love you very much. And I don't know how to let you go."

Etty closed her eyes, holding him close, and then kissed the kneeling giant. A warm kiss on the lips which tasted of her tears.

"I love you too, George Williams," she said. "You're a big fat ginger jerk. But you're a good man. You're a kind man. And you're so adorable I could burst. If we ever get back to Earth, I'm going to kiss you a thousand more times. Remember this not as our last kiss. But as a promise of many more." She smiled. "Something to look forward to."

She left him there, dazed. She scuttled up the fence, cut the barbed wire, then turned and looked back. George stood below, a towering shadow in the night, the most courageous man she knew. Etty gave him a last smile, not sure if he could see. Then she hopped and vanished into the dark jungle.

Chapter Thirty-Four
The Living

She journeyed south alone.

She was a deserter. A criminal. If she was caught, she would spend years in prison.

Etty didn't care.

"I refuse to be evil," she whispered.

She had seen so much evil in her life. Her parents—slaughtered. Her homeland—brutalized. She was Israeli. Her people had suffered throughout history. Invasion after invasion. Slavery and captivity. Genocide after genocide. All the horrors of humanity had been inflicted upon her nation, and now Etty found herself here.

On Bahay.

A soldier inflicting evil upon others.

A soldier in a genocidal empire.

Tears flowed as Etty walked through fields of devastation.

"I betrayed my family," she whispered. "I betrayed my people. I betrayed humanity. And I betrayed myself."

True, she had not murdered civilians herself. Not in Santa Rosa, at least. But she had fired rifles into the jungle. Who's to say she had not killed good men and women, honest peasants fighting for their homes? She had fired artillery shells onto Basilica. Who's to say some of those shells had not killed an innocent family?

Etty looked at her hands. Small, slender hands. Dust and grime covered them. But to Etty's eyes, they were covered in blood.

All around her, across the wilderness of Bahay, spread the work of Earth.

Charred forests, their ancient ecosystems destroyed.

Smoldering villages, bombed or brutalized.

Mutated peasants crawled, eyeless, starving.

Bahay—a world so beautiful, a jewel of the cosmos. Earth had come, and Earth had destroyed.

"For what?" Etty whispered. "Just because the Santelmos brought people here. Just because they're aliens. Just because other aliens hurt us long ago, and we're so afraid. And our fear destroyed a world."

When she looked around her, more than she saw evil or cruelty, Etty saw fear. Earth's terrible fear. Her lingering shell shock from the Alien Wars a century ago. That fear exploded here with fire and shrapnel.

She looked at her battlesuit. The uniform of the Human Defense Force.

Once Etty had been so proud to wear this battlesuit. The HDF—the military the Golden Lioness had once commanded! Etty's heroine! The military that had beaten back the scum, the marauders, the grays, the cyborgs. The military that had birthed legendary warriors like Marco Emery, Addy Linden, Lailani de la Rosa—war heroes everyone on Earth idolized. As a child, Etty had hung posters of those heroes on her bedroom walls.

The first day Etty had donned this uniform, her chest had swelled with pride. She had felt like Einav Ben-Ari, the Golden Lioness.

Now Etty ripped the insignia off her sleeves. She threw the chevrons at the charred forests.

Then, after a moment's thought, she ripped off the entire battlesuit. She tossed it aside, remaining in her undershirt and boxer shorts. To hell with it.

A donkey brayed.

A man sang.

Wood rattled.

Etty turned. A cart was trundling along the dirt road. Peasants sat inside, huddled together. They were bandaged. Some were scarred with burns. All seemed to be starving. The cart driver was an old man with a long white beard. He sang a sad song of Bahay.

Behind the cart walked many other peasants. A hundred or more. They wore rags. A few of the children were naked. Everyone was scarred, burnt, cut. Many were diseased. One child stumbled and fell. She was too thin, maybe dying. A man lifted her, shuffled onward.

Etty approached the group.

"Who are you?"

A few peasants recoiled.

"An Earthling!"

"Run!"

"She'll hurt us!"

"I won't hurt you," Etty said. "I'm no longer a soldier."

They cast fearful looks at her rifle.

"With those weapons, you slaughter us!" said an old woman.

"With this weapon, I will protect you," Etty said. "I'm going to Mindao. Can I join you?"

Gradually they accepted her, and Etty walked with them. A young mother walked beside Etty, holding her baby. The baby was deformed. Its eyes bugged out, nearly popping from the sockets. Its head tapered into a point. It kept crying.

Poisoned, Etty knew.

Another mother walked ahead. She looked so young, barely into her teens. Yet she too had a baby. This baby was healthy, but it had blond hair and blue eyes. A mixed child. A *mestizo*. A child of rape, born of a Bahayan girl and an Earthling soldier. It would not have an easy life, perhaps no easier than those kissed by Mister Weird.

A young boy walked beside Etty. He had one leg, and he limped on crutches. He spoke of a battle in the jungle, of dead brothers.

A hundred people walked here—and each one had a story. A tragedy. And Etty felt at home with them. She felt like she belonged here. More than she had ever belonged in the Human Defense Force. More than she had ever belonged in America. She was not a Bahayan, but nor did she feel like an Earthling. Not anymore.

I'm just an empty husk in the wind, Etty thought. *I'm nothing. I'm no one. I'm already dead.*

They shuffled forward. Refugees. The undead.

As the days went by, they kept singing. Even wounded, starving, mourning—the people sang. They embraced. Held hands. Comforted one another. Carried those who collapsed. Buried those who died. They moved ever onward. They clung to hope.

I was wrong, Etty thought.

They were not the undead. She herself was not dead already. She realized that they were more alive than they had ever been. They were life triumphant. They were survivors. They were the true spirit of humanity that craved life, that fought for life through the unbearable darkness. And she was proud to walk among these refugees, for here on this sundering world, they were more noble than the mightiest brigade of soldiers.

She reached into her pocket, and she felt the codechip there. A little data file, containing the photos from Santa Rosa. The evidence of Earth's cruelty. Evidence she had to share.

She walked onward, weak but in many ways stronger than ever. They saw it in the distance past smoke and scattered fires—Mindao, the great city in the south. Etty walked with more vigor.

From here I will unleash the truth like a dove from an ark. I must send these photos home.

Chapter Thirty-Five
Etty's Sacrifice

"Maria, Maria!" The child ran toward her, barefoot. "Maria, you must come to the Go Go Cowgirl at once."

Maria was in an alleyway, feeding soup to hungry orphans. She often came to these alleys, bringing not only her camera but food and clean water, whatever she could collect from the clubs. Millions of children lived in Mindao, most of them homeless, many of them orphaned. They were everywhere. They begged outside the neon clubs. They huddled in alleyways or hid in shanties. They slept along the train tracks, waiting to run alongside any train that rolled by, to beg for scraps, to catch whatever passengers threw. They crawled over landfills, seeking bones and peels to eat.

Maria could not save them all. Not speak to them all. She could record a few of their stories. She could give what little she had. She could save a life, maybe two, bringing an orphan back from the brink of starvation.

But if she wanted to truly save this world, she needed to end this war.

She needed to shame Earth.

She needed to bring Hale down.

And so Holy Maria walked the alleyways, feeding, healing, listening. Recording.

Now a child ran toward her, out of breath, eyes wide. "Maria, Maria! You must come now! To the Go Go!"

Maria recognized the child. One of Charlie's boys. He was *mestizo*, the son of an Earthling soldier. He had the dark, almond-shaped eyes of a Bahayan, but his hair was brown instead of black, and his skin was pale. He was a beautiful boy but doomed to a life of hardship. Even among the poorest Bahayans, *mestizos* were a class below, the untouchables among the untouchables.

I wonder what my child with Jon will look like. She placed her hand on her belly. *Will he have Bahayan eyes like mine, or round blue eyes like Jon's? Will he have brown skin like mine, or white skin like his? Will he look like this boy who runs to me?*

"Rodrigo, what is it?" Maria said.

"Come, Maria! My mom says you need to come!"

The boy turned and ran out of the alley. Maria hesitated for a moment. Rodrigo had already visited the Go Go Cowgirl once. Would he be waiting there? Was this a trap?

I'll take that chance, Maria decided. She patted her skirt, feeling the pistol strapped to her leg. If Ernesto was there, good. She would finish this.

She ran, following the boy.

They ran down the Blue Boulevard, the city's entertainment strip. It looked so different during the day. At night, this was a dizzying wonderland of neon and music, of bargirls strutting in miniskirts, or drunken soldiers carousing, hunting for booze and flesh. The poverty of the city disappeared during those nights, fading behind the neon glow. But now, in the daylight, it was everywhere. Now, with the neon signs dimmed, Maria could see the concrete foundations of the clubs, decaying and stained. She could see the rusty balconies. Half-completed upper floors. Roofs of rusting steel held down by tires. She could see the poor beggars lying on the curb. It all seemed not only poorer but smaller somehow, the boulevard narrow, the buildings squat, a place of bitter reality after a fanciful dream.

But the street was unusually subdued, even for the daytime. Normally countless people bustled here back and forth, day and night, frenzied bees in a field of intoxicating nectar. But now people were gathering outside shops and kiosks and clubs. A few radios were on, leaking snippets of crackly news reports.

"… across the northern border. Early reports say the massacre has claimed…" The radio crackled, muffling a few words. "The Luminous Army had vowed retaliation, and—" More static. "South Bahayan President Santiago is expected to make a statement in—"

Maria kept running, following the boy. She could hear no more.

They approached the Go Go Cowgirl. The club, so flashy at night, seemed particularly miserable during the day. Just a decaying box of concrete and plywood, rotting away. The cowgirl sign, which at night draped the club with a luminous garment of particolored light, was now dark. A few of the *unanos*—the club's midget boxers—sat on the curb, snorting shabu, wasting away their paltry earnings.

Maria stepped inside to find a club like a graveyard. There was no music. No dancing.

The Magic Man and his bargirls sat at a booth, surrounding a shadowy figure. The Magic Man turned toward Maria, and she paused, expecting him to grab her, to chastise her for fleeing his club. But he only gave her a somber look, then turned his back to her.

Maria approached slowly, her heart thudding.

She joined the other girls at the booth, and then she saw the shadowy stranger.

It was an Earthling soldier. A young woman with black hair, skin as dark as a Bahayan's, and startlingly green eyes, as large and bright as a tarsier's.

"Etty!" Maria said, gasping. "You're back!"

Etty looked up, and Maria took a step back.

She clutched her cross. *My God.*

The young Earthling looked like she had been to hell and back. Her eyes, once full of light and laughter, now seemed dead. Bruises and scratches marred her face and arms.

"Maria," she whispered.

Charlie rose from the table. The beautiful bargirl, queen of the cowgirls, stared at Maria with mournful eyes. She stepped closer and held Maria's hand.

"Come, little sister," she said. "Sit with us. Etty has a tale to tell." She wiped a tear from her eye. "And you need to record it."

Maria sat with the others, and she pulled out her camera.

And Etty spoke.

For a long time, Maria listened and filmed. And her tears flowed.

Etty spoke of the massacre at Santa Rosa.

She spoke of the hundreds of dead.

She spoke of the rape. The soldiers laughing as they shot babies. As they dumped corpses into wells.

She spoke of a village wiped out.

And she showed them the photos.

"Jon took these," she whispered, looking at Maria. "Your husband is a good man. He wanted the world to know."

Maria looked at the first photo. Bodies strewn across a road, piled up. Babies on top.

She wept.

"I left," Etty said. "I ran. I had to run. I couldn't be part of this army anymore." She cradled a mug of beer, not drinking. "I had to leave. I had to tell you. Earth must know."

"Earth will know," Maria vowed.

The club's front door banged open.

Several Military Police officers stormed inside, guns drawn.

The Magic Man hopped to his feet, his golden chains jangling. "What are you doing in here? This is a private club! This—" When a gun pointed at him, the pimp cringed. "Um, I will go… get you some beers. Bye bye!"

With a flash of his purple coat, he retreated into the kitchen. They heard him storm out the back door.

The Military Police stomped toward the booth.

"Corporal Ettinger?" one said, voice emerging metallic from his helmet. "Come with me."

Etty sat still, head lowered, staring into her mug.

Maria leaped to her feet and faced the police. They towered above her. She barely even reached their shoulders. But she stood firmly before them, chin raised.

"You'll have to get through me first."

Charlie looked at the scene, and her eyes seemed sad. Then they hardened, and she stood up too.

"And through me."

The other bargirls all rose, hands on hips.

"Get lost, *pute*!" one bargirl said, an eyebrow raised.

"Yeah, get out of here!" said another bargirl, chin thrust out.

"Out of our club."

"Get off this world!"

"Earthlings go home!"

The chant spread among the bargirls. "Earthlings go home! Earthlings go home!"

The soldiers cocked their guns. They aimed the barrels at the bargirls.

Maria found herself staring into an open muzzle.

Fear flooded her, but she refused to back down.

She drew her own gun, and—

"Wait." Etty stood up. "I'll go with them. It's all right, girls. I knew what I was getting into. I went AWOL. That makes me a criminal."

She held out her wrists. The military police handcuffed her and grabbed her arms.

As they led Etty away, Maria ran after them, clutching the damning photos against her chest. On the sidewalk, she leaned toward Etty and spoke urgently in her ear.

"I'll let them know, Etty. What happened in the village. What happened to you. I'll let everyone know. You're not alone."

Without anyone seeing, Etty slipped something into Maria's hand. A little piece of metal.

A codechip.

"Get back, slit!" grunted an MP.

The soldier shoved Maria. She hit the ground, banging her tailbone. For long moments, she could barely see or breathe with pain.

When the agony finally cleared, Etty was gone. Maria was left sitting on the curb, the photos scattered around her, shreds of tragedy scuttling across the pavement.

Chapter Thirty-Six
The River

The Bargirl Bureau was giving goodbye kisses when the storm came, both a storm of rain and furious Earth vengeance.

It was a miserable morning in Mindao. Monsoon season had come, and the rain kept falling, washing through the streets, carrying away trash, human waste, and collapsed shanties. Throughout the city, the surviving shanties teetered on stilts, and the water glistened everywhere, silvery and pure and almost beautiful in a city of such decay.

The city shut down during a monsoon. Streets flooded, pulling jeepneys and rickshaws downstream like a child sweeping aside colorful blocks. A few intrepid people built makeshift rafts from particleboard, and they rowed back and forth, rescuing stranded orphans and cats stuck on rusty roofs. In a few days, Maria knew, the water would recede and the people would rebuild. They would collect driftwood, metal sheets, and windblown scraps of tarpaulin, and the stilts would rise anew, and new shanties would pop up like mushrooms after the rain. The people of Bahay would survive and move on.

If only we can survive this war too, Maria thought. *We are sturdy people. We are brave and optimistic and industrious. We are only Bahayans, not mighty Earthlings with their towering height, big muscles, and clever technology. We are lowly compared to those gods. But even the mightiest hurricane blows over. Even the wettest monsoon floats away on the wind.*

Like a storm, their empire will scatter in the wind, and the sun will shine again. And we will live on.

Yes, the city was flooded, and the rain kept falling. But the military complex churned on. Shuttles still took off and landed, transporting troops to and from space. The planes still flew over the rainforest, bombing and bombing. Sometimes, when lightning flashed, Maria could glimpse the shadow of motherships beyond the clouds. It was said those grand starships were the size of cities, able to travel between the stars within only weeks.

The Earthlings are so powerful, Maria thought. *Yet so easy to seduce with just a kiss or the curve of a hip.*

"Goodbye kisses, come and get your goodbye kisses!" Charlie said, strutting across the stage, hips swaying. A tarpaulin canopy protected the stage, sagging low with rain. Some water made its way through to drench the parading bargirls, and their wet clothes clung to their bodies—much to the delight of the Earthling troops.

Another hundred Earthlings were heading home today. They lined up, ready to enter Marco Emery Spaceport and blast into orbit, the first leg of their journey home. On the way to their shuttles, they kept approaching the stage to kiss the girls goodbye.

With every kiss, Maria planted a codechip in a man's pocket, whispered into his ear, asked him to share her truth. With every kiss, she sent another little arrow into the war machine's engines.

"Thank you, Holy Maria," a sergeant whispered to her, still blushing from her kiss. "I've heard of you from my brother. Your videos are shared all over Earth. I'll share this too."

Maria blinked. "You've… heard of me?"

He nodded. "Everyone has! Some of us are just here for kisses. The others to help the Bargirl Bureau."

The sergeant gave her another quick kiss, then retreated with her codechip.

Maria's heart fluttered like a trapped bird.

More soldiers were lining up below. Charlie, Pippi, and the other girls were busy leaning forward, kissing them, slipping them more codechips.

They know, Maria thought, her legs shaking now. *They all know. That means…*

"Charlie." Maria inched toward her friend. "We have to get out of here."

Charlie leaned back from kissing a soldier, patted the man's cheek, and turned toward Maria.

"What?" Her eyebrow rose. "We're only getting started, *Nini*! We have so many codechips left, you know."

Maria looked at the crowd. At the sheets of rain, and the water spreading through the city. A city full of soldiers.

They all know…

"Charlie, we have to go." She grabbed her friend's hand. "*Now.*"

Pippi was busy giving a soldier a long, passionate kiss. She turned toward them. Her red pigtails and schoolgirl uniform were sopping wet, and her makeup was dripping, making her look like a psychotic doll.

"What are you two chattering about?" she said. "We have goodbye kisses to give, and…"

Her words faded away.

Maria saw them in the crowd. Marching toward the stand.

Twenty or more. Earth's Military Police.

"Girls, run!" Maria said.

She leaped backstage.

The police swarmed.

Bargirls screamed, and Maria looked over her shoulder. The police were running onto the stage, grabbing girls. One man caught Pippi, who began to scream bloody murder. Another policeman clutched Charlie, who kicked and bit and howled. The police wrestled a few girls down, began handcuffing them. Below the stage, the departing soldiers booed.

"Let 'em go, pigs!" a sergeant said and tossed a bottle.

But when the MP turned toward the soldiers, the men grumbled and walked away. Nobody wanted to end their tour of Bahay in handcuffs.

Dammit! Maria thought.

She ran back onto the stage.

"Maria, no, run away!" Charlie cried.

But Maria raced toward her. "Not without you!" She began hitting the policeman holding her friend. "Let her go, let her—"

A policeman grabbed Maria.

She screamed.

She kicked wildly, but the man was so strong, pinning her arms to her sides. She was only a Bahayan woman, not even half his size.

"You treasonous little whore!" the policeman hissed in her ear. His breath reeked. "We Earthlings came here to liberate you. And we find you leaking classified material. You'll hang for this, you fucking little slit."

Maria bit his hand. So hard she tasted blood.

The policeman screamed and released her, and Maria drew her gun.

The world seemed to expand around her. Everything was pulsing, zooming in and out, a vibration of space and time, and her chest trembled, and when the policeman came at her again, she pulled the trigger.

He fell, clutching his chest.

Maria's hands shook so badly she almost dropped the gun.

For a moment—everything was silent.

Then the remaining policemen drew their guns, and Maria leaped away.

She landed behind the stage, and bullets whistled overhead. Her heart fluttered.

I took a life. Oh God, I killed again.

But she had no time for horror now.

"Charlie!" she cried. "Pippi!"

But the military police was dragging them away.

"Run, Maria!" Charlie's voice came from across the stage. "Run!"

More bullets flew. One hit the ground beside Maria. Another grazed her arm, drawing blood, and she screamed.

She returned fire. She emptied her magazine, and another policeman fell.

Then Maria finally turned and ran, tears on her cheeks.

I'm sorry, girls. I'm so sorry.

She ran into the alleyways of Mindao. The water was up to her knees. The police followed, but they were slow and clunky, and the water caught them. They slipped and fell, but Maria de la Cruz was from the provinces, had been raised a rice farmer. She had spent most of her life in the wet paddies. She waded forward with ease.

A bullet streaked overhead.

A man, an innocent bystander on a raft, screamed and fell into the water.

Maria wanted to dive after him. To try to save him. But more bullets flew, and the police was still chasing, and she was out of ammo.

She kept running.

She left the innocent man behind.

He died because of me.

"You slit!" a policeman shouted, firing.

Bullets slammed into the shanties. A wooden stilt cracked and fell. A shanty collapsed into the water. Children screamed inside, crawling out through holes, only for the river to pull them away.

Maria raced behind the pile of plywood, scurried up a pole, and scrambled into a shanty. A family huddled inside around a pot of aromatic *adobo.* Maria ran by them, jumped out the window, and hopped into another shanty. A family was here too—grandparents, parents, children, twenty or more people living inside this little room, no larger than a bedroom in the Go Go Cowgirl club.

Maria hopped from shanty to shanty, in and out of windows, vanishing into this labyrinth of plywood and rust. The police ran below, moving between the stilts, but slow. So slow. The water kept tugging them down, and the rain kept falling.

She moved. Room to room. All the shanties blurred together, becoming one massive maze, an entire city, a great honeycomb, family after family huddling inside for shelter. Living out their lives. Endless stories and dramas and generations here in the slums.

"Holy Maria!" they cried after her. They knew her. They all knew.

If they all know me, and the police knows me, then Ernesto knows too.

She kept running until she reached a rickety, abandoned shanty, home only to cats and mice. Lightning flashed, and between slats of particle board, she beheld the city. The shantytown rolled toward the train tracks. Beyond them snaked the Blue Boulevard, a strip of neon, glistening in the rain like a river of molten light. Farther out, the azure cathedral grew from the slums, an angel rising over a pit of hell. Farther still rose the landfills, the concrete towers of the city center, and the barracks of the Earthlings.

Thunder boomed.

The shanty rocked beneath Maria's feet, then pitched forward.

Maria screamed, and then the shanty was falling, crashing, and particle boards shattered, and the structure crashed into the water.

Thunder boomed again and again, and Maria struggled, caught in the flood, as wood rained around her. A sheet of tarpaulin fell over her, and she clung to it, gasping, head rising above the water.

The river pulled her along. Needles, paper cups, and the corpses of animals floated around her. Everywhere the lightning flashed, and the winds stormed, and torrents of rain pounded the city. She clung onto the tarpaulin, an ant clinging to a leaf, as the storm raged.

The police were gone now. They must have fallen behind, and perhaps the rain would take them too. Perhaps the rivers would cleanse all the evil from this city. The disease. The prostitution. The hunger. The Earthlings who had come from so far away. Maria imagined that the water could purify it all, and that in the morning, she would find a reborn city, transfigured into something holy and glistening like the cathedral on the distant hill.

Yet when the rain eased, and the winds died, she found herself in an alleyway among fallen palm trees. And the city still wept. And the world still mourned. She was alive, but her friends were gone, and her hope flowed away with the river.

Chapter Thirty-Seven
Metal and Tears

The news hit Kaelyn like a bullet.

She sat before the computer, staring blankly at the screen, unable to believe what she was seeing.

Photo after photo. Smuggled to Earth by the so-called Bargirl Bureau of Bahay.

Photos of a massacre.

A village called Santa Rosa—destroyed.

Tears ran down Kaelyn's face. She forced herself to keep looking. To scroll through the photos. To see the piles of dead. Hundreds of them. All of them innocent villagers. Men. Women. Babies too. Piled up on the roadsides. She saw photos of soldiers lining up to rape women. Tossing babies into the air and shooting them.

She saw inhumanity. Barbarism. Evil.

And then—even worse—she saw the name of the unit. Of the platoon that had done this.

Horus Battalion, Cronus Company, Lions Platoon.

George and Jon's platoon.

Kaelyn's heart broke.

"Hey, Kaelyn, want some coffee? I hope so, because I already made you a cup! Kaelyn?"

Lizzy came into the living room, wearing pajamas, holding two steaming cups of Joe.

She looked at the computer where Kaelyn sat.

Her cups fell and shattered, and coffee spilled across the floor.

Kaelyn had been living here since her father had kicked her out. It was a small apartment in Queens, New York. Lizzy paid for it, using her humble disability pension, some money from her grandparents, and a night shift working a parking lot booth. Over the past few weeks, the apartment had been a hub of activity. Every day, more activists came here, crowding the little place. They pored over the leaks coming from Bahay, built placards, uploaded videos. Every day, they planned their war against the war. Every day, they marched. They protested. They clashed with police.

And every night, it was just Kaelyn and Lizzy here. It was a studio apartment, all they could afford. Lizzy slept on the bed, and Kaelyn slept on the couch, but even at night they were not alone. At night the nightmares came. Lizzy often woke up screaming, drenched in cold sweat, and Kaelyn would sit beside her for long hours, soothing her, sometimes singing to her, until the sergeant calmed.

Days of protests. Nights of horror. This had become Kaelyn's life. She had found a new meaning here, and a new fire blazed inside her. She had not felt such burning purpose since singing for Symphonica. That old dream had died. Here was her new quest.

But today… today was not like other days.

Today Kaelyn was staring at photos of a massacre. The work of her brother's platoon.

"It wasn't them," Lizzy whispered, face pale, lips trembling. "It can't have been them. Not my platoon."

But in one photo they saw a faded figure of a giant. He stood in the background, grainy, barely visible at all. But they recognized him by his size. It was George.

"No," Kaelyn whispered, looking at her brother. "It can't be you. It can't…"

She trembled. It was impossible! Her brother was a gentle giant. As a child, he would cry whenever their father crushed an insect. And Jon! Jon was the sweetest boy Kaelyn knew, a boy who lived for poetry, who walked alone in autumn forests and gazed upon the stars. Neither boy had gotten into a fight since kindergarten. How could they have done this? Butchered hundreds of innocents?

"It wasn't them," Lizzy said. "Maybe it was their platoon. But Jon and George took no part."

Kaelyn sniffed, wiped her tears, and looked at the sergeant. "How do you know?"

"I know!" Lizzy said. "I trained them. I fought with them. I was their sergeant. With all due respect, I probably know Jon and George better than you do. As soldiers, at least. And I'm telling you: those boys did *not* commit this crime." Her voice softened. "And neither did Carter."

Kaelyn tilted her head. "Who's Carter?"

Lizzy lowered her head, for a moment silent. "The platoon's commander. A man I love. He would never have allowed this. If it's truly the Lions who carried out this atrocity… Carter is dead."

And now a tear rolled down her cheek. It splashed onto her lap.

"Wait." Kaelyn leaned closer to the monitor. She tapped the photo. "Look. George is standing apart from the other soldiers. And one of his hands is raised. As if…" Kaelyn gasped. "He's trying to stop the others!"

She clicked to another photograph. This one showed villagers lying dead in a ditch, tied and executed. A few soldiers stood above them, laughing. She could see George here too, standing in the distance. Again, he was apart from the others. He was shouting. Howling in silent anguish.

He was grieving.

She kept scrolling through photographs. Most didn't show George. But the ones where he appeared—he was weeping. In one photo, it looked like some soldiers were restraining him. Pulling him back.

Kaelyn's tears flowed. "My brother didn't kill anyone. He tried to stop the massacre. And Jon! Jon isn't in the photos." She let out a sob. "Of course not. Jon took the photographs. He wanted the world to see. And the world will see! We will use these photos. We will bring Hale down!"

She turned toward Lizzy, panting with excitement, then recoiled.

Lizzy was looking at another photograph.

Not one on a monitor. Not the photos distributed online around the world. But a photograph she had pulled from her pocket.

It showed her standing with a young officer. A handsome, somber young man with dark skin, closely-cropped hair, and intelligent eyes. The insignia of a lieutenant adorned his shoulder straps.

"Oh, Lizzy, I'm sorry," Kaelyn whispered. "I'm so sorry. Maybe he's still alive. Maybe…"

But then Lizzy turned on the news, and along with reports of the massacre, they saw the list of the dead.

Dozens of new names.

Among them—Captain Michael Carter. He had died a captain.

Kaelyn pulled Lizzy into an embrace. For a long time, they held each other, weeping.

*****

A million people gathered that autumn day to march.

The came from around Earth, even from colonies as far as Mars and Titan. They were rich and poor. Young and old. Veterans and those who had never served. They were ruffled and shabby. Some had long hair and scraggly beards. Some wore business suits. Some wore tattered jeans and rumpled coats. Some wore military jackets, their medals pinned to their breasts. They smoked weed and they drank from flasks, medicine to forget the horrors. Some walked on crutches. Many rolled in wheelchairs. Some were elders with crooked backs and wobbling canes. Some were just children riding on their parents' shoulders.

They were all different.

And they were all angry.

They converged in New York City, and they moved through Central Park, heading toward the presidential palace.

Earth had united under a single government long ago, following the devastating Cataclysm, an alien invasion that had brutalized the planet. For over a century, Earth's presidents had come from around the world. There was no central headquarters for the world government. No worldwide White House or 10 Downing Street. Traditionally, the president governed from his or her home.

The last president, Einav Ben-Ari, had lived in a humble home in Jerusalem. For decades, she had ruled the Human Commonwealth from that little house on the mountain. President Hale was American, and he lived here in New York, reigning from his palace in Central Park.

Lizzy was still in pain, still weak from her wounds. But she walked here with the million. She walked at their head. She had to lean on Kaelyn, but she walked on, ignoring the pain.

She had run, howling, firing bullets into the enemy hordes. She had run into fire and death. Now she limped toward a golden palace. And this was the longest walk of her life. And this was her greatest battle.

Her missing hand still ached, a phantom pain, even with the prosthetic attached to her nerves. The bullet through her lung had left her weak and wheezing. The nightmares of her captivity forever filled her mind, an eternal pain. But she was lucky. She had survived a war that had slain so many. And she was stronger than ever before.

She still wore her military uniform, and her medals clanked on her coat. Medals for courage under fire. But she no longer wore this uniform with pride. She wore it with shame. It was who she was. What she had done. A soldier in an unjust war. And she would not deny it.

She could hardly believe that only five years ago, she had been such a different person. Lizzy the popular high school girl. Always smiling. Always laughing. Captain of her volleyball team. A girl who lit up every room. Who loved dogs and volunteered at the retirement home.

That girl had died somewhere in the burning jungles of Bahay.

This was all that remained now. Sergeant Lizzy Pascal. A broken shell around a hardened soul. A soldier with medals on her uniform. With a hole through her chest. With a hole in her heart.

Her beloved Carter was gone.

Her platoon had slain hundreds.

All Lizzy had left was her rage.

And so she walked, and other veterans walked with her, medals clinking. Behind them walked a million souls. Raising banners. Singing songs. Chanting to end the war. To bring the sons and daughters of Earth home.

But the veterans did not sing, did not cheer. They walked with grim, silent purpose. Some on crutches. Some leaning on friends. And in their memories, they were walking again through the jungles of Bahay.

The palace rose before them, dominating Central Park. It was built in Neo-Nouveau style, all soaring white lines, pale arches, and crests of gold. During Ben-Ari's reign, Earth had risen from the ashes of the Cataclysm, defeated its alien enemies, and become a local power in the galaxy. The Golden Lioness had ushered in a golden age. Across the world rose grand structures, emulating the roaring 1920s a few centuries earlier, boasting of new optimism and prosperity. Ward Palace took Neo-Nouveau architecture to the extreme, forging a shining beacon, perhaps the grandest palace on Earth.

It was nothing like the humble little house on the hills of Jerusalem. Ben-Ari had been like Moses, shepherding her people through the desert to the promised land. Ward was a decadent king, grown fat on inherited wealth.

And we, the soldiers, are the hosts of Joshua, Lizzy thought. *We were given a land of milk and honey, and we smite our enemies with ruthless abandon.*

She reached the palace gates. Metal bars sealed off the palace from the rest of the park. Armed guards stood here, wearing riot gear, rifles in hand. An attack helicopter hovered above, guns unfurled.

A few of the protesters hurled cans, bottles, and stones at the guards.

"Break through the fence!" somebody cried.

"Tear down the walls!" somebody shouted.

More shouts rose.

"Break into the palace!"

"Drag Ward out!"

The guards stiffened. A few raised their guns. Lizzy turned toward the crowd. She lifted a megaphone.

"Do not use violence here!" she said. "I am Sergeant Lizzy Pascal. I fought and killed and watched men die on Bahay. I've had enough of violence. Do not fight the guards, friends! Sing instead! Sing and chant and make your voices heard!"

The procession halted at the palace gates. The million people spread across the park, covering its paths and lawns. And they all chanted together. They sang songs of protest. They did not back down even as the military helicopter flew right above them, rotor blades blasting them with air. Their voices only grew stronger. And Lizzy remembered the helicopters and planes flying over Bahay. Soldiers leaning out the sides to strafe villagers. Mister Weird raining his poison. Fire spreading.

She turned toward the palace and raised her megaphone. She spoke to the palace. She knew President Ward could hear.

"I am Sergeant Lizzy Pascal from New Mexico! I served two tours in Bahay."

People in the crowd roared. Some seemed to boo, perhaps scornful of her service, scornful of all veterans. Others cheered, perhaps supporting her courage to come here.

Lizzy continued speaking.

"I won a Silver Star medal for gallantry in action during the Battle of New Cebu."

She pulled the medal off her chest, showing it to the crowd. Tears filled her eyes. She remembered that battle. Her first battle. She had killed two men. She had watched friends die.

"I won this medal for killing peasants who dared rise up against me. I won this medal for killing two honest men defending their home. President Ward—take it back!"

Her tears flowed. Lizzy hurled the medal—between the gate bars and onto the palace lawn.

A cheer rose from the crowd.

Lizzy ripped another medal off her coat. She held it overhead.

"I won this Purple Heart for being captured in Bahay. Tortured. Burned. For losing my hand." She raised the medal higher, showing it to the crowd—and the prosthetic hand holding it. "Take it back!"

She tossed the medal at the palace.

Everyone was still cheering. Many had tears on their cheeks.

She pulled off another medal. "I won a second Purple Heart for being shot in the chest. Take it back!"

She threw it at the palace.

People surrounded her. They lifted her overhead. She rose above the crowd, nearly as high as the fence around the palace. Drones flew above, and Lizzy cringed, expecting them to fire. But these were media drones. Their cameras rolled, and the world was watching.

She took her last medal off her coat.

"I won this Golden Heart, a medal of Distinguished Service, the highest honor bestowed upon soldiers." Her voice was choked. Her eyes were red. "Only a handful of soldiers have ever been awarded a Golden Heart. You approved this medal yourself, President Ward. You pinned it on my chest with your own bloodstained hands." She let out a hoarse cry. "Take it back!"

She tossed her last medal at the palace.

The crowd cheered and wept.

Across the park, other veterans tore off their medals. Medals earned with courage under fire. With blood and tears spilled on Bahay. Medals that came with bloodstained hands and shattered souls. Medals for unyielding bravery and unspeakable horrors.

And they all threw them.

"Take them back!" they cried.

Hundreds of medals flew and clattered around the palace walls.

New helicopters rumbled and began to spray gas.

Lizzy coughed. Her eyes watered and stung. People bent over, vomiting.

Tear gas, Lizzy knew.

Through her tearing eyes, she saw troops marching into Central Park, all in riot gear. The held large shields, and gas masks hid their faces. There were hundreds.

Lizzy could not fight them. Even if she could—she would not. She had shed too much blood.

She gazed toward the palace, struggling to keep her burning eyes open. On the balcony, she saw him. A tall man with a tanned face and white hair. With cold dark eyes. President Ward was looking right at her. And she thought that he was smiling.

Then she collapsed, coughing, vomiting. Policemen twisted her arms, handcuffed her wrists behind her back, kicked her, beat her with batons. They were beating everyone, and blood splattered the grass.

Lizzy ended that night in jail, sitting beside Kaelyn and handful of other bruised, battered protesters.

"We lost," Kaelyn said, one eye swollen shut, lip bruised.

Lizzy shook her head. "No. We did not lose. The world saw. The world heard. We won this battle. And the war is just beginning."

Chapter Thirty-Eight
An Old Friend

They were gone.

All of them.

The Bargirl Bureau—destroyed.

Maria had not seen the others since the military police raid.

She wandered the city in a daze, her dress in tatters, her hair scraggly and wet. She had visited the clubs. The alleyways. The sleazy strip bars.

"Have you seen Charlie? Have you seen Pippi?"

She showed them photos. She had some on her camera. But everybody turned away, pale.

"I don't know!" said one club owner, going pale. "I've never seen them. Go away! Go now."

"Never heard of them!" barked a bartender, and his hands shook. "Leave now. Go! You bring trouble."

Wherever she went, faces turned away. She felt like a leper. But it was not a disease that clung to her. It was the specter of the military police.

She had been Holy Maria, the blessed saint of the slums. She had become a pariah.

After long hours, exploring the city, she had to admit it to herself. Nobody else from the Bargirl Bureau had escaped the raid. The girls were probably rotting in an Earthling prison—or buried in a mass grave.

They might as well have never existed at all.

When finally she dared visit the Go Go Cowgirl, the Magic Man did not rail at her, did not strike her, did not try to force her back into service. Instead, he seemed almost mournful.

"You're in trouble, Maria," the pimp told her. "The MPs are looking for you. They were here this morning, asking about you. You must hide. You must never come back here again." He slumped into a seat and covered his face. "I'm ruined. Ruined! All my best princesses are gone. Oh, I curse the day I ever let Holy Maria into my home!"

She left the club.

She wandered the city in despair, feeling like a ghost. When she placed her hand on her belly, she could feel the child kick inside. She feared the day he would emerge into this nightmare.

Finally she returned to the cemetery. She had nowhere else to go. She was like the dead already. She climbed into a stone coffin, curled up among bones, and closed her eyes.

* * * * *

"It's you. It's really you, isn't it? Holy Maria."

The soldier walked through the cemetery, towering in the shadows, an assault rifle hanging at his side.

Maria's heart pounded. She leaped back, slamming into a stack of coffins. They tilted, nearly falling over. A skeleton spilled out and clattered to the ground.

Maria couldn't see much in the darkness, and shadows cloaked the moons. With shaking hands, she drew her gun and aimed it.

"Stand back!"

"Whoa, whoa!" The soldier raised his hands. "I'm not going to hurt you. It's me." Suddenly his voice was choked, as if struggling through tears. "It's David."

Maria frowned. *David…*

She stepped closer between the tombstones. He stood before her, more than a foot taller but so thin. The clouds parted, and Bahay's two moons shone. She could see his face now, gaunt and honest. He gave her a shaky smile, and his eyes were damp.

Maria gasped.

It was him.

The memories pounded through her.

Her war in the jungle last year. Fighting with the Kalayaan. The battle at the Earthling base.

Slitting a man's throat.

Shooting a man in the chest.

The coppery smell of hot blood.

And him—David. An Earthling soldier. So much taller and stronger than Maria. The man she had taken captive, despite being a third his size. The man Ernesto had tortured. The man she had freed.

And there he was again, nearly a year later, standing before her. David. The reason she had left the Kalayaan and ended up here in this city of tears.

"David," she whispered. "Is it really you?"

"It's me, Maria. I—" His cheeks flushed. "Can I hug you?"

She leaped onto him and embraced him tightly, nearly crushing him. He wrapped his arms around her. For a long moment, they merely stood together, holding each other.

"David. I'm so happy to see you." She caressed his cheek, then realized the cheek was still scarred. A scar shaped like a clothing iron. The scar Ernesto had given him.

"It doesn't hurt," he said. "It hurt for a long time. I'm no longer in pain. I'm just ugly now." He winked.

She shook her head. "No. You're not ugly. You're very handsome. You look good."

She remembered the last time she had seen him. A bleeding, burnt wreck of a man.

"Maria." He held her hands. "You saved my life that night. They sent me back to Earth. I spent a while in a hospital. They said I could remain on Earth for the rest of the war, get an office job, even leave the army early. But I had to come back. I volunteered for another tour of duty. All so I could see you again. So I could thank you."

Maria couldn't help but laugh, even as tears stung her eyes. "You could have written me a letter!"

But David remained somber. He looked into her eyes. "I had to come back, Maria. Because I knew it was you. When the videos appeared in protests. When they began popping up everywhere online. When people spoke of Holy Maria walking through Mindao, recording stories. I knew it was you, the girl who saved my life. I had to come back. I had to see you. To thank you for saving me—and for sharing the stories of this world."

She smiled sadly and wiped away her tears. "The videos I took?" More tears flowed. "They really reached Earth? I was never sure…"

David nodded. "They reached Earth, Maria. And millions of people saw them."

And suddenly Maria could not help it.

She began to weep.

"Maria!" David held her hands. "Are you all right?"

She wiped her damp eyes. "They're tears of relief. All that work I did. The people who suffered for our cause. I never knew if it made a difference."

All she had been through. Seeing, hearing, living all this suffering. The long days and nights, moving through the city of despair, recording her stories. The long hours at the Goodbye Kisses booth, kissing the soldiers who had killed so many of her people, slipping secret codechips into their clothes. The other bargirls—arrested, vanished.

I thought it was for nothing.

"Some of them watched," she whispered, tears on her lips. "Some of the soldiers watched my videos. And they shared them." She let out a sob. "They shared them with Earth."

"They're everywhere now," David said. "Across Earth. Hale is trying to crack down, to hide the videos. But they're spreading like wildfire, fueling an anti-war movement. Sergeant Lizzy Pascal has been leading the protests. You know her, I think."

Maria gasped. "Yes! She drank at the Go Go Cowgirl a few times. She was shot there. I didn't know she survived."

"She survived all right," David said. "And she's stronger than ever. She used to fight against Bahay. Now she's fighting for it. And she's a serious fighter."

A flicker of hope filled Maria, faint yet blessed like a Santelmo in the dark.

"Will it be enough?" she whispered. "To sway hearts and minds? To bring President Hale down?"

David sat on a coffin, and his shoulders slumped. "President Hale is still strong. The anti-war movement is growing, yes, but Hale is arresting protesters. Dismissing the videos. Calling it alien propaganda. Some people believe Lizzy, others believe Hale. There is slow change. It will take time. Maybe years." David lowered his head. "According to the polls, Hale is expected to win the upcoming election and secure another term. And the war will continue."

Maria felt weak. She nearly collapsed. She managed to sit down beside David, but the weight of Earth itself seemed to crush her.

"So this *was* all for nothing," she whispered.

"It's a beginning," David said. "An important first step. Hearts and minds can't be changed overnight. We just need more time."

Maria placed a hand on her belly. She wasn't showing yet. But she felt the child growing inside. Jon's child.

I don't have more time.

She stood up and paced between the sarcophagi. "Bahay can't survive another term of Hale in power. We probably can't even survive another year. Earth is too powerful. They're killing too many. Millions are dying. If we can't stop Earth soon, nothing will be left of Bahay but poison and bones."

And my child will be born into a world of ruin.

David paced beside her. "I know. But there are billions of people on Earth. It has over a thousand times the population of Bahay. To change their minds, to show them the war is wrong—we'll do that! Video by video. Story by story. We—"

"No." Maria shook her head, despair clutching her chest. "Not step by step. This will not be a war of attrition." She clenched her fist. "I must deliver a blow straight to Earth's heart."

She began to walk between the tombstones.

David hurried to follow. Even with his long legs, he struggled to keep up. "Maria, where are you going?"

She narrowed her eyes. "To end this war."

Chapter Thirty-Nine
The Madman is King

He lurked in the dark waters.

He waited for his prey.

He was a reptile, a monster of the rivers, ravenous but patient. Stalking. His hunger a ticking bomb.

Ernesto Santos had been stalking for a long time. Still as a stone. Deadly as a crocodile's bite. And now, finally, he approached his prey.

There she was. Walking down the alleyways of Mindao. A beautiful young woman, her hair black and smooth, her figure graceful. The most beautiful woman in the world.

His woman.

His betrothed.

His prey.

"Maria," he hissed.

He had been in the shadows for too long. Hiding in the rivers. Huddling in the urban warrens and burrows. He had needed this time. To let his rage fester. To let his wound heal. The metal plate was now bolted into his skull. It hurt. It never stopped hurting. The pain fueled him.

For weeks, he had hunted smaller prey. Becoming faster. Stronger. Perfecting the art. He caught mutated fish that swam beneath the rivers of trash. He caught rats that scurried among the shanties. He caught children and practiced twisting their necks until they snapped. He feasted upon some of those he hunted. He absorbed their power, and now Ernesto was stronger than he had ever been.

He was no longer the same man. Not the villager from San Luna, that burnt piece of seared memories. Not even the Kalayaan warrior, a guerrilla of the jungles.

The bullet had changed that.

Jon had changed that.

A piece of my mind was lost that day, Ernesto thought. *Jon's bullet took a part of me. The weaker part. The human part. I am now pure hunter. A predator of the urban jungle.*

Perhaps he had gone mad.

Perhaps that was a good thing.

War is madness, he thought. *In an insane world, the madman is king.*

He slunk through the river. It flowed beside the street, polluted, filled with floating debris. Only his head rose above the surface. Maria walked along the bank, graceful as a gazelle, unaware of the crocodile stalking her.

A fish swam before him.

Ernesto reached out. Grabbed it. Tore into it. His teeth ripped through scales and flesh and guts. The heart popped like a cherry tomato in his mouth, squiring juices. He devoured his prey. Growing even stronger. And he kept swimming.

He knew that Maria was carrying a gun. But he was bulletproof. He had survived a bullet to the head—and he still hunted. Maria had burned him before. But he was fireproof. He had passed through fire and risen stronger.

I have become immortal. A god of Bahay.

Maria turned away from the river. Sweet, graceful prey. She walked down a dark alleyway, as innocent as a fawn.

Ernesto licked his lips. What a delectable morsel.

He paddled toward the riverbank. He rose from the water, dripping pollution, algae, and strands of plastic. A grin spread across his face. Maria had still not noticed him. She was walking down the alley, a dark place, with only children and stray cats between the narrow walls.

A perfect place to attack.

He stalked her, shedding moss, dripping oil. His arms spread out. He filled the alleyway like a demon risen from the depths. Cats and orphans fled before him.

Halfway down the alleyway, Maria froze.

She spun around, gun raised.

She fired.

Ernesto swerved left.

Her bullet flew over his right shoulder, missing his head.

Stupid girl. Aiming for the head instead of the larger torso. She would pay for that mistake.

Ernesto pounced.

He knocked Maria down. He pinned her to the ground. She screamed, and Ernesto sank his teeth into her flesh.

Chapter Forty
The Luminous Army

So here I am, Jon thought. *The proud warrior, defending a priceless strategic asset.*

By strategic asset, he meant a useless, godforsaken hill in the middle of the jungle.

By defending, he meant sitting in a wooden guard tower, leafing through a dog-eared paperback.

"Go Earth!" he muttered.

Jon sighed.

The book was an old Western, not particularly good. It was full of cliches, stilted dialog, and Tom Swifties. But the previous guard had left only two paperbacks behind, and *Cowboys of Atlantis* seemed preferable. It was that or *Alien Temptresses: Pinups from the Stars!*

The rainforest rustled below the tower, a green sea spreading toward haze. The real sea glimmered along the eastern horizon, a strip of blue under Bahay's two suns. Jon was deep in the northern wilderness. The war was flaring. It burned hotter than ever across this woeful planet. But it was hard to be anxious here. The land was just too beautiful.

Most of Bahay was ugly now. Earth's starships had bombed the land. Her planes had poisoned forests and fields. Her soldiers had swept through villages, burning and killing. But standing here, Jon saw the real Bahay. The world that had been.

The planet's wild beauty spread around him, the last remnant of a dying world.

It hurt to see. Jon did not know how much longer this beauty would last.

He returned his eyes to his book, needing some escape. He read a few more pages in *Cowboys of Atlantis*. The cowboys had found a race of giant seahorses a few pages ago. They were now riding them to battle against an evil kraken, hoping to free a buxom mermaid from its grip. When bandits appeared on shark-back, Jon put the book down and glanced at *Alien Temptresses*. Maybe it wouldn't be so bad after all.

He flipped to the first page of *Temptresses*. It featured a garish illustration. A reptilian woman gazed seductively from the page, her three breasts bare. The artist had lovingly painted her lounging over a pile of alien corpses. Jon wasn't sure why a reptile would need breasts, but the artist had clearly thought three of them were necessary.

He closed the book and yawned. It was boring up here. Guard duty was mostly boring. Hell, war itself was mostly boring. At least when it wasn't utterly terrifying. War was full of horror and battles and blood and death. But a lot of it, even most of it, was just like this. Sitting in some godforsaken tower, guarding some godforsaken hill, trying not to go mad with boredom.

Jon glanced down toward the camp. They were just a squad of soldiers here on the hill. No officers. No NCOs. Just a handful of privates and corporals. A few were sleeping under the trees. Others were brewing coffee over a campfire. George sat on a log, whittling a chunk of wood. Despite his enormous hands, George had become an accomplished whittler in the army, carving figurines of Bahayan animals. Jon leaned from the guard tower, focused his binoculars, and looked down at his friend's work. George seemed to be sculpting an *ungoy*, a local monkey with several tails arranged in a ring.

Three junglers parked beside the squad. Jon had to admit—they were sweet rides. Especially after months in a damn jeep. Only scouts and guards in the farthest outposts got junglers. Most of the HDF's vehicles on Bahay were old; many had seen service during the Ganymede Uprising twenty years ago. Junglers were newer and sleeker, built specifically for the Bahay War. Unlike armacars, tanks, and jeeps, they didn't require deforestation. Mister Weird's services were not required here, thank you very much. And unlike planes or starfighters, junglers weren't ridiculously expensive, and they didn't require years of training. Even a dumb grunt like Jon could fly a jungler.

They were essentially glorified hovercraft, designed to float over the jungle canopy—at insane speeds. They were silent, aerodynamic, and painted with camouflage patterns, making them quite stealthy. A jungler could glide over the rainforest like a hawk, barely disturbing the leaves below.

Flying a jungler here, the wind in his hair, had actually been kind of fun. And fun was hard to come by in this war. Jon was looking forward to flying one back to Camp Apollo in five days. Then another squad would fly up here, and let them suffer through *Alien Temptresses.*

"Hey guys!" Jon called down to his squad. "My shift's almost over. Who's next?"

They looked up at him. A few soldiers flipped him off.

"You still got twenty minutes up there, dipshit!" George called up.

Jon sighed. Up here on the guard tower, twenty minutes felt like a year. He was going mad with boredom.

But no, he realized. It wasn't the boredom that was bothering him.

There was another feeling inside him. Cold and gray. Almost a physical sensation, growing from his belly like a tumor, spreading icy tendrils through his body. Fear? Guilt? Grief? It was a bit of all those things. The best way Jon could describe it was despair.

It was the memory of the people he had killed.

It was the lingering horror from the Santa Rosa massacre.

It was missing Etty, who had gone AWOL, and missing Maria, who was probably still a bargirl far south. It was missing home.

It was the tense wait for the battles ahead.

It was the knowledge that he might never return to Earth.

It was shell shock. And in the loneliness of this guard tower, without his friends to distract him, it expanded inside him, claiming every cell.

Jon forced himself to take deep breaths.

"This will be over soon," he whispered. "This whole damn war. And I'll be with you again, Maria. I'll take you to Earth with me. We'll all gather in Lindenville. George will play his drums, and Etty promised she'll learn to play bass. You and Kaelyn will sing. We'll make music together and we'll be happy. We'll be far from all this pain. Just a little bit longer, Maria, and we'll—"

A distant horn sounded, barely audible.

Jon frowned and stared north.

He lost his breath.

"Holy shit," he blurted out.

*****

Jon leaned over the guard tower's wooden railing. He squinted, trying to see more clearly.

"My God," he whispered.

They were rising over the horizon. Enormous vessels. Bloated and silvery. Floating over the forest.

Jon raised his binoculars and a chill flooded him.

A dozen gargantuan ships were sailing through the sky. They looked like blimps, but they spread out many slender tentacles. They reminded Jon of jellyfish, and he wondered if they were living beings. But no—they were machines. He could make out exhaust pipes, headlights, and cannons.

Smaller vessels flew beneath the blimps. A hundred or more. They were long, aerodynamic, and silvery, slicing the sky like arrowheads. They were smaller than the blimps, perhaps the size of fighter jets.

Those must be balisongs, Jon thought.

He had heard of balisongs, which meant "butterfly knives" in Tagalog. They were supposedly the fighter jets of the Luminous Air Force, appearing in North Bahayan propaganda reels. But no Earthling had ever seen one in real life. The Human Defense Force considered them a myth. Well, here flew a bunch of myths.

Farther down, trudging through the jungle, came the strangest vehicles Jon had ever seen. They had round bodies and spindly legs. They looked like spiders with wonky proportions, the legs ridiculously long and thin. From a distance, the legs barely seemed wider than ropes, and they swayed every which way. Yet those legs were strong enough to propel the vehicles forward. Jon adjusted his binoculars, zooming in on one spiderlike machine. He saw a round, silvery hull lined with windows. Men stood inside.

The hulls were painted with red inverted crosses. Sigil of the Red Cardinal.

"The Luminous Army," Jon whispered. "*His* army."

But that was impossible! The Lumis barely even had jeeps and planes, let alone tech like this! Hell, even Earth didn't have anything this advanced.

And then Jon saw it.

Glowing orbs. They floated among the machinery. More and more rose from behind the horizon, a thousand little sunrises.

Santelmos.

Santelmos and Bahayans—working together. A joint army—sweeping south. Right toward Jon.

For long, critical seconds, Jon could just stare in stunned silence. Then horns blared, shattering his paralysis. War horns. Luminous Army horns. Hundreds of horns sang, calling for victory.

Jon spun around. He leaned over the guard tower, facing the squad below.

"Enemy incoming!" he shouted.

The troops were already standing, clutching their rifles. They had heard the horns too.

"How many?" George shouted from the forest floor.

"All of them!" Jon cried. "I'll stream your binoculars the data."

George and the other soldiers lifted their binoculars. Jon hit a button on his, transmitting a live stream from the tower. The enemy was even closer now. The soldiers below cursed.

"Jon, get your ass down here!" George yelled. "We're flying back to base."

"Excellent idea," Jon said, trying to control the tremor in his voice. "Let me just broadcast Camp Apollo a warning."

He looked again at the incoming army. Damn, they were moving fast. Those blimps, planes, and arachnid walkers were swallowing the distance. Cursing, Jon reached for his radio, began to dial Camp Apollo, which was located a hundred kilometers south.

"Hello, Apollo?" he spoke into the receiver. "This is—"

Beams of light flared from the incoming army.

The light blazed over Jon, blinding and hot. The pain seared through him like a thousand suns.

He screamed.

It lasted for only a few seconds. When the light dimmed, the pain vanished. Jon was surprised to find himself alive.

The radio had no such luck. The controls were fried. Jon's electronic binoculars were just as dead. Some kind of EMP attack?

"Jon!" George shouted from below. "Hurry!"

Jon shuddered. The enemy kept coming closer. They would reach him within mere minutes.

He scrambled down the guard tower, thumped onto the mossy hilltop, and ran toward his squad.

The other soldiers were already in their junglers, ready to take off. Jon hopped into the middle jungler. George was squeezed into the cockpit, barely fitting, his knees pulled to his chest. Jon took the gunnery station behind the giant. He sat inside a bubble turret, which could swivel in every direction.

The three slender, camouflaged junglers leaped into the air.

Jon rattled in his seat. His helmet wobbled on his head. He clutched the machine gun as the jungler stormed forward, skimming the jungle canopy. Normally junglers were a smooth ride. But George, understandably nervous, was flying erratically. The jungler kept dipping down, cracking branches, and lurching like a drunk bird. The trees bent and creaked below. Leaves tore free from branches, spraying everywhere like confetti.

"George, are you drunk?" Jon shouted.

"Stop backseat driving!" the giant replied from the cockpit.

The three junglers streaked south, gliding just above the canopy. They had no wings. They could not rise higher. They glided on a carpet of air, moving at breakneck speed. Jon clenched his jaw and struggled not to pass out. It was like riding the world's fastest motorboat, skimming over green water.

The junglers tightened their formation. Apollo Base was still too far to see.

Dammit, we'll never make it, Jon thought.

He tugged a lever. He swiveled the gun turret around, facing backwards.

Good. He breathed a sigh of relief. He could no longer see the enemy. The Luminous Army was behind the horizon.

"At least we're faster than you guys," Jon muttered.

But his relief didn't last long.

Over the hill, they rose—a dozen enemy balisongs. The dreaded butterfly fighter jets.

Far away, so small Jon could barely see it, rose the guard tower on the hill. The same tower Jon had manned just moments ago. A balisong smashed through it. The jet kept flying, leaving a pile of rubble.

Goodbye, Cowboys of Atlantis, Jon thought.

The balisongs thundered through the air, moving with terrifying speed. They flew without wings, leaving trails of white light. This had to be Santelmo tech. But when Jon squinted, he could make out humans in the cockpits. Bahayan pilots.

Jon grimaced.

We bombed the Santelmos who dwelled in Basilica, he thought. *Now they will spare no effort to arm our enemy. We awoke a sleeping giant.*

The balisongs roared closer.

Jon decided to take the first shot. He aimed the jungler's rotary cannon. He pulled the trigger, unleashing his fury.

He hit. A perfect hit! His bullets sparked against a balisong. Hope leaped in Jon's heart.

The two other junglers opened fire too, peppering the enemy.

But the bullets did not penetrate the silvery hulls. And the balisongs returned fire.

Beams of searing white light blazed.

"George!" Jon shouted.

His friend was already swerving the jungler.

A beam just missed them. It hit trees below. The forest crumbled. Another beam shot just overhead, missing the jungler by a mere foot or two. It was so hot Jon thought his helmet would melt.

Beside them, a beam hit a jungler.

It exploded.

Jon clenched his jaw. He had known the three soldiers inside. They were friends.

That left two junglers. Both kept firing at the balisongs. Jon held down his trigger, ripping through ammunition belts, pounding the enemy.

One balisong crashed into the forest.

Jon grunted in satisfaction. Good. So the bastards weren't invincible.

But ten or more balisongs were still pursuing the two junglers. And countless still flew beyond the horizon.

"George, faster!" Jon shouted.

"The pedal's to the metal!" the giant roared. "Hold them off!"

The silvery balisongs rose toward the sun. Jon could barely see them. More searing beams rained down.

George swerved, but a beam hit the side of their jungler. A section of hull melted. The jungler spun madly. Jon screamed. George wrestled the yoke, struggling to steady the careening vehicle. Trees caught fire below.

More beams flew. Beside them, the second jungler crashed and burned.

It was only Jon and George now.

They raced onward.

Jon couldn't see Camp Apollo yet.

They wouldn't last another minute in the air.

"George, into the forest!" Jon cried.

"Junglers are meant to fly *above* the forest!"

"Dammit, George, now!"

George shoved the yoke forward. The jungler plunged down. Jon's stomach lurched. They dropped through the canopy, and suddenly they were flying inside the jungle. The tree trunks rose all around.

Beams blazed from the heavens. Trees burned. Holes tore into the ground. But the enemy couldn't see them here. The beams were all missing.

"George, watch it!" Jon shouted.

They were racing toward an enormous tree—it was the size of a Redwood. George tugged the yoke. They swerved, narrowly dodging the trunk. A second later, George had to swerve the other way, avoiding another tree.

"I told you, stop backseat driving!" George said. "I got this!"

They zigzagged through the forest. Beams blasted downward with the fury of gods. Boulders cracked open like eggs. Trees burst into flame.

One beam grazed the jungler.

They jerked sideways, glanced off a tree, careened forward. Chunks of bark flew. Jon nearly tumbled from the turret. He clung to the machine gun, inadvertently releasing a hailstorm of bullets.

And then balisongs were plunging through the canopy, shattering branches, and storming through the forest.

"Copycats!" George shouted.

Jon sneered and opened fire.

He hit a balisong. His bullets pinged off the hull, not penetrating it. But it was enough to knock the balisong into a tree. The silver jet exploded. The tree crashed down, crushing another balisong.

"Good job, buddy!" George said.

"Two butterflies with one stone," Jon muttered.

He fired again and again. The forest burned. Branches crashed down. George kept zigzagging around trees. Jon jerked from side to side in the turret, firing all the while.

Beams blazed above. Below. Everywhere. One grazed Jon's gun turret, searing off a chunk of chassis. The silica canopy cracked, and wind roared into the jungler, thick with leaves and dirt and slivers of bark.

More balisongs descended into the forest.

More beams flew, searing all in their path.

Trees collapsed. Birds crashed down dead. Jon waited for the end.

Then he saw it ahead.

Between the trees, down in a valley—wooden palisades topped with barbed wire. Beyond them—rows of tents.

Camp Apollo.

"Hold on!" George shouted, and their jungler soared, smashed through branches, and emerged into open sky.

The balisongs followed.

The lone jungler flew toward the camp, almost there…

Another beam hit them.

An engine caught fire.

They weren't going to make it.

I'm sorry, Maria. I'm sorry.

And then, from inside Camp Apollo, the guns of Earth fired.

Cannons boomed.

Shells flew.

A balisong exploded. Another. A third.

The burning jungler flew over the palisade.

The artillery fired again and again, pounding the enemy, and the last balisong exploded.

But those are just a few drops in the ocean, Jon knew. *The rest of that ocean is roaring forward in a tidal wave.*

One engine aflame, hull seared and dented, the jungler crash-landed inside the camp.

Jon and George leaped from the burning vehicle.

"Enemy approaching!" Jon shouted. "Where's Pascal? Enemy approaching!"

A jeep roared toward them. The white-haired colonel hopped out.

"What in tarnation is going on?" Pascal shouted.

"Sir, they're only moments away!" Jon said, panting. "A combined Bahayan and Santelmo army. Warships. Fighter jets. Blimps. A huge army, coming in from the north. We tried to call. They fried our radios with an EMP attack. They're almost here."

Pascal grabbed a megaphone. His voice boomed from speakers across the base.

"Red alert! All soldiers—to your positions! Red alert!"

Klaxons blared. Thousands of soldiers ran to the walls, cannons, and tanks. Attack helicopters took flight. Artillery batteries swiveled north. Guards raced along the walls, manning machine guns.

Pascal looked at Jon and George. "You two. With me. Onto the northern wall."

They ran toward the palisade, climbed a ladder, and manned the battlements. Other soldiers stood along the wooden walkway, guns in hand.

From up here, Jon could see the jungle spread to the northern horizon.

And he could see the enemy.

The tentacled blimps floated above the trees like storm clouds. More balisongs flew around them, protecting their larger brethren. The strange arachnids loped forward, their bodies rising above the canopy, their slender legs piercing the forest.

And from the trees, the foot soldiers emerged.

Countless Bahayan infantrymen marched, wearing black battlesuits, holding rifles. With them floated orbs of light—Santelmos furious over the loss of their comrades.

It was the largest army this war had ever seen.

With blaring horns, with howls and shrieks and roaring engines, the Luminous Army stormed toward Camp Apollo's wooden walls.

Goodbye, Maria, Jon thought. *I love you.*

He loaded his rifle, aimed at the enemy, and prepared to kill and die.

The story continues in

Earthling's War

Soldiers of Earthrise III

NOVELS BY DANIEL ARENSON

Earthrise:

Earth Alone

Earth Lost

Earth Rising

Earth Fire

Earth Shadows

Earth Valor

Earth Reborn

Earth Honor

Earth Eternal

Soldiers of Earthrise:

The Earthling

Earthlings

Earthling's War

I, Earthling

The Earthling's Daughter

We Are Earthlings

Children of Earthrise:

The Heirs of Earth

A Memory of Earth

An Echo of Earth

The War for Earth

The Song of Earth

The Legacy of Earth

The Moth Saga:

Moth

Empires of Moth

Secrets of Moth

Daughter of Moth

Shadows of Moth

Legacy of Moth

Dawn of Dragons:

Requiem's Song

Requiem's Hope

Requiem's Prayer

Song of Dragons:

Blood of Requiem

Tears of Requiem

Light of Requiem

Dragonlore:

A Dawn of Dragonfire

A Day of Dragon Blood

A Night of Dragon Wings

The Dragon War:

A Legacy of Light

A Birthright of Blood

A Memory of Fire

Requiem for Dragons:

Dragons Lost

Dragons Reborn

Dragons Rising

Flame of Requiem:

Forged in Dragonfire

Crown of Dragonfire

Pillars of Dragonfire

Misfit Heroes:

Eye of the Wizard

Wand of the Witch

Kingdoms of Sand:

Kings of Ruin

Crowns of Rust

Thrones of Ash

Temples of Dust

Halls of Shadow

Echoes of Light

Alien Hunters:

Alien Hunters

Alien Sky

Alien Shadows

Standalones:

Firefly Island

Flaming Dove

The Gods of Dream

Utopia 58

KEEP IN TOUCH

www.DanielArenson.com
Daniel@DanielArenson.com
Facebook.com/DanielArenson
Twitter.com/DanielArenson

Made in the USA
Coppell, TX
15 December 2019

12935705R00203